Praise for Joan Johnston

"Joan Johnston does short contemporary
Westerns to perfection."
—*Publishers Weekly*

"Like LaVyrle Spencer, Ms. Johnston writes
of intense emotions and tender passions
that seem so real that the readers will feel
each one of them."
—Rave Reviews

"Johnston warms your heart and
tickles your fancy."
—New York *Daily News*

"Joan Johnston continually gives us
everything we want . . . fabulous details
and atmosphere, memorable characters,
a story that you wish would never end,
and lots of tension and sensuality."
—*Romantic Times*

"Joan Johnston [creates] unforgettable
subplots and characters who make every
fine thread weave into a touching tapestry."
—*Affaire de Coeur*

JOAN JOHNSTON

THE COWBOY

DELL
NEW YORK

2013 Dell Mass Market Edition

Copyright © 2000 by Joan Mertens Johnston, Inc.

Published in the United States by Dell,
an imprint of The Random House Publishing Group,
a division of Random House, Inc., New York.

DELL is a registered trademark of Random House, Inc.,
and the colophon is a trademark of Random House, Inc.

Originally published in the United States by Dell,
an imprint of The Random House Publishing Group,
a division of Random House, Inc., in 2000.

ISBN 978-0-440-22380-1
eBook ISBN 978-0-307-56932-5

Cover design: Lynn Andreozzi
Cover illustration: Alan Ayers

Printed in the United States of America

www.bantamdell.com

22 24 26 27 25 23 21

Dell mass market edition: August 2013

This book is dedicated to my favorite native Texans,
Heather and Blake

ACKNOWLEDGMENTS

I want to thank a number of individuals without whose knowledge and assistance this book could not have been written.

My former law school study group partner, Cheryl Hole, now an assistant district attorney in Edinburg, Texas, was kind enough to introduce me to her friend, attorney Charles W. Hury, who—over a spicy Mexican dinner—helped me to contrive a great many of the financial difficulties that plague the Creed family.

Angela Strittmatter, Public Relations Manager for the National Cutting Horse Association, made me feel more than welcome at the Will Rogers Memorial Complex in Fort Worth during the 1998 World Championship Futurity and initiated me into the world of "cutters." A special thank-you to Kathy Shaughnessy for finding me a seat for the sold-out Charles Goodnight Gala, and to all the "cutters" who willingly allowed themselves to be interviewed.

My longtime friends Jack and Carolyn Lampe, in Uvalde, Texas, helped me to connect with Robin

Clark, a field inspector for the Texas and Southwestern Cattle Raisers Association. Thank you, Robin, for all the information about brucellosis and the work of a TSCRA field inspector.

The King Ranch in Kingsville, Texas, provides tours to anyone who would like to see its ranching operation and maintains a museum of King Ranch memorabilia. I want to thank the individuals who shared their knowledge and pride in the heritage of the King Ranch with me, including archivist Lisa Neely.

I'm indebted to Captain Doug Giacobbe of the Miramar, Florida, police department for information and instruction on the use of varmint rifles.

People always want to know what sparks a writer's imagination. I owe a debt of gratitude to my trainer Charlie Mihlstin for helping me to get in shape—and for informing me that a can of PAM has 433 servings, which inspired a scene in this book.

And finally, to my friend Fran Garfunkel, thank you for being such a faithful reader, avid researcher, and kind critic.

Prologue

CALLIE COULDN'T STOP TREMBLING. HER knees turned to mush, and she landed on the edge of the bed as the phone clattered back into its cradle. "Trace . . ." she croaked.

The sheet wrapped around Trace's waist as he turned over and leaned up on one elbow, brushing at the sleep in his eyes. It was only a little after four in the afternoon, but they'd both dropped off to sleep after some pretty incredible sex. He took one look at her and sat up abruptly. "What's the matter? Who was that on the phone?"

Callie's heart clutched at the mere sight of him, she loved him that much. His features were too angular to be handsome, but she loved the slash of mouth, the blade of nose, and the hint of rough, dark beard that made it necessary for him to shave again in the evening if he wanted to go out.

She captured the moment in her mind, knowing that whatever small chance had existed for a life with this man had ended with the phone call she had just received. Her gaze met the ice-blue eyes that had so frightened her the first time she had spoken to him. Ruthless eyes. Predatory eyes. She saw the growing concern in those eyes as she struggled to find words to tell him what had happened.

Speech was impossible.

"Who was that on the phone?" he demanded, muscles flexing in his shoulders and arms as he shoved himself toward her. "What the hell is wrong, Callie?"

Tears blurred her vision. Her hands clutched the bottom edge of the thigh-length T-shirt that was all she wore. "There's b-been an accident. My b-brother Sam—" She broke down, unable to tell him the rest.

She felt Trace's strong arms close around her as he dragged her into his lap.

"You're trembling." He pulled her close and held her snug and warm against his big body. "What happened? Is he dead?"

"No. Something m-much worse."

"What could be worse—"

"He b-broke his neck. He won't ever walk again. They d-don't even know if he'll live!"

"Damn. I'm so sorry, Callie."

She clutched him around the neck, muffling her sobs against his throat, for fear someone in the hallway would hear her and come to investigate. Trace wasn't supposed to be in her dorm room, and they'd both be in big trouble if someone found them together.

She laughed at herself, but what came out were hysterical sobs. Imagine worrying about something as stupid as getting caught with a man on the girls' floor before visiting hours when Sam was never going to walk again. When any chance of a life with Trace had ended forever.

Callie felt Trace's big hands smoothing her hair, rubbing her back, a mute promise of support. But nothing could help now. She hadn't told him the whole story. He had no idea of the depth of the disaster that had befallen them.

His voice rumbled in her ear. "Tell me what happened."

Callie cried harder. Their whole world had just been turned upside down, that's what had happened. It was a miracle they had found each other at all, in light of the ongoing feud between their families. She still found it hard to believe that they had become lovers . . . that they had fallen in love.

She had never let her gaze linger on Trace during high school, even though she found him attractive, and not just because he was a senior and she was a freshman, or because his father's South Texas ranch was ten times as large as her father's. It was a simple case of having the wrong names. He was a Blackthorne, and she was a Creed. Blackthornes and Creeds had hated each other since the Civil War, and the fight had never been more bitter than it was between Trace's father and her own.

But the University of Texas at Austin campus was a long way from home. She'd been lost those first few days amongst such a huge college population, and even though Trace had been "the enemy," he'd also been the only familiar face she'd seen. So she'd asked him for directions.

Callie shivered as she remembered how harsh his voice had sounded when he'd given them to her. She'd been surprised when Trace offered to show her the way. Amazed when he asked her to go out with him. Astonished at herself for saying yes.

She would never forget their first kiss. The memory

was filled with sensations. The wind lifting the hair on his brow and tugging at the silk scarf holding her ponytail. The shifting shadows beyond the bright porch light at the front door to the dormitory. The rough bark of the live oak at her back, and the rustle of leaves above their heads. The quiver of expectation as his callused fingertips grazed her nape.

She had felt a shiver of fear as she braced for the unknown, and her gaze had lowered to focus on the third pearl snap on his Western shirt. She had felt his warm breath against her cheek, and finally, the exquisite softness of his mouth on hers and the certain knowledge that beneath his gentleness lay an urgency, a need, a desire so powerful it made her breath catch in her throat.

She had felt clumsy, because she hadn't had much practice kissing. She had tentatively touched his shoulders and marveled at their strength, then held her breath, as she felt his arm slide around her waist and draw her tightly against the full length of an aroused male for the first time in her life.

She had blocked out all knowledge of who he was and who she was and lost herself in his kiss. He had teased her lips with his tongue seeking more, demanding more, and she had let him in, answering the thrust of his tongue with her own. Her body had squeezed up inside as though someone had pulled a lasso tight.

She had ignored the warning bell jangling deep inside, reminding her that this man was a Blackthorne and she was a Creed. She had clung to Trace, believing in her heart that they were meant to be together, two ragged halves of one perfect whole.

Even then it was too late to save her heart from break-

4

ing. It was his from the first moment he had asked for it eight months ago.

They had long since decided to defy their parents and get married when Trace graduated in May. They had planned to honeymoon over the summer in Australia, where they both had distant relatives. Only that wasn't going to happen now . . . or likely ever.

"Callie, sweetheart, please. Tell me what happened. Let me help," Trace murmured.

There was no sense putting it off any longer. Callie did her best to control the tears, but it was a losing battle. "Sam was at f-football practice after school. He leaped up for a pass and got hit really hard. When he came down, he f-fell wrong and b-broke his neck."

She felt Trace's arms tighten around her.

"I want to be there with you, Callie. At the hospital, I mean. I guess there was never going to be an easy way to let our families know we're a couple. But I don't want you to have to go through this alone. We might as well tell your father now that we don't intend to let this insane feud of his with my dad separate us ever again."

She shrugged herself free of his embrace and slid off his lap, staring at the sheet that was tangled around him. "You c-can't come home with me, Trace."

"Why not?"

She stood and walked away, putting the first distance between them, then turned and spoke. "Your brother Owen was the one who tackled Sam. Your brother Owen is the one who broke his neck."

She watched the color leach from Trace's face before he met her gaze and said, "Sam getting hurt on the football field has nothing to do with us loving each other." He gripped the sheet in hands that had become fists. "It was an *accident* for Christ's sake!"

"My father doesn't think so."

"He can't believe Owen did it on purpose! Owen doesn't have a mean bone in his body."

"What words could I use to explain why I've brought you with me? What could I possibly say? 'Oh, by the way, Daddy, I'm going to marry the brother of the man responsible for putting Sam in a wheelchair for the rest of his life. We can let bygones be bygones, can't we?' My father would throw me out and tell me never to come back."

Trace rose, letting the sheet drop. "So? You can come live with me." His eyes asked her to give them a chance. His lips slowly curved into a cajoling smile.

Callie couldn't take her eyes off him. She focused on the smile first, because he flashed it so seldom, and then on the powerful, rangy body that had given her so much pleasure. His frame was lean and ropey with muscle, his chest covered with black hair that narrowed into a single line of black down at his navel.

She forced her gaze upward and saw the anticipation in his eyes of her imminent surrender. She held a hand up, palm out, to stop him in place. "I can't abandon my family, Trace. They need me."

"I need you, too."

"Not as much as they do."

She saw the flare of hurt in his eyes before he reached for his Jockey shorts and jeans. "You either love me or you don't!" he said, stuffing his legs into worn Levi's and buttoning them up. He snatched a Texas Longhorns T-shirt off the floor and tugged it down over his head. "Which is it?"

She stared at him in disbelief. "You know I do! But surely you can understand—"

"I understand our fathers have made it impossible for us to live our lives the way we want," he said, yanking on Nikes and tying knots with fists that looked ready to strangle flesh. "I'm done playing their games. I'm leaving the States in May, with or without you."

She took a step toward him. "If you could just wait—"

"One year? Two?" He shoved a hand through his dark hair to get it out of his eyes. "How long before someone else in my family offends or embarrasses—or cripples—someone else in yours? Or vice versa? That goddamned feud is never going to end! The best thing for us to do is start a new life away from all of them."

"I love my parents and my brothers and sister. I don't want to be separated from them forever."

"Not even if it's the only way we can be together?" He crossed the room in two strides and grabbed her by the arms. She could feel the desperation in his grasp, see it in his eyes as they bored into hers, hear it in his panting breaths. "I love you, Callie. I want to spend my life with you. Doesn't that mean anything?"

"You're being unreasonable," she argued.

His arms suddenly folded around her, and he nestled his nose against her throat. She could feel the effort it took for him to gentle his strength. His powerful hands caressed her with infinite care. "Callie," he murmured in her ear. "I need you. Let me go home with you. We can make your father understand. Give us a chance, sweetheart. Please."

Callie closed her eyes and bit her lower lip to keep from agreeing. Trace had rarely asked her for anything.

This request was especially difficult to refuse, with Trace holding her so tenderly in his arms, reminding her of what she would be giving up if she forced him out of her life.

His lips moved across her throat, leaving a trail of lingering pleasure. He made a carnal sound, as he molded their bodies together. Callie felt herself responding to the raw animal heat that had never failed to excite her. In a moment, it would be too late to escape without causing both of them more pain.

"Trace, no. Stop." She shoved at his chest with the heels of her hands. When he lifted his head, she met his wary gaze and said, "I can't. I'm sorry. It's over."

He let her go abruptly and took a step back. She rubbed her arms, holding herself tightly as she watched the dawning realization in his eyes of what she had known since she'd let the phone drop back into the cradle. They were not going to live happily ever after.

It had been a long shot from the start because of the feud, but also because they'd been raised with such different values. Perhaps because the Blackthornes had always had so much land— and had never been in any danger of losing it—Trace took his heritage, and the financial security that went along with it, for granted. He had grown up as a young prince in his family's Texas kingdom, bowing to no man—except, of course, to his father, the king.

Trace's father, Jackson Blackthorne, was called Boss to his face and Blackjack behind his back. Callie had heard several versions of how he'd acquired his nickname. One was simply that he had hair as black as a crow's wing. Another was that he liked to gamble and usually won—by fair means or foul. Her father claimed that Jackson Blackthorne was called Blackjack because he had a coal-black soul.

Callie had accepted her father's version of how Blackjack had earned his nickname—until she'd gotten to know Trace. She didn't think someone with a coal-black soul could have raised a son like Trace. He had his father's crow-wing black hair, all right, but Trace was honest and fair. And loving. Where would he have learned such attributes, if Blackjack were really as sinister as her father had painted him?

But Blackjack hadn't been a perfect father, either. He'd taught Trace everything he needed to know to run the Bitter Creek Cattle Company, then made it plain he had no intention of relinquishing control of the day-to-day operations of the ranch to his eldest son anytime soon.

Callie knew Trace chafed at his father's strictures. She knew he wanted to make his own way in the world, away from his father's vast sphere of influence. She had tried very hard to want what he wanted. But her needs were very different from his.

The Creeds had always lived on the brink of financial disaster. Callie had learned early to make do, to cut corners, to bargain and plead and placate. She treasured her home at Three Oaks all the more because she knew at any moment it could be lost. As the eldest, she had always been given a great deal of responsibility. Her father had needed her help just to make ends meet. She had yearned for the financial security, and the freedom to get up and go, that Trace took so much for granted.

She couldn't walk away from her family, because they needed her. He couldn't bear to stay with his, because they didn't.

There were things she could say that would make Trace stay with her, but there was no hope that anytime in the near future her father would welcome a Blackthorne across his threshold. So what was the point?

"I love you, Trace," she said sadly.

"Just not enough to defy your father and marry me," Trace replied bitterly. "I should have known better than to get involved with a Creed. My father always said you couldn't be trusted. What about the promises you made to me, Callie? Were those all a bunch of lies?"

Callie's stomach clenched. "Please, Trace. You're angry and upset right now because we can't be together, but—"

"You're the one pushing me away, Callie. You're the one afraid to take a chance. Remember that. Because I won't come crawling back."

Callie felt the acid rising in her throat. *Not now. Oh, God. Not now.*

Trace grabbed his canvas backpack on the way to the door. "I don't have to get my teeth kicked in more than once to learn my lesson. I'm out of here."

The door slammed, and she was alone. Not quite alone. She let her hand rest on the small mound below her waist. She swallowed several times, but it was a losing battle. Callie raced for the bathroom.

Afterward, she pressed a cool, damp washcloth against her mouth as she stared at herself in the mirror. Eighteen and pregnant. And unmarried.

You should have told him.

I will. Someday. If he ever comes back.

Chapter 1

ELEVEN YEARS LATER.

"YOU BLACKTHORNES ARE ALL GREEDY, thieving sons-of-bitches!"

Trace kept his features even, but his heart was thudding, and beneath the ancient oak desk, his hands were fisted on rock-hard thighs. He barely resisted blurting, *Those are fighting words, Dusty.*

They were, of course. But it sounded too much like dialogue from the barroom showdown in a western B movie. The scenario was classic Louis L'Amour, but Trace resisted the comparison, because he would have been forced to cast himself as villain, rather than hero.

"Just sign the papers, Dusty," he said in a level voice.

But the young man sitting across from him had apparently crossed some threshold between rational being and trapped animal. Dusty Simpson scrabbled for the pair of crutches lying beside his chair. One crutch fell beyond the carpet, clattering across the polished hardwood floor. He shoved himself upright on the crutch he had left and stood, wavering on a single leg, the other having been amputated just above the knee. "Come and get me, Trace. Come on, take a swing!" Dusty yelled.

Trace met Dusty's furious gaze—furious, he knew, because Dusty must have felt so impotent—and said, "I don't fight cripples."

He watched the blood drain from Dusty's face, taking the fight along with it.

"Sit down, Dusty."

The one-legged man, his whole body quivering with anger, stubbornly balanced himself between his booted foot and the crutch. "How do you live with yourself? Mine isn't the first small ranch that's been gobbled up by you Blackthornes. But you were best man at my wedding! You're godfather to my two girls! What kind of friend are you?"

"I'm only following orders," Trace said through tight jaws.

"Yeah. I know," Dusty replied, a sneer twisting his features. "If Blackjack told you to jump off a cliff, you'd find yourself dead in the rocks below by sundown."

Trace's eyes narrowed. He'd made the mistake, when he'd had one too many Lone Stars on Dusty's back porch, of confiding the truth to his friend. It might look to the world like Trace Blackthorne had managed the Bitter Creek Cattle Company since his father's heart attack three months ago, but Blackjack held a tight rein on everything Trace did and roweled with sharp, painful spurs when he wanted his dirty work done. Like now.

Trace watched as tears welled in his friend's eyes. He'd sat beside Dusty's wife Lou Ann at the hospital while Dusty had the surgery that took off his leg, leaving him unable to compete in the arena on a cutting horse and thus unable to pay the mortgage on his ranch. Trace hated what Blackjack was forcing him to do. But he had no choice.

"What happened to you, losing your leg in that car accident, was a tragedy," Trace said. "But if we hadn't bought the Rafter S, it would have gone into foreclosure."

"Blackjack owns the bank that holds my mortgage, Trace. Are you saying you couldn't have talked to your dad, maybe persuaded him to give me a little more time to get back on my feet? Aw, hell. On my one damned foot?"

Trace bit back an apology for his father's ruthlessness. He'd learned some hard lessons at Blackjack's side. Dusty was like a calf choking on a string of barbed wire tangled around its throat. When Trace was ten years old, he'd ignored his father's order to kill the animal and tried to untangle the wire. But the harder he'd worked to unwind the deadly garrote, the harder the calf had struggled, and the more it had suffered. He'd learned it was more merciful to simply kill the calf and end its pain.

"Sign the papers, so we can get this over with," Trace said.

Dusty sank into the horn and cowhide chair, defeated. The crutch landed with a thump on the handwoven Turkish carpet that framed the two chairs in front of the desk.

"What am I going to do, Trace? How am I going to support Lou Ann and the girls? Without my leg, I'll never ride well enough to work as a trainer. It would have been better for everyone if I'd died in that crash!"

"Don't talk like a fool."

"I've never said anything in my life that made more sense," Dusty said. "The mortgage insurance would have paid off the ranch, and my life insurance would have given Lou Ann and the kids something to live on. Instead, my kids are being forced to leave the only home they've ever known, and Lou Ann is . . . is stuck with half a man."

Trace opened his mouth to frame a denial, but Dusty cut him off.

"Before I came over here this morning, I sat in the barn for a long time with the barrel of my grandfather's Navy Colt stuck in my mouth."

Trace felt his heart take an extra beat. "Dusty—"

"I figured killing myself was the best thing I could do for them." Dusty's hands gripped the arms of the chair so hard his knuckles turned bone white. He glanced fleetingly at Trace, then away. "But I couldn't make myself pull the trigger. So here I am."

Trace's insides tightened, as though he were looking at a savage open wound. His friend was hurting, and he needed desperately to do something to take away his pain. But Dusty wasn't some poor, dumb animal that could be put out of its misery.

Trace said the first thing that came into his head, an idea he'd been mulling over but had delayed acting upon, because he knew it would mean another fight with his father.

"I wasn't going to mention this until later," he said, "but now is as good a time as any to ask. How would you like to work for me?"

Dusty grimaced. "You mean work for Blackjack? I'd rather starve in the street."

"No. I mean work for me. I'm starting up my own quarter horse operation."

"Since when?" Dusty asked suspiciously.

Trace managed a crooked smile. "Since you became available to run a breeding program for me. Who knows better what makes a good cutting horse than the man who's ridden a horse in the finals of the Futurity, the Stakes, and the Derby?" Dusty was one of only a few riders to make the finals in all three events in the triple crown of cutting horse competitions.

Dusty rubbed the sandy-colored stubble on his chin. "I could do it, Trace. There isn't a man in South Texas who knows more about quarter horse conformation than I do. And when it comes to cutting a cow from the herd, I can spot a horse with a knack for stopping and starting better than just about anybody."

"I know. That's why I want you. Will you do it?"

"How does Blackjack feel about hiring a cripple?"

Trace regretted using the word earlier. He waited until Dusty met his gaze before he said, "Blackjack isn't making the hiring decisions. I am."

He saw the skeptical look on Dusty's face and had cause again to regret baring his soul to his friend. He'd made a number of suggestions over the past couple of months for modernization and diversification at Bitter Creek, which Dusty knew his father had vetoed.

Once Blackjack had said no, the subject was no longer open for discussion. Whenever Trace had persisted, his mother had intervened, reminding him that his father shouldn't be upset, and that Trace ought to have some consideration for Blackjack's ailing heart. More than once since his father had gotten home from the hospital, Trace had repressed the urge to bolt.

But there was no one else to take his place.

Trace had known from the time he was old enough to understand speech that as the eldest, he would one day inherit the hundreds of thousands of acres of South Texas ranchland that some noble English ancestor had won on a bet. He'd figured all that would have changed after what he'd done.

He'd gone on a trip after graduation that had taken him around the world . . . and simply hadn't come home. Not for Christmas. Not for Easter. Not for eleven years. Not until he'd been summoned to his dying father's bedside.

Only Blackjack hadn't died.

Trace had been surprised, on his return home, to discover that his younger twin brothers Clay and Owen, and his baby sister Summer, had created lives for themselves that didn't tie them to Bitter Creek.

Owen, following in the footsteps of several Blackthorne forebears, had become a Texas Ranger. Clay had recently been elected, at age thirty, the youngest Attorney General of the State of Texas. Summer, bless her rebellious little heart, had managed to get herself kicked out of every university Blackjack had insisted she attend and was home raising hell until Blackjack could make yet another generous contribution to some institution of higher learning.

It was as though, despite all evidence to the contrary, Blackjack had known Trace was coming home someday, so there was no need to train anyone to take his place. Trace still wasn't sure why he'd returned. There was nothing he wanted in Bitter Creek, Texas.

Except the one thing he couldn't have.

Trace gritted his teeth against the pain that was still there, even after all these years. The wound of betrayal had gone deep and healed badly. Callie had married her father's wrangler, Nolan Monroe, a man at least twenty years her senior, a matter of weeks after Trace had left Texas. She hadn't waited to see if things would settle down so they could get married. She had shut him out of her life for good.

So why had he come back?

Because, for the first time in his life, his father had needed him. And because, damn his soul, he'd heard Callie Creed Monroe's husband had died and left her a widow.

Trace had agreed to stay only until Blackjack could resume his duties. He'd figured he'd be around for six weeks at most, while his father recuperated from bypass surgery, and that he'd deal with Callie when their paths crossed, as they surely would. But Blackjack had never recovered sufficiently to handle all the day-to-day responsibilities of the ranch. And Trace hadn't seen hide nor hair of Callie Creed Monroe.

This business with Dusty was the last straw. Trace hadn't spoken yet with Blackjack about his desire to start a quarter horse operation, but he wasn't going to take no for an answer. He looked at his friend and said, "If you want the job, Dusty, it's yours."

Dusty's face revealed relief, and his brown eyes were misted with a sheen of hope. "I'll have to talk it over with Lou Ann. Where are you going to set up this operation of yours?"

"For the moment, right here at Bitter Creek."

Dusty pursed his mouth thoughtfully. "That northwest section has a pasture perfect for yearlings. Is that where you mean?"

"Yeah, that's it," Trace said. That's where he'd tell Blackjack he was putting his quarter horse operation. As soon as he told his father there was going to be a quarter horse operation.

"Look," Dusty said, his voice excited, "I was working with this three-year-old stud when . . ." He swallowed and continued, "When I had that wreck. Best cutting horse I've had under me in a long time. I had Smart Little Doc signed up for the NCHA World Championship Futurity later this year, but now he's going to auction with the rest of my stock. I think you ought to buy him."

"Just let me know when and where he's being sold," Trace said.

"I'll do that." Dusty lifted his Stetson, brushed his shaggy, dust-colored hair back, and resettled the hat low on his forehead. "I came a hair's breadth from killing myself this morning. And now . . ." He looked at Trace, his eyes full of wonder and disbelief. "Lou Ann . . . the girls . . ."

His voice broke and Trace looked down at the desk to give his friend time to recover himself.

"I'll find out which of the managers' houses here at Bitter Creek is vacant," Trace said to fill the silence.

"Trace, I—"

"I'd be providing a home for whoever managed the operation," Trace interrupted. "Just tell Lou Ann I'll need to know what color to have the walls painted."

He kept his gaze focused on the papers in front of him while Dusty swiped at his eyes with a red kerchief he dragged from the back pocket of his jeans. Then Trace shoved the documents across the desk and handed Dusty a pen. "Sign everywhere the lawyer marked with an X."

When Dusty was done, he dropped the pen on the desk

and slid back in the cowhide chair. "Would you mind getting that other crutch for me?"

"Sure." Trace crossed around the desk and retrieved the crutch that had slid across the floor, then handed it to Dusty, who was already standing, balancing himself on one foot and the other crutch. "When are you getting your prosthesis?" Trace asked.

"I was supposed to start therapy with it a while ago, but—"

"Like a stubborn mule, you've been putting it off," Trace finished for him. "Get yourself another leg, you jackass," he said, laying a supporting arm across Dusty's back. "You're going to need it."

"You bet, Boss," Dusty said with a grin.

"We won't be taking possession of the Rafter S for a while yet," Trace said, as they headed into the high-ceilinged central hallway. "How about inviting me over for supper, so I can enjoy some of your wife's home cooking?"

"Sure. Meanwhile, I'll take a look at what brood mares are available at upcoming auctions and make a list of what you ought to buy."

Trace was hoping to get Dusty out of the ranch house before his mother and father returned from a board meeting at the Bitter Creek First National Bank, but they encountered his parents just as they were entering the front door.

Trace felt Dusty recoil at the sight of Blackjack. His father was a tall man, broad in the chest, an imposing figure with flinty gray eyes that had a way of staring right through a man. He still had a headful of thick black hair, most of which was hidden right now beneath an expensive Resistol with a Buster Welch double crease in the crown.

Though Buster had long since retired from competitive cutting, he was about the best cutter alive, and many a cowboy had emulated the way he creased his hat. To Buster, a cutting horse wasn't just a show animal, he was a link to a vanishing way of life. Last year, at the gala held in Fort Worth during the final week of the Championship Futurity, Buster had received the Charles Goodnight Award, named after cattleman and nineteenth-century trailblazer Charles Goodnight.

Blackjack had recently learned he'd be receiving the prestigious Goodnight award himself at the upcoming Futurity in December. Being there to see his father receive the award was one more reason Blackjack had given Trace for staying at Bitter Creek long after he'd planned to be gone.

"You finished signing everything?" Blackjack said by way of greeting to Dusty.

"We're done," Trace said, speaking before Dusty could say anything to worsen the situation. "Dusty was just leaving."

"I was so sorry to hear about your misfortune," his mother said. "How is . . . ?"

It was clear to Trace that his mother couldn't remember Lou Ann's name. Eve Blackthorne had never been the sort of PTA mom who consorted with other parents and knew the names of her children's friends. Whenever Trace had wanted to find his mother as a boy, he'd sought her out in the upstairs studio where she spent her days and nights producing the most beautiful oil paintings he'd ever seen. Whenever he hugged his mother, he smelled paint thinner, rather than perfume.

His mother frequently seemed distracted, as though she were listening to another conversation besides the one in which she was engaged. Watching his mother over the months he'd spent as an adult in his parents' home, Trace had decided that when she wasn't actually painting on canvas, she was mentally creating her next work in her head.

It was hard to resent her total dedication to her work, because the art she produced was so unique. He wasn't the only one who thought her work distinctive. Her paintings had been hung in some of the finest galleries in the country. But sometimes, like now, it was irksome to realize how totally out of touch she was with the real world.

"Lou Ann is fine, Mrs. Blackthorne," Dusty said, leaning his armpits onto his crutches as he reached up to touch his hat brim in greeting.

"I saw her waiting outside," his mother said. She frowned at the pinned-up denim that covered Dusty's stump, then added, "I guess you can't drive."

"No, ma'am," Dusty said.

"Well, you mustn't keep her waiting in this heat," his mother said.

"No, ma'am."

As Dusty headed for the door, Trace turned to his father and said, "I'll meet you in the library as soon as I see Dusty out."

He followed Dusty down the front steps and out to the black Chevy Silverado parked in the shade of one of a dozen elegant magnolia trees that lined the circular drive. Lou Ann was waiting in the driver's seat. She wasn't wearing any makeup, and the ravages of the past few months were visible in the new lines around her eyes and mouth. He watched as she anxiously followed Dusty's progress around the extended cab pickup.

"We're all done," Trace said, momentarily drawing her gaze in his direction. "I'll let Dusty tell you the good news."

She glanced at Dusty, who was hopping toward the passenger's seat after dropping his crutches in the bed of the truck. "What good news?" she asked Dusty.

Dusty used his arms to lever himself onto the torn leather seat before he answered, "I'm going to manage a quarter horse breeding operation for Trace."

Trace felt guilty at the grateful look Lou Ann shot him. It hadn't been charity. Dusty knew quarter horses—and more specifically, quarter horses bred for cutting—like a prairie dog knew its own hole.

"Thank you, Trace," she said, reaching out to cover his hand where it lay on the windowsill of the pickup.

"Dusty's the one doing me a favor," Trace said, pulling his hand free and thumping the dented door of the Silverado with the flat of his hand. "But I'll accept an invitation to supper, if you want to thank me anyway."

"You've got it," Lou Ann said, her face looking years younger with the radiant smile she now wore.

Trace waited until the Chevy had exited the paved circular drive and was heading down the road that led back ten miles to the entrance to Bitter Creek, before he turned and walked back to the house.

He found his mother sitting at the desk in the library, pen in hand, while his father stood behind her, pointing to the places where she should sign.

Blackjack looked up and said, "He give you any trouble?"

"No." Trace saw the fleeting look of censure flash across his father's face when he left off the "sir" that should have followed his reply. The "sir" had been automatic when he was a boy, even through college. He hadn't used it once since he'd come home.

Blackjack was too smart to confront him over the matter head-on, because that might have given Trace the opening he needed to discuss the changes time had wrought—and to ask either for the authority to act without consulting his father or to be relieved of the duties he'd assumed, so he could leave.

The quarter horse operation was a compromise, a way Trace could accomplish one of his own goals while still helping out his father until Blackjack was well enough to take over the ranch work himself—or willing to admit he never would. The need to employ Dusty was finally going to force the long-postponed confrontation between them.

"Am I done?" his mother asked.

Blackjack sorted through the papers and said, "One more."

Trace decided to make his move now, while his mother was here. After all, as the papers she was signing pointed out, his mother owned half of everything. If he could convince her to say yes to his proposal, Blackjack might go along to avoid an argument. His parents didn't wrangle often, but when they did, the rafters rattled.

"I've been thinking about buying a quarter horse stud and some good mares," Trace said.

Blackjack never looked up. "We have all we need, but I suppose we can afford a few more."

"I plan to breed them for cutting," Trace said.

His father straightened and focused his gaze on Trace. "That would require quite an investment of capital. If I'm not mistaken, the best two-year-old cutter went for about $80,000 at the NCHA Select Futurity Sale last year."

"You're not mistaken." Trace kept his body outwardly relaxed, but he could feel his pulse begin to pound. He resisted the urge to explain or defend his proposal, merely kept his eyes locked with his father's.

He watched the small frown lines form and ease along Blackjack's forehead before his father's hand settled on the back of his mother's chair. "Too much risk. Too little reward," he said.

"I wasn't asking for permission," Trace replied. "I was stating a fact. I'm going to buy some quarter horse stock and start up a breeding operation."

"If you're so interested in breeding something, how about marrying the eldest Creed girl and breeding me a few grandsons," Blackjack retorted. "She's been a widow damn near a year. Can't believe you haven't rushed her to the altar."

"I don't love—"

His father made a barking sound to cut him off. "Hellfire and damnation. I didn't love your mother, either, when I married her, but she brought me fifty thousand acres of good DeWitt grassland. That Creed girl can do the same for you. She's next in line to inherit Three Oaks."

Trace glanced at his mother, expecting to see some reaction to his father's callous admission. But her gaze was focused on the documents before her, as though she were oblivious to his verbal stab.

He wondered why his father stayed married to his mother, since there seemed so little love between them, but he knew the answer without asking. Texas was a community property state. If his father couldn't bear to share the responsibility of the ranch with his son, he would hate like hell giving up half of the wealth he'd accumulated during thirty-three years of marriage—and the land his mother had brought to the union—in a divorce.

That didn't explain why his mother stayed with his father. Trace had asked her, after his parents' most recent shouting match, why she didn't divorce Blackjack. Her answer had surprised him.

"I love him. I always have."

He understood all too well the pain of loving someone who didn't love you back. Which was why he had no intention of marrying Callie Creed Monroe.

"You'd do well to hog-tie that little filly before some other cowboy figures out what a prize she is and steals her out from under your nose," his father said. "I'd give my left nut to see Jesse Creed's face the day my son married his daughter."

"I'm not—"

"Imagine the bitter bile of knowing a Blackthorne will own Three Oaks when he's gone," Blackjack continued. "That parcel of Creed land smack-dab in the middle of my ranch has been like a stone in my boot for as long as I can remember. I'll be damned glad to get rid of the irritation once and for all."

During the course of his father's speech, Trace was remembering the first time Blackjack had suggested he court and marry Callie Creed. He'd been a senior in high school, Callie a freshman. At the time, Blackjack had been enraged at having been thwarted yet again in his attempt to buy Three Oaks from Jesse Creed. During an angry tirade, he'd suggested that if Trace got Callie pregnant, her father would have to let them marry. Then, when Jesse died, Trace and Callie would inherit Three Oaks.

The result of his father's suggestion had been to make Trace keep his distance from Callie Creed. He wasn't about to be forced into marrying some girl just so his father could spite her father. Besides, at eighteen, he was determined to run his own life, free of his father's meddling.

But because of that tirade, he'd taken his first good look at Callie Creed. Although they'd gone to school together their whole lives, he'd never paid much attention to her, because she was four years younger. But once he'd let himself look, he couldn't keep his eyes off her. Perhaps because he'd forbidden himself any contact with her, she became even more attractive to him.

He spent his entire senior year resisting the urge to ask her out on a date. He refused to give his father the satisfaction of thinking he'd been manipulated into it. He went away to college without ever speaking to Callie Creed, without running his fingers through her tawny hair, without looking deep into her sky-blue eyes or kissing her bowed, pouty lips.

Four years later, she'd asked him for directions to the LBJ Library, looking lost and scared and more lovely than any female had a right to look. He'd fallen hard and fast. And she'd left him high and dry.

"I'm not marrying Callie Creed Monroe," he said in a hard voice. "I'm starting a quarter horse breeding program."

"The hell you are!" his father retorted.

His mother looked up at Trace, then over her shoulder at his father, as though she'd just noticed the antagonism between them. "Please don't argue," she said.

His father patted his mother on the shoulder. "We're just having a friendly discussion, Eve."

"I could hear you all the way in the kitchen."

All three of them turned to find his sister standing in the open doorway to the library.

"Get out and close the door behind you," Blackjack said.

Summer strolled in, leaving the door opened wide. Her naturally curly blond hair was falling out of a ponytail, and her tailored Western shirt showed signs of having been nuzzled by a grass-eating horse. She wore skin-tight jeans that made Trace wonder how she could get her leg up over the saddle and scuffed boots that had to be almost as old as she was.

"You can't keep ordering Trace around, Daddy, without giving him a chance to do anything on his own," Summer said.

"Thanks, Summer. But I can fight my own battles," Trace said, both exasperated and touched by her interference.

"It sounded to me like you were losing," she pointed out with a grin, as she crossed the room toward their father. She seemed utterly confident of Blackjack's acceptance of her presence, despite his order to get out. Sure enough, as her arm slid around Blackjack's waist, his arm circled her shoulders. She stood on tiptoe and kissed his cheek, then grinned and said, "You know I'm right, Daddy."

Blackjack made a grunting sound in his throat, but he didn't contradict her.

No wonder his sister was such a brat, Trace thought. She had their father wrapped around her little finger.

"Why can't Trace start a quarter horse operation?" Summer asked, her candid hazel eyes focused up at Blackjack.

"He wouldn't know a good cutting horse from a nag," Blackjack said. "How can he hope to breed a winner?"

Trace bit his tongue rather than defend himself.

Summer winked at Trace, then said, "Well, Daddy, there's one sure way to settle the matter."

"What's that?" Blackjack asked.

"I'd be willing to bet you Trace can pick a horse that makes it into the top ten at the Open finals of the Futurity in Fort Worth."

Blackjack laughed. "There must be a thousand horses entered in that competition."

"More like twelve hundred," Summer said with a grin. "And my bet is still on the table."

"What are the stakes?" her father asked, his eyes narrowed.

"If Trace's horse finishes in the top ten, you fund whatever operation he wants here at Bitter Creek."

"And if it doesn't?" Blackjack asked.

"You don't have to fund the operation," Summer said with a shrug.

The fact that his father was playing this sort of game with his sister convinced Trace that it wasn't the idea of a breeding operation Blackjack objected to, so much as the fact that it was Trace who'd come up with it.

"The stakes aren't high enough," Blackjack said.

Summer shot a look at Trace that warned him he'd better win, then said, "All right. If Trace's horse doesn't make it into the top ten, you don't fund the operation *and* I'll go back to college and get my degree."

Trace watched his father eye Summer speculatively. "If I thought you really meant that—"

"I do," Summer interrupted.

"If I agree to this bargain of yours, I'm going to hold you to it," Blackjack warned.

"You know I'd never welsh on a bet, Daddy. You've taught me better than that."

Trace watched as his immovable rock of a father let himself be shifted like a handful of pebbles by his only daughter's irresistible charm.

"What do you say, Daddy? Is it a deal?"

"Deal!" Blackjack said, reaching out to shake her hand.

"Wait a minute," Trace said. "How the hell am I supposed to come up with a horse that can finish in the top ten at the Futurity barely five months before the event? And why should I have to?"

Blackjack turned to Trace and said, "I'm giving you a chance to have things your way. Take it or leave it."

Trace hesitated, shot a look at his sister, then stuck out his hand. "I'll take it."

Chapter 2

CALLIE CREED MONROE COULD COUNT ON ONE hand the number of regrets she'd accumulated in twenty-eight years of living. Ever since that first gigantic leap off a cliff without looking to see where she'd land, Callie had lived a reasoned, cautious, carefully considered existence. But she deeply regretted not branding the four registered quarter horses that had been stolen from Three Oaks the night before.

It was bad enough losing the horses, because her family lived on a knotted shoestring, and this disaster had broken it for about the last time. But to Callie's horror and dismay, Owen Blackthorne had shown up at the horse barn at dawn, wearing a badge, asking questions, and giving her father answers he didn't want to hear.

"What the hell do you mean you can't find them if they weren't branded," her father was ranting. "I've got color photos of every damned one of them!"

Callie had to give Owen credit. He'd remained patient and even-tempered despite Jesse's abusive harangue. But she was convinced the rippling tension between the two men had less to do with her father's fury over the stolen

30

horses, than with the fact that her eldest brother Sam lived in a wheelchair, and Owen Blackthorne had put him there.

"I understand your frustration," Owen said. "We can post the photos at slaughterhouses around the state—"

"Slaughterhouses?" Callie interrupted, appalled at the thought of her beautiful quarter horses being turned into dog food, or worse, being served at some European dinner table, where horse meat was a delicacy. "Those two-year-olds are worth tens of thousands of dollars each at auction."

"It's possible they might be sold at a small auction somewhere," Owen conceded. "The truth is, horse thieves don't normally take that risk. It's a damned shame you didn't brand them."

Callie felt the weight of blame on her shoulders. The four fillies had been born and raised at Three Oaks. She had meant to have them freeze-branded, which allowed the hair to grow back in a lighter color instead of leaving a scar. But over the past hectic year since Nolan had died, so many things that weren't absolutely necessary had fallen through the cracks. And she had believed, with good reason, that the fillies were safe from thieves.

Three Oaks was a virtual island, 65,000 acres of rich Creed grassland completely surrounded by 745,000 acres of fenced Blackthorne property. There were plenty of roads crisscrossing Three Oaks, but there was only one way in or out, a single easement that wound across Bitter Creek Ranch, through at least a dozen gates, to the world beyond. Callie had made the terrible mistake of assuming no horse thief would dare to steal livestock from Three Oaks, when he could be so easily apprehended on the way in or out.

Her father must have had the same idea, because his eyes narrowed as he said, "The only person who could get a horse trailer in or out of here without being detected is someone able to move freely over Blackthorne land. I may not be able to pin this on your father, but I know he's responsible."

"My father doesn't need four more horses," Owen said.

Callie could see her father was incensed by Owen's implication that what was everything to the Creeds was a pittance to the Blackthornes.

"Blackjack has been trying to force me into selling Three Oaks ever since I stole the woman he loved from under his nose," her father snarled. "He can try every dirty trick in the book, but I'll never let him break me. I'll give this place to charity before I'll sign it over to him!"

"Are you accusing my father of stealing your stock?"

"It wouldn't be the first time one of you Blackthornes hit below the belt!"

Owen's body visibly tautened at the jibe. He opened his mouth to speak, then clamped his jaw tight without replying. Callie knew there were no words to defend what he'd done. Too many people had seen the cheap shot he'd taken on the football field that had put Sam in a wheelchair.

She remembered how miserable—and defiant—Owen had looked as he walked down the hall at the hospital and stood before her father, chin up, shoulders squared, to apologize.

"It was an accident, Mr. Creed," he'd said. "I'm really sorry."

"Sorry won't bring my boy's legs back!" her father had shot back.

"If there's anything I can do to help—"

"You can keep your Blackthorne charity!" her father had shouted. "And get the hell out of here!"

The one time Owen had come to the house after Sam was home from the hospital, her father had met him at the kitchen door with a double-pump shotgun. Now her father was being asked to put his trust in a man he despised.

"Why the hell did you come here, if you don't intend to help?" her father demanded.

"I'm here to do my job," Owen said.

"Get off my property. Get out! Go!"

Owen stood his ground. "I'm not through—"

"I sure as hell am!"

Callie saw that her father intended to shove the Texas Ranger out of his way as he stomped past him, but Owen deftly stepped aside, and the two avoided coming to physical blows.

Callie tugged her Stetson down low on her forehead, aware as she did so that her hand was shaking. She stuck her hands in the back pockets of her Levi's to hide her agitation, eyed Owen ruefully from beneath the brim of her hat, and ventured, "That went pretty well, all things considered."

Owen, who had the tall, lanky look of all the Blackthorne men, along with a shock of black hair and piercing gray eyes, shook his head and chuffed out a laugh. "I figure it's a good day when no shots are fired."

Callie caught herself smiling but sobered as the enormity of the loss struck her with renewed force. "Are you sure there isn't any way to trace those four fillies without a brand?" she asked. "Freckles Fancy has such a distinctive blaze. Surely you could send out a description that would get her recognized."

Owen sighed and resettled his hat. "There are a hundred thousand horses in Texas with distinctive blazes. My suggestion is to brand what you have left that hasn't been branded. It won't prevent theft, but it'll give us a better chance of recovering your stock if this ever happens again."

Callie lifted her gaze to meet Owen's. "You think this might happen again?"

"Face it, Callie. You made yourself an easy mark. If you don't do something to improve the situation, what's to keep the thieves from coming back to help themselves again?"

"I can't figure out how they managed to get in and out without getting caught the first time," Callie replied. "Unless they had the kind of help my father suggested."

"You're barking up the wrong tree if you think my family had anything to do with this."

"You did it all right!" a childish voice behind Owen accused.

Owen stepped aside as Callie's ten-year-old son Eli took an angry step forward. The boy glared at Owen, his hands clenched at his sides. Callie drew a sharp breath, wondering if Owen would see the resemblance, so obvious to her, between her son and Owen's brother Trace.

Eli was tall for his age but rail thin, with narrow shoulders and big feet he had yet to grow into. His eyes were the same sky blue as her own, but his sharp cheekbones and square jaw and slash of mouth were all Blackthorne.

Callie had been careful over the years to ensure that Eli

did not cross paths with any Blackthornes. She had convinced her family that Nolan Monroe was Eli's father with the story that they had slept together when she was home from college for the long Christmas holiday. But Owen knew about her relationship with Trace.

Callie held her breath as Owen surveyed the boy from top to toe, expecting him to ask why she'd kept Trace's son a secret from him. Owen merely observed, "A man can cause a lot of harm making accusations without proof."

"You're a Blackthorne. That's all the proof I need!" Eli retorted.

"Eli! Apologize to Mr. Blackthorne."

"I won't!"

"I'm sorry, Owen," Callie said. "Ever since Nolan died—" Callie felt the sting in her nose that warned of tears. She closed her eyes to hold them back, but there was nothing she could do to stop the quiver in her chin. The thickness in her throat made it painful to swallow.

Every time she thought she was over Nolan's death, something like this would happen to remind her how much she missed him. Nolan had not been her first love, but she had grown to love him. And he was the only father Eli had ever known.

Callie opened her eyes in time to see the stricken look on Eli's face before he glowered at Owen and said, "This is all your fault!"

Callie understood her son's behavior. Eli had been mad at the world since his father's death, and the Blackthornes made a convenient target for his anger. But there was no way the Blackthornes could be blamed for Nolan's death from colon cancer. "Go back to the house, Eli."

"Gram says to tell you breakfast is on the table," Eli said. "You're not invited," he spat at Owen.

"Eli!" Callie said, appalled at her son's rudeness.

"No Blackthorne is ever gonna sit at our table, Mom. Grampa says they're all lying, cheating—"

"That's enough!" Callie said, cutting off her son. "Go back to the house. I'll be there as soon as I've finished here."

Her son shot a look of disdain in Owen's direction, then turned and stalked away.

"Lot of hate in that kid," Owen murmured. He turned and sought her gaze. "Kind of hoped you'd be the one to put an end to that."

Well, he hadn't forgotten she'd once loved a Blackthorne. Owen had discovered her relationship with Trace during his sophomore year at Texas A&M University in College Station, when he and his twin brother Clay had driven down to Austin one weekend to visit Trace and caught Callie in his bedroom.

"I've done my best to convince Eli the Blackthornes aren't the devil in disguise," she said. "But it hasn't been easy when his grandfather blames all his troubles on your father."

"Even when the accusations aren't justified," Owen pointed out.

"Don't defend Blackjack to me," Callie retorted. "Your father has done enough harm over the years to warrant the black name he bears, and my brother lives in a wheelchair because of you!"

Owen's gray eyes flared with anger. And pain. It was the pain that made her wish back the words she'd spoken. But it was too late for that.

"How is Sam?" Owen asked at last.

He's an embittered, antisocial alcoholic.

Callie held her tongue. They wouldn't be making a TV movie-of-the-week anytime soon featuring Sam Creed coping nobly with his paralysis. Sam had railed violently and vehemently against his fate ever since he'd woken up in the hospital and learned he would never walk again. But she would never betray her brother's shortcomings to anyone outside the family. Especially not to the man who had made Sam so much less than he could have been.

"Sorry I asked," Owen muttered when she didn't answer.

Owen had already turned to leave when she said, "Sam's become something of a computer whiz. He keeps himself busy doing the ranch paperwork." *When he's sober.*

Owen managed a smile over his shoulder. "I'm glad to hear it. I'll call you if I get any word on your stolen stock."

Callie spent the time it took her to walk the distance from the horse barn to the ranch house trying to regain some measure of inner calm. It was a losing battle.

The official visit from Owen Blackthorne had brought the past barreling back, and all her fears along with it. Callie had managed to avoid Trace Blackthorne during the three months he'd been back at Bitter Creek, but if he stayed around, it was inevitable that she would meet him again face-to-face. How would he look at her? What could she say to him?

Callie knew she had hurt Trace when she married No-lan, but she hadn't known what else to do. If she had remained single, it was too likely Trace would have figured out Eli was his son. As badly as Sam had coped with his paralysis, marrying Trace had been out of the question. And she had refused to take the chance that Trace would settle for having Eli, if he couldn't have them both.

She had made a good life with Nolan Monroe. She'd learned to love Nolan for his kindness and his gentleness and his unwavering support. But she'd missed the passion she'd shared with Trace. Nolan Monroe was not the other half of her soul.

On his deathbed, Nolan had urged her to tell Trace about his son, but Callie had been careful never to promise she would. She was afraid of what Trace might do if he ever found out the truth. What if he wanted custody of his son? In this part of Texas, the Blackthornes generally got what they wanted. She would never give up her son. And she could never marry his father. So what choice did she have but to keep Eli a secret from Trace?

" 'Bout time you showed up," her father said as she crossed the wooden back porch and shoved open the screen door. The hardwood floor creaked as she stepped inside the kitchen to be greeted by the smell of bacon and strong, black coffee. The house was old, and had become more decrepit in the years since Sam's accident, when they'd been so pinched for cash. But Callie loved every curling piece of flowered wallpaper, every water-stained ceiling, and every warped floorboard of it.

The original Three Oaks, built even before the days of the Texas Republic, had been a cotton plantation along the Brazos River, but the Southern mansion where the first Creed ancestors were born and had died had burned down during the Civil War. Southern Major Jacob Tyler Creed had built a new house similar to the first Three Oaks but much farther south, on the small bit of land along Bitter Creek that was all he had left after a man who called himself, "Blackthorne, without the mister," had stolen his inheritance.

The two-story antebellum mansion where Callie had been born, with its tall columns across the face and porch on the second floor, was situated near a stand of live oaks that provided wonderful shade in the summer. The kitchen was large enough to accommodate an immense trestle table, which was filled now with her family.

"Is that sonofabitch gone?" Sam demanded when he spotted her.

Callie shot Sam a reproving look, the reason for which became apparent when her four-year-old daughter Hannah parroted, "Is that sun-bitch gone?"

Callie crossed and lifted Hannah out of her brother's lap. She glared at him over Hannah's head, noting his brown eyes were bloodshot before he guiltily dropped his glance. "Yes, he's gone," she said as she settled her daughter into the youth chair next to Sam's wheelchair.

"Would you bring some more butter to the table?" her mother asked.

Callie watched as Eli crawled up onto one knee in his chair and stretched across the length of the table for another biscuit. She tugged his ear to get his attention as she passed by on her way to the refrigerator. "Ask Gram to please pass the biscuits," she instructed.

Eli dropped back into his seat with a sullen look and said, "Pass the biscuits, Gram."

"*Please* pass the biscuits, Gram," Callie corrected. She stood by the refrigerator door, her eyes focused on her son, noting the mutinous thrust of his chin, wishing Nolan were here, knowing that Eli was testing her. His behavior had become increasingly defiant during the last months of Nolan's illness. Since Nolan's death, he had become nearly incorrigible. She kept hoping that if she were patient, yet persistent in demanding courtesy, his attitude would improve.

"Stop nagging the boy," her father said. And in the same breath to Eli, "Do what your mother says."

"*Please, please, please* pass the biscuits," her son said in an aggrieved voice.

"For cripe's sake, take them!"

Callie groaned in disbelief as her teenage brother Luke lobbed the basket of biscuits across the table into her son's outstretched hands.

Callie crossed back to the table with a stick of butter, unwrapped it, and dropped it into the chipped saucer they were using for a butter dish, before she settled into the chair next to her daughter.

There were two empty seats on the opposite side of the table. One had been occupied by Nolan. The other belonged to her sister Bayleigh, who was away completing her final year of clinical work toward her degree in veterinary medicine at Texas A&M. They had both been her allies in a household that was divided by the difficult financial choices that were constantly being forced upon them. Like the one they would have to make now.

"Your father has been telling me we can't expect to recover the stolen fillies," her mother said as Callie served herself a spoonful of scrambled eggs and two slices of bacon.

"It's doubtful," Callie conceded. She saw Freckles

Fancy in her mind's eye, then thought of the playful filly cut up for steaks. Suddenly, she had no appetite.

"What are we supposed to do now?" Luke asked. "I told you we should have gotten some insurance."

"We couldn't afford insurance," Callie reminded him. She heard the fear in Luke's voice. At sixteen, her brother was old enough to understand the desperate nature of their financial situation, but still too young to be of any real help improving it. Callie took a deep breath and said, "We'll just have to lease our pasture to hunters for the season."

"No," her father said in a hard voice. "I won't have those corporate bigwigs from Dallas and Houston tramping around my property pretending to be the Great White Hunter and mistaking my fence posts for turkeys, my trucks for wild boar, and my cows for deer!"

Sam, Luke, and Eli laughed, and Callie couldn't help smiling at the picture her father had painted. Actually, he wasn't far off the mark. The corporate honchos from around the country who leased tracts of Texas pasture for hunting were likely to be novices. It was entirely possible they would lose a cow or two to a stray bullet or find one of their trucks peppered with buckshot pellets.

But they could earn far more leasing the land for hunting than they could putting it to use merely as pasture for cattle, and the land would do double duty if it were leased, since they could still use it to graze their stock. Unlike the Blackthornes, they had no oil under their land to provide a financial cushion in hard times.

"We need the money," she said flatly.

"How much can we realistically expect to get if we lease the land to hunters?" Sam asked.

"The going rate is $10,000 per gun, per season, and that's for a small pasture of ten thousand acres," Callie said.

Luke whistled, and his brown eyes lit up. "We could make a fortune, Dad. I could get a Harley!"

"No motorcycle, Luke," her mother said. "They're too dangerous."

Her father's features remained obdurate. "We'd have strangers all over the damned place."

"I think that's a price we have to pay," Callie said.

"Never."

"What else can we do?" Callie asked.

"I'll borrow from the bank," her father said.

"They won't loan us any more money. Three Oaks is mortgaged to the hilt. We're in hock with every supplier we have. The market for beef is down, and without some form of income, now that the two-year-olds I planned to sell at the Futurity auction are gone, we'll be lucky to make it past Christmas without going belly-up."

"Blackjack did this," her father muttered. "He stole those fillies. I know he did."

"We don't know that," Callie said. "We certainly can't prove it. Right now, we have to figure out how to replace our missing stock. And the best way to get some quick capital is to lease our pasture for hunting."

To Callie's surprise, her mother took her side in the argument. "Sometimes we have to make sacrifices," she said. "Do what's best, even if it isn't what we'd like."

The words were familiar to Callie, a refrain she'd heard all her life. *Sacrifices have to be made.* She had her mother as an example, who did without Vera Wang dresses or season tickets to the Houston Opera or a racy little Mercedes Benz coupe or any of the other luxuries she might have expected from life on a ranch the size of Three Oaks—which was small only in comparison to an operation like the Bitter Creek Cattle Company—and never complained.

She admired her mother and had tried hard all her life to emulate her. "Mom's right, Dad," she said. "We have to do what's necessary to survive, whether we like it or not."

"It's only for a year, Jesse," her mother said.

"It's only for a year, Jesse," Callie's four-year-old daughter chirped.

Her father's eyes focused on Hannah's tiny, cherubic face, before he met her mother's steady gaze. Callie watched her father's shoulders sag in defeat.

"Aw, hell," he said. "Lease the damned land. I'll roast in hell before I let Blackjack beat me."

"All right, Dad. I'll take care of it." Callie had won, but she didn't feel triumphant.

"The Rafter S put a Notice of Auction in the *Bitter Creek Chronicle*," Sam said. "Dusty Simpson ought to have some pretty good stock we can buy at bargain prices."

"Thanks, Sam," Callie said.

"We might as well pick up whatever scraps Blackjack has left," her father muttered.

"What do you mean?" Callie asked.

"Blackjack stole the Rafter S from Dusty Simpson the same way he's been trying all these years to steal Three Oaks from me."

"Dusty Simpson lost his ranch because he lost his leg in a car accident," Callie said.

"What makes you think that 'accident' was an 'accident'?" her father said, lifting a brow. "You only have to take one look at your brother to know the depths the Blackthornes will sink to when they want something. The only way Clay Blackthorne could become wide receiver for the Bitter Creek Coyotes was if Sam was out of the way. So Owen took care of the matter for him."

"It was an accident," Callie protested.

"Yeah," her father said sarcastically. "Like Dusty Simpson 'accidentally' lost his leg in a hit-and-run. And those four fillies were 'accidentally' stolen a few months before the Futurity sale."

Callie was disturbed by her father's fixation on Jackson Blackthorne as the root of all evil. She couldn't believe Blackjack would resort to such underhanded methods to get what he wanted. He was simply too rich to need Dusty Simpson's small ranch. And though she didn't doubt Blackjack wanted Three Oaks, he wasn't entirely responsible for their current financial straits. As Owen had pointed out, Blackjack could hardly have much use for four two-year-old quarter horses. They wouldn't even be eligible to enter the major cutting competitions for another year.

But her father's suspicions were grounded on facts. Clay Blackthorne had become the wide receiver for the Bitter Creek Coyotes. Someone had managed to get a horse trailer in and out of Three Oaks without being noticed by anyone on Blackthorne property. And the Blackthornes had ended up with Dusty Simpson's ranch.

"Too bad the days of frontier justice are past, when you could hang a horse thief," her father said. "I'd pay good money to see Jackson Blackthorne jerking at the end of a rope."

Callie heard a gasp. Her gaze darted to her mother, whose eyes were wide with shock and dismay.

"There will be no more of that kind of talk," she said.

"You can't deny—"

"Jesse, please," her mother said, cutting off her father.

"Jesse, please," Hannah mimicked.

Callie clamped a hand over her daughter's mouth. She could feel the tension stretching the distance of the table between her parents, like a piece of barbed wire strung too tight and ready to snap.

Callie had heard enough arguments between her parents over the years to know her father was still jealous of her mother's long-ago relationship with Jackson Blackthorne. She had never even seen her mother speak to Blackjack, but to hear her father talk, their romance had never ended.

It was impossible for Callie to imagine her mother in love with Jackson Blackthorne. Even more difficult to imagine Blackjack in love with her mother. And if they'd been in love with one another, as her father suspected, why hadn't they gotten married? To hear her father talk, all Blackjack would have needed to do was crook his finger, and her mother would have come running. So what had gone wrong?

Callie had never asked. Would never ask. And her mother had never volunteered to tell. But Callie couldn't help wondering. Was rage over losing her mother the reason Blackjack seemed so determined to ruin them financially? Or was he merely carrying on the tradition begun by previous generations of Blackthornes and Creeds?

In the end, her father was no match for the pleading look in her mother's eyes. "All right, Ren," he said. "I'll let it go . . . and see about getting some flak jackets for my cows."

Her mother smiled. "Thank you, Jesse."

"Will you come to the auction at the Rafter S with me, Dad?" Callie asked. "I could use your help." With everything at risk, she didn't want to make a mistake.

"Sure," he said. "Count me in."

"Can I come, Mom?" Eli asked.

"Can I come, Mom?" Hannah echoed.

"We'll see," Callie said.

"That means no," Eli moaned. "Can I come, Grampa?"

"We'll see," he said with a smile and a glance at Callie.

Callie made a face at her father. Eli was more excited by a flashy-looking horse than one with the right bloodlines, but maybe she ought to take him along. It wasn't too early for Eli to start learning what he needed to know. Someday he'd be helping Luke to manage the ranch.

Assuming Blackjack didn't figure out a way to swallow Three Oaks whole . . . and spit the Creeds back out.

Chapter 5

"I'VE FOUND A HORSE I THINK CAN WIN THAT bet for me," Trace said. "He's being auctioned here at the Rafter S this afternoon. I want your okay to buy him."

Blackjack thumbed away the condensation on the ice-cold bottle of Lone Star that sat on the red-checked tablecloth before him, then looked up and said, "You're wasting your time."

"It's my time."

"But my money," Blackjack pointed out.

Trace didn't plead. He didn't cajole. He didn't demand. He kept his eyes shuttered, his body still, as though his father's answer mattered not at all.

"All right. Go ahead," Blackjack said at last. "If you see anything else you like, help yourself. I've got deep pockets."

Trace forcibly held his tongue.

"Hey, Boss!" a cowboy called.

"What is it—"

"What do you want—"

Trace cut himself off, realizing he and Blackjack had

both answered the summons. Trace tipped his head, conceding the role to his father.

"What is it, Whitey?" Blackjack asked.

"Uh . . . I was . . ." The cowboy took off his sweat-stained hat and swatted it against his jeans, raising a cloud of dust.

"Spit it out," Blackjack ordered.

"Trace said I was to come and get him when the auctioneer got around to the cutting stock," the cowboy answered.

Trace felt his gut twist as an anguished look flickered briefly in his father's eyes.

"You've delivered your message," Blackjack said, dismissing the cowboy. He took one last swallow of his beer, then, without another word, shoved his chair back and headed toward the corral where Dusty Simpson's stock was being sold. Trace followed a respectful step behind him.

Trace was more than willing to play the dutiful son for the benefit of their neighbors, not to mention the myriad strangers who'd shown up at the Rafter S wearing Larry Mahan hats, silver belt buckles, and ostrich boots. It seemed half the state of Texas was hoping to buy a small piece of Dusty Simpson's life.

The auction had the look of an upscale fair, with a striped food tent that offered the choice of free champagne, cold beer, or iced tea with the catered barbecue. A clown entertained the children with balloon tricks, and bleachers had been set up near the corral where several girls in tight jeans and white hats handed out printed four-color brochures giving details of the sale. The late August day was sunny and hot, with no threat of rain.

"You two hold up there while I get your picture."

"Sure, Mom." Trace waited for his father to sling an arm around him and pull him close, as he might have when Trace was a boy, but Blackjack stuck his thumbs in his front pockets. Trace stood next to him, his hip cocked, as his mother snapped away with her Nikon. She did all of her paintings from photographs and had come along with them to the Rafter S, camera in hand, in search of a subject for her next work.

"Smile, Trace," his mother coaxed.

Trace tipped his hat back off his forehead and bared his teeth.

"You, too, Jackson," his mother ordered his father, snapping away.

He and his father glanced at each other, saw the corresponding grimaces, and broke out laughing.

"Wonderful!" his mother said.

Trace's gaze slid beyond his father to a commotion in front of the reviewing stands near the corral. A sorrel stallion with the numeral 2 painted on its hip was rearing, trumpeting its fear and rage as it struggled to pull free of the handler showing it off in the ring. Trace's smile faded as he recognized the woman hauling a boy off his perch on the corral and out of harm's way.

"Callie," he murmured.

She fiercely hugged the skinny shoulders of the long-legged boy, while a little blond girl clung tightly to her knee. He realized they must be her kids.

He looked for the changes time had wrought, but for her, it seemed time had stood still. The delicate lines at the corners of her eyes hadn't been there eleven years ago, but he recognized the familiar fullness of her breasts, her still-slim waist, and trim hips. The sun kissed a long blond braid where it trailed down her back beneath a battered black Stetson. An erotic memory flashed of her silky hair spread across his flesh.

Trace didn't want to remember. He turned away and heard his father murmur something under his breath. He followed his father's gaze and saw what had caught Blackjack's attention.

"Ren," his father repeated. "And Jesse."

Trace had expected Jesse to show up for the sale. It was common knowledge in town that the Creeds needed stock to replace what had been stolen a few weeks ago. But he hadn't expected to see Jesse's wife. Or his daughter. Or her kids.

Trace felt an ache in his chest, almost a physical pain, as he watched Callie brush at a stubborn cowlick in the boy's short black hair. The kid ducked out of her reach, bending to retrieve his lacquered straw hat from the dust where it had fallen. She gave him a quick, reassuring pat on the butt before he climbed onto the bottom rail of the corral, lapping his elbows over the top rail to steady himself.

Callie then picked up the little girl, who clasped her legs around Callie's hips. She tousled the girl's fine blond curls, then kissed her on the nose and gave her another hug, before crossing back to stand beside Jesse and Ren near the bleachers.

She should have been my wife, he thought. *Those should have been my kids.* He fought to control the anger that had been so carefully banked, but it flared to ferocious life. He clenched his fists, struggling to find some measure of control.

"Come on."

Trace felt his father's hand on his shoulder, urging him in the direction of the stands. It was the last place he wanted to go.

But maybe it was time—hell, it was long past time—he confronted Callie, time he exorcised the memories of her he had carried with him for the past eleven years. Once and for all he wanted her out of his heart and his head. He probably should have confronted her sooner, but he'd been too afraid of what he might say or do. Feeling the way he did right now, he was glad he hadn't sought her out. It was bound to be safer to meet her in a crowd, where he would be forced to keep a rein on his temper.

"Hello, Jesse. Ren," Blackjack said.

Trace's gaze had never left Callie's face as he approached her, so Jesse's snarled reply came as a shock.

"Get your goddamned eyes off my wife."

Trace felt the sudden tension between the two men, who reminded him of nothing so much as two barnyard dogs faced off over a bitch in heat, fangs bared and neck hairs hackled. He'd always known his father wanted Three Oaks. He'd never realized how much he hated Jesse Creed.

After one narrow-eyed glance at Jesse, his father's eyes lingered provocatively on Jesse's wife. "You always were a fool, Jesse," Blackjack said in a condescending voice. "There's nothing between me and your wife—"

Jesse's fist caught Blackjack completely by surprise and staggered him backward. He would have fallen, except Trace grabbed his father's arm and kept him upright.

"I should have killed you a long time ago," Blackjack said through gritted teeth.

"You can always try," Jesse replied menacingly.

Lauren Creed's sob of distress distracted Blackjack just as Jesse launched another blow. Instinctively, Trace caught Jesse's fist before it could reach his father's jaw.

"I see you need your boy to fight your battles now," Jesse taunted.

"I can take care of myself," his father bit out.

Too late, Trace realized his error. It would have been far less humiliating for his father if Trace had simply let the second punch land.

"Jesse, let's go," Ren pleaded.

"I'm not finished here," Jesse said, shrugging off his wife's hand and pulling himself free of Trace's hold.

"Dad, come on," Trace said.

"Stay the hell out of this!" his father snapped at him.

"Jackson."

At the sound of his name, his father's head swung around like a Longhorn bull facing a pack of wolves. Trace thought his mother had—for once—intervened. But it turned out to be Jesse's wife who'd spoken.

Trace would have given anything not to witness the glance of longing and despair that passed between Ren and his father. He turned quickly to locate his mother and saw that she was still snapping pictures. There was nothing beautiful here for her to capture, Trace thought. The scene was as ugly as it could get.

Then a whirling dervish attacked Blackjack.

"You leave my grampa alone!" Callie's scrawny boy slugged away with his fists at Blackjack's belly and kicked with his booted feet at Blackjack's unprotected shins.

"What the hell?" Blackjack grunted.

"Get him, Eli!" the little girl in Callie's arms shouted.

"Stop it, Eli!" Callie cried.

Trace hesitated only an instant before grabbing the boy around his middle like an orphaned calf and holding him snug against his hip.

"Put me down, you yellow-bellied, toad-eating varmint!" the boy shouted, fists and feet thrashing helplessly in the air.

"What do you want me to do with this prickly piece of cactus?" he asked Callie.

"Give him to me," she said in a shaky voice. "We're leaving."

Jesse stepped forward. "No! I'll take the boy home. You stay and get us those horses we picked out."

"Daddy, I—"

"Set the boy down," Jesse ordered.

Trace set the boy down.

Before the kid could launch himself at Trace, Jesse snagged the boy's arm and pulled him close. "Get the hell out of my way," he said to Blackjack.

Trace was certain his father would have stood his ground, except Ren moved between the two men to take the little girl from Callie's arms. "I think Hannah should go with us," she said.

Ren remained as a buffer until Jesse and the boy had passed and were well on their way to the parking area. She looked up at Blackjack with stricken eyes, then followed after her husband.

"I'm out of film."

Trace realized his mother had crossed to his father's side. She slipped her arm through his and said, "Will you take me home please, Jackson? I need to get this film developed immediately. I believe I've found the subject for my next painting, and I want to get started right away."

His father shot him a look that asked for deliverance, but Trace wasn't feeling too charitable toward him at the moment. Someone had to drive his mother home, and he had unfinished business with Callie Monroe. "I'll see you later, Dad. I hope those pictures turn out, Mom."

"I'm sure I've got something I can use," his mother said.

A moment later, Trace was left facing Callie, with half the population of Bitter Creek watching to see what they would do.

Callie could feel the tension radiating from Trace. She forced herself to meet his gaze and then wished she hadn't. The ruthless predator was back. If she ran, he would only come after her. The only way to survive was to stand her ground. Her mouth was dry, her voice harsh to her ears when she spoke. "Hello, Trace."

"Hello, Callie."

There was a world of malice in those two words. Callie felt only pain. And fear. Had Trace recognized his son? It seemed he had not, but maybe he was baiting her, playing with her as a cat plays with a mouse it can crush at its leisure. Her heart pounded so loud she thought Trace must be able to hear it.

She became aware of the silence around them and realized they were being watched. She couldn't afford for people to notice them together. Someone else might put two and two together and come up with three—Callie and Trace and Eli. She had to get away from him.

Callie lifted her chin and said, "Good-bye, Trace."

He caught her wrist before she'd taken two steps. "Take a seat, Callie."

She fought her terror by speaking with all the disdain she could muster. "You're hurting me."

He let her go, but Callie knew there was no escape. She didn't dare make a scene, and besides, she had horses to buy. She turned to survey the stands and saw a spot where there was a single seat left between two cowboys. She climbed up two rows and squeezed in, relieved to have outmaneuvered Trace.

A moment later, she watched Trace stare down the cowboy sitting on the aisle next to her. The young man rose, touched the brim of his hat, and excused himself. Trace took his place, but he was larger than the cowboy who'd given up his seat, and his leg was jammed tight against the entire length of her thigh.

Callie edged away to the opposite side, so their bodies were no longer touching, but it was too late. The damage was already done. She had already felt the heat of his flesh. She had already experienced the rush of unwanted desire.

She viciously squelched the feeling. Trace had abandoned her. He had refused to wait, even a little while, to see if they could work things out. And he had made sure she knew how easily she could be replaced. She had heard stories in Bitter Creek about the women who had come and gone from his bed. The first had been told within three weeks of their separation.

She had died inside. She had cried bitter, resentful

tears. Until Nolan had found her and comforted her. And married her.

Callie had wondered how she would feel when she saw Trace again. She had wondered what he would say, what he would do. Well, she had her answer.

He was nothing like the man she remembered. There was nothing honest and fair about his behavior. Trace seemed every bit as ruthless as his father, every bit as callous and uncaring of the harm he might cause by coming back into her life. It seemed, after all, that the apple didn't fall far from the tree.

She focused her gaze on their parents as they retreated to the parking lot. "All these years, and nothing has changed," she murmured.

Except her love had died a lingering death. And Trace felt nothing but contempt for her.

"What do you want from me, Trace?" she asked brusquely.

"You're still a beautiful woman, Callie."

Her gaze collided with his. But it wasn't love she saw in his eyes, it was lust. Callie felt a spurt of panic.

"Don't do this, Trace. Please. I'm begging you."

"The Callie I knew wouldn't have begged anyone for anything."

"I don't have that luxury anymore," she retorted. "I have a family that depends on me. I can't afford to indulge myself—"

"Is that what we did? Indulged ourselves? I thought we were in love."

"How dare you speak of love," she hissed at him, keeping her voice low. "You walked away. You were the one who left!"

"And you stayed. And married within— How long did you wait for me, Callie? A month? Two months?"

He had left her first, but she didn't dare argue the point. She didn't want him counting the months between her marriage and the birth of his son. "Nolan loved me. He didn't want to wait to get married," she said defiantly.

"And he gave you a son," Trace accused, "that should have been mine. *Mine*, Callie, not his."

He believes Eli is Nolan's son.

Callie felt a profound rush of relief.

Before she could change the subject, Trace said, "That kid of yours is as rank a colt as I've ever seen. It's been a while since Blackjack had his shins kicked."

"Eli doesn't normally fly off the handle like that," she shot back in defense of her son. "He was provoked. Blackjack shouldn't—"

"I don't blame him for jumping into the fray. In fact, the kid reminded me of myself once upon a time."

Callie was terrified Trace would make a physical comparison and blurted the first thing that came into her head. "You mean knobby-kneed and skinny as a sapling?"

His lips curved in a wry smile. "I was thinking full of fire and brimstone, ready to fight the world. With his teeth bared like that, and his eyes . . ." He waited until she looked at him and said, "He has your eyes, Callie."

Callie's throat tightened with emotion. *And your nose and cheeks and chin. Oh, Trace, I wish* . . . She tore her gaze away and stared down at her hands, which were twisting the rolled-up sales brochure into a tighter spiral. Callie cursed herself for a fool. She couldn't afford sentiment. She couldn't afford to wish and dream about what might have been.

"I suppose the boy must be missing his father," Trace said. "I'm sorry for your loss, Callie."

Her hands stilled. Callie swallowed painfully over the knot in her throat. She didn't want Trace's sympathy. She didn't want him being kind. She met his gaze and said, "Eli loved Nolan. And so did I."

She wanted Trace to know she'd gotten over him. She wanted him to know she'd gone on with her life. She wanted him to know that she'd even loved again. That she'd borne another man's children. She wanted to hurt him with the knowledge of all he'd missed by leaving her behind.

She looked into his cold blue eyes, searching for the pain she wanted him to feel. And saw a flicker of something that might have been anguish.

"Callie . . . I—"

She jerked away when his fingertips grazed her cheek. "Don't!" She struggled against the hand he had clamped on her arm to keep her from bolting. "Let go of me, Trace."

A two-year-old filly whinnied with fear. Callie's eyes were drawn by the terrified sound. She saw the whites of the animal's eyes and then the number 6 painted on its hip. She froze in place.

"Damn, damn, damn," she muttered, fumbling to unroll the curled-up brochure. "That's one of the horses I'm supposed to bid on."

She and her father had evaluated all the animals before the auction, and she'd written $40,000 in red Flair pen as the amount above which it was no longer profitable for her to bid on the number six animal.

In the cutting horse business, the price of an animal

was tied not only to how well the horse for sale had performed, but equally, or even more importantly, to how well the previous two generations had performed as cutters, how much money they had won, and how much their progeny had won.

The number six horse, Hickory Angel, was by Doc's Hickory, AQHA High Point Cutting Stallion, NCHA Futurity semifinalist, and Equistate #5 All-Time Leading Cutting Sire, siring the earners of nearly twelve million dollars, and out of Osages Little Angel, sired by Peppy San Badger, NCHA Open Futurity and Derby Champion, NCIIA Open Reserve World Champion, and #1 All-Time Leading Cutting Sire.

Trace said, "She looks a little long in the back to me."

"A little," Callie agreed, eyeing the horse critically. "But her hocks are nice and short. I saw her working earlier this morning. She can turn on a button and never scratch it." She bit her lip, suddenly realizing that she was sharing information Trace might use against her, if he decided to bid on the animal himself.

The filly jumped when the auctioneer's microphoned voice began its patter, and the handler turned her in a circle to show her off and calm her down. "What am I bid for this two-year-old filly? This little lady has the very best bloodlines."

Callie caught Trace staring at her. "What are you looking at?" she asked irritably.

He eyed the frayed ends of her collar. "If you'd been my wife, I'd have taken better care of you than Nolan Monroe apparently did."

"In all the ways that mattered, Nolan took excellent care of me," she replied scornfully.

He gazed at her with heavy-lidded eyes. "Was he good in bed, Callie?"

A quiver of sensual need rolled through her. "I won't dignify that with an answer."

Their eyes remained locked in a battle of wills, Trace demanding a carnal response from her, and Callie refusing to give him one. Abruptly she turned away, focusing her gaze on the ring, where the bidding was underway. "I have work to do," she said curtly.

"Callie—"

"No, Trace."

She heard the desperation in her voice as she answered the question Trace had not been given the chance to ask. There wasn't going to be a resumption of their love affair. Not when all that remained between them was lust.

"I like the looks of that filly," he said.

She glanced at him warily. "She's going to cost a pretty penny," she said neutrally.

"I can afford it."

Callie braced her shoulders, as though for a blow. Surely he wasn't going to bid on Hickory Angel just to keep her from getting the animal. "Why would you want to buy this horse?" she asked. "She's been bred for competitive cutting."

"I've decided to start my own breeding operation at Bitter Creek," Trace said.

She stared at him in dismay. He couldn't be planning to go into business in competition with her. "There must be a million other investments that would give you a better return on your money. Why cutting horses?"

"Riding a really good cutter is about the biggest rush there is," he said. "Almost as good as sex," he added with a provocative smile. "I got a hankering for it when I competed on the cutting circuit as a teenager. Guess you never outgrow it."

"And you Blackthornes are rich enough to gratify your every whim," she said contemptuously.

"Yes," he said. "We are."

The bidding on Hickory Angel had slowed until there were only two other bidders. Callie raised her index and middle finger to bid $35,000.

"Now thirty-five," the auctioneer said. "Do I hear thirty-five-five? Now thirty-five-five-do-I-hear-thirty-six? Now thirty-six-now-thirty-six-five."

The rancher from Dallas dropped out. Callie was now bidding against a well-known California cutter.

"Now thirty-seven. Now-thirty-seven-five-thirty-seven-five."

The California cutter dropped out. Callie had the high bid at $37,500.

"This little lady is a beauty. Don't let her get away. Now thirty-seven-five."

Trace touched the brim of his hat.

"Now thirty-eight," the auctioneer said.

Callie's eyes went wide with alarm. She lifted a finger and the auctioneer said, "Now thirty-eight-five-thirty-eight-five."

"Forty," Trace said, jumping the bid to the limit Callie knew he must have seen written in her brochure. She met his gaze. His eyes were cold and hard and uncaring.

"I need that filly, Trace."

"So do I."

"Looks like the gent wants this little lady," the auctioneer said. "Now forty-now-forty-now-forty."

Callie turned away, lifted her finger, and bid $40,500. Trace must know as well as she did the value of the filly. She could hedge a little, maybe pay another thousand or so more, but beyond that, they wouldn't make the profit they'd need to justify feeding and training the animal for a year.

"Forty-five," Trace said.

Callie hissed in a breath. Well. Now she knew. It wasn't over between them, even if she wanted it to be. He wanted to hurt her every bit as much as she had wanted to hurt him. Unfortunately, she wasn't the only one who would suffer from Trace's vengeance. If she wasn't careful, her family could lose Three Oaks.

"Why are you punishing me like this?" she whispered.

"This isn't personal, Callie. It's business."

"Well, folks. I have forty-five thousand. Do I have another bid?"

Callie felt a shiver of fear crawl up her spine. Should she test his resolve? Should she bid more, to see if he would go higher? Callie sighed inwardly. She couldn't take the risk that Trace would allow her to win the bid at a price that would cost her family money.

It was crystal clear now, if it hadn't been before, that what had once been a deep and abiding love between them had become something else entirely, something dangerous.

"Now forty-five-forty-five-forty-five. Do I have another bid? Forty-five once. Forty-five twice. Sold to the gentleman in the black hat for forty-five thousand."

"Hey, Trace," Dusty said, tipping his Stetson. "That filly will be a great addition to your stable."

"Price went a little high," Trace said, eyeing Callie.

Dusty winked at Callie. "You're welcome to drive up the prices all you want. See you later, Trace. Don't forget. Number twenty-three."

Callie paged through the auction materials. "Number twenty-three is Smart Little Doc," she said. "Isn't he the stud Dusty was training when he had his accident?"

"He's got him signed up for the Futurity," Trace confirmed.

"Good bloodlines," Callie observed.

Trace stared over her shoulder and read the statistics on Smart Little Doc. Championship cutters on both sides. Millions in competition earnings.

Callie looked up at him and said, "Who are you going to get to train and ride him at this late date?"

"I haven't thought too much about it."

Trace knew as well as she did that competitive cutting was the one sport where the animal was the real athlete. The rider had to loosen the reins once the cow was cut from the herd. It was then up to the horse to use its "cow sense" to stay one step ahead of the cow. Winning horses often crouched down like a cat and stayed nose to nose with a steer to keep it cut from the herd.

But Trace would have no hope of winning the Futurity without a top-notch rider. The rider had to be good enough to stay in the saddle through some awesomely abrupt turns and smart enough to let the horse do its job.

"How about you?" Trace said. "You've trained and ridden winners—both at the Stakes and the Derby. Want the job?"

"No."

"Just no? No explanation why not?"

"I don't have to give you a reason."

"I mean to win the Futurity, Callie."

"You and a thousand other cutters who've signed up to compete," she said. "Including me."

"You've got a horse entered in the Futurity?"

Callie's chin came up in response to the frown on Trace's face. "I've got a mare that's been performing well, Sugar Pep. I think she can win the Open."

"I guess that puts us in competition."

"If you can find a rider," Callie said.

"Oh, I'll find a rider," Trace replied. "Even if I have to compete against you myself."

Callie rose abruptly.

Trace caught her wrist. "Where are you going?"

"I'm leaving."

"Without buying the stock you need to replace what was lost?"

She felt the eyes of their neighbors focused on them, but stubbornly remained standing. "I can't afford to out-bid you, Trace."

She noticed he didn't contradict her or bother to suggest they might be bidding on different horses. She was certain he would have picked out the best horses to buy, just as she and her father had. And she was equally certain he would outbid her just for spite.

The sooner she took herself out of his way, the better. There were other auctions she could attend where Trace Blackthorne would not be there to remind her of how easily his family's money could be used to punish her. She would have to be especially careful to keep Eli out of his way. If he was this determined to hurt her just for marrying Nolan, imagine what he would do if he ever discovered Eli was his son!

"How will you get home?" he asked.

Callie had completely forgotten that her parents had left her stranded when they'd departed in such a rush. "I'll call Daddy and have him send someone for me," she said. "Let go of me, Trace."

"Will you be coming back for the barn dance tonight?"

"I won't dance with you, Trace."

"Then you'll be there?"

Too late, Callie realized her mistake. She had promised Lou Ann she would keep an eye on the punch bowl to make sure some cowboy didn't spike it. She could beg off. But she refused to give Trace the satisfaction of seeing her routed.

She stared at his hand, where it manacled her wrist, but didn't repeat her request to be set free.

"I'll see you tonight, Callie," he said as he let her go. "Save a dance for me."

Chapter 4

CALLIE STOOD BEHIND THE REFRESHMENT TA-
ble along the east wall of Dusty Simpson's barn with a
knot in her stomach and a headache throbbing at the base
of her skull, waiting for Trace to appear and claim his
dance. As the hours passed, the crowd from the auction
thinned until only a few locals were left two-stepping to
the sad wail of a violin, an emphatic drummer, and a very
loud electric guitar.

She had spent the entire evening imagining every possible way of refusing Trace and his resulting chagrin,
embarrassment, and fury. All her planning had been for
naught, because with only fifteen minutes left before the
band quit for the night, it seemed the sonofabitch wasn't
even going to show. Callie was chagrined, embarrassed,
and furious at how much time she'd spent worrying over
nothing.

"Hey, Callie, wake up!"

Callie tore her gaze from the barn entrance and focused it on her brother Luke, who was waving both hands
in front of her face. Her father had agreed to send Luke to
pick her up, but only after insisting that she stay for the

rest of the auction—and bid on the horses they'd decided they wanted. It had been a very long, very frustrating day, and Callie was glad it was almost over.

"What do you want, Luke?" she asked.

"Are you ready to leave yet?"

Callie glanced at her watch. "I promised Lou Ann I'd stay until midnight. Can you wait fifteen more minutes?"

Luke made a face. "I need to get outta here. That Coburn girl has been dogging my footsteps all night."

Callie followed his glance to the very tall, very red-headed girl standing like an exotic wallflower near the exit. "Why don't you ask her to dance?"

"She'll think I like her," Luke protested.

"What's wrong with that?"

"She's a freak."

Callie glanced at the girl. "In what way?"

"She's the giant and Jack's beanstalk all rolled into one."

Callie felt a pang of sorrow for the Coburn girl. Her father Johnny Ray, and her older brother "Bad" Billy, both of whom were known troublemakers, worked part-time for Blackjack when they weren't taking care of their own run-down ranch. Emma Coburn couldn't have been more than fourteen or fifteen, but she was easily six feet tall and as skinny as a bed slat.

"It isn't Emma's fault she's taller than you," Callie said. "She's probably very nice. Have you spoken to her?"

Luke rolled his eyes. "I'll wait for you outside."

Callie watched her brother stalk past Emma Coburn as though she were a cedar fence post. The girl hesitated a moment, then followed him. Callie looked around the barn in agitation. Where was Lou Ann? She'd left Callie at the punch bowl over an hour ago and promised she'd be right back.

Callie didn't want to leave Luke alone with the Coburn girl, who'd apparently gone after him, because she didn't trust her brother not to hurt the girl's feelings. She considered abandoning the punch bowl. This late in the evening, it probably wouldn't matter if some cowboy spiked the punch.

"I believe this is my dance."

Callie froze, then turned to find Trace standing close enough that she could feel the heat of his body. Memories assaulted her. How it felt to run her hands over ridged muscle and bone. The softness of his hair against her breasts and belly. The sleek thrust of his tongue in her mouth. She felt her body clench with desire and forced herself to see the man who stood before her, not the memory.

He wore a white, Western-cut shirt, open at the throat, the sleeves rolled up to bare sinewy forearms. His jeans looked old and butter soft and molded his body. His hat was pulled low on his forehead, leaving his eyes in shadow, revealing a strong chin stubbled with beard.

If she were meeting him for the first time, she might have been a little frightened. He looked dark and dangerous. But this man was no stranger. She knew his body as well as she knew her own. And she wasn't going to be intimidated into dancing with him.

She cocked her head and said, "You're a little late, aren't you, cowboy?"

"Did you think I wasn't coming?" Trace replied, his lips curving in a winsome smile.

She refused to be charmed. "The dance is over."

"Not quite," Trace said, as the band began playing "Crazy," a slow, sentimental Patsy Cline tune.

"I have to watch the punch bowl." Callie was appalled to realize that she was breathless and that her pulse was racing.

"I'm here, Callie," Lou Ann said with a smile, as she stepped up beside Callie. "Trace and Dusty and I were going over some figures in the house. Sorry I'm so late getting back to relieve you. Trace told me you'd promised him a dance."

Callie stared at Trace's outstretched hand, looked up to catch the gleam in his eye and the arrogant arch of his brow, and realized how neatly she'd been trapped.

It's only a dance. One dance can't matter.

Callie set her hand in the one Trace held outstretched to her. It was warm and strong, the fingertips rough and callused. She shivered as the flat of his hand palmed the small of her back. She rested her hand on his shoulder, feeling the hard, too-familiar play of muscle and bone beneath her fingertips.

This isn't the same man you once loved, she reminded herself. She looked for changes and found them.

His nose had a bump on the bridge that hadn't been there in college, and he had a new scar running through his left eyebrow. She realized she had no idea what he'd been doing during the long years he'd been gone from Texas, or even where he'd been. Except, whatever he'd been doing had kept him outside, because the sun and the wind had etched lines around his eyes and mouth. And his work had required physical labor, because his shoulders seemed broader and his body looked even leaner and harder than it had when he was a younger man.

"Do you remember the last time we danced, Callie?" Trace asked as he moved her around the sawdusted wooden floor to the seductive country tune.

Callie felt her heart skip a beat. She wondered if there was any significance to his question. The last time they had danced was in college, on Valentine's Day. They had left the dance floor that night and driven out into the hill country to a spot along the Colorado River where they could be alone, with only the stars overhead and the cool grass beneath them.

She remembered how much they'd laughed that night, how boyishly Trace had smiled at her in the moonlight, before he pulled her sweater up over her head, leaving her wearing only a plain white bra. It was the only time she had truly regretted being poor. She'd wished she had on some expensive French lingerie, something made of delicate lace that would make her beautiful for him.

Trace hadn't minded. He'd grinned and told her how glad he was that the bra clasp was at her back, because he had an excuse to put his arms around her. He'd made her feel beautiful without the need for rich, expensive things.

That long, lazy night they had spent together on the banks of the Colorado, they'd loved one another with reverence and abandon and delight. She had become a woman in his arms that night. And they had created their son.

"I remember," she murmured.

"I found you enchanting, Callie." He turned her in a circle that forced their bodies close.

Callie barely had time to register the fact that he'd

phrased his compliment in the past tense before he added, "You look tired."

"It's been a long day," she said, aggravated that she could feel hurt that he no longer found her enchanting. She kept her eyes determinedly focused over his shoulder. She considered staying silent, but decided it would be safer to direct the conversation herself. "Congratulations on winning the bid on the number twenty-three animal. Smart Little Doc was a steal at $76,000."

"That colt you got wasn't bad, either," he said.

"You mean the one colt you let me have." Callie bit her tongue to keep from saying more.

"I didn't expect you to return after you left the stands," Trace said. "Why did you?"

"My father called me a quitter."

He hesitated, then said, "And you're not?"

"You left me, Trace, not the other way around."

"And now I'm back," he said quietly.

"You've been back nearly four months," she said, her eyes flashing. "Today is the first I've seen of you. Am I supposed to fall at your feet—or into your bed? I'm a widow now, the mother of two children."

His jaw flexed. "I'm not likely to forget either condition. That doesn't change the fact that I still find you desirable."

"But not enchanting?" Callie flushed as she realized what she'd revealed.

"I never said you weren't enchanting, Callie," he said as he met her gaze. "I merely observed that you look tired, which you do. You've obviously been working too hard. I could make life easier for you, if you'd let me."

"More Blackthorne charity? I don't need it, and I don't want it."

"You may not want it. But you need it," Trace contradicted.

Callie refused to argue the point.

"Since Dusty's bum leg put him out of business, I need someone to train my new stud for the Futurity," he said. "I'll pay you a premium wage for your time and half the purse, if Smart Little Doc finishes in the top ten."

"I will never, ever work for you."

"Don't make promises you can't keep, Callie." He pulled her close so her breasts grazed his chest.

She pushed at his shoulder, caught a neighbor watching with raised brows, and muttered, "Let me go, Trace."

"The dance isn't over, Callie."

He might as well have said *I'm not done with you.* She'd gotten the message loud and clear. "We don't know each other anymore, Trace. We might as well be strangers."

"I know you in every way there is for a man to know a woman."

"I've changed," she said. "I'm not the girl who fell foolishly in love with you."

His eyes focused intently on her. "So much the better."

"What do you want from me?"

"That should be obvious."

His hand pressed against the small of her back, drawing her close enough to feel his hardness against her softness. A frisson of awareness streaked through her. She gasped, tried to catch the sound, but was too late.

"Look at me, Callie," he commanded.

Callie tried to jerk free, but Trace tightened his hold. She raised her chin and glared at him. "Whatever we had between us is over and done."

"Not quite," he said.

She eyed him warily, her heart thumping crazily. "What is that supposed to mean?"

"I haven't had my fill of you."

She snorted derisively. "You make me sound like a bottle of beer you haven't finished swilling."

His voice was low and seductive. "I was thinking of something utterly soft and incredibly sweet I haven't finished sampling."

Callie felt the flush creeping up her throat, but could do nothing to stop it. "I don't love you anymore, Trace."

"Who said anything about love?"

She was startled into meeting his gaze. His blue eyes were icy and unfathomable. Ruthless and predatory. This was the merciless man who had so frightened her the first day she had spoken to him. Back again to haunt her. To hunt her.

But she was no longer the naive girl of seventeen who had given him her virginity. Who had loved him with her entire being. Whom he had professed to love and then abandoned with a willingness that had left her aching inside for years afterward.

Callie lowered her gaze as she acknowledged the truth. She had never really gotten over the pain of losing Trace. Nolan had applied a balm to soothe it, but the anguish of Trace's betrayal had been buried deep inside her, where it remained to this day. "This is not the place—"

"My thoughts exactly." He danced her out of the barn and into the cool, quiet night, then clasped her hand in his and dragged her behind him along the length of the barn and into the darkness.

"Let go of me, Trace."

A moment later she found herself backed up against the rough wooden barn, with Trace's hard body pressed against hers from breasts to thighs. His hands stapled hers against the weathered wood on either side of her head, and his face was so close she could feel his moist breath against her cheek, smell the musky scent of a man who had spent the day under a hot sun.

"We have unfinished business, Callie."

She stared up into hooded eyes and felt all the heat and desire—and regret and anger—she had tried so hard to put behind her. She was tempted to give in to the moment, to taste him, to feel the passion and the frenzy of loving him just one more time.

But she could never become Trace's wife. And if she became his lover, they would be forced to hide their relationship from his family and from hers. She had long ago said farewell to the fairy tale. She had to live in the real world.

"No, Trace."

"Yes, Callie."

Callie held her breath as Trace's mouth lowered toward hers. She turned her face so his lips only caressed her cheek. She felt her throat swell with the loss of all that might have been.

"I'm not going to let you turn away from me this time," he said in a harsh voice. His hand grasped her chin and turned her face up to his as his mouth came down, devouring hers, hungry and seeking satisfaction.

When he thrust his tongue into her mouth, her body

began to tremble. He released her hands as his own went seeking. She put her hands on his shoulders to push him away, but found herself holding on instead, as his hands sought her breasts and then moved down between her legs to the heat and the heart of her. Her cry of need was swallowed by his punishing kiss.

For an instant she let herself feel, and then she panicked, struggling against the powerful emotions that had surged within her. She shoved at his shoulders, as she made her body rigid. "I won't let you do this to me again!"

He lifted his head to look at her, his eyes glittering in the light from the doorway. There was no sign of the fascination that had once filled his eyes when he looked at her. No sign of tenderness, of love or caring. Only carnal desire.

"I'll fight you, Trace."

"Go ahead." He lowered his head toward her mouth, then abruptly turned away. "What was that?"

Callie froze. Oh, dear God. What if Luke had come looking for her? She shoved at Trace with all her strength, fighting to be free. And then she heard it, too. A woman's cry for help.

"Someone's in trouble," she said.

But Trace had already headed in the direction of the woman's voice, pulling her along behind him.

Trace heard the sounds of the fight—the *thwack* of flesh hitting flesh, the *oomph!* of air being forced from lungs, the female screech of terror and rage—long before he and Callie reached the combatants. His adrenaline began to pump when the stream of yellow light from the open door of the barn revealed that his sister Summer was smack in the middle of the fracas.

Summer had her arms wrapped around Bad Billy Coburn from behind, while he slugged away with both fists at a tall, skin-and-bones boy. It was Luke Creed.

Another female had hold of the bloodied Creed boy— who was also swinging wildly with bared knuckles—trying to drag him away. The boy leaned to dodge a blow, and Trace identified the second girl as Emma Coburn.

To his disgust, a half-dozen cowboys, including several Bitter Creek cowhands, were egging the fighters on.

"Get him, Billy!"

"Did you see that? Hit him again, boy!"

"Jesus, Billy kicked him!"

"Don't let him get to ya, Luke!"

As Trace scanned the crowd, he was disgusted to discover that Bad Billy's father, Johnny Ray Coburn, was yelling the loudest.

Bad Billy suddenly ducked, and a roundhouse punch from Luke intended for Billy's chin ended up hitting Summer's nose, causing it to spurt blood, and knocking her to the ground.

"That's enough," Trace said in a voice that demanded obedience. He glanced at Summer and saw she had her hand cupped against her bloodied nose. He put himself between the two men and ordered, "Both of you take a step back."

Bad Billy held his ground, glaring insolently at Trace.

Luke did as he was told, but tripped over Emma Coburn, who was standing too close behind him. Hands windmilling, he lost his balance and fell, taking Emma down with him.

"Luke, you asshole!" Bad Billy slurred in a drunken voice. "That's my sister you just put on the ground."

Billy kicked out savagely at the downed boy, but Trace knocked his boot aside and hit Billy once, hard, in the stomach. Billy grunted in pain as he fell to his knees, retching.

Trace fixed a steely eye on the now-silent cowboys, and ordered curtly, "Hector, Slim, pick up the Creed boy and have Mrs. Monroe show you where her truck is parked. Johnny Ray, see to your girl."

Trace felt a hand on his arm and turned to find Callie standing beside him.

"Trace, I . . . How can I thank you?"

He almost let the moment pass without taking advantage of it. But he didn't have time to be subtle. "You can be my date for the gala at the Houston Museum of Fine Arts next weekend."

She looked stunned. "I . . . ." He saw the struggle that went on before she smiled and said, "I don't have anything to wear to something like that."

He found himself smiling back at her. "No problem. We'll go shopping first at Neiman Marcus."

"Trace, I—"

"Señor Trace," Hector interrupted, reminding him that his cowhands were still holding Luke Creed.

"Your brother needs some attention," Trace said. "I'll pick you up Saturday at noon."

"I'll meet you in town," she countered. "At Bobbie Jo's Café."

"Done," he said.

Once Callie was gone, Trace crossed to Summer. She was on her knees beside Bad Billy, who lay groaning on the ground. Trace could smell the yeasty stench of too many beers, and shook his head in disgust. "You're fired, Billy."

"Trace, you can't do that," Summer protested, as she rose to confront him.

Trace's lip curled in disgust at his sister's defense of Bad Billy Coburn. "He's a drunken brawler. I don't need his kind working for me."

"You don't know a thing about him!" she cried. "Luke started it by insulting Emma. Billy was only defending his sister."

Trace's gaze shifted to the tall, redheaded Coburn girl, who was being dragged away by her father. It was then he realized Johnny Ray Coburn had left his son lying on the ground without even checking on him. What kind of father was he, Trace wondered, to let his children get involved in a fight without interfering to save them from harm?

Trace saw the older man weaving and stumbling away with his daughter and realized Johnny Ray's son had grown up to be just like his father—a drunken, scrapping, care-for-nobody.

He turned back to Summer. "Don't defend that bast—" He cut himself off. Now she had him swearing in front of her. "Don't defend Bad Billy Coburn to me, Summer. Any man who was a man, wouldn't fight where women might get hurt."

"Don't spout platitudes at me, Trace," Summer retorted, jabbing him in the chest with her pointed finger.

"You hit Billy with a sucker punch, showing off for Callie Creed."

"I was not—" Trace cut off his denial. Maybe Summer was right. He wanted Callie's admiration. But he'd sunk pretty low, if he was reduced to fighting for it.

Trace felt like hitting something. Unfortunately, his cowhands were keeping their distance. And Bad Billy Coburn was still flat on his back.

Trace frowned as Summer knelt beside the fallen cowboy. His brow furrowed more deeply when she brushed the sweaty black hair from Bad Billy's brow and pulled the bandanna from Billy's pocket to dab at the blood streaming from his mouth and nose.

He'd thought Summer had merely stumbled onto the fight and gotten involved in an attempt to help the Creed boy, who was younger and slighter and had less experience brawling than Bad Billy. But as Summer spoke in soothing tones to the downed man, it became increasingly apparent that his sister was somehow involved with the drunken cowboy.

"Summer, it's time to go," he said.

"Billy's hurt. He needs medical attention."

"Leave him," Trace ordered.

"No," she said flatly. "I've got to take Billy home. He can't drive in this condition."

Trace looked around for someone who could take Bad Billy home, but all of his cowhands had slunk quietly away. "Dammit all to hell," he muttered under his breath. He was tempted to leave Bad Billy lying in his own vomit, but one look at the obstinate tilt of Summer's chin convinced him he wasn't going to get away with doing that.

At least, not without hauling his sister home kicking and screaming all the way.

"Aw, hell." Trace leaned down and grabbed Bad Billy by the arms and hauled him upright, then hefted him over his shoulder like a sack of feed. "Let's go," he said.

He ignored Summer's protest when he dumped Bad Billy into the bed of his pickup without a care for the bruises it would cause. When Summer started to climb in with the boy, he caught her wrist and said, "Get into the cab. We need to talk."

Her chin came up—when didn't it?—and she stalked to the front of the truck and got in. Trace caught himself sighing and pressed his lips flat. It would be a cold day in hell before he allowed his little sister to be wasted on the likes of Bad Billy Coburn.

The Coburn ranch was twenty-five miles in the opposite direction from Bitter Creek, which would give them plenty of time to talk. Trace held his tongue, waiting to see what Summer would have to say for herself. He wanted to hear what kind of defense she intended to mount for the jug-bitten cowboy.

Her stubborn silence gave him too much time to think, and his thoughts were all about Callie Creed Monroe.

Trace had told himself over and over since she'd walked away from him at the auction that the smart move was to keep his distance. He'd remained in the house with Dusty and Lou Ann in order to avoid seeing Callie, despite his taunt of claiming a dance. But she'd been in his head the whole time, the same way she was lodged in his heart.

He'd tried to cut her out. He'd tried not to want her. But she was under his skin, and there was no getting rid of her without peeling himself away a layer at a time, until there would be nothing left. Trace knew what he wanted from Callie. He just wasn't sure of the best way to get it.

Maybe if he could get her into bed he'd discover that the memories he had of the time they'd spent together wouldn't measure up. That what he remembered as pure gold would turn out to be dross.

But merely kissing her against the rough wall of the barn had turned him inside out, so that all the pain of loss and the wealth of need were right there on the surface, aching and demanding. He'd wanted to possess her. Needed to possess her. Intended to possess her before he left this place once and for all and went back to where he'd come from.

He'd made up his mind about that tonight.

"Trace, you can't fire Billy for fighting," Summer said into the silence. "Especially when the fight wasn't his fault."

Trace turned to survey his sister, whose nose looked dark and swollen in the light from the dash. "He was fighting. That makes whatever happened his fault."

"I told you he had no choice. Luke Creed told Billy's sister Emma to get lost. He called her a bloodsucking leech."

Trace lifted a brow. "What was Emma doing out there in the dark with Luke in the first place? No, hold that question. What were *you* doing out there in the dark with Bad Billy Coburn?"

"We were having a beer together," Summer said defiantly. "So what?"

Trace swore under his breath. "Bad Billy—"

"Stop calling him that. His name is Billy," Summer

said irritably. "He isn't a bad person. And it isn't fair to label him as one."

"He was fall-down drunk, Summer. The man is a troublemaker, a nothing, a nobody. I would've cut him loose a long time ago, except he's about the best man I've ever seen with a rope. I won't have him at Bitter Creek—"

"Bitter Creek doesn't belong to you. You aren't the boss. When I tell Daddy—"

"When I tell Dad you were out drinking with Bad Billy Coburn, he'll—"

"Trace, you can't tell!" Summer cried.

"Why not? Was there something more going on between you and Billy Coburn in the dark than just drinking a few beers together?"

"No. Nothing. We're just friends!" Summer insisted. "But Daddy wouldn't understand."

"I don't understand, either. The man isn't worth a bucket of spit, Summer. Are you sure you aren't slumming with that saddle tramp just to get back at Dad for making you break up with that last boy you were dating?"

"No! I just—Billy and I— Oh, you'll never understand, so there's no sense trying to explain it to you."

"Try me," Trace said.

"Billy never had a chance to be 'good,' Trace. His father's treated him like dirt all his life."

"How does that give the two of you anything in common?" Trace questioned.

"Let me finish," Summer said. "Billy wants to do better, but nobody around here will give him half a chance. Everybody has already decided he's 'bad' Billy Coburn, and nothing he does makes any difference."

"I still don't see the parallel between the two of you," Trace said.

Summer shot him a frustrated glance. "Don't you see? He isn't what people think he is. And neither am I."

"You're not a spoiled brat?" Trace teased gently.

Summer crossed her arms under her breasts. "I don't know why I even bothered to try and explain. You don't want to understand. Nobody does."

"I understand one thing, and you'd better understand it, too," Trace said. "If Dad catches you anywhere near Bad Billy Coburn, there's going to be hell to pay."

"You're not going to tell him about us, are you?"

"Not if you agree to stay away from Billy."

"What about you and Callie Monroe?" Summer shot back. "What's Daddy going to say when I tell him I saw you kissing her tonight?"

Trace glared at his younger sister. "I'm a grown man—"

"And I'm a grown woman!"

"You're my baby sister—"

"I'm not a little girl anymore," Summer said. "I grew up while you were off gallivanting around the world. I can manage my own life, thank you very much, without any help from you!"

"You're bound to get hurt if you hang around with Ba—" Trace corrected himself. "With Billy Coburn."

"And you're out of your mind to be kissing Callie Creed Monroe," Summer countered. "But you don't see me trying to stop you from following your heart."

Trace hissed in a breath. "Are you in love with that bum?"

"Of course not! I told you, we're just friends. Which is more than you can say about Callie Monroe."

"Callie and I—" Trace cut himself off. He wasn't about to explain to his sister that he'd been exorcising demons, not pursuing romance, with Callie. Instead he said, "Billy Coburn will only break your heart."

"It's my heart," Summer said. "And if I want to take a chance on having it broken, that's my business and nobody else's."

"I'm warning you," Trace said. "Stay away from him."

"Or what?" Summer demanded. "Are you going to tattle to Daddy?"

Trace met his sister's rebellious gaze and said, "I'll get rid of Billy myself."

"You do, and I'll make you sorry you did," Summer threatened.

"Look, Summer, be reasonable. You can't be friends—"

"I can and I will. You're not going to make me change my mind."

He braked the Chevy truck to a dust-raising stop in back of the Coburns' dilapidated ranch house. The porch roof sagged, and one of the wooden steps that led up to the kitchen had rotted through. The back door screen curled away from the frame in the corner, leaving an opening for flies. Trace could see a chipped red Formica table and four mismatched chairs in the light from the single uncovered bulb that lit the kitchen.

An aproned woman stood at the kitchen sink, her brown hair stuck in a bun at her crown. When she turned,

Trace realized it was Dora Coburn, Billy's mother. She crossed and shoved open the screen door, which squealed on its hinges.

"Stay in the car," Trace ordered his sister. "I'll take care of this."

"But—"

"Who's there?" Mrs. Coburn called.

"It's Trace Blackthorne, Mrs. Coburn," Trace said, stepping out of the pickup. "I've brought Billy home."

"Is he all right?" The woman hurried toward him, letting the screen door slam behind her. "Is he hurt?"

"He's passed out drunk. He's been fighting, but he's not seriously hurt."

He saw the resignation in the woman's face, saw her shoulders sag as she looked up and met his gaze. "Would you bring him inside for me, please?"

Trace let down the back of the pickup and hauled Billy up and over his shoulder. To his consternation, he found Summer by his side as he stretched his legs over the broken step and carried the drunken man inside.

"Follow me," Mrs. Coburn said as she led them through the kitchen and living room and down a dark, narrow hall. "His room is this way."

Trace saw the look of distaste on his sister's face when she saw the filth in which Billy Coburn lived. His bed was unmade, and his room, about the size of a jail cell, Trace noted ironically, was strewn with empty beer cans and ranch magazines and dirty clothes.

Mrs. Coburn shoved the rumpled covers aside and said, "Lay him down, please."

Trace let Billy fall onto the bed, which sagged down at

the center with the weight of his body. He exchanged a look with his sister, whose chin, for once, wasn't jutting. Her eyes were troubled, confused, even a little sad.

"Can I help you with anything, Mrs. Coburn?" she asked.

"I think it would be best to let him sleep it off," she said.

"His face—"

"It'll mend," the woman said sharply. "Don't you Blackthornes be worrying about my boy. He'll be fine."

Trace watched Summer recoil at the woman's harsh words. He put an arm around her shoulders and said, "We'll be going now."

"I'll make sure he's up for work tomorrow," Mrs. Coburn said.

"There's no need—" Trace began.

"Oh, he'll want to be up in time for work. We need the money too much for him to skip a day," she said bitterly.

"Mrs. Coburn—" Trace felt Summer's hand on his arm, felt the plea for mercy. But he was doing this for her own good. "Billy doesn't need to show up for work tomorrow. I fired him tonight."

"Oh. Oh," the woman said, looking flustered. "Couldn't you . . . Wouldn't you reconsider?"

"No, ma'am," Trace said.

Summer took a step away and stared at him accusingly.

"Come on," he said, as he clamped a hand on her wrist and began dragging her from the house. "It's time we got home."

When the screen door slammed behind them, Summer turned on him. "How could you stand there and tell her

Billy was fired, when it's so obvious they need every penny to make ends meet?"

"I fired him, and he's staying fired," Trace said. "I don't go back on my word."

"You're a heartless sonofabitch, Trace Blackthorne." Trace didn't bother denying it.

Chapter 5

CALLIE HAD NO INTENTION OF LETTING TRACE buy her a dress. But in the few seconds she'd had to make a decision whether to accept his invitation to the gala, Callie had realized they needed time alone to put the past to rest. And Houston was a nice, safe distance from her family and from his.

But she'd been a nervous wreck ever since she'd agreed to go with him, trying to figure out a way to absent herself from Three Oaks overnight without raising eyebrows or provoking questions from her family that she didn't want to answer.

"There's an auction in Houston I think I should attend," she announced at the supper table on Wednesday.

She was expecting an argument, but her father merely said, "Sounds like a good idea."

Her mother asked, "Where will you stay?"

"Someplace cheap," she replied.

"Can I come along?" Luke asked.

"I need you here," her father said.

As simply as that, her escape had been arranged.

Of course, she was going to have to attend the auction,

but she didn't think that would be a problem. The sale was being held on Saturday afternoon. The event at the museum wasn't until later that evening. But she'd have to leave for Houston earlier than the time she'd agreed to meet Trace in town.

Callie debated the best way of contacting Trace to let him know they'd be traveling separately to Houston and to set the ground rules for their "date." Finally, she decided to ask Lou Ann Simpson for help. They'd been friends all through high school, but Lou Ann had gotten married instead of going to college. Callie had never confided to her friend about her relationship with Trace, because Lou Ann would have given her too hard a time about "sleeping with the enemy."

Callie had never told her best friend the truth about Eli, so Lou Ann had no reason to suspect the relationship that had existed between Callie and Trace in the past. At the same time, Lou Ann already knew Trace was interested in Callie, because she'd heard him ask Callie to dance.

Wednesday night she called Lou Ann and said, "Can you do me a favor?"

"What do you need?" Lou Ann asked.

"Invite Trace Blackthorne over for supper on Friday night."

"No problem. I owe him a dinner anyway. What's the special occasion?"

"I need a chance to talk with him before Saturday."

"What's happening Saturday?"

"Trace asked me out on a date. In Houston."

Lou Ann whistled. "I could see the sparks flying between the two of you on the dance floor, but my dear girl, I had no idea things had gone so far. Trace Blackthorne and Callie Creed. I would never have figured the two of you together."

"It's Callie Monroe," Callie reminded her. "And I only agreed to be his date for some charity event at the Museum of Fine Arts. Will you do it?"

"Sure. Just call me Cupid."

"That isn't funny," Callie said.

Lou Ann laughed. "See you on Friday at seven."

It was easy to get away from the house on Friday. Callie simply told the truth. "Lou Ann invited me over for supper. I won't be late."

Of course that meant no dressing up. No wearing makeup. Not that she needed—or wanted—to dress up for Trace. There was no need to impress him. They weren't an item, even if Lou Ann planned to play Cupid. Callie put her hair into a French braid, slipped on a clean pair of jeans and a plaid Western shirt, and gave her boots a quick buffing.

It was too late to change when she noticed the worn-through elbow on her shirt. She told herself she wouldn't have changed shirts anyway. Not everyone was as rich as the Blackthornes. Most people had to get the fullest use out of the material things they owned before they could discard them. She wasn't about to let Trace make her feel uncomfortable about a frayed shirt.

Trace was sitting in a wicker chair next to Dusty on the back porch of the Rafter S ranch house, drinking a Lone Star, when Callie arrived.

"Don't get up," she said to both men as she stepped down from her pickup.

Trace was clearly surprised to see her. She'd assumed

Lou Ann would have told him she was coming, since her friend was notoriously bad at keeping secrets.

Had he always been so handsome? Callie wondered. His black hair was wet, as though he'd just come from the shower, and he'd shaved, since his cheeks and chin were smooth. She thought of the time he'd left whisker burn on her cheeks when they'd spent an evening necking, and how ever after he'd insisted on shaving before he came to her. She'd missed the rough, prickly feel of his beard against her skin.

Suddenly, she realized he was eating her with his eyes as voraciously as she'd been consuming him. She brushed absently at a strand of hair that blew across her cheek as her body responded to the gleam of fascination in Trace's eyes—oh, yes, she could remember how delicious it felt!—as he gazed back at her.

"Lou Ann's in the kitchen," Dusty said. "She'll be out in a minute. Make yourself comfortable." He gestured toward the hanging porch swing that he knew was Callie's favorite place to sit.

Callie would have been more comfortable in the kitchen with Lou Ann, but she settled herself in the wooden swing as Trace handed her an opened longneck from the bucket of iced beer sitting on the porch between the two men. She managed to take the Lone Star from Trace without touching his hand and took a greedy gulp. The ice-cold beer tasted wonderful going down, and the bottle gave Callie something to do with her nervous hands.

"I didn't expect to see you before tomorrow," Trace said.

"That's why I came," she said. "We have to talk."

"Uh-oh."

"I'm still going to Houston," she hurried to say. "But there are complications we need to discuss."

"There you are, right on time," Lou Ann said as she used her hip to shove open the screen door. An immense stack of picnic items was balanced precariously in her hands and tucked up under her chin.

"Let me help you with some of that," Callie offered, leaping to her feet and grabbing for the bottle of catsup, the mustard, and a jar of pickles. She followed Lou Ann to the picnic table just beyond the porch, where Lou Ann let everything tumble out of her hands onto a checked tablecloth. Silverware placed strategically at the four corners kept the wind from sending the cloth flying.

"I decided on a cook-out, because the day turned out so nice," Lou Ann said. Giant hamburgers sizzled as Lou Ann dropped them one at a time onto the hot grill.

"Where are the girls?" Callie asked as she helped Lou Ann arrange plates and condiments on the picnic table.

"Sallie and Frannie are on a Girl Scout camp-out this weekend. Leaving me and Dusty all alone," she said, her eyebrows wagging up and down suggestively.

Dusty blushed. "Aw, hell, Lou Ann. Not in front of the neighbors."

"Trace and Callie know we sleep together, darling," Lou Ann said, as she crossed and sat down on Dusty's lap. She wrapped her arms around his neck and said, "For once, I'm not giving away any secrets."

Dusty's blush deepened.

Trace's laugh was cut off when Lou Ann turned to him and said, "What I want to know is where you two are planning to sleep this weekend."

Callie choked on a swallow of beer. She avoided looking at Trace as she replied, "In different hotels."

Lou Ann laughed. "If you say so."

"I thought you were planning to stay in your parents' penthouse on Woodway," Dusty said to Trace.

"Callie and I are going to take a walk," Trace said, rising from his chair. He snagged her hand, set both their beers on the picnic table, then headed toward the shade of some cottonwoods along Bitter Creek.

"Don't hurry back," Dusty said, as his arms encircled his wife.

"Don't forget about the hamburgers," Callie called over her shoulder.

"Hamburgers?" Lou Ann replied with a dazed look in her eyes, as Dusty nuzzled her neck.

"Come on," Trace said, tugging on Callie's hand. "The sooner we finish our business, the less charred my hamburger's going to be."

Trace held on to her hand until they reached the creek. He released it to bend down and pick up a stone, then skipped it across the creek. It quickly plopped in.

"I used to be better at this," he said, bending down for another stone.

Callie leaned back against a cottonwood, to avoid joining him. She didn't want to be friends. She just wanted things settled between them, so that Trace could go back to wherever he'd come from and leave her alone.

"What complications need to be resolved?" Trace asked, when the second stone performed no better than the first.

"I have to leave early in the morning, in order to attend an auction in the afternoon in Houston."

"No sweat. I'll fly you over in the morning. Next problem."

Callie was stunned. "There really isn't any other problem. But I can't—"

"Don't tell me you wouldn't rather fly than face that drive on Route 59," Trace said. "What time do you need to be in Houston?"

"The two-year-olds go on sale at one o'clock."

"We'll leave at eight. That'll give us time to shop at Neiman's for a dress, then freshen up at the penthouse before you—"

"I'm not staying with you, Trace."

"Why not? It'll save you the cost of a room."

"I won't sleep with you," she corrected.

He skipped a stone halfway across the creek. "You can have your own bedroom."

She thought of the kind of motel room she could afford, then imagined the luxury of the Blackthornes' penthouse apartment in Houston. She was tempted to agree to his offer. But she knew better. There were dangerous pitfalls lying in wait, if she spent the night under the same roof as Trace.

"Nothing is going to happen that you don't want to happen, Callie."

She looked at Trace, startled at the way he'd read her mind. The problem was, she wasn't sure what she wanted. She felt entirely too vulnerable. She hadn't been held in a man's arms for a very long time. And Trace was not just any man. They had once been lovers. They had once been in love.

In the end, her practicality won out. It was foolish to spend the money for a room when she had the offer of a place to stay for free. "All right," she said. "I'll stay at your parents' penthouse. But only because it'll be more convenient for both of us. And I'll take that separate bedroom."

"Fine. Now that we've worked everything out—"

"One more thing."

"What?"

"I don't want you buying any clothes for me."

"No dress?" Trace said with a boyish grin.

"No dress."

He crossed to her and slid an arm around her shoulders in the way he often had when they were in college, as though they were just good pals. "We'd better get back to the house," he said. "I can smell our hamburgers burning."

It wasn't until they were in the air headed toward Houston that Callie realized she was a captive, with nowhere to go if Trace started asking questions she didn't want to answer. She decided the safe move was to direct the conversation herself and keep it aimed at neutral topics.

"Nice airplane," she said. "I was expecting a twin-engine Cessna, not a corporate jet."

"Actually, we don't own this yet. I'm trying to talk Dad into buying it."

"It's beautiful, sleek, and fast. Why wouldn't he want to buy it?" Callie asked, smoothing her hand across the leather seat.

"Because I suggested it."

"Oh."

"Let's change the subject," Trace said. "What are you going to do with the rest of your life?"

Callie's jaw dropped. Then she laughed. "How am I supposed to answer a question like that?"

"Honestly."

She shrugged. "Live it, I guess."

He shook his head. "That's no answer. Do you plan to keep on working for your father?"

"Why wouldn't I? It's work I love. And I'm good at it."

"Fair enough," Trace said. "What if someone offered you more money to do the same work somewhere else?"

"My family needs me."

The words were out before Callie could stop them. She watched Trace's mouth thin and harden. She waited for him to chide her for putting her family first, but he changed the subject entirely.

"What are you wearing tonight?"

"A dress."

"I figured that," he said, his lips curving wryly. "What color?"

"Why does it matter?" she asked.

"I thought I might get you a corsage."

"I love gardenias," Callie said wistfully.

"I know. Fortunately, they go with anything. All right, gardenias it is."

Callie laughed. "You don't have to buy me flowers, Trace. This isn't the prom."

"I never got to take you to the prom. You went with Henry Featherstone. And you wore a peach-colored dress."

"How could you possibly know that?" Callie asked.

"Because I saw you walk in with him."

"You didn't know I was alive in high school," Callie scoffed.

"You had algebra first period, across the hall from my trig class. You ate a sack lunch with the same three girls every day, Lou Ann, Becky, and Robbie Sue. You spent your free period in the library reading Hemingway and Steinbeck. And you went straight home after school without doing any extracurricular activities, except on Thursdays. For some reason, on Thursdays you showed up at football practice. Why was that, Callie?"

Callie was confused. How could Trace possibly know so much about her activities in high school? They hadn't even met until she showed up at the University of Texas campus. "I don't understand," she said.

"You haven't answered my question. Why did you come to football practice on Thursdays?"

"Because that was the day I did the grocery shopping, and I didn't have to be home until later."

"Why were you there, Callie?"

Callie stared into his eyes, afraid to admit the truth. But what difference could it possibly make now? She swallowed hard and said, "I was there to see you."

He gave a sigh of satisfaction. "I hoped that was it. But I never knew for sure."

Callie's brow furrowed. "You wanted me to notice you?"

"I noticed you. Couldn't you feel my eyes on you? Didn't you ever sense the force of my boyish lust? I had it bad for you my senior year. I couldn't walk past you in the hall without needing to hold my books in my lap when I sat down in the next class."

"You're kidding, right?"

Trace chuckled. "I wish I were."

"Then it wasn't an accident, our meeting like that at UT?"

"That's the miracle of it," Trace said. "It was entirely by accident. Fate. Kismet. Karma. Whatever you want to call it. I would never have sought you out, Callie."

"Why not? Why didn't you just ask me out, if you wanted me so much?"

"Let's just say I wouldn't give my father the satisfaction and leave it at that."

Callie could imagine what he wasn't telling her. "A whole year," she murmured. "A whole extra year we could have had together."

"There's nothing keeping us apart now," Trace said. "You're single, and so am I."

"But you hate me!" she blurted.

"I've never hated you, Callie. I hated the choice you made."

"I wasn't the only one who made a choice, Trace."

He nodded his head. "True."

She waited for him to accept more of the blame for their separation. But he said nothing. "So what are you suggesting?" she asked. "What happens now?"

"I don't know," Trace said. "Maybe we can figure that out this weekend."

She stared out the window at the wide open Texas sky, wishing Trace hadn't revealed his high school infatuation. Wishing he hadn't suggested a world of limitless opportunities just waiting to be seized. Wishing he hadn't given her hope.

Did she want to get together with Trace? Was it possible to marry him and live happily ever after? Oh, it hurt too much to hope. What if he only wanted a sexual fling? What if he made her love him again and then left her behind? The temptation to reach out to him was so great, she threaded her hands together in her lap, to keep them to herself.

She'd wanted a chance to settle things between them on this trip. She'd hoped for a truce, a cessation of the war of wills, that would last until Trace could return to wherever he'd come from. She hadn't realized how dangerous it could be to talk as they used to do, and to discover that she still wanted him as much as he wanted her.

A limousine was waiting for them when they arrived at Houston's Hobby International Airport. Callie asked Trace to drop her off at the stockyards where the auction was being held, rather than take her by the penthouse first. "I'd like a chance to look over the horses before the bidding starts," she said. "I'll call you when I'm ready to be picked up."

She'd expected Trace to argue, but he said, "Fine."

To Callie's delight, she was able to purchase two more fillies during the afternoon at a price she could afford. And she'd have the horses to convince her family that she'd merely attended the auction while she was in Houston.

Trace wasn't in the limo when it arrived to pick her up. Callie was grateful for the opportunity to gather her wits before she had to do battle with him again. She had no doubt that a confrontation was coming sometime during the evening. Trace would make his move, and she would either have to accept his advances or rebuff them. Callie still hadn't made up her mind what she wanted to do.

She got the key from the concierge at the front desk and took the elevator to the penthouse. She expected Trace to be there, but when she entered and called his name, there was no answer.

She stepped inside and gasped at what she found. The place reeked of gardenias. Callie laughed in delight as she ran from vase to vase sniffing the pungent flowers. "Trace, you idiot!" she said, grinning from ear to ear. She was more pleased by his gesture than she wanted to admit.

It took a moment longer to focus her attention on the penthouse itself. She had expected it to be furnished elegantly and expensively, and it was. What surprised her were the homey touches that gave the place personality. A photograph on the credenza of the four Blackthorne kids wearing T-shirts and cut-off jeans, with one of the twins grinning broadly as he held a catfish aloft. A collection of rodeo belt buckles, apparently won by Blackjack, displayed under a glass tabletop. An antique tricycle shaped like a horse, with a worn leather seat.

She found a note from Trace on the dining room table that told her to make herself at home, that her bedroom was the second one down the hall, and that he would be there to pick her up at eight sharp for the reception. Callie wondered where he was and what he could possibly be doing so late in the day. Then she realized she had only two hours to get herself ready. She would need every minute of it to make herself beautiful. And she wanted very much to be beautiful for Trace.

There were more framed photos hanging in the hall, and Callie took a few minutes to peruse them. Trace at nine or ten, standing between Clay and Owen, with an arm around each brother's shoulders. Trace in his football uniform. Clay and Owen in football uniforms. Summer on horseback. Summer sitting on Trace's lap. Summer between Clay and Owen, her arms around their waists. They all looked happy. As though they hadn't a care in the world.

Which was what had created the chasm between her and Trace in the first place. Could Trace really have changed so much in eleven years? Could they really make a life together when they'd come from such different backgrounds?

Callie glanced at her watch and realized she had to hurry. She opened the door to the bedroom Trace had given her and stopped dead. On the antique four-poster bed lay the most beautiful cocktail dress she'd ever seen.

"Oh, Trace, I asked you not to do this," Callie whispered in a voice filled with awe.

She walked toward the dress, unable to resist touching it, then holding it up to admire it. It was red. Bright red. Made of heavy silk, strapless, with a fitted bodice, and a skirt cut on the bias which, unless she was very much mistaken, would hit her somewhere about mid-thigh. A fringed silk shawl lay on the bed beside a black merry widow, a lacy black garter belt, and black nylons.

"I can't wear any of this," she said aloud.

But she wanted desperately to wear it. She forced herself to set the dress back down on the bed. She opened her suitcase and took out the simple black wool sheath she'd brought with her. The style was ageless. The dress was old. It had been in her closet for years. She'd last worn it to Nolan's funeral.

Callie hung the black dress up and headed for the shower. "First things first," she said aloud. She could make the decision which dress to wear after she'd taken a shower and put on her makeup.

Callie was just stepping out of the shower when the doorbell rang. She couldn't imagine who it could be, unless there was only one key, and Trace was locked out. Hair dripping, she wrapped herself in a towel and trotted to the front door. She leaned her ear against the wooden panel and called, "Who's there?"

"Mrs. Monroe?"

"Yes," Callie answered.

"I'm here to give you a manicure."

"I didn't arrange for a manicure," Callie said.

"Mr. Blackthorne made the appointment."

Callie looked down at her rough hands, at the ragged nails and torn cuticles. How dare he notice! Some people had to work for a living! She was about to send the woman away when she heard a second female voice talking to the first.

"Mrs. Monroe?" the second voice said.

"Yes. Who is it?"

"I'm here to do your hair and makeup."

Callie pulled the door open. "I don't need—"

The two women marched in without invitation.

"He said you might resist at first," the manicurist said. "But that we shouldn't take no for an answer."

"You can sit here," the hairdresser said, pulling out a chair at the dining room table and pressing Callie into it. She set a tray containing combs, brushes, a hair dryer, and curling iron on the lacquered surface and dropped another, equally heavy bag of makeup, on the floor.

"Will this give you enough room to work?" she asked the manicurist.

"I've got a table I can set up in front of her," the other woman replied, "if you turn her chair around."

"I'm Wanda," the hairdresser said as she angled the chair Callie was sitting in so the manicurist could set up a table in front of her. "Is there any particular way you'd like me to fix your hair?"

"I'd like you both to leave," Callie said, crossing her arms over her chest and tucking her ragged nails into her armpits where they couldn't be seen.

"Mr. Blackthorne said I should tell you that we work for a living, too," Wanda said. "And that if we leave, we won't get paid."

Callie stared at the hairdresser for a moment in astonishment, then laughed and held her hands up in surrender. "I'd like my hair in a French twist."

Wanda tipped Callie's chin up and surveyed her features. "Good choice. That'll show off those nice cheekbones of yours."

Callie flushed with pleasure at the compliment.

"I'm Harriet," the manicurist said. "If you'll just put your hands in this warm water, we can get started."

Callie had never felt so pampered. She couldn't help wondering whether Trace had ever done this before—for some other woman. "Has Mr. Blackthorne ever employed you before?" she asked Wanda.

"Oh, no, but his sister has. Summer Blackthorne calls first thing when she arrives in town."

Callie expelled a sigh of relief. Of course. Trace had asked, and Summer had told him who to call. She wanted to resent his high-handed behavior, but she was enjoying herself too much.

Harriet's manicure was followed by a foot massage

and pedicure, a hedonistic pleasure Callie had never experienced.

"Mr. Blackthorne specified Ravishing Red polish for your toenails," Harriet said. "Said it would match your dress."

Callie looked down at her polished toenails, which would, indeed, match the cocktail dress Trace had bought. Callie realized that sometime during the past hour, she'd decided to wear the dress. Why not? If she was going to play Cinderella and go to the ball, she might as well be dressed for the part.

She and Wanda and Harriet were fast friends by the time Callie showed them out the door. When she returned to the bedroom, she discovered a pair of strappy, open-toed high heels in a box on the floor beside the bed. No wonder Trace had wanted her toenail polish to match! He'd even provided his Cinderella with glass slippers.

Callie wondered how Trace had known what sizes to buy, then realized her figure hadn't changed in eleven years. He'd often helped her dress—and undress—in college. In any case, everything fit perfectly. Even the lacy—and extraordinarily tiny—French underwear she'd found beneath the merry widow.

When she heard the doorbell ring again, she hurried to answer it, expecting Trace to be there. While Callie stared in astonishment, a waiter wheeled in a magnum of iced Dom Perignon champagne, two crystal flutes, and a bowl of strawberries.

She was still staring at the strawberries when Trace arrived, tipped the waiter, and closed the door behind him.

Their eyes locked.

"Hi," he said.

"Hi," she replied.

"You look beautiful."

"Thank you. So do you."

He gave her a roguish smile, looked down at the tailored black Armani tuxedo he had on, and said, "In this old thing?"

Callie laughed. He was charming. She was charmed.

"Would you like some champagne?" he asked.

She nodded, no longer able to speak over the lump of emotion in her throat.

He uncorked the champagne in a way that made it plain he'd done it many times. She held the flutes while he filled them, then handed him his glass.

"Want a strawberry?" he asked.

She shook her head.

"Guess I'll have one," he said.

She took the strawberry out of his hand and held it up to his lips by the stem. Gazing steadily into her eyes, he leaned down and bit it off close to her fingertips. Callie's insides did a somersault when his tongue flicked out to catch a bit of juice that remained on his lips. She watched his Adam's apple bob as he swallowed the fruit, then met his gaze again.

"Callie."

Nothing more. Nothing more needed to be said. She turned into his body and angled her head up for his kiss. His mouth was soft on hers, hesitant, searching. Callie slid her tongue along the seam of his lips, and he opened to her. She went up on tiptoe, leaning into him.

He tasted of strawberries and champagne.

"You taste sweet," he murmured.

Callie laughed. "You're the one who's been eating strawberries."

His lips caressed the left side of her mouth and then the right, before his tongue teased the seam of her mouth. When she would have opened to him, he lifted his head and said teasingly, "I'd like another strawberry."

Callie set down her champagne flute. She realized her hand was trembling as she reached for the ripe red berry and held it up to his lips. His hand covered hers as he ate the fruit down to the stem, then took the stem away and kissed her fingertips.

"We can't have you going out tonight with sticky fingers," he said as he sucked each one clean.

Callie's knees felt ready to buckle, and she laid her free hand on Trace's shoulder to hold herself upright. The sexual teasing was something new, something they'd never done when they were younger, because they'd always been in too much of a hurry. His gaze was tender, and she felt the heat of it warm a cold place deep inside her.

She traced his ear with her fingertip, then leaned up to nibble on his lobe. She was rewarded with a satisfying groan. "Now, that's what I call sweet," she murmured in his ear.

"Oh, God, Callie," he moaned as his mouth latched on to her throat.

She'd always loved it when he kissed her throat, always worried he'd leave a mark of passion, of possession, and always felt disappointed when she'd looked later to find he hadn't. She let her head fall back to give him greater access to her throat and made a carnal sound as he pleasured her with his mouth and teeth and tongue.

"Trace, please," she whispered as her hands slid up around his neck.

It was a plea for satisfaction. And for absolution. How could they have a future together, when she couldn't find the strength to tell him the truth about his son? When she feared his anger and his vengeance? But that didn't stop her from needing his hands on her, needing the succor she found in his kiss, wanting to join her body with his.

She let her hand slide down his chest, down across his belly, down his trousers until she was cupping him in her hand. He leaned into her touch and groaned.

Abruptly, he stepped back, his breathing tortured, his eyes heavy-lidded. "We're late," he said. "We have to go."

Callie put a hand to her lips, shocked at what she'd done, even more surprised that Trace had ended the interlude. He'd woven a spell around her—the beautiful dress, people to pamper her, champagne and strawberries—and at the moment of her surrender, he'd broken it. Why?

"I don't want us to be rushed," he said in answer to her unspoken question. "I want us to have plenty of time to enjoy each other."

Callie flushed at his assumption that she was ready to slip into bed with him. Of course, he was right. If they'd kept on kissing and touching, they would have ended up in bed. But that was before she'd come to her senses—with a little help from him.

She took a step back. All of this was a fairy tale. In the morning she'd be going home to Three Oaks. "I feel like a fool."

"Don't," he said, laying a hand on her bare shoulder. His hand felt warm against her cool flesh. She held herself still as his fingertips moved across her breastbone. When his thumb finally came to rest on the pulse at her throat, her body was quivering with need. She looked up at him and asked in a shaky voice, "What are you doing, Trace?"

"Finding my way," he said.

Callie felt herself sliding down a slippery slope. How was he able to seduce her with so little effort? "We have to go," she said.

"I know," he said, his voice filled with regret.

He picked up her shawl from where it lay across the back of the sofa and wrapped it around her shoulders. They rode in silence down the elevator. Spoke not a word during the drive to the Museum of Fine Arts on Bissonnet. As they headed inside, Trace said, "I'm expected to shake hands in the receiving line as a stand-in for my mother. Feel free to look around. I'll find you as soon as I'm done."

Callie spent the time Trace was greeting the other attendees surveying the collection of Western art, which included several of his mother's paintings. It seemed no time at all before he was slipping his arm around her waist.

"There are some people I want to introduce to you," he said as he turned her around.

"Oh, Trace, I don't think—"

"Callie, I'd like you to meet my godparents, Marla and George Carpenter. Marla, George, this is Callie Monroe," Trace said to the short, elderly couple she found herself facing.

They were both white-haired and both dressed very plainly but elegantly. The only obvious evidence of their wealth was the five- or six-carat marquise-cut diamond on Marla's ring finger and the diamond clasp on the three-strand rope of pearls around her neck.

"We've heard so much about you," Marla said. "All of it good," she hastened to reassure Callie.

Callie shot Trace a questioning look. She hadn't been aware he'd discussed her with anyone, let alone his god-parents.

"Trace has told us how good you are with cutting horses," George said.

"Oh, thank you," Callie said, relieved at the thought that Trace hadn't revealed their personal relationship. "It's very nice to meet you."

"And you, too," Marla said, taking Callie's hand in hers. "I despaired that this boy would ever find his way back to you. I'm so glad he did. He was devastated when the two of you broke up."

Callie barely managed to keep her jaw from dropping. It seemed Marla and George were very much aware of her personal relationship with Trace. And approved of it!

"We're very proud of all Trace has accomplished," George said. "When he finally contacted us from—"

"That's enough, you two," Trace said, interrupting his godfather. "You'll have me blushing. Come on, Callie, there are some other people I'd like you to meet."

He presented a half dozen other couples to her, all people he'd obviously known for a very long time and with whom he was comfortable. Callie felt the distance between herself and Trace looming greater with every introduction. Trace laughed and joked and made small talk with these people as though he'd been doing it all his life.

And he had, Callie realized. She was a poor match for Trace when it came to social experience. Her family had worked hard on several regional events to earn funds for the Miami Project to Cure Paralysis, but otherwise she'd spent her life in blue jeans and boots.

"I don't belong here," she whispered to Trace. "I don't know what to say to these people."

"How can you say that? Everyone is charmed by you. Including me."

Callie felt that treacherous warmth inside again.

Just then Marla crossed to Trace with a very tall, distinguished-looking gentleman at her side and said, "There's someone here who wants to say hello to you."

Callie paled. It was the governor of Texas. She stood beside Trace as he smiled—and then shared a bear hug with the man.

"Hi, Pete," Trace said. "Dad said I'd probably see you. How's Shirley?"

"Fine," the governor said. "Who is this beautiful lady with you?"

Trace pulled her close and let his eyes linger on her face. "She is beautiful, isn't she?"

"No argument from me," the governor said with a laugh.

Callie blushed with pleasure and barely managed not to hide her face against Trace's shoulder. "Thank you," she murmured.

"Callie, I'd like you to meet my friend Governor Pete Hanson."

"How do you do, Governor Hanson?" Callie said.

"Please, call me Pete," the governor replied with a smile and a wink.

"I will," she said, but couldn't make herself do it. Callie wasn't necessarily impressed by men in positions of power, but that didn't mean she was comfortable with them either. Trace didn't seem to notice her nervousness, and she was certain those she'd met had been considerate of her for Trace's sake.

Trace had been introducing her to people as though he expected her to become a part of his life. As though they had a future together. As though there were no differences between them that needed to be resolved.

"Will you excuse me?" she said to Trace. "I need to powder my nose."

Trace grinned, then kissed the tip of her nose. "Your nose looks fine. Don't run too far, Callie. We're seated at the head table."

Callie turned her back and walked blindly in the direction of the powder room. She felt like her insides were flying apart, and closed her arms around her middle to hang on. She could see where the evening was headed. If she went back to the penthouse with Trace, they would end up in bed together. What would that prove? That they were physically attracted to one another? She conceded the fact. But they hadn't a snowball's chance in hell of building a life together. Not when he was a Blackthorne and she was a Creed.

All right, technically she was a Monroe. But that didn't change the facts. Marriage between them was still as impossible now as it had been eleven years ago. If she let herself love him again, she would only have to find a way to pick up the pieces when he was gone. She didn't want any more pain in her life.

Not even for one night of indescribable pleasure?

Callie turned and headed for the exit, making sure she stayed out of Trace's sight. When she got outside, she found the limo they'd come in and told the driver, "Please take me back to the penthouse."

Coward. The word reverberated in her head. Maybe she was. But how much pain was one person expected to survive? She couldn't bear to lose Trace again. It was better not to let herself start caring again.

Callie left the beautiful red dress on the bed. She left Cinderella's slippers on the floor. She didn't want to take time to find underclothes to wear, so she put her plain black wool dress on over the sexy lingerie Trace had bought for her, feeling an ache of regret as she conceded how much she would have enjoyed having him take it off her, one piece at a time.

She left a note for Trace, thanking him for the plane ride and the afternoon of make-believe. An hour later, she was headed southwest on US Route 59 in a rented Ford Taurus.

It wasn't quite midnight, but her fairy tale was over.

Chapter 6

IN THE FIRST DAYS AFTER SHE HAD PANICKED and run from Trace, Callie kept expecting him to show up at her doorstep and demand an explanation. But for the past three weeks, there hadn't been one word from him. She wondered if he was angry with her, or whether her behavior had finally convinced him of the futility of pursuing her. She still hurt inside. But life had gone on. Once again she had made her choice, and Trace seemed willing to let her live with it.

Callie stood on the back porch and eyed the setting sun, then turned her gaze toward the south pasture, where she'd sent her parents at noon with a picnic basket. Conversations between her parents had been brittle for the past three weeks since the incident with Blackjack at the Rafter S, and it had been her idea to send them off together to mend their fences.

"You two are going on a picnic this afternoon," she'd announced at breakfast. She'd been prepared for the argument that had followed, and she hadn't given up or given in.

"All right," her father had finally conceded. "I'll take

your mother on a picnic. Who knows," he said with a wink at her mother. "We might even have time for a little—"

"We'd better get to work," her mother had interrupted, her cheeks pink. "Or the chores won't be finished in time to go."

Callie's mother had a habit of postponing pleasure, if there was work to be done. Unfortunately, with as little hired help as they had, and as much work as there was to do, pleasure for its own sake was seldom a part of their lives. Callie was determined that today would be an exception.

At noon, as her father headed out the kitchen door, Callie had unclipped his cell phone from his belt, chiding, "Otherwise you'll be calling me every five minutes to see what I'm doing."

She had sent them off in a battered '51 Chevy pickup, the only ranch vehicle without a CB radio. "Have fun!" she'd called, as she waved goodbye from the back porch. "Enjoy yourselves. Don't even think about coming back until after you've had a lazy lunch."

It was long past lunchtime. In fifteen minutes it would be dark. Callie had hoped her mother would manage to keep her father from coming home before they'd consumed the contents of the picnic basket, but she'd never expected them to be gone this long. She told herself not to worry. She told herself it was a good sign that they'd taken the whole afternoon for themselves. But she fervently wished she hadn't relieved her father of his cell phone.

Callie couldn't help thinking about the hunters she'd seen earlier in the day trying to manipulate the bump gate that led into the north pasture. The double-wide gate swung on a central pivot. Hit it too hard, and the left side would swing around and smack the driver's door before he could get his truck through. Hit it too softly, and the gate would swing back closed on the front end of the truck before it could pass beyond the opening. Even an experienced cowboy sometimes mistook his speed and ended up crinkling his fender.

When she'd come upon them, the hunter driving the rented Jeep Cherokee had already crumpled the driver's side door. She'd driven up and said, "You might want to—"

He'd cut her off briskly. "I've done this before, honey. You don't need to give me instructions."

Callie tried not to bristle at the offending endearment. She took a look at the other three men in the car, all dressed like the driver in military camouflage with bright orange neon vests, and realized the portly executive was going to lose face if he didn't manage to get through the gate on his own. She'd smiled sweetly and driven away, then grinned with wicked satisfaction as her rearview mirror revealed the bump gate smacking into the Jeep's front fender.

She wasn't grinning now. Four idiots with hunting rifles had spent the day wandering around out there shooting at wild boar—the only large game in season year round—in the north pasture. What if they'd crossed fences and ended up where they shouldn't be?

"Any sign of Mom and Dad?"

Callie turned to find Luke standing at her shoulder. "Not yet," she said.

"Maybe we'd better go looking for them," Luke said, his forehead wrinkled with worry.

"Mom and Dad can take care of themselves."

"I've never known Dad to be out of touch this long," Luke said. "Sam thinks something bad happened."

"Sam's been drinking all day." Callie bit her tongue on the bitter accusation, but it was too late.

"You ought to cut him some slack," Luke said in his brother's defense. "He's got a reason to drink."

Callie didn't argue. Luke was too young to remember how great a brother Sam had been before the accident. She missed Sam's sense of humor, his strong back, and his willing help. "Will you keep an eye on Eli and Hannah while I go take a look around?"

"Sam can baby-sit. I want to go, too."

"Sam's drunk," Callie said sharply. "I need you to stay here."

"Shit."

Callie gave Luke a sharp look, and he dropped his gaze to his boots.

"All right. I'll stay," he muttered. "But take Dad's cell phone and call me when you find them."

"You'll probably have to call me when they show up here," Callie said, bumping her shoulder against Luke's in a gesture meant to reassure him. "Most likely they're just having a good time together and don't want it to end."

"Yeah. You're probably right," Luke said.

Callie could tell from the worried look in his eyes that he didn't believe that any more than she did.

Callie spent the next three hours driving every road in the north, middle, and south pastures without seeing any sign of her parents in the meager illumination provided by her headlights. They seemed to have disappeared. She stopped the pickup and pressed the button on the cell phone that was preprogrammed for the ranch house.

Luke answered the phone with, "Did you find them?"

Callie felt her heart sink. "I thought they might have contacted you."

"They didn't. We have to call in some help, Callie. We have to find them. Something's happened. Something's wrong. They wouldn't stay gone this long."

Callie chewed on her lower lip. Her parents would be mortified if she called the sheriff and reported them missing, and they showed up from their picnic with swollen lips and tousled hair. It was possible.

But it wasn't probable. More likely, something had happened. Callie hoped it was simply a mechanical failure on the truck. That was entirely possible with that old heap. This was all her fault. She should have let them take a truck with a CB, so they could call for help when the truck conked out. Or left her father his cell phone.

Maybe they'd started walking home and one of them had stumbled into a prairie dog hole and sprained an ankle and they'd decided to wait together for help to come.

Maybe one of them had been shot by one of those corporate idiots who'd gone where he shouldn't have gone and shot what he couldn't clearly see.

Callie shivered. Better to have her parents embarrassed than to wait and discover later that they'd needed help and she'd been too proud to call for it.

"Look in the drawer by the refrigerator," she instructed Luke. "You'll find a list of important phone numbers. Give me the number for the sheriff."

Callie listened to the number, then disconnected her brother and dialed the county sheriff's office. "This is Callie Monroe at Three Oaks," she said. "I want to report two missing persons."

"Who's missing?" a deputy asked.

"My mother and father, Lauren and Jesse Creed."

"How long have they been gone?"

"Since this morning."

"It's only been dark a couple of hours," the deputy replied with exasperation. "What makes you think they're missing?"

"They would have come back if—"

"Look. I'm sorry you can't find them. But you'll have to wait twenty-four hours before you can file a missing persons report."

"But I—" Callie found herself listening to dead air. She pounded the steering wheel and swore every epithet she knew. She'd never relied much on anybody to help her out of a jam because of precisely the response she'd gotten. If you didn't ask, you didn't have to deal with being turned down. You didn't leave yourself feeling helpless and hopeless and defeated.

Callie's throat tightened until it was painful to swallow. Something was wrong. She knew it. But there was nothing she could do in the dark. She started the engine on the Chevy pickup and turned it toward home.

Every light in the house was on when she pulled up to the kitchen door. She stopped the engine and listened. There were no voices to be heard through the screen door. A moment later she heard boots pounding on the hardwood floor and Luke, Eli, and Hannah showed up at the screen door and peered out.

"Is it them?" she heard Eli ask.

"Naw. It's your mom," Luke answered.

Callie got out of the truck and gathered her children in her arms on the back porch, as they spilled out the screen door.

"What's happened to Gram and Grampa?" Eli demanded. "You made them go! Where are they?"

"Where are they?" Hannah parroted.

"They'll be home soon. Have you had any supper?"

"I'm not hungry," Eli said.

"I'm not hungry," Hannah echoed.

"Well, I am," Callie said, though she was certain she wouldn't be able to choke anything down. The children needed to eat, and she needed the normalcy of preparing them a meal.

Sam had retired to his bedroom to sleep off his Jack Daniels, and she was just setting grilled cheese sandwiches in front of Hannah, Eli, and Luke, when the phone rang.

She barely managed to beat Luke to the phone. "Dad? Is that you?"

"Is it them?" Luke asked, hanging over her shoulder

"Is it them?" Eli and Hannah repeated, jumping up and down around her.

She covered the mouthpiece and said, "No, it's Trace Blackthorne."

"What does he want?" Luke said with a sneer.

"If you'll give me some peace and quiet, I'll find out," Callie said, turning her back on Luke and taking her hand from the mouthpiece. "What do you want, Trace?"

Callie listened, not quite believing what she was hearing, especially in light of the way she'd abandoned him without a word in Houston. "What are you suggesting?"

"What does he want?" Luke asked, hovering nearby.

Callie covered the mouthpiece and said, "He wants to know if we need any help looking for Mom and Dad."

"How does he know they're missing?" Luke asked suspiciously.

"His brother Owen was at the sheriff's office when my call came in. He called Trace and told him about it. Trace is offering to come over and help with the search."

"We don't need help from any Blackthornes!" Luke growled.

Callie took her hand off the mouthpiece and said, "How long will it take you to get over here?" She listened to his answer, said, "I'll expect you then," and hung up.

"Why did you do that?" Luke demanded angrily.

"Yeah, Mom! Why?" Eli asked.

"Because he's got a vehicle with a searchlight mounted on the front fender, and I'm not going to sit here on my hands doing nothing if there's any chance Mom and Dad are in trouble."

"One searchlight isn't going to make much difference," Luke said belligerently.

"Maybe not," Callie replied. But Trace had also promised he'd have every cowhand who worked at Bitter Creek help with the search come dawn. Callie thought it wiser to keep that bit of information to herself for now. With any luck, they would locate her parents tonight.

"Why is Trace Blackthorne so interested in helping us?" Luke asked. "What's in it for him?"

Callie didn't want to think about that. "He's just being neighborly, I suppose."

Luke scoffed. "Blackthornes being neighborly to Creeds? In a pig's eye! He wants something. Or he knows something. Maybe he had something to do with Mom and Dad disappearing. Maybe he wants to be there when they're found, so he can cover up whatever evidence—"

"That's enough, Luke," Callie said, as she saw the growing fear in Eli's eyes. "I'm accepting Trace's offer of help. I don't want to hear any more speculation about why he's helping."

But as she ushered her children back to the table, she found herself wondering why Trace had offered to get involved in something that was really none of his business. Trace Blackthorne no longer had a relationship with anyone in the Creed family. Callie's gaze strayed to Eli. Or at least, none that he knew about.

So why had Trace agreed to help? He must want to ingratiate himself with her, Callie decided. He must still have hopes of an affair with her. Perhaps he thought she would change her mind about getting involved with him, if she owed him a favor.

She wondered what excuse Trace would give Blackjack if it became necessary for him to order the Bitter Creek cowboys away from their work to search for her parents. Callie shuddered. Something had happened to them. She knew it. Something bad.

She used the time it would take Trace to drive to Three Oaks to get Eli and Hannah ready for bed. During her marriage to Nolan, they had lived in the foreman's house. During the last six months of Nolan's life, Callie had spent so much time at the hospital, it had been necessary to move into the big house, so her mother could more easily take care of the children. After Nolan's death, it had been the path of least resistance to stay where they were.

She ushered the children upstairs and made sure they brushed their teeth before they put on their pajamas. A bath would have to wait for another night. They slept in twin beds in the same room, a situation Callie was aware couldn't go on much longer. Eli was getting old enough to need and want some privacy. But she knew the children took comfort now from each other's presence.

"How come I have to go to bed the same time as Hannah?" Eli grumbled.

"If you're not sleepy, you can use the time to read," Callie said as she pulled the covers up under Hannah's arms.

"Tuck me in, Mommy," Hannah said.

Callie tucked the covers against Hannah's body all the way down one side, under her feet at the bottom and up the other side. "Snug as a bug in a rug," she said when she was done, tweaking Hannah's nose playfully.

Hannah giggled. "Sleep tight. Don't let the bedbugs bite," she recited in return.

Callie bent over and kissed Hannah's forehead, smelling her hair, resisting the urge to pick her up and cuddle her. She fought tears and bit back a curse of frustration that she still wept so easily. She turned to Eli and saw he was just finishing the same tucking ritual, having done it for himself. Their eyes met, hers stark, his bleak.

Nolan had performed the ritual for Eli, as she had performed it tonight for Hannah. But Nolan was gone, and Eli had informed her on the day Nolan went into the hospital for the last time, that he was too old for his mother to be tucking him into bed.

She crossed and sat beside him, adjusting the pillow behind him, so he could sit up to read. "Don't stay up too late reading," she said.

He shrank away when she leaned over to kiss his cheek. He quickly swiped away the kiss, much too old, his pointed look told her, for such signs of maternal devotion. He opened a Christopher Pike novel and pretended she wasn't still sitting beside him.

Callie rose and made it to the doorway before she turned back to check one last time on her children. Hannah was turned on her side away from the small reading light beside Eli's bed, a faded yellow Pooh bear snuggled under her arm, her eyelashes dark on her plump cheeks, her thumb in her mouth.

Eli was engrossed in the horror novel, his eyebrows arrowed down in concentration, his knees drawn up to make a rest for the book. She had seen Trace in the same pose. Callie frowned. It was understandable the scene would remind her of Trace, rather than Nolan. Nolan hadn't liked to read. But Nolan had been Eli's father. Nolan was the one who had loved him and raised him from a baby. It was Nolan Eli would remember when he was a grown man recalling his father.

Callie stepped out of the room and drew the door almost closed behind her. She hurried downstairs, wanting to be outside to greet Trace, rather than take the chance of Luke confronting him in the kitchen.

"Listen closely for Hannah," she told Luke. "And make sure Eli turns the light out by ten-thirty."

"Why don't you stay, and let me go?" Luke suggested.

"Trace offered to take me," Callie replied.

"All the more reason I should go," Luke said. "How do we know he won't make a move on you?"

Callie felt the blush crawling up her throat and turned away to grab her Levi's jacket from the antler coatrack. "I can take care of myself," she said as she shoved open the screen door.

"Callie!" Luke called.

She turned back to him impatiently. "What is it, Luke?"

"Call as soon as . . . I mean if you . . . that is, when you find them."

She crossed back inside and gave Luke a quick, hard hug. He hesitated only an instant before he hugged her back. "Don't worry," she said in his ear. "It's probably something ridiculous that's making them so late, like that stupid truck wouldn't start."

She backed away from the desolate look in his eyes and hurried outside. The air was cool and damp, almost chilly. She thought of the spaghetti-strapped yellow sundress she'd talked her mother into wearing with a pair of white sandals. Her father would probably offer her mother his Western shirt to cover her bare shoulders, but he never wore an undershirt, so even if Callie imagined her mother warm, her father's skin would have to be prickling in the cool night air.

Sandals. Her mother would have a hard time walking in the brush in sandals. No worse than her father would have walking in boots intended to be worn by a man who spent his day in a saddle. Damn. What had she been thinking?

Callie hurried toward the bright stream of headlights, forcing Trace to skid to a stop in order to avoid running her down. Once her eyes adjusted to the glare, she stopped cold and stared at the wide-bodied, definitely-not-standard, white-on-white Buick 88 convertible Trace had described merely as "a vehicle with a spotlight mounted on the fender."

The first thing she noticed was the flashy chrome hood ornament bearing the Blackthorne brand, the Circle B. A heavy-duty chrome bumper had been mounted to protect the front end of the car from bump gates and brush. There were movable chrome spotlights on both front fenders.

She ran her hand along the oversize front fender as she headed for the passenger door, noting the three shotgun holders molded into the metal frame. A quick look confirmed there were three more on the other side of the car. Two of the slots on her side held guns in rawhide cases.

"This is quite a car," Callie said as she stared at the open convertible.

"Think of it as an upgraded jeep."

"I've never seen a jeep that looked remotely like this."

"It's a hunting vehicle," Trace said. "Come on, get in."

"It sure beats my pickup," Callie muttered. The Circle B brand appeared again beside the inset chrome door handle. She couldn't help noticing the complete refreshment center along the backseat as she stepped up onto the chrome running board.

An antique-looking car phone was attached beneath the burled wood dash, and the glove box also bore the Circle B brand, but this time engraved in silver. Callie found the brand on the circular chrome radio knobs as well. The leather seat was wide enough for three men to sit comfortably, with lots of leg room, but she hugged the seat near the window, leaving a chasm of leather between them.

It wasn't enough.

Trace's presence filled the car. The night shadows emphasized the crow's feet around his eyes and the deep brackets around his mouth. He looked tired, and she could easily imagine he'd spent a long day working at some physically demanding job. She could tell he'd showered, because his hair was still damp, but he hadn't shaved, and beard darkened his cheeks and chin. He obviously hadn't planned to go out again.

"Thank you for coming," she said.

"You're welcome."

She felt a need to fill the silence, so he wouldn't bring up her behavior the weekend she'd run away from him in Houston. "Why haven't I ever seen this car before?" she asked.

"It's been in a garage, along with a few horse-drawn carriages used by the first Blackthornes at Bitter Creek."

"Who customized it for you?"

"It was a gift to my grandfather."

When Trace didn't mention the donor, Callie asked, "Who gave it to him?"

Trace shot her a deprecating smile. "President Eisenhower. He used to come for hunting parties at Bitter Creek."

"I see." The car, which apparently dated from the 1950s, looked brand new. It was one more sign of the difference between their two families. Any carriages her forebears had used had long since worn out. And there were no presents from presidents who'd been hunting buddies.

"No word from your parents?" Trace asked as he backed the oversize car and headed for the main road.

"Nothing," she said, staring straight ahead to avoid his gaze.

"Where do you want to start looking?"

"I sent them to the south pasture. We might as well start there," Callie said.

"Sent them?"

Callie folded her hands on her lap to keep from fidgeting. "Ever since the Rafter S auction—" She stopped herself. It was none of Trace's business that her parents had been having marital difficulties. "They went on a picnic this afternoon," she said instead. "And they haven't come back."

"Did they have a cell phone? A CB?" Trace asked.

Callie shook her head. "I wanted them to have some time alone to—" She cut herself off again. "The truck might have broken down."

"How many miles could they be from the nearest road if they're in the south pasture?" Trace asked.

Callie thought for a moment. Three Oaks consisted of sixty-five thousand acres of grassland, which was just over one hundred square miles of property. It had a rectangular shape that ran five miles from east to west, and a little more than twenty miles from north to south. The ranch house was situated in the middle pasture, along the widest part of Bitter Creek.

Callie did the math and didn't like the answer she came up with. "They would never have to walk more than five miles from any place in the south pasture to reach a road."

"They could have walked that in a little more than an hour. You've driven all the roads, I presume."

Callie nodded soberly. "I spent three hours driving up and down every gravel track they might have crossed getting home from the south pasture, and I checked out the camp house, where we feed the crew during roundup. I didn't find them."

"One of them must be hurt."

Callie's heart skipped a beat. "Why do you say that?"

Trace met her gaze, then turned his attention back to the road. "Nothing else makes sense. Unless you think they might have run away from home."

Callie snorted in disgust. "They went on a picnic." But Trace's words made her think of something else that hadn't previously occurred to her. Another scenario that was so unpalatable, so unbelievable, that she hadn't let herself consider it.

Her father was notoriously jealous. What if, instead of making up, her parents had argued about Blackjack? What if her father had struck her mother and accidentally—What if he'd taken her body and—

Callie shivered.

"Cold?" Trace asked. "I can turn up the heater."

"No," Callie said. "I was just thinking."

"Why did they go off without a cell phone or a CB?" Trace asked.

"I wanted them to have some time alone. I never dreamed anything like this would happen."

"Life is full of unexpected turns," Trace said.

And too many of the turns in her life had been unexpectedly tragic, Callie thought. Losing Trace. Losing Nolan. And maybe losing—Callie refused to let her mind dwell on what they might find. "I was surprised you offered to help, after what I . . . Why did you?"

"Can't a neighbor help out a neighbor?"

"Not when one is a Blackthorne and the other is a Creed," Callie said.

"Let's just say I did it for old time's sake, and leave it at that."

Callie eyed Trace warily. "This isn't going to change my mind. I'm not going to get involved with you again, Trace."

"No?"

"No."

He didn't argue, simply aimed both fender-mounted spotlights into the thick brush on either side of the road and drove slowly along the perimeter of alternating steel and mesquite fence posts that framed the south pasture. The shiny steel posts were there to keep the fence standing if a range fire burned out the wooden ones, while the mesquite would keep the fence standing if cattle leaned against the less sturdy metal posts to scratch and knocked them down.

"Lot of rotten posts down," Trace noted. "You ought to replace that mesquite with cedar."

Callie pressed her lips flat to keep from replying. Mesquite rotted from the inside out, so it was hard to tell when a post needed to be replaced unless it actually fell down. On the other hand, cedar rotted from the outside in, so the signs of wear were more visible and repairs could be made in a timely fashion. But mesquite was available for free, since it grew all over Three Oaks. Cedar posts had to be bought, with money they didn't have.

She caught Trace staring at her and said, "I know what you're thinking."

"What am I thinking?"

"That we Creeds might as well give up and sell Three Oaks to you Blackthornes right now, because you'll get it from us sooner or later," Callie said bitterly.

"That's probably true," Trace said with a half smile. "But I was wishing it was eleven years ago, and that I knew then what I know now."

"Meaning what?"

"Meaning that I didn't know then what I was giving up when I left you behind."

Callie felt the hairs stand up on her neck and turned, expecting Trace to tell her he had discovered Eli was his son. When he didn't speak, she said, "We can't turn back the clock, Trace. What's done is done."

"What's done can be undone," he contradicted. "Wounds can be healed."

"Scars don't go away. Scars are there for a lifetime."

Callie leaned out into the brisk wind to listen. The salt cedar and mesquite and huisache trees stood so thick, their leaves made an amazing amount of noise brushing against each other in the breeze, while the grass whispered a song all its own.

She could hear cattle lowing, the cry of a kiskadee, the keening notes of a mourning dove. Every so often the spotlight caught on a pair of reflected eyes, but it always turned out to be a white-tailed deer, or a Nilgai—the African antelope that had first been introduced to Texas by the King Ranch, or a Santa Gertrudis cow.

"Honk your horn," Callie said. "Maybe they'll hear that, even if they can't see the spotlight."

"If it's noise you want, why not try a couple of shots." He gestured with a finger toward the front fender. "The gun in the front case is a Remington 700 rifle. I loaded it before I left the house."

"I suppose it's worth a try," Callie said.

Trace stopped the car. "You want to do it? Or shall I?"

"I'll do it," Callie said.

"There are more bullets in the chrome box mounted at the front of the running board," Trace said.

The .223 caliber varmint rifle was illegal for large game, like deer and feral hogs, because the bullet was too small to humanely kill with one shot, but it was accurate at long range and perfect for rabbits. And humans.

Callie shuddered, then mentally shook herself. She had to stop imagining the worst. She was going to feel pretty stupid when her parents showed up with some story of how they'd decided to take a little time for a second honeymoon.

She removed the rifle from the leather case, checked the load, made sure Trace was still sitting in the driver's seat, then braced the stock and fired into the air.

When the explosion of sound diminished, Callie listened for human voices. All she heard was a cacophony of beating wings and the angry cries of a flock of great-tailed grackles that had been flushed into the spotlight. Too soon, it was quiet again, except for the percussive trees and the singing grass.

"Do you want to head back home?" Trace asked, when they'd covered every road that ran through the hundred square miles of Three Oaks at least twice.

Callie looked at her watch in the green light from the dash. The time had flown by, yet the night had seemed endless. "It's not long until dawn. The camp house I mentioned, the one we use during roundup, is just a quarter mile down the road. It's got a woodstove and a pump and some Coleman lanterns, and we keep it stocked with coffee. Let's go there."

Trace glanced at her, but she was grateful he didn't point out the obvious, that dayligh. was a good hour and a half away, and that she could be home in twenty minutes and get a cup of coffee there.

Callie didn't want to go home. The fact that she hadn't gotten a call meant there was no good news waiting for her there. She pointed Trace in the direction of the rustic wood-frame camp house, but when they arrived, she sat without moving.

"I'm so afraid," she whispered.

"I know," Trace said.

She turned on him, venting her fear and frustration. "How can you possibly know what I'm feeling? You've never known what it was to be scared—of anything! What are we going to do if Momma and Daddy—" She clenched her teeth to bite back a sob.

"Come here." Trace reached over, grabbed her by the waist, and settled her sideways in his lap.

She sat stiffly, unyielding. "Don't you dare try to comfort me. Not now. It's too late, Trace. Eleven years too late. You were never there when I needed you. When I cried for you. When I died inside for the want of your arms around me, holding me—"

One strong arm circled her shoulders, while his large hand cupped her head and urged it against his shoulder. "Go ahead and let it all out," he crooned.

She pressed her mouth hard against his muscular

shoulder, keeping the sounds of anguish inside. Her hands clutched fistfuls of his shirt as her body sought the warmth and comfort of his.

"I'm here now. Lean on me, Callie."

He was like the serpent in the Garden of Eden, tempting her to trust him. But once she took a bite, once she gave in, all would be lost. She shoved her hands against his shoulders and pushed herself upright, resisting the offer of solace. "No, Trace. No."

His hand slipped to her nape, his callused fingertips caressing the tension there. She kept her body rigid, but she was melting inside. Her gaze focused on the day's growth of black beard on his cheeks and chin. She wanted to feel the harsh brush of it against her flesh. She wanted to feel the softness of his lips against hers. She lifted her eyes to his hooded gaze and saw a need that matched her own. She wanted to lose herself inside him, safe from the frightening, unfathomable future.

She closed her eyes and succumbed to temptation.

Chapter 7

IT WAS LIKE COMING HOME. IT WAS AS THOUGH the years they'd been apart had passed in the blink of an eye, and they were once again exuberant college kids who loved one another with the whole of their beings. She moaned as his hands cupped her breasts, sighed into his mouth as it captured hers. She threaded her fingers into his hair as she lost herself in the familiar taste and smell of the man who was the other half of her.

"Callie," he murmured against her mouth. "I've wanted you for so long."

"Oh, God, Trace." She turned to him hungrily, greedily, desperately seeking solace from the terror that waited in the darkness, oblivion from the fear of what she might discover in the light of day.

He pulled off her boots, then stripped her bare, lifted her, shifted her, until she was straddling his waist, facing him body to body on the soft leather seat.

She had already unbuckled his belt, already unbuttoned his jeans and dragged them down his hips, already reached for him, so that once she was naked there was nothing to stop them from joining. She slid down onto his shaft, felt him filling her, stretching her.

He caught her groan of satisfaction with his mouth, mimicked with his tongue the intrusion of flesh into flesh. She bucked against him, rode him hard and wild, took what she needed and gave all he asked. And found passion beyond feeling, pleasure beyond bearing. She fought against the final culmination, fought against the end, wanting the moment to last.

But there was no stopping the inevitable. She felt herself at the edge of a cliff with no choice but to leap with him, to relish the moments of soaring ecstasy before they must once again touch solid ground. Her cry of exultation ended in a sob of despair.

Callie's sweaty cheek was burrowed against Trace's equally sweaty neck. She was panting, trying to suck enough air to keep her alive. The race had been run, the battle fought. The cliff had definitely been leaped.

And she had come crashing back to earth.

"Oh, God," she whispered. "What have I done?"

Callie shoved herself off Trace, felt their bodies separate, felt the chill air against her damp flesh. There was enough predawn light to see the wary look in his eyes. To see the downturn of his mouth as she scrambled to find her panties, which seemed to have gotten lost in the shadowed depths of the vast front seat. She finally pulled on her jeans without them and stuffed her feet back in her boots.

She found her bra on the burled dashboard. As she snapped herself into it, she couldn't help noticing how calmly Trace shifted his briefs and jeans back up over his hips, how he buttoned them up with one slow, easy hand, while his eyes remained steady on her. The rattle of his belt being buckled unnerved her, and she met his gaze. And wished she hadn't.

She wanted out of this confined space with a predator she was certain had not had his fill of her.

Trace reached for her, and she jerked away. "No! Don't touch me." She grabbed her wrinkled Western shirt from the spotted cowhide carpeting under her feet and shoved her arms into the sleeves, then pushed open the door. Before she could step down, a cell phone rang.

Callie froze. Where was her phone? What had she done with it? It had been in her Levi's jacket. Where was her jacket? She bent down to search under the seat, then looked in the seat behind her, where she discovered her plain cotton panties hanging from a crystal decanter. She grabbed them and stuffed them into her front jeans pocket.

"It's mine," Trace said.

"What?"

"It's not your phone, it's mine."

Callie watched as Trace retrieved his cell phone from the pocket of his jacket and answered it. She listened to the side of the conversation she could hear.

"No, we haven't found them, Russ. Organize the men in pairs. Have them meet me—" He turned to her and said, "Where do you want everyone to meet?"

Callie realized it would be awkward—maybe even dangerous—to have a dozen Bitter Creek cowboys show up at the door to Three Oaks. "How about right here?"

Trace gave directions to the camp house to the Bitter Creek *segundo,* the middle-aged cowboy who'd been his father's right-hand man as long as he could remember, then disconnected the call. "Let's go make some coffee," he said. "We're going to need it."

Callie bristled at the idea of taking orders from Trace, but realized he was only asking her to do what she knew she ought to be doing anyway. Fortunately, the camp house was set up to provide meals for working cowboys. She paused before entering the house and stared at the sunrise. The sky was bigger in Texas, every Texas sunrise more extravagant than the last. Pinks and oranges and yellows lit the immense sky.

"I love the dawn, the hope of a new day. It's always so beautiful," Callie said wistfully.

"Yeah," Trace agreed as he came up behind her. "It was never quite like this in—" He cut himself off.

She angled her head and eyed him over her shoulder. "Where?" She turned and confronted him. "Where have you been all these years, Trace?"

"Here and there," he said with a teasing wink. "We'd better get that coffee started." He took her hand and walked with her into the camp house.

What was the big mystery? Callie wondered. Why was Trace being so secretive about his past? What had he been doing that was so great—or so awful—that he didn't want her to know about it?

Callie had no time to ponder the question. Or to consider what the results of her lapse with Trace might be. They had left things unfinished in Houston. This morning she'd acted without caution, recklessly seeking the escape she'd found in his embrace.

But whatever solace she'd found had long since disappeared. Callie was edgy and anxious, frightened and fretful. She called home and told a worried Sam—he'd

sobered up overnight and insisted on speaking to her—
that some neighbors had volunteered to help her continue
the search.

"No. Don't call Bay yet," she told him. "There's no
need to worry her at school until we know . . . until we
have more information about . . . Just don't call her,"
she finished in frustration.

She asked to speak to Luke and ended up having to
both beg and threaten to convince him he could help most
by taking care of Eli and Hannah. "I'll explain to the
school later why you and Eli took off today." Though she
didn't say it, it was understood that Luke was also to keep
an eye on Sam.

Callie barely had time to get a fire started in the stove
and get coffee made before the first of the cowhands arrived.

Russell Handy, the Bitter Creek *segundo*, was the perfect mix of deferential cowboy and authoritative leader.
That is to say, he deferred to Trace and made sure every
cowboy in the bunch that showed up obeyed him without
question. He looked like most working cowboys Callie
had known, lean and wiry, with skin tanned to leather by
the sun.

He could have been any age from thirty to fifty, but
Callie figured he was somewhere in between. He had a
thick mustache trimmed to the edge of his lips, a straight,
thin nose, and eyes so dark brown they looked black in the
shadow of the straw Stetson he'd pulled low on his forehead.

"Sorry to hear about your parents bein' lost, Mizz
Monroe," Handy said, touching a finger to his hat brim.

"Don't you worry none. If they're out there, we'll find 'em."

"Thank you, Mr. Handy," Callie replied.

Callie had feared she'd get stuck making coffee all day at the camp house, but the *segundo* had brought along a cook with rations of frijoles and tortillas to feed the men if their search should go beyond noon. Callie was grateful for his foresight and terrified at the thought her parents could remain unfound for so long.

"You might want to give the sheriff's office another call," Trace said.

"They said I had to wait a full twenty-four hours," Callie said, her voice catching. "I'll bet if your parents were missing, every lawman in the county would be out looking for them right now."

"You'd never catch my parents on a picnic together," Trace said with a wry smile.

Callie looked up when she heard the distinctive WHUP-WHUP-WHUP of a helicopter, shading her eyes to locate it against the sun. "Yours?" she asked Trace.

"I decided it might save us some time if we can locate your father's truck from the air."

Callie felt her throat swell with gratitude. Three Oaks also used a chopper for rounding up cattle, but they hadn't been able to keep up the payments on the one they'd briefly owned, so now they rented one when they needed it. "What is Blackjack going to say when he finds out you appropriated a Bitter Creek helicopter to search for my parents?"

"He'll be glad the search was shortened," Trace said with a grin. "Especially since work at Bitter Creek is going to be at a standstill until we find your parents."

"Oh," Callie said. "Oh, God."

"What is it?"

"I think I know where they might have gone."

"Somewhere in the south pasture?"

"No. There's a stock pond in the middle pasture. Daddy forbade us to go there, because there's a sinkhole nearby. It's fenced, but he was always afraid one of us— But he would have been sure of being alone there. I don't know why I didn't think of it yesterday. I checked every pond, every shady spot I could think of in the south pasture. I just never thought—"

"Give me directions, and I'll have the helicopter take a look," Trace said.

Callie wanted to jump in Trace's hunting car and drive there, but Trace insisted she wait until the helicopter could fly over the area.

Minutes later Trace got a radio response. "My pilot found the truck. It looks abandoned. He didn't see any sign of your parents."

Callie's heart was in her throat. "They must be there. We have to go there."

The drive to the middle pasture seemed interminable. By cell phone, Trace had directed Russell Handy to have his men head there to continue the search. As they drove up to the pond, her stomach tightened at the sight of buzzards circling overhead.

Handy was waiting for them. "We found them," he said.

"Where are they? How are they?" Callie asked as she tumbled out of the luxurious convertible.

Handy didn't answer her, merely looked at Trace and shook his head. She felt Trace slide a supporting arm around her waist. She wanted to shrug it off, but her knees threatened to buckle, and she was afraid that without his support she would fall. Her chest felt as though she'd been kicked by a mule, and she couldn't seem to catch her breath.

"Where are they?" Callie managed to say. "I want to see them."

"Your mom's alive," Handy said.

Which meant her father was not. Callie felt her insides go flying and mentally coiled a rope around herself to pull things in tight. She couldn't fall apart. Everyone was depending on her. She'd been needed by her family all her life, but never so much as now.

"They've been shot," Handy said.

For half an instant Callie thought her father might have shot her mother in a jealous rage.

"Looks like the bullet hit your father in the back, went through him, and struck your mother."

That couldn't have been a self-inflicted wound, Callie realized. So someone else had shot them. But who? And why?

"We haven't moved her yet," she heard Handy say. "I think the bullet might have broken her shoulder. She doesn't seem to be hurt anywhere else. She won't let go of your dad, and we didn't want to force her. Maybe you can talk to her."

That meant her mother was conscious. That meant her mother was talking. That was good news.

Callie wished she hadn't gotten her hopes up, because they fell like hail, hard and painful, when she caught sight of her parents lying half on, half off the gray wool blanket she'd packed for them to use as a ground cover the previous day. The woven straw picnic basket lay open, the contents scattered. Two paper plates that bore the remnants of fried chicken and potato salad were covered with black ants.

Nature was consuming the dead. She glanced up at the circling buzzards. And waiting for the dying.

Callie forced her gaze back to the grizzly tableau. Her father had fallen on top of her mother and lay almost on his side, half covering her. There was a small brown stain on the back of his plaid Western shirt, but otherwise she could see nothing wrong with him. The entire bodice of her mother's beautiful yellow sundress was stained an ugly brown with dried blood.

Her mother had one arm wrapped around her father's neck. The other arm lay still at her side. Her shoulder had a ragged wound filled with a black pool of seeping blood, where the bullet had torn the thin strap in half. The copper smell of blood was cloying, and the incessant buzzing of the circling flies made Callie feel nauseated.

The wail escaped without warning. Callie put her hands over her mouth to stifle the sound, but there was no shutting off her grief. It spilled from her eyes in huge tears that blinded her. She reached for Trace with a groping hand as her body sagged, but a moment later she pulled free and was on her knees beside her parents.

She swiped at her eyes with her fingertips, wanting to see. And was devastated by what she found. Another wail of anguish escaped as she focused on her father's still, gray face. She brushed futilely at the flies, which buzzed angrily, then returned. Her skin crawled, as though the irksome insects were walking on her own sensitive flesh.

"Callie . . . your father is dead," her mother said in a whispery voice.

"I know, Momma," Callie croaked. "We have to get you to the hospital. You have to let him go now."

There was no new blood, only dried, crusted brown covering her mother's hand, where it clutched her father's collar. Callie felt another tear slide down her cheek and licked it away when it reached her mouth. She untangled her mother's stiff fingers from the soft fabric, then looked up at Trace.

"I'm afraid to move her. I don't want to hurt her."

"The sooner we get her to a hospital, the better," Trace said.

Her mother's glazed eyes were barely open, but her lips were moving. Callie put her ear next to her mother's mouth to catch the faint sound and couldn't help inhaling the sickly sweet smell of blood. Though her nose wrinkled against the stench, she forced herself to remain still and listen.

"Your father said . . . he loves you all."

Callie choked back the sob in her throat, afraid she would miss something her mother said. It was appalling to realize her father hadn't died right away, that if she had let him take his cell phone along, her parents might have called for help. He might be alive right now. This was all her fault!

"Not your fault," her mother rasped, as though she had read Callie's mind. "Died too fast . . . for help . . ."

"Don't talk," Callie whispered past the knot in her throat. "Save your strength."

She felt her mother's fingertips tighten against her own.

"May not . . . make it. Take care of . . . everybody. Up to you . . ."

Her mother's eyes rolled up in her head, and Callie felt a surge of panic. "Don't die, Momma! Please, don't die!" She frantically searched for a pulse at her mother's throat. "I can't find her pulse!"

Trace knelt beside her and put his fingertips to her mother's throat. "It's thready, but it's there."

"What are we waiting for?" Callie demanded. "We have to get her to the hospital!"

"As thick as the mesquite is, there's no place around here where we can set down the helicopter," Trace said. "We can rig a soft pallet for her in the bed of one of the trucks."

"What if we hurt her worse by moving her?" Callie asked.

"We don't have much choice," Trace said reasonably. He took Callie by her shoulders and pulled her to her feet. "Or much time."

Callie looked at the Bitter Creek *segundo* and the other cowboy standing nearby, waiting for orders from Trace. "All right," she said. "But be careful. Don't hurt her!"

Trace gestured to Handy and the other cowboy, and they shifted her father's body off her mother. Then Trace bent down and slid one arm under her mother's shoulders and another under her knees. Her mother's eyes fluttered open, and she whimpered in pain as Trace lifted her, but she didn't cry out. The fear of making noise was inbred from generations of living in a country where being discovered could result in getting scalped by a savage or eaten by some wild beast.

"Did you find anything to indicate who did this?" Callie asked the *segundo*, as they followed Trace to Handy's pickup.

"Best we can tell, they were shot from long range," Handy replied.

"It must have been one of those hunters!" Callie cried.

"What hunters?" Trace asked.

"Four idiots were hunting in the north pasture yesterday. One of them must have crossed the boundaries of the land we leased to them and ended up in the middle pasture. Find them, and you'll find the man who did this!"

Handy had already arranged a pallet of blankets in the back of his pickup, and as soon as Trace laid her mother down, Callie scrambled in to sit beside her.

"Drive fast! No, drive slow. I don't want her to be jostled," Callie ordered breathlessly.

"I can't do both, Callie."

"Just be careful!" she cried.

The drive to the hospital was an agony. Her mother clenched her teeth against the pain, but every hissed-in breath, every moan, made Callie's stomach lurch.

Callie hadn't allowed herself to consider how much blood her mother had lost. Or whether she might succumb to shock. Apparently, she'd been kept warm overnight by her father's dead body. Just the thought of it made Callie shiver. And she couldn't seem to stop.

"The doctors will take her, Callie. You can let her go now."

Callie was hardly aware of Trace helping her out of the sun-heated metal truck bed. For some reason her knees wouldn't work, and he picked her up rather than let her fall. She clutched his neck and buried her face against his throat and hung on for dear life. She was cold, and he was warmth. She was lost, and he could help her find her way.

She knew they were in the hospital somewhere because the smell of antiseptic burned her nose, and she could hear the clatter of metal instruments against a metal surface. And then they were somewhere blessedly quiet, somewhere she could only hear the hum of an ancient air conditioner, somewhere the blazing sun was muted by venetian blinds.

"Do you want to call your brothers? Or do you want me to do it?" she heard Trace murmur.

Callie couldn't imagine calling Sam and Luke and telling them Daddy was dead, and that Momma was in surgery, and no, she didn't know whether Momma was going to be all right. And no, she didn't have answers to their questions: Who was going to run the ranch now? Who was going to manage things? How were they going to survive this catastrophe? Each person in the family had been a cog in a well-oiled machine. Without her father and mother, the whole thing was going to grind to a halt.

She felt Trace's hand smoothing her hair. "You don't have to do this all by yourself, Callie," he said. "I'm here to help."

Callie wanted to let Trace handle everything. It would be so easy to let him handle it. She lifted her gaze to his face. And saw her son's nose and jaw and chin. She couldn't allow Trace to get close. She couldn't take the chance.

She pushed herself away from him and made herself stand, though she wavered at first, like a colt trying its legs for the first time. Trace stood up as well and kept her from falling until she got her legs under her. Then she took a step away.

"There's nothing I can do here while Momma's in surgery," she said. "I want to go home. I have to make arrangements for Daddy. I have to call Bay. And I want to give Sam and Luke . . . I want to tell them in person," she finished.

"I'll drive you."

"No. I don't think that would be a good idea."

"You came with me. I'll take you home."

Callie wanted to refuse him, but on the spur of the moment, she couldn't think of any other way to get home. There was no such thing as cab service in Bitter Creek. She could call Luke and have him come get her, but then he'd have to know where she was. She could call Lou Ann Simpson, but she didn't want to deal with Lou Ann's concern or her questions right now.

"All right," she conceded. "You can take me home. But I don't want you coming inside."

"Fine. Is there anything I can help with? Anything your father might have left undone?"

About a hundred things, Callie thought. But there was no way she could allow Trace Blackthorne to do any of them. "We can manage."

He lifted a skeptical brow.

"We'll be fine. Don't worry. We Creeds have survived Comanche attacks and Mexican soldiers and Yankee carpetbaggers." *And bushwhacking Blackthornes.* "We can survive this."

"Fine, Callie. But if you change your mind—"

"I won't," Callie said. "And, Trace . . ."

Her throat was thick, and it was hard to talk, but she

knew she had to speak. "You won't be invited to the funeral."

"I'm sorry to hear that. Once upon a time I thought Jesse Creed was going to be my father-in-law. Believe it or not, I'm sorry he's gone, because—" He cut himself off. "I'm sorry he's gone, Callie."

She met his gaze. "I'm grateful for all your help. Really, I am. But I think, under the circumstances, it wouldn't be a good idea for you to be there."

"What circumstances?" Trace challenged. "The mere fact that I'm a Blackthorne, and you're a Creed?"

Callie sighed. "You represent everything my father fought against his whole life. To have you there . . . It would hurt too much."

"Fine. I'll stay away."

Just as he had stayed away from the hospital when Sam was hurt. She could see he was angry, but she didn't back down.

Her family came to the kitchen door at the sound of the truck on the gravel drive. She didn't hesitate, simply said, "Good-bye, Trace," and headed for the back door to Three Oaks on the run.

"Callie, wait! I want to—"

She was inside before he could finish his sentence.

Her eyes were so blurred by tears, she could hardly see her family. Sam was in his wheelchair. Eli was hanging on her arm, and Hannah was clutching her knee. Luke stood at her shoulder, his eyes watchful and wary.

"Sam called Bay anyway," Luke informed her. "She's on her way home."

"That's good," Callie said. "Because the news is bad."

"They're dead," Sam said flatly.

Hannah wailed. Callie picked up her tiny daughter and held her tight. "No! Momma is alive. She's in the hospital, in surgery."

"Where's Daddy?" Luke asked.

"Daddy is . . . He didn't make it." Callie said.

"Like I sssaid, he'sss dead," Sam said in a slurred, drunken voice.

"Yes, he is," Callie replied, her voice cracking. "And because he is, I'm going to need all of you to help around here. Which means you, too, Sam!"

"Is Grampa really dead?" Eli asked.

Callie's knees started to buckle, and she settled into a kitchen chair. She reached out to Eli and pulled him close. "I'm afraid so, sweetheart."

"How?" Luke asked. "What happened? Was the truck in an accident?"

"No. They were shot."

"Shot!" Luke cried. "Who shot them?"

Callie had opened her mouth to answer, when Sam interrupted.

"Who the hell do you think?" he said. "Thossse goddamned Blackthornes! Now they'll get Three Oaks for shhure."

Callie had been ready to contradict Sam, to say it was a hunter's stray bullet that had killed their father. But the last half of Sam's statement arrested her. "There's nothing to keep us from running Three Oaks like we always have. We'll all just have to work a little harder."

Sam snorted derisively. "You're forgetting sssomething. Something I'm shhure Blackjack hasn't forgotten."

"What's that?" Callie asked.

"Inheritance taxesss. The government takes its shhare—fifty-five percent of everything in Dad's estate—before Mom gets a penny! Or had you forgotten that?"

Callie felt her heart skip a beat. Oh, God. How would they manage to survive, if they had to come up with an enormous sum to pay the government inheritance taxes? There was nothing left to mortgage. Nothing left to hock. Nowhere else they could go for a loan.

"We're not giving up Three Oaks," she said aloud.

"I don't sssee where we have much choice," Sam retorted.

"We're not giving up Three Oaks," she repeated. "There must be some way to get the money to pay the government. All I have to do is figure it out."

Chapter 8

"Did you shoot Jesse yourself? Or did you hire someone to do it for you?"

Trace carefully observed his father's expression as he lifted his gaze from the paperwork on his desk to respond to the accusation.

"Are you telling me Jesse Creed has been shot?" Blackjack said, a smile growing on his face.

"Jesse and his wife both."

Blackjack leapt to his feet, and the smile disappeared. "Ren's been shot? When? Where? How is she?"

Trace suddenly realized his father wouldn't have shot Jesse in any circumstances that might have endangered Lauren Creed's life. Blackjack was too concerned—disgracefully, disgustingly concerned—for the well-being of the other man's wife. But all Trace had been able to think of since he'd seen those two blood-caked bodies was the way Jesse Creed had humiliated his father three weeks ago, and Blackjack's venomous threat against the other man.

But his father's surprise appeared genuine. Maybe it had been a hunting accident after all. Or maybe his father was damned good at feigning innocence. It seemed too coincidental that Jesse Creed had been killed "accidentally." Trace didn't put much faith in flukes. It seemed more likely that chance had been helped along.

"I can't believe you're just hearing about this, Dad. I've had every cowhand on the payroll out searching for the pair of them since dawn."

"How the hell would I know that?" Blackjack retorted. "Ninety-five percent of the time you don't tell me what you're doing around here. And I asked you a question. How is Ren? Where is she?"

"What's all the shouting about?"

Trace turned to find his brother Owen standing in the library doorway. His brother the lawman. "I was just accusing Dad of murdering Jesse Creed."

Owen stiffened. "He's dead?"

"As a door nail," Trace said.

"Goddammit, Trace! Stop that nonsense and tell me what's happened to Jesse's wife!" Blackjack shouted.

"The bullet that killed Jesse passed through him, struck Mrs. Creed, and broke her shoulder," Trace said. "She spent last night out in the cold—blanketed by her dead husband. I left the hospital before she got out of surgery, so I don't know what her prognosis is."

"I guess I'll have to find out for myself," Blackjack muttered as headed for the door.

Trace had figured his father might call the hospital to inquire about Lauren Creed's condition. He was appalled to realize his father intended to go there. "You can't go to the hospital, Dad."

Blackjack was drawn up short. "Why not?"

"Because the whole Creed family will be there."

"So?"

"They hate your guts."

"That's not my problem," Blackjack said as he took another step.

Trace was surprised when Owen put out a hand to stop their father.

"No, Dad," Owen said.

"Get out of my way, Owen," Blackjack said.

Owen took a step forward, blocking Blackjack's path. For the first time, Trace noticed Owen was wearing his badge above his heart. "You don't want to make yourself any more of a suspect than you already are," Owen said.

Blackjack made a dismissive sound. "Don't pull that Texas Ranger bullshit with me, son. I diapered your bottom."

"You've never touched a diaper in your life," Owen countered.

"I was making a point," Blackjack snapped. He shot a glance from Owen to Trace and back again. "I don't need my sons telling me what I can and can't do."

"You'll take my advice on this," Owen said. "Stay away from Mrs. Creed."

"Who the hell do you think—"

"What on God's green earth is going on down here?"

"Hello, Mother," Trace said as his mother stepped into the space between Owen and Blackjack, forcing Owen to drop his hand.

Her short-cropped blond hair bore a splash of copper at the temple, and Trace saw a similar dab of dried oil paint on her right forefinger. She was dressed in a khaki painting smock that looked like a cross between Joseph's coat-of-many-colors and a safari jacket, and she held a long, delicate, red-daubed paintbrush between her fingers, as though she had stopped in mid-stroke to come and investigate.

"I was starting on the red-checked tablecloth, when I heard such a commotion down here I couldn't concentrate. Will someone please tell me what all this ruckus is about?"

"We've had some disturbing news, Mother," Trace said.

"What is it?" she asked, glancing from Blackjack to Trace.

Trace noticed she never once looked at Owen—and that Owen knew he was being slighted. It was difficult for Trace to accept the fact that his mother preferred one twin over the other. After all, Owen and Clay were identical, born two minutes apart, Owen first, and then Clay. But she had made her choice when the twins were still boys, and for some reason, she had chosen Clay over Owen.

"There's been an accident," Trace said, moderating the story for his mother's ears. "Jesse Creed has been killed, apparently by some hunter's stray bullet."

"What about Mrs. Creed?" his mother inquired of Trace.

"She was wounded in the same incident, but she's alive," Trace said. "She's in surgery right now."

"That's too bad," his mother murmured. "When will we know whether she's going to make it?"

"I have no idea," Trace confessed.

His mother turned to his father. "And you want to go see how she is, Jackson?"

His father nodded.

Trace felt his heart constrict as he observed the carefully neutral expression on his mother's face. He felt the humiliation she refused to express and despised his father for it.

"I've advised Dad not to go to the hospital," Owen interjected.

"Why not?" his mother asked.

Owen grimaced. "You know why not, Mother."

"All right. Then I'll go," she said.

"What?" all three men said together.

"I'll go," his mother announced. "We're neighbors. It's only natural that we express our concern. I suppose I can buy Ren some flowers at the hospital." She hesitated and said, "Assuming she survives the surgery."

Trace watched his father's face turn white. His mouth looked pinched, and his shoulders hunched forward, as though he were in pain. "You stay and take care of Dad," Trace said to his mother. "I'll go."

He watched as his mother laid a solicitous hand over his father's heart.

"Are you all right, Jackson? You're not having another attack, are you?" she asked.

"Dammit, woman. Stop treating me like an invalid!" his father said, shoving her hand away. A startling streak of red paint appeared like a bleeding cut when her brush caught on his yoked white Western shirt.

This time, Trace found the wounded look in his mother's eyes. He glanced at Owen, wondering if his younger brother felt any sympathy for their mother's plight. But Owen's face was stoic, his gray eyes unreadable. "I'll call you from the hospital," Trace said, as he headed for the door.

Owen lifted an eyebrow as he passed by. "They won't want to see you, either."

"I helped with the search," Trace retorted. "That ought to count for something."

"You're a Blackthorne," Owen said. "That counts for a helluva lot more."

Owen used his badge of office as an excuse to attend the interment of Jesse Creed in the small family cemetery at Three Oaks that was the final resting place of generations of Creeds. He was dressed in uniform, although his Texas Ranger uniform consisted of a Stetson, white shirt, tie, Wrangler pants, and boots. He also wore his badge, a Texas five-pointed star surrounded by a circle. His had been cut from a gold Mexican peso by a Blackthorne forebear who'd served in one of the Ranger regiments in Zachary Taylor's army during the war against Mexico in 1846.

Supposedly, Owen was there to see if anyone showed up who might have wanted Jesse Creed dead badly enough to have murdered him in cold blood. He was actually there to see someone he expected to attend the ceremony. Owen was pretty sure the person who had most wanted Jesse Creed dead was his own father.

Blackjack had made no secret of how glad he was that his nemesis was being planted six feet underground. He hadn't even waited for the funeral before he offered to purchase Three Oaks. And it was no secret—at least to his son, the Texas Ranger, hell, probably to the whole county—that Blackjack was, and maybe always had been, in love with Jesse's wife.

Owen had heard Trace's accusation of murder from the hallway. It was what had lured him into the library. But his father had seemed too surprised and upset that Lauren Creed had also been shot. If Blackjack had hired a hit man to kill Jesse Creed, there wouldn't have been another victim, especially not Lauren Creed.

Maybe it had been a hunter after all.

Likely they would never know the truth for sure. The four executives from Houston that Callie Monroe had seen entering the north pasture had been questioned, but they'd brought along rifles big enough to hunt elephants—including a .300 Magnum Weatherby Mark V— which meant they'd probably been hunting deer out of season. But that was a problem for the Texas Parks and Wildlife folks.

It was possible some trespasser—some local teenager?—had been out hunting rabbits with a varmint rifle, and his shot had gone astray. But it was going to be difficult to identify the culprit, because the .223 caliber slug that had killed Jesse had been flattened and splintered by Lauren Creed's shoulder bone. Ballistics on what was left of the bullet weren't sufficient for use in identifying the gun used to shoot Jesse Creed.

After a preliminary investigation, the sheriff's office had declared Jesse Creed's death a hunting accident.

Owen stood at the edge of the crowd of mourners and looked for someone who might be grieving more than normal or acting strangely, anyone exhibiting remorse for the accidental act, whom he might question further. But all he found was a family devastated by tragedy and neighbors who were shocked and sympathetic.

He had done his duty before he turned to the real

reason he had come to the funeral. He needed to see the boy who'd been paralyzed all those years ago, wanted to discover for himself what had become of the reclusive figure. Owen hadn't laid eyes on Sam Creed in more than ten years. He was stunned at what he found.

Owen had tried to imagine how Sam's body might shrivel, confined in a wheelchair, without the use of his legs. His knees certainly appeared bony in the black trousers, but Sam's broad shoulders were just as broad, his arms even more powerfully muscled, in the buttoned-up white, long-sleeved shirt that was flattened by the wind against his body. Lank brown hair hung two inches over his collar, and his mouth, cheeks, and chin were hidden behind an untrimmed, reddish-brown beard. He looked dissipated, unkempt, uncaring.

Owen's gut twisted. *What a waste of a human being!*

They had never been friends, but they'd been teammates, forced to practice together, and then to pull together to win football games throughout high school. They had roughhoused in the locker room, patted each other's butt on the playing field, secretively drunk bottles of Pearl or Lone Star on the back of the school bus coming home from away games, punching each other and giggling behind their hands when they got drunk, to hide their reckless behavior from Coach Kuykendall.

Sam had been paralyzed; but Owen had never stopped suffering. Sometimes he could barely stand to look at himself in the mirror. He should have . . . If only he had . . . He consoled himself now, as he had all these years, with the knowledge that no matter how the incident had looked to others, it had been an accident.

His lips tilted up at one edge in bitter irony, as he

watched Jesse's casket being lowered into the ground. The Creeds certainly were accident prone. He wondered again if a Blackthorne was as much responsible for Jesse's "accident" as one was for Sam's.

His gaze shifted back to the man in the wheelchair. He studied Sam, wishing he had the nerve to approach him, to speak the apology he had never been allowed to voice. But this wasn't the time. Sam's eyes were puffy and bloodshot. Had he been crying? His complexion, above the ragged beard, was sallow. He looked like he had a bad hangover.

Sam wavered in the wheelchair, and his sister Bayleigh—the pretty, auburn-haired sister who'd been away at veterinary school—steadied him. It would be no wonder if Sam had gotten drunk, Owen thought. The Creeds were in dire financial straits, and everybody knew it.

The latest estimate Owen had heard was that the family needed around five million dollars to pay the inheritance taxes on Jesse Creed's estate. He didn't know how accommodating the government was in cases like this. Had no idea whether the taxes could be paid in installments, and if so, how long the family had to come up with the first payment.

He'd heard they were planning to sell their Santa Gertrudis breeding stock, so their situation must be as desperate as gossip suggested. The roundup was set to follow the funeral by a matter of days.

His mind had been wandering, so he was disconcerted, when he focused on Sam again, to find Sam staring back at him. The virulent hatred in the other man's eyes was an ugly thing to behold. Owen watched as Sam turned to speak to his sister, then saw Bay's gaze turn in his direction. She leaned close to her brother, listened, and shook her head. Sam continued talking, looking agitated, until Bay gripped her brother's shoulder and nodded.

Owen steeled himself for the confrontation he suspected was coming. He almost put his hands on his hips, but realized how ridiculous that was. Bayleigh Creed was a slip of a girl, who didn't even reach his shoulder. She wore her auburn hair in a ponytail, with a fringe of bangs that made her look like a teenager. How old was she? She was nearly done with vet school, so she had to be twenty-three, maybe twenty-four.

She wore a sleeveless black dress that followed her slight figure all the way to her knees and short, practical heels that didn't sink into the sandy Texas soil. When she got closer, he could see she wasn't wearing any makeup, and that her nose was dotted with freckles that added to the illusion of youth. It wasn't until she raised her eyes to his that he saw the wariness of a woman who'd learned not to trust. Whatever youthful innocence she'd possessed was long gone.

He was arrested by the color of her eyes—the purple-blue of bluebonnets—and the frank evaluation she was making of him as she approached. He felt a sensual tug in his groin, the pull of male to shapely, attractive female, before he reminded himself who she was.

"My brother would like you to leave," she announced as she stopped in front of him.

"I'm here on official business."

"The sheriff's office has already closed the investigation into my father's 'accidental' death," she said, making it clear with sarcasm that she didn't agree with their conclusion. "Are you here to suggest it wasn't an accident?"

"I thought I might see who showed up today," he said. As excuses went, it sounded lame.

"And did you find a murderer in our midst?" she asked.

"No," he admitted.

"Then I'd appreciate it if you'd honor my brother's request and leave."

"Will you tell him I'm sorry?"

Owen was appalled at what he'd said. He saw the surprise in her eyes before they narrowed.

"You're a few years late with an apology, if you're referring to what happened on the football field."

"It was an accident." Why was he persisting? Why couldn't he just let it go? "Why won't anyone believe that?"

He felt her hand touch his forearm, then drop away. He sought her gaze and found her distressed blue eyes focused intently on his face.

"I can't feel sorry for you, Mr. Blackthorne. All my sympathy has been used up on Sam."

"He looks . . . He doesn't look well," Owen said, glancing at Sam.

She looked over her shoulder, and Owen knew she must have seen the scowl on Sam's face, seen him gesture her back to his side. She turned her back on Sam and said, "There's nothing you can do to make amends. Sam is stuck in that chair for the rest of his life. And you put him there."

"I said I was sorry!" Owen didn't know where the

anger had come from, but he could feel the adrenaline shooting through his veins.

"Prove it," she said.

Owen frowned. "How would you suggest I do that?"

"Find the man who murdered my father."

The frown became a scowl. "You know that's an impossible request."

"Why? Because your own father is the murderer?"

Owen was startled by the accusation. "My father didn't do it."

She shrugged. "Maybe he didn't hold the gun. But I believe he's responsible. Three weeks ago, your father threatened mine. Now he's dead. Since my father's death—which has dropped us in a financial hole we'll have the devil of a time climbing out of—your father has made an offer to buy a ranch he's coveted for as long as I've drawn breath.

"Your father tried in every way he could to bring my father to the brink of financial ruin without success. Have you, by the way, found the thieves who stole our quarter horses?"

"No," Owen said in a low voice.

"When your father couldn't force my father into selling any other way—and having been provoked and humiliated in public—your father put mine in his grave."

Owen was at a loss for words. What she said made perfect sense. What she hadn't mentioned was his father's obvious infatuation—he wasn't willing to call it love—for her mother, which was a motive all its own for murder.

"Well?" she challenged. "Do you still think your father's innocent?"

"There's no way to prove who shot your father," Owen said. "The bullet that killed him—"

"Don't go looking for the gun that killed my father," she said. "Find the man who held the gun. He can tell you who hired him to kill my father."

She was right. If someone had, in fact, been hired to murder her father. "I have no idea—"

She made a disgusted sound and shook her head, then spoke slowly and carefully, as though to an idiot. "It's someone who works for your father. It shouldn't be too hard to figure it out. Who's been with him the longest? Who'd do whatever he was ordered to do, no questions asked? Who'd die before he'd betray your father to the authorities?"

"You should have been a cop," Owen said with grudging admiration.

"I have to figure out where an animal's hurting, even when it can't tell me in words what the trouble is," she answered. "I have to look for clues, search out evidence of what's wrong. Surely you've learned as much in your job."

He had. "There's only one thing wrong with your theory."

"What's that?" she asked.

"You're assuming my father is the guilty party."

"And you believe he's innocent?"

"I do."

She hesitated, then said, "Even though you've seen how he looks at my mother? Maybe it isn't the land he's wanted all along. Maybe it's her."

Owen drew in a sharp breath. So his father's infatuation was no secret to the Creeds, either. Blackjack had always wanted Three Oaks, but Owen believed his father had hopes that an alliance between his brother Trace and Callie Creed Monroe would resolve that issue. So acquiring Three Oaks didn't seem like motivation enough for Blackjack to have Jesse killed.

On the other hand, in order for him to have Lauren Creed, Jesse had to be out of the way. Love was a powerful emotion, and an all-too-common motive for murder.

Owen thought a little more, then shook his head, rejecting her suggestion. "No. He wouldn't have bothered."

"Why not?"

"You're forgetting something," Owen said.

"What's that?"

"My mother."

Bay's lips curved in a smug, secretive smile that reminded him of da Vinci's *Mona Lisa.* "You're awfully naive, Mr. Blackthorne, if you think your father can't rid himself of your mother. There's always divorce."

"He wouldn't do that."

"Why not?"

Because he'd have to give her back the land she brought with her as a dowry and half—maybe more, if she could convince the judge she deserved it—of what they've accumulated during their marriage, Owen thought. He said, "My father doesn't believe in divorce."

"I notice you didn't mention that your father would never divorce your mother because he loves her," Bay pointed out.

"That goes without saying," Owen said.

Bay smiled that infuriating, all-knowing smile again. "Of course."

"You're barking up the wrong tree, Miss Creed."

"Prove it."

She walked away without another word. To his disgust, Owen found himself admiring the sway of her hips in the black sheath. She never looked back at him, never looked at him again, as she wheeled her brother toward the pickup they'd come in. He wondered why they didn't buy one of those vans that were set up for folks in wheelchairs and realized the answer before the question was fully formed in his mind.

Sam didn't go out much, and a van designed for his needs wouldn't be as cost-effective on a low-margin ranch like Three Oaks as another pickup truck. He watched as Callie got on one side of Sam and her brother Luke on the other. He saw the struggle on their faces as they hefted Sam out of the wheelchair and levered him into the cab of the pickup. For a moment, he feared they would drop the crippled man.

They could have asked for help from any one of a dozen distant relatives or neighbors. He found it significant that they did not. It made a powerful statement: the Creeds took care of their own, without help from anyone.

He watched Sam take his weight on his arms as they edged him onto the seat. Callie's boy, Eli, folded up the wheelchair, and Bayleigh hefted it into the back of the pickup. She was stronger than her diminutive size suggested. But she'd have to be, if she was going to be a large animal vet.

Owen was startled when he felt an arm laced through his own. He looked down to find his sister leaning her head against his shoulder. "What are you doing here, Summer?"

Instead of answering his question, she said, "What were you and Bayleigh Creed talking about?"

"None of your business."

"She's very pretty, isn't she?" Summer said.

"What does that have to do with the price of cattle?"

"Then you do think she's pretty," Summer said with a cajoling smile.

Owen laughed. "All right, she's got beautiful eyes," he conceded. "Now tell me what you're doing here."

• She gestured with her chin toward the crowd of mourners. "I came because of him."

Owen looked in the direction she'd pointed, seeking someone he could connect with his sister. The only people left at graveside were Johnny Ray Coburn and his wife and their two kids, the tall, skinny girl and the even taller son. Owen had reason to know the son, because he'd stopped Bad Billy Coburn for drunk driving. They were distant kin to the Creeds, since Lauren Creed had been a Coburn before she married Jesse.

"I give up," Owen said as he turned back to his sister. "Who is it you came to see?"

"Billy Coburn."

Owen frowned. "Bad Billy?"

"I've already had this conversation with Trace," she said with asperity. "His name is Billy. Just Billy."

"Stay away from him."

Summer laughed. "You and Trace act like I'm some innocent virgin who—"

Owen caught her arm with enough force to cut her off. "Are you sleeping with that bastard?"

Summer's eyes glittered with angry tears, and her chin tilted up. Once upon a time, the tears might have swayed him, but Owen had seen her turn on the waterworks too many times to be moved by them. "I asked you a question. What's going on between you and Billy Coburn?"

"That's none of your business."

Owen felt acid churn in his stomach. He looked down at his sister—barely twenty and with her whole life ahead of her—and sent his gaze searching for Bad Billy Coburn. The boy looked almost decent dressed up in a suit. But his black hair needed a cut, and his tieless shirt wasn't ironed. The extra shirt cuff showing at each sleeve revealed that he'd long ago outgrown the suit jacket. His face was cut in hard planes, and there was a wild, feral look in his eyes.

"He's going to wind up in prison, Summer. That boy's no damn good. Look at his father. He comes from bad blood."

"He's not at all like Johnny Ray," Summer protested. "Billy's got hopes and dreams for the future."

Owen made a dismissive sound in his throat. "From the looks of those purple bruises on his chin and that black eye, I'd say about all that boy's got on his mind is fighting."

Summer pulled herself free of his grasp. "Billy and I are friends. I like him."

"Why don't you find yourself a nice man and get married and have a houseful of kids?"

She stared at him as though he were a two-headed calf. "That's the most chauvinistic, backward-thinking, Neanderthal remark I've heard in a long time. Ever hear of women's liberation? A woman doesn't need a man—"

Owen laughed. "Whoa. Whoa. I take it all back. Then why don't you find yourself a nice career—"

"You would say that! Have you ever thought that maybe I'd like to manage Bitter Creek someday?"

Owen's brows rose toward his hairline.

"I thought not," she said scornfully. "Just because I'm a girl—"

"The baby girl in the family," Owen pointed out.

"I'm not a baby anymore, I'm a grown woman."

"You're twenty. You're not even old enough to sit at a bar."

"No, but I'm old enough to get married to the 'right man' and have babies," she said angrily.

"Uh-oh. Did someone else bring up matrimony?"

"That was mother's suggestion. Daddy sees me as a piece of flesh he can barter to the highest bidder for more land!"

Owen saw the desperation in his sister's eyes and felt sorry for her. He'd never been important enough to either of his parents to suffer their interference in his life. He put an arm around her shoulder, tightening his grasp when she tried to shrug it off. "Hey. It's me. I'm on your side."

"You'd never know it," she grumbled.

"Just be careful around Billy Coburn, all right? Use some common sense."

"Someday you're all going to realize I'm right about Billy," Summer said. "Someday—"

He gave her a comforting squeeze, and aimed her toward the dirt road where they'd left their cars. "Yeah. Someday we're all going to live happily ever after."

Chapter 9

CALLIE WAVED HER STETSON AT THE NOISY helicopter overhead, the signal she'd prearranged to let her sister Bay know her work driving the herd of cherry-red Santa Gertrudis cattle from the north pasture to the loading chutes was done. At least they'd saved the cost of a pilot by having Bay fly the rented copter. Callie had hired a few cowboys to load the herd onto the tractor-trailer trucks that would take them to the auction house in Bitter Creek. Right now, every penny counted.

It was only noon, and the bulk of the work was done. But here and there, pockets of wiser cows remained hidden in the thick underbrush. It would probably take Callie, Luke, and Eli the rest of the day to flush them out on horseback and drive them to the loading chutes. Even four-year-old Hannah was helping with the roundup. The little girl had been riding horseback since she was two, and Callie figured her daughter was safer out on the range than she was at home with Sam, who'd spent his days since their father's death drinking himself into a stupor.

The mesquite was thick and scraped across Callie's chaps as she rode. She made a mental note to do a controlled burn in the north pasture in January, when deer and turkey seasons were over, to get rid of the troublesome mesquite, which extended its roots as much as a hundred feet across the ground, competing with the grass for moisture. She watched a red-tailed hawk swoop down and grasp a mouse in its talons and felt herself identifying with the helpless mouse.

Predators were on the loose. There was no hiding from the disaster that loomed.

The government was allowing them to pay off the inheritance taxes in installments over seven years. Huge installments. The price of cattle was up, so Callie had decided to wean the calves early and sell her Santa Gertrudis cows. Their cow/calf operation was going to be sorely depleted with the sale of so much stock, but they had no choice if the government was going to be paid its pound of flesh on time.

Unfortunately, selling the cattle would provide only half the cash needed to pay the first installment of taxes. Callie had to find some way to earn the other $375,000. She could train and sell the horses she'd bought to replace the stolen fillies and come up with a hundred thousand. And the prize money in the NCHA World Championship Futurity in Fort Worth could be as much as $200,000 if she won on Sugar Pep.

But she couldn't count on winning. She was going to have to eat some crow—and take Trace up on his offer to train Smart Little Doc. With the fees for training Trace's horse, and with any luck, her share of the prize money he'd offered if his horse made it into the top ten, she might be able to pay off the government in time to avoid owing interest and penalties on top of the taxes.

Of course, she was going to have to eat a lot of peanut butter and jelly sandwiches along with crow over the next year, but at least they'd still have Three Oaks.

But for how long?

Callie didn't allow herself to contemplate the grim future that lay ahead of them. Her mother was still in the hospital, and though she was expected to recover completely, Callie was disturbed at how despondent her mother had seemed the last time she'd visited her.

"Maybe we should sell," her mother had suggested.

"That isn't necessary, Mom," she'd countered. "We can come up with the money to pay the taxes."

"For seven years? How are the two of us going to keep the ranch going and pay off that kind of debt?"

"We'll manage. Bay will be done with school in a year and—"

"How can we afford to send Bay back to school next semester?"

"Bay can borrow whatever she needs to finish up. Don't worry, Mom. Just get well."

"How is Sam handling all this?"

He's turned into a real pain in the ass. "Sam's having some trouble dealing with Dad's death," Callie said. "But we all have to find a way to go on."

"Why?" her mother had asked. "Why keep fighting a battle we're losing?"

"Because Three Oaks is our home. It's where we belong."

Callie never got to finish her speech. The nurse had interrupted her. So she never said to her mother, "Where else would we go? What else would we do?"

The truth was, Callie could probably get work training

cutting horses for somebody in California or Texas. And once Bay got her degree, she could get licensed as a large animal vet pretty much anywhere. But what would happen to Sam and her mother and Luke? Callie wasn't about to abandon her family, and she couldn't support all of them on what she would make working for somebody else.

And there was history to consider. The Creeds could trace their heritage back to the youngest of three sisters, Sloan, Bayleigh, and Creighton Stewart, who'd grown up on a cotton plantation called Three Oaks when Texas was still a Republic.

Creighton Stewart had married Texas Ranger Jarrett Creed, and they'd raised a family of four sons on a plantation called Lion's Dare. During the Civil War, Cricket had gone to live with her widowed sister, Sloan, on her vast Southwest Texas cattle ranch, Dolorosa.

But everything the Stewart sisters owned was stolen by a conniving Englishman called Blackthorne. And when Creighton's eldest son Jake came home from the war— the only survivor among his father and brothers—he'd built himself a home on the comparatively small piece of land along Bitter Creek that was all he had left of his inheritance.

Callie and her family lived in that house, which had been handed down from generation to generation for more than a hundred and fifty years. The family had struggled too hard to keep Three Oaks. Callie wasn't about to be the one to give it up to somebody else, especially when that somebody would almost certainly be Jackson Blackthorne.

Callie had spent more than a little time contemplating Sam's accusation that Blackjack had something to do with her father's death. Violence had always been a possibility between the two men. But why now? Had the incident at the Rafter S been the spark? Did Blackjack want Callie's mother badly enough to kill her father in order to have her? But her mother would have to want Blackjack in return, and that was just plain crazy. And what about Eve Blackthorne? Callie hadn't heard anything about an impending divorce.

Callie shook her head. No, she didn't think Blackjack had killed her father. But she would be damned if he was going to benefit from her father's death. She would never give her father's bitterest enemy the satisfaction of having Three Oaks during her lifetime, not if there was any way she could hang on to it. She owed her father that much, at least.

The cell phone in her shirt pocket rang, and Callie pulled her horse to a stop to retrieve it.

"Callie here. What kind of problem? That's impossible! Don't do anything until I get there."

"What is it, Callie?" Luke asked.

"Something's come up at the auction barn. You finish driving these cows to the loading chutes. I'll meet you there after I've taken care of this little glitch."

"You sure you don't need any help?"

Callie stared into Luke's worried eyes. "Thanks for the offer, Luke, but I can handle this. I appreciate you doing a man's job."

Leather creaked as Luke shifted his weight in the saddle. He lifted his eyes from the ragged buckskin gloves that protected his hands, which were perched one on top of the other on the saddle horn, to meet her gaze. "I could do more, Callie. I could be a big help. I don't have to finish high school."

She laid a hand on Luke's thigh, then shifted it to avoid the searing heat from one of the silver conchas decorating the leather pockets on his chaps. "You're a big help right now. I'm counting on you to finish up here. I'll see you at the loading chutes later on."

Callie spurred her horse to get away before Luke saw the tears stinging her eyes. She couldn't believe another disaster had befallen them, especially not the one Bay had called to explain. *Brucellosis.* The vet at the auction barn was claiming one of their cows had tested positive for brucellosis!

Brucellosis was a sexually transmitted undulant fever that caused cows to abort their fetuses. Their cows had all recently dropped healthy calves. Therefore, they didn't have—couldn't have—brucellosis.

According to Bay, an inspector from the Texas Animal Health Commission had quarantined their cows based on the determination by the vet that their cattle were infected. Which meant they couldn't be sold—except for slaughter—until the quarantine was lifted.

Of all the bad luck! The cows were worth only half as much if they were sold for beef, rather than breeding stock. And lifting the quarantine could take months! They wouldn't be able to make the first payment to the government. Three Oaks would be seized and sold for taxes!

There must have been a mistake. Callie wanted to see the results of the card test—the blood drawn from one of her cows and put on a cardboard card that revealed the disease—with her own eyes.

Callie shouldn't have been surprised to find Blackjack

at the auction arena, but she was. Corporate buyers stood by the rail smoking unfiltered cigarettes, eyes narrowed against the smoke, or sat in clumps in the stands swatting at flies, observing the beef cattle being herded into the arena, checking to see whether they had been fed to a grade of "choice" or "prime." Although with everybody nowadays so worried about cholesterol and calories, there wasn't much market for the marbled fat found in a "prime" piece of beef.

Callie crossed to the small stand of wooden bleachers beside the covered, pipe-railed auction arena and climbed up the several rows to where Blackjack sat with his *segundo,* Russell Handy. It seemed Blackjack had come, like a vulture, to wait for her last dying breaths, so he could feed on what carrion was left.

"What are you doing here?" she demanded.

"I'm auctioning one of my bulls," he said, gesturing to an enclosed pen beyond the arena.

That made sense. It was also very coincidental. "Have you heard what happened?"

He nodded, as though in commiseration, but he couldn't keep his lips from quirking. "Too bad about your cows. My offer for Three Oaks stands. It's a fair price, considering I can probably pick up your land at a tax sale for a lot less."

"There's been some mistake," Callie said.

Blackjack lifted a black brow. "Is that so? Did you have your cows vaccinated?"

"No, and you knew very well why I didn't!" Not only was Strain 19 vaccine expensive, it was risky to vaccinate cows for brucellosis, because sometimes a cow infected with live *Brucella abortis* bacteria would get hot and go wall-eyed and turn into a "banger," and you'd get precisely the result you'd been trying to avoid.

Even if that didn't happen, the brucellosis antibodies could give you a false positive on the card test at auction, and your vaccinated cow would get a big red *B* painted on its flank to indicate it could be sold only for slaughter.

"There are no bangers in my herd," Callie said.

"You'll have to talk to the vet about that," Blackjack said.

"That's exactly what I intend to do." Callie started down the risers, then stopped and turned around. "You know, we have a common fence line. If my cows end up quarantined for brucellosis, yours could end up being quarantined as well."

Blackjack shrugged. "Wasn't planning on selling any cows anytime soon," he said. "Guess I'll have to take my chances when the time comes."

Callie felt the anger welling inside her, that feeling of helpless frustration she'd had too often in the days when Nolan was dying of cancer and the doctors shook their heads and said there was nothing they could do. She'd stopped praying to a God who seemed to have abandoned her. She'd thought He'd done his worst when she'd found her father dead.

But it seemed there was worse to come.

Callie left the stands without another word and headed for the outdoor pens, where cattle were unloaded from the trucks. It occurred to her long before she got where she was going that Blackjack had most likely loaded the deck in his favor.

He was president of the local Texas and Southwestern Cattle Raisers Association, which was responsible for hiring the auction vet. Which meant the man Callie was about to confront had been handpicked by Blackjack and held his job only so long as he kept him happy.

"Dr. Guerrero!" she called over the noise of the bawling cattle.

When Tony Guerrero turned to face her, Callie was startled to discover that he'd been talking to Trace. She hid her distress as best she could and crossed to the vet's side. "What's this I hear about one of my cows turning up a banger?" she demanded.

The vet pulled a card out of his shirt pocket and held it out to her. "Read it and weep," he said sympathetically.

Callie was sure he didn't mean his words literally, but it was all she could do not to burst into tears. She turned on Trace and said, "How could you let Blackjack do this?"

"Callie, my father—"

"Your father owns the vet, and as sure as I'm standing here, he arranged for that positive card test."

The vet shook his head. "That's not true, Mrs. Monroe."

"Oh, really?" she said, doing nothing to hide the sarcasm in her voice. "Who took the blood that supposedly turned out positive on that card test?"

"I hire a couple of men to draw blood," the vet said.

Callie was surprised. She'd thought the vet did it himself. She looked around to see if she knew the cowboys who'd drawn the sample. Maybe she could find out the truth from one of them. "Who did you hire?"

"Just a couple of drifters looking for day work," the vet said. "And Billy Coburn."

Callie felt her heart skip a beat. "Bad Billy Coburn?"

"I think they call him that," the vet said.

Callie rounded on Trace. "Doesn't he work for your father?"

"Not anymore. I fired him for fighting with your brother the night of the Rafter S auction. Remember?"

Callie rubbed her temples in an attempt to ward off the headache that was threatening. Was it possible Bad Billy Coburn blamed her brother Luke for losing his job? Had Billy faked the positive card test to get back at the Creeds because he'd been fired? "I want to talk to him," Callie said.

The vet stood on the bottom rail of the corral, stuck two fingers in his mouth, and whistled shrilly. When he had Billy's attention, he waved him over.

It took Billy a few minutes to weave his way between the cattle and reach them, and Callie watched his face the whole way, hoping for some clue as to whether he was the guilty party.

When Billy reached the other side of the fence, he stopped, stuck a boot up on the bottom rail, and touched his fingertip to the brim of his hat. "Mizz Monroe."

Bad Billy Coburn reminded Callie of a young James Dean. His black hair lay in waves beneath the brim of his hat, and his dark brown eyes glittered with defiance. There was something raw and animalistic about his sharply defined features that appealed to her as a woman. Callie felt a shiver of unwelcome response as his heavy-lidded gaze slid over her body.

"Did you draw the blood that tested positive, Billy?" she asked.

"That depends," he said, eyeing the three of them.

"Answer the question," Trace said.

Billy shot an insolent look in Trace's direction. "I don't work for you anymore, big man."

Callie spoke before the situation could worsen. "I'm trying to find out if someone fixed a card test on one of my cows."

"I didn't do the card tests," Billy said.

Callie frowned. "I don't understand."

Billy took a final drag on his cigarette and flicked it into the dirt. "I gave the blood samples to the guy who was working with me, and he put it on the cards."

Callie turned to the vet. "Is that how it's usually done?"

The vet shrugged. "We do it all kinds of ways. That way works as well as any."

"Where's the cowboy who was working with you?" Callie asked Billy.

"Don't know. He left a while ago for lunch. Hasn't come back."

Callie turned to the vet. "Doesn't that sound a little suspicious?"

"Not necessarily," the vet said. "Cowboys come and go around here. The work's hot and dusty, and we don't pay much."

"Are you done interrogating me?" Billy demanded.

"Oh. I'm sorry. Yes. I appreciate your cooperation," Callie said.

Billy took another long, lazy look at her, then met her gaze with suggestive eyes and said, "Anytime, ma'am." He tugged his had brim low over his eyes and sauntered away.

"That kid is pure-D trouble," the vet muttered.

Callie agreed, but she didn't think Bad Billy Coburn

had anything to do with the positive test results. "How many of my cows tested positive?" she asked.

"Just one," the vet replied.

"One. Just one." Callie laughed with relief. "So the rest of the herd—"

"Is quarantined," the vet said.

"But you can't do that!" Callie protested. "One suspicious test—"

"There's nothing suspicious about the results on this card," the vet said, holding it out to her. He pointed with his finger. "That result is positive."

"What if that missing cowboy substituted a vial of blood for one Billy gave him?" Callie said. "What if the test was fixed!"

The vet's face reddened. "Are you suggesting I'd do such a thing? Because I can assure you—"

Callie could see she was losing ground. "No, no. Of course you wouldn't. But don't you see? What do we know about that missing cowboy? Couldn't you retest my cows?"

"Wouldn't do any good. Have to quarantine them for a bit to see if any bangers show up."

"But—"

"What's the problem here?"

Callie turned to find the local field inspector, Harvey Miller, standing with his hands perched on his hips beneath a burgeoning belly. He wore a TSCRA badge framed in leather—a Longhorn etched on a star within a silver circle—that hung from his breast pocket. The field inspector carried a Colt .45 on his hip and had the power to arrest wrongdoers. Callie wondered if Blackjack had sent him over to intimidate her.

"I came to see whether you want to sell your cows for slaughter or load them back onto your trucks," Harvey said.

"I want my cows tested again. I don't believe you'll find any bangers, because my cows all recently dropped calves!"

"That doesn't mean they can't—or won't—abort next time," Harvey said reasonably. "What's it gonna be?"

"I can't afford to have my cows butchered," Callie said, her voice rising sharply.

"Then I'll have the boys load 'em back up," Harvey said.

"This is insane!" Callie said. "My cows are perfectly healthy."

"Well, you can always have the Texas Animal Health Commissioner come down from Austin and certify—"

"It could take months— And by then the prices— I need this situation straightened out now!" Callie cried.

"There's nothing you can do, Callie," Trace said.

She turned on him, her eyes flashing with anger. "Your father made this happen! I know he did! At first, I didn't think he had my father killed, but now I'm starting to wonder just how far he's willing to go to get Three Oaks!"

"You know that's crazy talk," Trace said.

"Is it?" She turned to the field inspector and said, "Load up my cows. I'm taking them home. I'll be in touch with the Animal Health Commissioner, and believe me, I'm going to report what happened here today." She turned to glare at the vet. "When I'm done, you'll be lucky if you still have your job!"

Callie made the threat even though she knew, as the vet

must also have known, that Jackson Blackthorne and the Texas Animal Health Commissioner were most likely good pals, and that if she could compel the commissioner to come and reinspect her cattle at all, it wouldn't be anytime soon—and certainly not before she was forced to sell Three Oaks to Jackson Blackthorne or lose it to the government for failure to pay her father's estate taxes.

Callie gave instructions to the cowboys who were working with her cattle about where to drop them off, then headed toward the stands where Blackjack still sat waiting for his bull to be auctioned. She was nearly there when she realized Trace was beside her, matching her stride for stride.

"What are you planning to do, Callie?" he asked.

"Tell your father exactly what I think of him."

"What purpose will that serve? Listen, Callie. I have a proposition."

She stopped and whirled to face him. "What could you possibly offer me that would be of any help now, Trace?"

"I can loan you the money to pay the first installment of taxes."

She stared at him, unblinking, for a full thirty seconds, then laughed. The laughter bubbled out of her, the force of it bending her in half. "That is rich. That is so funny."

"I'm not joking, Callie."

"Where would you get that kind of money—that didn't come out of your father's pocket?"

"I have money of my own," he said quietly.

Her laughter stopped abruptly. "You're serious."

He nodded.

"I don't understand. What do you get out of this?"

"You."

She should have known there would be a fly in the ointment. She didn't ask what he meant. She could guess what he had in mind. "That makes me a pretty expensive whore."

"If that's the way you want to look at it."

"There isn't any other way of looking at it," Callie said bluntly. "You're asking me to have sex with you for money."

His expression hardened as he waited for her answer.

"How much will I be paid for my services? How many times—"

"Till I'm tired of you," he said brusquely.

"How am I supposed to explain this 'business arrangement' to my family?"

"There's no reason they have to know about it."

She laughed again, only this time it was an ugly sound. "My brothers aren't stupid. They'll want to know where I got the money to pay the taxes. I'll have to tell them something."

"Tell them you talked the bank into giving you a loan—based on the future sale of your cattle. They'll believe it, because they'll want to believe it."

Callie knew he was right.

"One more thing," he said.

"What's that?"

"I want you to train my stud for the Futurity—with the understanding you'll be paid the share of winnings I promised you if my horse finishes in the top ten."

"Anything else?"

"No. That's all."

Callie began walking again, and Trace kept pace with her. She really had no choice. Where else was she going to find the money to save Three Oaks? She opened her mouth to agree, but what came out was, "I won't do it."

"Fine."

She stopped and stared at him. "Is that all you have to say?"

"You've made your decision. What else can I say?"

Callie had expected him to cajole, to bargain and plead. She was taken aback by his willingness to abandon the whole idea. She was right back where she'd started—woefully short of funds to pay the first installment of her father's estate taxes.

She started walking again. "I'm not saying I'd ever agree to such an outrageous proposal, but if I did, where would these interludes take place?"

"My father has a hunting cabin. We can go there."

"Oh, God." Callie laughed. "This is absurd. I can't believe I'm even discussing this with you."

"It's a fair trade," Trace said.

Callie stopped and stared at him. "I guess I don't know you as well as I thought. The Trace I knew wouldn't have tried to buy love with money."

"I'm not interested in love. Just sex."

"Oh, and that makes it okay?"

He shrugged. "I was only trying to help you out."

"Thanks for nothing." Callie shook her head, sighed, then said, "I need time to think about your offer."

"You've got until sundown tonight."

"What's the rush?" she asked, eyeing him sideways.

"I'm not going to be in Texas much longer. I want to get full value for my investment."

"How soon are you leaving?"

"Soon enough," he answered evasively.

Part of Callie's unwillingness to sell herself to Trace was the fact that she had no idea how long she'd have to surrender herself to his sexual whims before she'd have paid him back for the loan. But if Trace was leaving Texas in the near future, that problem would solve itself.

She couldn't believe she was even considering his proposal. He wanted the use of her body, but he'd be buying her soul. She hadn't believed she could stoop so low. But when she thought of the alternative—losing Three Oaks to Blackjack—she didn't see where she had much choice.

She felt sick to her stomach.

"I need more time to think about it," she said.

"No."

Callie made a growling sound of frustration in her throat. She was certain if she just had a little more time, she could figure out a way to save both herself and the ranch.

Suddenly, Callie realized how she could take Trace's money and still keep her self-respect. If he wanted sex, that's what he would get, without the warmth and affection that normally accompanied such an intimate joining. He couldn't say she hadn't kept her part of the bargain. And the first installment on her father's estate taxes would be paid before he realized how little he'd gotten for his money.

"I don't need to wait until sundown," she said at last.

He raised a brow, but said nothing.

"I agree to the deal."

"What changed your mind?" he asked.

She shrugged nonchalantly. "I need the money. Shall we shake on it?" She held out her hand, and it was swallowed by his. Her skin tingled, and her blood began to race in her veins.

"Do you still want to talk to my father?" he asked.

"No. I don't think there's anything further that needs to be said."

"Then I'll bring my stud over tomorrow after church."

She looked down at the hand she'd used to make a devil's bargain and pulled herself free. "What will you tell your father?" she said. "He'll know I didn't borrow the money from the bank."

"I'll tell him I'm courting you."

She frowned. "I don't understand."

Trace sighed. "My father's wanted me to marry you for a long time. It'll please him to think he'll be getting Three Oaks without having to do more than pay inheritance taxes."

"I see." He'd hinted as much to her on the plane, then told her they'd met at UT entirely by accident. What if they hadn't? It would be punishment enough to open her body to a man who no longer wanted her love. It would be a nightmare to make love to someone who'd never seen her as anything other than a means to an end.

"Tomorrow," she said. "I'll see you tomorrow." Callie forced herself to walk away. You never ran from a predator. It only made him hungrier for the kill.

Chapter 10

"What's he doing here, Mom?"

Callie glanced at the horse trailer pulling up to the barn. *He's here to lay claim to what he bought yesterday.*

She cupped a reassuring—and restraining—hand around Eli's nape and said, "I'm going to be training Mr. Blackthorne's horse for the Futurity."

"Sheesh. You gotta be kidding! Why?"

"Because we need the money. I expect you to be nice," she said, as Trace stepped down from the cab of the pickup hauling the top-of-the-line Sooner two-horse trailer.

"Do I hafta?" Eli said.

Callie felt the muscles in her son's shoulders tense. "Please, Eli. Do this for me."

He made a face, then gave a curt nod.

"Where do you want him?" Trace asked as he headed for the back of the horse trailer to let down the ramp.

"Put him in the corral for now. I still need to fix the door on his stall. It's not hanging properly."

As Trace backed the bay stallion out of the trailer, Callie couldn't help admiring Smart Little Doc. The intelligent look in the horse's eyes, and the dance in his step, suggested he was something special. She already knew he was exciting to watch at work. She'd seen him move with a cow like the two of them were puppets attached to the same string.

At the same time, Callie couldn't help being aware of Trace. His powerful body moved with lithe grace over the ground, and his commands to the horse were quiet and sure. She felt her insides squeeze as his large, callused hand moved over the horse, down its arched neck, up across its withers and then down its back, the proud owner of an excellent piece of horseflesh.

Trace owned her body too. He'd bought the right to handle her as thoroughly as he was now handling Smart Little Doc. Callie realized, to her dismay, that she wouldn't mind being touched by Trace as much as she should, under the circumstances.

"Get the corral gate please, Eli," Callie said.

The boy hurried to do her bidding, but Callie should have known better than to think Eli would behave himself. An instant before Smart Little Doc was inside and clear of the gate, Eli let go, and it swung closed on the horse's rear end. Smart Little Doc leapt forward, hitting Trace in the shoulder and sending him spinning. Trace let go of the halter rope, rather than jerk the horse's head, and landed on his rear end in the sand.

Eli climbed onto the corral gate and hung over the top rail, a smirk of deviltry on his face. "Oops. Guess I let it go a little too soon."

Trace was so slow to rise, Callie thought he might be injured. He wasn't hurt. He was angry. Once he was on his feet and had ensured his horse was all right, he headed straight for the gate—and Eli.

"Trace, wait!" Callie cried, heading toward her son to protect him.

Callie could see Trace was going to reach Eli first. Eli saw the same thing, and came down off the gate and headed in her direction on the run. Trace was too fast. He vaulted the corral as though it wasn't there and caught Eli by the scruff of his shirt.

"Hold up there, son."

"I'm not your son!" Eli said, wriggling and kicking.

Trace held the boy away from him, so Eli's kicking feet couldn't reach his shins, and said, "That animal never did a thing to you. It wasn't fair to punish him because you don't like me."

"I hate you!" Eli shouted.

"It doesn't matter a bucket of spit what you think of me. If I ever see you mistreat another animal, I'll put you over my knee and wallop your backside till you can't sit down for a week."

"Mom, help! He says he's gonna beat me! Mom!"

Callie met Trace's furious gaze and said in a voice she might use to calm an excitable horse, "I can handle my son. You can let him go now."

"Let me go, you murdering Blackthorne!" Eli ranted.

A muscle in Trace's jaw jerked. For a moment, Callie thought he would follow through with his threat right then and there. But he released his hold on Eli's shirt, took a step back, and said to her, "Keep that boy away from me."

That was fine with Callie. The less Trace saw of his son, the better for everyone. "Eli, I think you'd better take some time out to think about what you've done. You can go help Henry finish mucking out stalls."

"Aw, Mom—"

Callie caught her son's chin as he slipped past her and turned his face up to hers. "We don't take out our troubles on animals that depend on us to care for them, Eli. Do you understand what I'm saying?"

Eli made a sound in his throat.

"Do you?"

"Yes, ma'am," the boy croaked.

A moment later Callie and Trace were alone. She turned to him and said, "I'm sorry. Eli's been upset—"

"Don't make excuses for the boy. What he did was wrong. End of story."

"Granted, but—"

"No buts."

Callie bit her lip. Had she been too tolerant of Eli's behavior? Should she have been punishing him for his outrageous antics, rather than trying so hard to understand his pain?

"You've got to set some limits, Callie, or the kid's going to turn into a bully."

Callie was stung by Trace's criticism. She might agree with him, but he had no rights where Eli was concerned. He'd given them up when he'd walked out of her life eleven years ago. "You're here to drop off your horse," she said in an icy voice. "I'll take care of my son."

"Fine. Just make sure your kid doesn't do anything to hurt my horse."

"Smart Little Doc will be perfectly safe."

"When can I see you?"

Callie stared at him, disconcerted by the abrupt change of subject. "What do you mean?"

"What time can I pick you up?"

"You mean today? I can't spend any time with you today," she said, aghast at how quickly Trace apparently intended to claim his right to her body. "I have too much work to do."

"Name a time, Callie."

"I can't—"

"Mommy! Mommy!"

Callie turned to see why she was being called and discovered her four-year-old daughter lying on her belly, hanging halfway out of the open door of the barn loft—twenty feet off the ground. "Hannah! Don't move, baby! Stay right where you are!"

Callie ran for the door to the barn, but was forced to stop just inside to let her eyes adjust to the dimness. Trace ran into her from behind.

He grabbed her shoulders to keep them both from falling and asked, "Where's the ladder to the loft?"

She pointed toward the north end of the barn and he was on his way again. She followed after him, but he was all the way up the ladder when she was still on the bottom rungs. "Be careful!" she cried. "Don't frighten her. She might fall."

When Callie got to the top of the ladder, her heart was pounding so hard she thought it would burst from her chest. She gave a garbled cry of relief when she saw Trace holding Hannah in his arms. She hurried across the width of the loft and took Hannah from him, clutching her so tightly Hannah protested.

"Mommy, you're squishing me!"

"What are you doing up here in the loft? You know you're not allowed up here!" Callie shouted. All her anger at Eli, who deserved to be punished, seemed to find its way into her condemnation of Hannah, who hadn't done anything worse than climb a ladder out of curiosity. The little girl burst into tears.

"Oh, Hannah. Oh, baby, I'm so sorry." She kissed away the tears on the cherubic face, brushed the straw out of her daughter's fine, flyaway curls. "Mommy was just so worried. What were you doing up here?"

"I heard kitties, Mommy. I heard them crying for their mommy." Hannah pointed toward the corner of the loft. "They're starving, Mommy. We have to feed them."

Trace walked toward where Hannah pointed, leaned over, and came up with a tiny calico kitten in each hand. "I guess this is what she heard."

Hannah reached out for a kitten, and Trace crossed and laid one in her arms. "See, Mommy? They need me."

At that moment, the orange-striped barn cat arrived and hurried to the straw nest where she'd left her kittens. After doing a quick survey, she crossed to where Trace stood and paced agitatedly before him.

"I think she wants her babies back, so she can feed them," Trace said to Hannah. "If you give me that one, I'll put them back."

To Callie's surprise, Hannah relinquished the kitten to Trace, and he gently placed both kittens back in the nest. As soon as he took a step back, the mother cat settled down and the kittens began to nurse.

"See? She just left them for a little while," Callie said. "Now we need to leave her alone, so she can feed them," Callie added, rubbing her nose against Hannah's.

She looked up and met Trace's gaze. "Thank you," she said.

"You need some help around here, Callie. You shouldn't be trying to do all this by yourself."

"Everybody who lives here does his fair share, Trace," she said.

He raised a brow. "Is that so? You look like you've been ridden hard and put away wet."

Callie bristled at his description of her exhausted condition, even though it very likely fit. "I suppose you want me rested up so I can—" She cut herself off, realizing that she had Hannah in her arms, and that her daughter had a notorious tendency to parrot everything she heard.

"You shouldn't be doing so much ranch work. Your kids need your attention," he said through clenched teeth.

"They get plenty of my attention," Callie retorted, heading for the ladder that led down from the loft.

Before she could start down the ladder with Hannah in her arms, Trace took the little girl from her and said, "She's too heavy for you."

Callie opened her mouth to protest, took one look at Trace's lowered brows, and snapped it shut. She had to choose her arguments, and the truth was, it would have been awkward to descend the nearly vertical ladder holding Hannah. What she found most astonishing was the fact that Hannah seemed perfectly happy in Trace's arms.

Callie pivoted and started down the ladder. She waited at the bottom, ready to take Hannah from Trace, but the little girl had her arms around Trace's neck and her head nestled against his shoulder and actually seemed reluctant to let go.

"Hannah," Callie said, tapping her daughter on the shoulder.

Hannah shook her head and snuggled her nose deeper against Trace's neck.

Callie felt her throat thicken. "She misses Nolan," she managed to say.

"Couldn't Sam or your sister be watching her for you?"

"Bay left to go back to school this morning. Sam is . . ." *Always drunk lately.* "I like having her with me," Callie said defiantly.

To her surprise, Trace didn't seem anxious to be rid of the clinging child. "Where's the stall door that needs fixing?" he asked.

"You don't have to worry—"

He met her gaze with another look that shut her up.

"This way." She headed toward the paddock that faced twenty wooden stalls in a row, each with its own door, most of which were open on top. She was embarrassed for Trace to see that the white paint was peeling and that more than one stall door hung crooked.

But the horses that hung their heads over the tops of the stall doors, ears cocked forward and nostrils flared to whinny a hello, were sleek and healthy. Callie caressed foreheads, noses, necks, and jowls as she passed by, greeting each horse by name.

"I can see Smart Little Doc is going to be a lot more pampered here than he would be at home," Trace said.

Callie angled her head so she could meet Trace's gaze. "Horses have feelings, too."

"I wasn't complaining, Callie."

Callie admitted to herself that she'd been expecting

criticism, so that's what she'd heard. But she couldn't stop herself from explaining, "The stalls could use a little paint, but the hay is changed daily and every horse gets bathed and groomed—"

"If I didn't think Smart Little Doc was going to be taken care of properly, I wouldn't be leaving him here," Trace interrupted.

They passed an empty stall with a wheelbarrow out front, half-filled with manure and straw. Callie paused and looked into the stall, expecting to see Eli with a pitchfork in his hands, but found Henry working alone.

"Where's Eli?" she asked, looking around for her son.

"He went to get a drink of water," Henry said.

"How long ago was that?" Callie asked.

Henry shrugged and went back to his work.

Callie was afraid to look at Trace, afraid she would see disapproval in his eyes, or worse, pity. She prayed he wouldn't say anything, because she couldn't bear to hear him criticize Eli, even though she knew Eli deserved to be chastised.

"Where's that stall door?" Trace asked.

Callie shot him a grateful look, then turned and hurried two stalls farther. "Here."

Tools littered the ground around the stall, and Callie felt the need, again, to explain. "I'd already started on this once today, but I got called away."

"You don't have to explain to me that you're pulled in a dozen directions at once. I can see that." Trace set Hannah on her feet and bent to pick up a wrench.

Hannah bent to pick up a screwdriver. "I want to help."

Callie started to pick her up, but Trace said, "She's not in my way. Why don't you go find your son?"

"Eli will be back soon," Callie said, praying that her son would show up without having to be sought out. "I'd rather stay here and help you."

"Suit yourself."

Trace was aware of the knot in his stomach but wasn't sure precisely what had put it there. He went to work tightening the bolts that held the stall door to the door frame, doing his best to ignore Callie, who made a point of holding the heavy stall door perpendicular to the ground while he worked.

"What can I do?" Hannah asked, peering up at him with serious, gray-green eyes.

"See if you can tighten those screws, Hannah," Trace said, pointing to the lowest screws on the door. He made a space for Hannah between his widespread legs as the little girl squatted on her haunches trying to fit the screwdriver into a screw at the bottom of the stall door.

He saw the anxiety on Callie's face and said, "She'll be safe there. Don't worry."

Some of the worry left her face, but her overall look of exhaustion remained. Her golden hair was lank, as though it needed washing, and her blue eyes looked like cold water at the bottom of a deep well. He sought words to describe her and didn't like the ones that came to mind. Haggard. Gaunt. Wasted.

He might have been too generous comparing Callie to a horse that had been ridden hard and put away wet. That horse at least had a chance of recuperating. Callie looked more like a horse down with colic—that might or might not survive the night.

You're not making her life any easier.

Trace wished he'd never offered to loan Callie the tax money she needed. And it had been pure folly to put conditions on the loan, making Callie sell her services like some two-bit whore. Well, not a two-bit whore. He was paying a great deal more than two bits for her services.

Trace chuckled.

"What's so funny?"

There was no way he could explain, so he asked, "How much help do you have around here?"

"Henry does most of the heavy work, now that Daddy—" Her voice cracked.

When she didn't speak again, he said, "Who else works for you besides Henry?"

"We have a few cowboys we call on when there's extra work to be done."

"So why didn't you call one of them to do this?" Trace asked, as he finished tightening the bolts.

She stared at him, her lips pressed flat.

No money, he surmised. "Where's Luke?" he asked, thinking her teenage brother ought to be some help.

"He spent the night with a friend."

Trace frowned. "With all the work that needs to be done around here?"

"He's entitled to some fun," Callie said defensively. "He's just a boy."

"Seems to me you had plenty of responsibility growing up. Maybe too much."

"My family needed me. I was happy to do my part."

"Like I said. Ridden hard and—"

"There isn't anybody else," she said sharply. "Not right now. I'm doing the best I can, and if you—"

"Whoa, there, sweetheart."

She glanced up sharply at his use of the endearment. "I'm not your sweetheart."

"I'm not your sweetheart," Hannah echoed.

Trace looked down at the tiny mite peering back up at him. He reached down, picked up Hannah, and settled her on his arm. "You're cute enough to be a sweetheart," he said, smiling at her.

Hannah smiled back.

Trace couldn't believe how good that smile made him feel inside. He glanced at Callie and was surprised at the stricken look on her face. She was probably remembering her husband. He felt that knot in his stomach again, but he wasn't going to set the little girl down. Callie would just have to deal with the situation.

He'd always liked kids. He was sorry he didn't have a couple of his own. He realized the little girl was probably used to male attention, since she had her brother, a couple of uncles, and until recently, a grandfather to dote on her. But he was glad she wasn't afraid of him, glad that she accepted his friendliness at face value.

Trace used his free hand to open and close the stall door. "That wasn't much of an adjustment, but it seems to be working fine now. Shall we go get my horse?"

The three of them walked toward the corral, Hannah still in Trace's arms.

"When is your mother due to come home from the hospital?" Trace asked.

"In a few days," Callie said.

"Do you have someone coming in to take care of her?"

Callie shook her head.

Trace stopped in his tracks. "How are you planning—"

"Look," she said, turning to face him, her hands on her hips. "That's my business, and I can handle it. You don't need to get involved."

"I have my own reasons for wanting you rested, Callie. Or had you forgotten?" he said. "I'll have someone—"

"You will do no such thing!" she interrupted. "You Blackthornes don't own Three Oaks yet, and God willing, you never will! I can take care of my family without any help from you."

He felt the little girl tense in his arms and draw back from him. "You're frightening Hannah," he said in a measured voice.

She reached for her daughter, and Trace let the little girl go, rather than risk upsetting her any further. But his arms felt bereft.

"You can leave now," Callie said brusquely. "I'll move your horse later."

With the extra weight of the child in her arms, she was wavering on her feet. Trace was afraid she might literally fall down. When he took a step toward her, his arms outstretched to take the child, Callie stiffened, and the little girl looked at him with wide, terrified eyes.

The knot had moved from his stomach to his throat. He hadn't understood, when he'd walked out of Callie's dorm room in a huff eleven years ago, how much her family demanded of her—and just how much she was willing to give them. Everything. They wanted everything, and she was willing to give what they asked. He didn't understand that kind of selflessness. Or that kind of need.

Even now his father didn't really *need* him. There were others who could carry the load if he wasn't there to manage things. No one had ever needed him. He'd offered Callie the money to save her ranch; she'd never asked for it. He willed Callie to ask for his help now. He wanted to be allowed to help her. But she was shutting him out, as she'd shut him out eleven years ago.

"Look, Callie," he began. "Why not let me hire a housekeeper to—"

"We Creeds can take care of ourselves," she snapped, cutting him off.

"The hell you can!" he roared, finally losing patience with her.

Hannah burst into tears, and Callie simply turned and walked away from him.

"Hannah, sweetheart, I'm not mad at you," Trace cooed to the child, as his long strides caught up with Callie. "But I'm furious with you," he said under his breath to Callie. "Don't walk away from me, Callie. We have to talk."

"Trace, I don't think—"

Callie was drawn up short as Eli stumbled to a stop before her.

"Mom," he gasped. He bent over, trying to catch his breath. "Mom. Mom."

"What's wrong? Are you hurt, Eli? Where are you hurt?" Callie shoved Hannah into Trace's arms and began running her hands over Eli, searching for an injury.

When the boy looked up at her, Trace saw tears streaking the powder of dust on his cheeks. His chin trembled, and then he broke down completely. Trace could barely understand the wail of sound that erupted from Eli's throat, but a chill went down his spine when he finally made out Eli's tear-choked words.

"I think . . . Sam is . . . dead!"

Chapter 11

CALLIE TOOK OFF AT A RUN FOR THE RANCH
house, with Eli hard on her heels. Trace tried to calm
Hannah, who was wailing loudly, as he quickly followed
after the other two. "It's all right, Hannah. Everything's
going to be fine. Don't cry, sweetheart."

The whole time he was crooning to Hannah, his mind
was awhirl with questions. How had Sam died? An accident? What kind of accident does a man in a wheelchair
have? Had Sam perhaps taken his own life? They hadn't
heard any gunshots, but that didn't mean Sam hadn't slit
his wrists or taken some pills, even if that wasn't the way
most men would have chosen to kill themselves.

Trace arrived at the house only a moment after the
other two, but the kitchen was empty. He followed Eli's
sobs to a bedroom at the far end of the house on the
ground floor. Callie was sitting on the unmade brass-rail
bed, her expression stark, her eyes staring sightlessly at
her brother, who was sitting slumped over in his wheelchair beside the bed. Eli was kneeling on the floor, holding Sam's lifeless hand and bawling like a branded calf.

Trace looked for some sign of violence, a gunshot

wound or slit wrists or even an empty bottle of pills, but saw nothing. The blood had drained from Sam's bloated face, leaving it a pale shade of gray. He certainly looked dead. "Were you expecting this? Was he sick?" he asked.

"Sick at heart," Callie answered in a desolate voice.

"Any idea what might have killed him?"

"He drank himself to death."

Trace stared at the man whose paralyzing accident so long ago had meant the end of any chance he'd had of marrying Callie Creed. It would have been better if Sam had died that day. He'd lived as a festering wound that had kept the feud between their families alive and well. And now, when Trace was only starting to know Callie again, he felt certain Sam's death was going to put another wedge between them.

He so much wanted Sam to be alive, that at first he didn't believe his eyes. *There's sweat on Sam's brow.* He set Hannah down carefully and bent over to put his fingertips to Sam's throat, where he supposed the carotid artery might be.

"He's got a pulse," Trace said, unable to keep the excitement from his voice.

Callie scrambled to put her own fingertips to Sam's neck on the other side. "Where? I can't find it!"

"Believe me, it's there. From the looks of him, he needs to see a doctor pronto, or he will be dead." Trace bent to disconnect Sam's foley catheter from the wheelchair.

"How did you know to do that?" Callie asked.

Trace didn't take the time to answer, since the answer seemed obvious: *I've spent time with a man in a wheelchair.* He simply picked Sam up in his arms and said,

"Grab some blankets for the back of your pickup. Eli, you take Hannah's hand, and make sure she gets into the cab of the truck okay."

"I don't have to—"

"Eli!" Callie said shrilly. "Do what you're told!"

Callie barely had the blankets laid in the back of her Chevy pickup before Trace was there with Sam. Callie climbed into the bed of the truck and Trace laid Sam's head in her lap, then made sure Sam's feet were inside and slammed the tailgate.

Trace had an awful feeling of déjà vu. He took one look at Callie's stricken face and wondered how many more of these calamities she could survive. "Hold on," he said. "I'll drive as carefully as I can."

"Forget careful," she said. "Drive fast!"

When Trace slipped into the cab of the pickup he saw that neither Eli nor Hannah was wearing a seat belt. "Belt yourself in," he ordered Eli, as he snapped the center belt around Hannah.

Eli glared at him. "I don't have to do what you say."

"This truck isn't moving until you're belted in. If your uncle dies—"

"All right," Eli retorted. "You win!"

The click of the belt came at the same time Trace hit the gas, so that all three of them were thrown back against the worn leather seat.

The trip to the hospital in Bitter Creek would have been silent without Hannah there to comment. As it was, Trace had to force himself not to snap responses to the child's remarks.

"You drive fast!" she exclaimed.

"Your uncle is very sick," Trace said. "We have to get him to the hospital in a hurry."

"Is Uncle Sam gonna die?" Hannah asked, peering up at him.

"I hope not," Trace answered, avoiding her wide-eyed gaze by keeping his eyes on the road.

"My grampa died," Hannah said.

"I know," Trace answered.

"I had to wear my black velvet Sunday school dress with the white collar and Mommy bought me a brand-new pair of white socks with lace on them and I got a brand-new pair of black patent leather shoes with buckles."

"Uh-huh."

"I don't like to go to the hospital," Hannah noted.

"Me neither," Trace said.

"Can I see Gram at the hospital?"

"I suppose so. You'll have to ask your mother."

"Where's Mommy?" Hannah asked anxiously, looking around, suddenly realizing her mother wasn't in the cab with them.

"She's in the back of the truck with your uncle Sam."

When Hannah tried to get up to look out the back window, Trace held her in place. "You need to stay buckled in."

"I want to see my mommy!" she shrieked.

"We'll be at the hospital in a few minutes. You can see her then. Eli, talk to your sister," Trace ordered. "Tell her she can see your mom—"

"Sit down, Hannah," Eli said in a voice that cracked. "Mom's in back with Uncle Sam. I'm here. I'll take care of you."

The little girl leaned against her brother, who put an

arm around her shoulders. "I'm scared, Eli," she confided.

Eli glanced at Trace, then whispered to Hannah, "Me, too."

Trace had called ahead with his cell phone, and when he pulled up to the emergency entrance at the Bitter Creek Regional Hospital, two orderlies met them with a gurney. "Stay in the truck," he ordered Eli. "And keep your sister with you."

"But—"

"Don't argue!" he snapped.

As he helped lift Sam onto the gurney and the orderlies began rolling him inside, the doctor began his preliminary examination.

"How long has he been in this condition?" the doctor asked.

Trace looked at Callie. When she didn't answer he said, "I don't know."

"Did he take any pills?"

Again Trace waited for Callie to answer, but she seemed to be in a stupor. "I don't know. Sam's been a paraplegic for eleven years. His nephew found him passed out in his wheelchair. His sister told me he's been drinking heavily."

The doctor leaned over to smell Sam's breath and shook his head. "Could be alcohol poisoning," he said. "We'll do some tests and find out."

Trace had heard of alcohol poisoning, but mostly in relation to teenage boys at college fraternity parties who played drinking games and consumed way too much hard liquor. Too much alcohol caused the body's systems to shut down. Then you died.

"Will Sam be all right?" Eli called from the cab of the truck.

"We'll do our best," the doctor said, as he disappeared inside with Sam.

Trace followed with Callie, but they didn't get far before the doctor disappeared behind a set of doors with the words EMERGENCY ROOM and AUTHORIZED PERSONNEL ONLY in red block lettering.

Callie was approached by a nurse informing her that she would need to provide insurance information. Trace put a hand to the small of her back to urge her toward the chest-high reception desk, but she didn't move.

"Callie, are you all right?" he said in her ear.

She turned to look at him with eyes that were frighteningly vacant. A row of furrows appeared on her brow, and she looked around her as though she had no idea where she was.

The nurse behind the barrier laid a pile of forms in front of Callie. "These papers need to be filled out."

Trace stood a little behind Callie, biting his tongue to keep from offering to pay Sam's expenses. He was sure Callie wouldn't welcome the offer, and he didn't want to make things between them any worse than they already were.

Callie stared at the papers without speaking. She made no move to reach for the pen the nurse provided.

Trace took a step forward and said, "The patient is Sam Creed. His mother, Lauren Creed, is a patient here. Perhaps you can use her information for him."

"Do they both have the same insurance carrier?" the nurse asked as she began typing on the computer. "Oh. Oh, dear."

"What's wrong?" Trace asked.

"Mrs. Creed has no insurance carrier. She paid a $20,000 cash guarantee upon admittance. Unless Mr. Creed has insurance, I'll need another $20,000. Cashier's check or credit card, please."

Callie wavered on her feet. Her eyes brimmed with tears, which began to spill over. When she opened her mouth to speak, her voice came out in a croak. "I . . . I don't think . . . Isn't there any way . . . ? Can't you . . . ?"

Trace caught her as she fainted.

"Get a doctor over here!" he yelled. "I need somebody NOW!"

"Oh, my," the nurse said, rising to stare over the counter at Callie. "Is she sick, too?"

Trace didn't answer the woman. His heart was racing too fast, and he was too angry—with Callie, mostly, for wearing herself out, but also at fate, for putting so many obstacles in the way of what he wanted.

"Dammit, Callie," he muttered. "Why the hell haven't you been taking care of yourself?"

He knew the answer. Because she was too busy taking care of everybody else. Well, that was going to stop. He had plans for her that required her to be healthy and rested. Starting right now, he was going to make sure that her family started carrying their share of the load.

A doctor showed up and asked, "What seems to be the problem?"

"I think she's just worn to the bone," Trace said. "But maybe you ought to check her out. Have you got a bed where I can put her?"

"Of course," the doctor said.

Before they could take a step, the nurse behind the reception desk leaned over and said, "First, we'll need a cash guarantee."

Trace shifted Callie higher in his arms, as he met the nurse's gaze with eyes narrowed in fury. "My name is Trace Blackthorne. My father is Jackson Blackthorne. I'll be responsible for all the hospital expenses for Mrs. Monroe and her brother. Now I need someone to show me a bed where I can lay Mrs. Monroe down so the doctor can examine her."

Trace didn't feel a bit ashamed of using his father's name to get what he wanted. His family had donated the funds to build the Bitter Creek Regional Hospital, and his parents both served on the board. He'd worry later about what he was going to say to Callie when she confronted him about paying Creed hospital bills with Blackthorne money.

The doctor led Trace to an examining room, where he laid Callie on a paper-covered, padded table. As he stepped back, Callie's eyes fluttered open and she tried to sit up.

"What's going on?" she asked.

"You fainted," Trace replied, as he laid a palm on her shoulder to keep her prone.

"I'm fine," Callie said, trying once more to rise.

"Let the doctor take a look at you," Trace said.

Callie rolled her eyes, but remained prone. "This is ridiculous."

The doctor smiled at her and said, "This won't take long."

The doctor did a quick check of her eyes, pulse, blood

pressure, and temperature. "Have you been having dizzy spells? Blurred vision? Headaches?"

"No," Callie said. "I just . . ." She shot a look at Trace. "I'm just worn out," she said defiantly.

The doctor smiled again. "Then I prescribe a great deal of bed rest, Mrs. Monroe."

"I can't—"

Trace cut her off. "I'll make sure she gets it."

After the doctor had left the examining room, Callie slowly sat up. "What happened to Sam? Did the hospital agree to treat him?"

"Sam's being cared for right now."

"Where are my kids? They didn't see me faint, did they?"

"I told them to stay in the truck."

"How long ago was that?"

"I don't know. A while."

Callie scooted off the examining table. "I need to check on Sam and the kids." She was wobbly on her feet but shrugged off the hand Trace offered to keep her steady. "I'm fine."

"You will be, after you've had some rest," Trace corrected. He figured he'd take her to the hunting cabin, but that meant finding someone to take care of her kids. There was no backup for Callie at home.

Callie ignored him and headed toward the emergency waiting room, where she asked a nurse, "Is there any word on my brother, Sam Creed?"

At that moment, the doctor who'd examined Sam came through the emergency room doors.

"How is my brother?" Callie asked anxiously.

"Definitely alcohol poisoning," the doctor said. "I can't promise you he'll live. We'll have to wait and see."

"When will you know for sure?" Callie asked.

"We'll keep a close eye on him through the night. We should know more by tomorrow morning."

Trace heard Callie moan, deep in her throat. "Are you all right?" he asked.

She took a deep breath and let it out, then said, "I have to check on my kids."

She marched out of the hospital with Trace a step behind her. Even before they reached the truck, Trace realized her kids were no longer in it. He felt a clutch of panic.

"They're not here!" Callie said. "Oh, God. Where could they have gone?"

"They must have gone looking for us."

"But they weren't in the emergency waiting room. Were they?"

"I didn't see them," Trace said. "Let's go back inside."

They didn't find them in the waiting room. Trace shoved open the red-lettered doors, but a nurse caught him and said, "You don't belong in here."

"I'm looking for two kids."

"Look somewhere else," the nurse said.

He found Callie at the reception desk asking, "Have you seen two kids, a tall, skinny boy about ten and a towheaded little girl?"

"No, ma'am. I have not."

"Can you tell me what room Lauren Creed is in?" Trace said.

"Of course!" Callie exclaimed. "They know my mother's here. That must be where they went."

"Visiting hours are over," the nurse replied.

Trace narrowed his eyes and stared at her.

"Room 342," the nurse said. "But you can't—"

Trace grabbed Callie's hand and headed for the elevator before the nurse could finish her protest. In a matter of minutes, they stood outside the open door to room 342. They paused and listened, as the children's grandmother spoke.

"It sounds like Mr. Blackthorne is a very kind and helpful man," she said.

"He was mean!" Eli said. "He yelled at me."

Trace would have argued the point. He'd spoken sternly; he hadn't yelled.

"You know he was right to make you wear your seat belt," Mrs. Creed said. "And if he asked you to stay in the truck, I imagine he's probably wondering where you are."

Trace and Callie stepped through the doorway.

"Hi, Mom," Callie said.

"How's Sam?" her mother asked.

"Hanging in there. The doctor says we'll know more by tomorrow morning."

Trace watched as the two women exchanged a look. He could see that Mrs. Creed realized the seriousness of Sam's situation.

Trace was surprised at how healthy Callie's mother appeared. One arm was tied in a white sling against her chest, but she was wearing a pretty robin's-egg-blue robe, and her long auburn hair was tied up in a youthful ponytail that left soft curls framing her face. She looked much younger and prettier than he remembered.

And now she was a single woman.

For an instant, he wondered whether his father would ever consider divorcing his mother to marry this woman. He would give his eyeteeth to know what had happened between Lauren Creed and his father all those years ago. Could the tie that had once bound them really have survived all these years? Then he thought of himself and Callie, and realized that the ties of the past could survive a great deal.

"Good afternoon, Trace," Mrs. Creed said with a welcoming smile that seemed genuine. "I hope you haven't been searching for these two scamps for very long."

"Callie and I figured out pretty quickly where they must have gone," Trace said.

"We thank you for your help," she said in a voice that told him he had her permission to leave now. She tightened her hold on the little girl, who was cuddled up next to her.

Eli slid off the bed and turned to confront him. "Why did you come up here? We don't want you here!"

He looked at Mrs. Creed as he explained to Eli, "Your mom is worn out. I'll be arranging for someone to come and stay with you and your sister, while she gets some rest."

Eli's jaw dropped. He quickly backed up toward the head of the bed and reached for his grandmother's hand. "You can't do that? Can he, Gram?"

"What's wrong with Callie?" Mrs. Creed asked, her gray-green eyes wide with alarm as she surveyed her daughter.

Callie rolled her eyes again. "Nothing's wrong with me that a good night's sleep won't cure."

"She fainted downstairs," Trace countered.

Callie glared at him.

"Is that true, Callie?" her mother asked.

"I was just tired, Mom."

"She needs a break," Trace said, pressing his advantage. "And I intend to see that she gets it. I have a hunting cabin where Callie can have some peace and quiet and get all the sleep she needs."

"What is it you plan to do with my daughter's children while she's getting some rest?" Mrs. Creed asked.

Trace cleared his throat. "I figured I'd take them home to Three Oaks and . . . uh . . . I thought I'd ask Rosalita—the Mexican woman who took care of me when I was growing up—to come over and stay with them."

"My son Luke can take care of them."

"That may be true, ma'am," Trace said. "But he wasn't home when we left. And won't he have school during the day? Somebody'll have to take care of the little girl while he's gone."

"How long did you plan to keep my daughter away from home?" Callie's mother asked.

"A night or two, I suppose."

"Mom, this is ridiculous," Callie protested. "I can sleep at home!"

"But apparently you haven't been sleeping," her mother said sharply. "You look exhausted. Someone has to make you take better care of yourself. Trace's plan sounds like the perfect solution."

"But, Mom—"

"What will happen to us if you fall ill, Callie? I think two days of rest sounds entirely reasonable."

Callie's chin jutted mulishly, but she finally said, "Fine."

"You can wait here with your mother while I take Eli and Hannah home," Trace said to Callie. "I'll be back to pick you up later."

Before Callie could object, her mother said, "Good. That'll give Callie and me a chance to catch up."

"I want Mom to come home with us!" Eli said, grabbing hold of the headrail of the bed with both hands. "Otherwise, I'm not leaving."

Mrs. Creed turned to Eli and said, "I need you to keep an eye on Hannah while your mother gets some rest."

"But, Gram—"

"We do what must be done, Eli, whether we like it or not," Mrs. Creed said. "You and Hannah have to give up a little of your mother's time and attention so that she can regain her strength. You don't want her to get sick, do you?"

Trace saw the stricken look on Eli's face as his gaze shifted to his mother's drawn features. "All right, Gram," he said at last.

Mrs. Creed gave Hannah a kiss on the forehead, smoothed her golden curls, and said, "Go with Mr. Blackthorne, Hannah."

Trace took the few steps necessary to put him close enough to reach Hannah. The little girl never hesitated; she simply reached her arms out to Trace as he picked her up. She clung to him like a possum, her arms surrounding his neck, her legs wrapped around his waist.

Hannah murmured, "Bye, Mommy," against Trace's throat.

Trace turned to the recalcitrant boy and said, "Come on, Eli. Time to go."

Eli let go of the rail and hugged his grandmother around the neck. "When are you coming home?" he asked her plaintively.

"Soon," she promised. "Very soon."

"You won't be gone long, will you, Mom?" the boy asked, turning to Callie.

"I'll be home tomorrow," Callie said, brushing at Eli's stubborn cowlick.

"Day after tomorrow," Trace corrected.

"Day after tomorrow," Callie conceded after a glance at her mother's pursed lips.

The boy headed for the doorway without looking at Trace. "I'll meet you at the truck," he said sullenly. He slipped past Trace, then galloped down the hall.

Trace had already turned to leave, when Callie stopped him.

"Trace."

He turned his head to meet her gaze and said, "Yes, Callie?"

"Take good care of my children."

"Like they were my own."

Trace saw a flicker of some emotion in her eyes, but it was gone before he could identify it.

Eli was not only sitting in the pickup by the time Trace got there, he was already buckled in. Trace slid Hannah in from the driver's side, buckled her in, and headed the pickup back toward Three Oaks. He used his cell phone to call Rosalita, who still lived in a house at Bitter Creek, though she had long since retired. She was delighted to hear from him and more than willing to stay with the children. But she was baby-sitting her own grandchildren at the moment.

"As soon as my daughter comes home, I will have her drop me off there. She promised not to be late," Rosalita said. "But she isn't always on time."

Trace disconnected the call feeling both relieved and anxious. He glanced at Eli and Hannah. If Luke wasn't home when he got to Three Oaks, he was going to end up doing some baby-sitting himself. He called Callie and advised her about the possible delay. She told him she thought she might spend some time sitting with Sam, and that he should look for her there, if she wasn't still with her mother.

"Do you have any idea how we can get hold of your uncle Luke?" he asked Eli.

"He's probably home by now," Eli said.

Using his cell phone, Trace called the number for Three Oaks that Eli gave him, but there was no answer. Trace figured he'd better give Luke some warning of the situation he'd find when he did get home, so he wasn't scared out of his wits.

"Any other suggestions where I might find him?"

Eli was silent for a moment before he said, "He stayed with a friend last night."

"What's his friend's name?"

A hesitation, then, "Jeff."

This was harder than pulling nails from oak. "Jeff who?" Trace asked, working hard to keep the irritation out of his voice.

"I don't know his last name," Eli said.

Trace gave up. If Luke didn't arrive home before

Rosalita showed up, Trace would leave instructions with Rosalita to have the boy call his grandmother.

Callie had left the house unlocked, a remnant of range hospitality from the days when no stranger was turned away without a cup of coffee and the offer of a night's lodging. Eli let himself in and headed straight upstairs to his room. Trace let him go.

"I'm hungry," Hannah said.

Trace looked at his watch. It was long past suppertime. He set Hannah down in the kitchen and said, "What should we fix for supper?"

"Blueberry pancakes," Hannah said without hesitation.

He didn't argue, because it sounded simple—except for the blueberry part—unless Callie was the sort who made pancakes from scratch. "Where does your mom keep the pancake mix?" he asked.

Hannah pointed to a cupboard next to the refrigerator. Trace opened the cupboard and couldn't believe his luck. On the shelf stood a box of Krusteaz blueberry pancake mix that said on the front, "Complete. Just Add Water."

"Thank the Lord for small favors," he murmured.

"I can help," Hannah said, crossing to a drawer to take out a set of aluminum measuring cups. "I can measure the water."

"You bet. Uh. Where's a bowl?"

Hannah pointed him to the correct cupboard. While he was retrieving a bowl, she pulled a kitchen chair over to the counter next to the sink and climbed up on it.

"Let's see," Trace said, looking at the directions on the back. "How many pancakes should we make?"

"The most," Hannah said with a grin. "I like pancakes."

Trace found himself grinning back at her. "So do I." He found the recipe for twenty-one to twenty-three four-inch pancakes, quickly measured out three cups of pancake mix, then said to Hannah, "We need two and one-quarter cups of water."

He turned on the faucet, then helped keep Hannah from losing her balance as she held the measuring cup under the water long enough to fill it. She spilled a bit of it before it got into the mix and looked up at him to see his reaction.

"No problem," he said. "We'll just add a little more at the end."

"Hmmm," he said after they'd added the water. "It says to use a wire whisk. Wonder where we might find one of those."

"I know!" Hannah said. She clambered down from the chair and crossed to a drawer beside the refrigerator, then pulled it open and rummaged through until she found a wire whisk. She held it up to him, beaming. "Here it is!"

Once the batter was whipped, Trace realized he hadn't heated up a skillet. "How are we going to cook these pancakes?" he asked Hannah.

She pointed to the top of the refrigerator, where he saw an electric skillet.

"Aha!" he said, retrieving it. "How about something to keep the pancakes from sticking to the pan?"

"Mommy uses the stuff with 433 servings per can," Hannah said.

"Wow! That many." Trace couldn't imagine a can that contained 433 servings of anything that would fit in one of the small wooden cupboards. "All right. I give up. What stuff?"

Hannah giggled. "PAM!"

Trace thought she was kidding. When he found the PAM in the cupboard where Hannah told him to look, it did, indeed, contain 433 servings—of a one-third-second spray. He generously sprayed the electric skillet with fifteen servings of PAM.

Trace was just dripping batter into the skillet from a large spoon, when Luke stepped into the kitchen. He automatically stuck his hat on a horseshoe hat rack inside the door, then stopped dead and stared. "What are you doing here?" he demanded.

Trace turned to face him, batter still dripping off the spoon, and said, "Your brother Sam's in the hospital with alcohol poisoning. Your sister's there with him and your mother. I'm baby-sitting."

"Is Sam going to be all right?" Luke asked.

"The doctor won't know for sure until tomorrow morning."

"You spilled some!" Hannah announced, pointing to the pool of blueberry pancake batter on the hardwood floor.

Trace set the spoon down, tore a paper towel off the roll attached under the cupboard, and handed it to Hannah. "Would you clean it up for me?"

"Okay," Hannah said, sitting down and sliding off the chair. She swiped at the batter, but her efforts merely spread it into a wider mess on the floor.

Luke crossed and bent down on one knee to help her. He stood with the paper towel in his hand and confronted

Trace. "You can leave now. I can handle things from here."

"There's a woman named Rosalita coming over to take care of the kids. She shouldn't be too late," Trace said.

"Tell her not to come," Luke said. "I can take care of things around here."

"What about tomorrow?"

Luke stared at him, uncomprehending.

"When you go to school," Trace said. "Who's going to take care of Hannah?"

"Callie should be home by then."

"Callie's taking a break for a couple of days to get some rest. Your mom insisted on it," he said when Luke opened his mouth to argue. "She won't be back until day after tomorrow."

"I can stay home from school tomorrow," Luke said stubbornly.

Hannah was back on her chair and announced, "The pancakes are burning."

"We forgot the spatula," Trace said to Hannah.

Luke grabbed a spatula from the drawer next to the sink, then stepped up to the skillet and flipped the pancakes. When he was done, he turned, holding the spatula as though it were a knife, to keep Trace at bay. "I said leave, and I mean it."

When Trace looked at the teenage boy, he didn't see the fisted hands posed aggressively or the narrow shoulders squared for action. He saw the freckles on his nose and the fear in his eyes.

Before he could insist on staying till Rosalita showed up, Eli stepped into the kitchen from the hallway.

"I thought I heard your voice," Eli said to Luke. "I'm

glad you're home. I was afraid this guy was going to hang around all night."

"I'm staying till Rosalita shows up," Trace said quietly. "To make sure she's welcomed when she gets here."

"I can take care of things around here all by myself," Luke insisted.

"The pancakes are burning!" Hannah said agitatedly.

As Luke stacked the pancakes one on top of the other, he said to Eli, "Get me a plate, will you? These things are going to be black on both sides."

Eli edged past Trace to retrieve a pretty flowered plate from the cupboard and handed it to Luke. Luke stacked the pancakes on it and said, "You and Hannah can start on these."

"Those are burned," Eli complained.

Luke glanced sideways at Trace, then back at Eli and hissed, "Just sit down and eat!"

"There's no silverware on the table," Eli pointed out.

"Then get some!" Luke said as he dipped batter for four more pancakes onto the smoking skillet.

"I can get it," Hannah offered. She leaned over and yanked open the silverware drawer, but pulled it out too far. When it came free, silverware clattered to the floor, followed by the drawer itself, which landed with a loud thump.

"Uh-oh." Hannah quickly climbed down from the chair to gather up the conglomeration of spoons and forks and knives, then glanced at Luke to see his reaction.

"Dammit, Hannah! You know better than that!" Luke yelled.

Hannah let out a wail and burst into tears. She looked

around for a friendly face, but neither her brother nor her uncle offered her any comfort.

Trace held out his arms, and the little girl came running to him. He gathered her up and felt her soft breath against his throat as he patted her on the back. "Don't worry, Hannah. Eli and Luke will take care of cleaning up everything."

Luke stared at him, furious and helpless.

Trace gestured Eli toward the silverware on the floor and said, "Help yourself."

"I don't need you to tell me what to do!" Eli said.

"Those pancakes might taste better with a little butter and syrup," Trace suggested.

He could see the two boys were torn. They didn't want to follow his suggestion, but they certainly didn't want to eat their pancakes dry, either. Luke decided the matter by crossing to the refrigerator and hauling out some butter on a chipped plate and a plastic container of Aunt Jemima syrup.

"Here," Luke said to Eli, as he dropped them both on the table.

"Luke," Trace said.

"What?" Luke retorted.

"Your pancakes are burning."

Chapter 12

"I DON'T UNDERSTAND WHY YOU GANGED UP with Trace Blackthorne against your own daughter," Callie said to her mother, feeling confused and surprisingly antagonistic.

"You need the rest," her mother said reasonably. "And it will give Trace a chance to spend time with his son."

Callie stared at her mother, her breath caught in her chest. "What makes you think—"

"I can count, Callie."

"You're mistaken. I—"

"Nolan told me the truth," her mother said. "Don't blame him for giving away your secret, Callie. He had no choice. I thought it was odd that if you got pregnant during the Christmas holiday, your baby should weigh barely six pounds, when it was supposedly three weeks overdue. I speculated that your calculations must have been off, or that there might be something wrong with Eli. Nolan was afraid I would say something to your father, and he knew that would be disastrous."

Callie sank into the molded plastic chair beside her mother's bed. "Why didn't you say something sooner?"

"I always hoped you'd tell me the truth yourself."

"Trace and I . . . I loved him, Mom." She looked up and was surprised to find tears in her mother's eyes.

"I thought maybe he didn't love you enough to marry you when he found out you were pregnant," her mother said. "But when I see how he looks at you now . . . What happened, Callie?"

"You're mistaken about Trace's feelings for me, Mom. And you know why I couldn't marry him. Daddy would have disowned me."

"True. But he couldn't have stopped you. Not if you really wanted to marry Trace."

"With Sam stuck in a wheelchair, you needed me at home."

"Also true. We might very well have lost Three Oaks without your help." Her mother's eyes focused on her hands, which were knotted in her lap. She glanced up at Callie and asked, "Do you regret the choice you made?"

Callie was startled by the question. "You're the one who taught me about sacrifice. I learned it at your knee. How could I not stay and help?"

"You haven't answered my question. Do you regret the choice you made?"

Callie's throat had swollen until it hurt to swallow. "Yes."

She hadn't realized she was going to admit such a thing until the word was spoken. She saw the pain in her mother's eyes.

"I know how that feels," her mother said quietly.

Callie went perfectly still. She was afraid to ask what her mother meant. She was afraid she already knew.

"Your father was right to be jealous."

"I don't want to hear this," Callie said, rising in agitation. "Don't tell me you didn't love Daddy. I won't believe you!"

"I loved him," her mother said. "I was never 'in love' with him. I didn't know what it meant to be 'in love' until it was too late."

"I told you I don't want to hear this!" Callie said, heading for the door.

"I was already pregnant with you when I realized I was in love with Jackson Blackthorne."

Callie stopped, the doorknob in her hand. She leaned her forehead against the cool wood. "Oh, Mom."

"I had to decide whether to take you away from your father, and let a man he hated raise his child. Or stay with your father, and give up the man I had come to love more than life itself. I made the sacrifice, Callie. I did the right thing. As you did, when the time came for you to make a choice. You chose to help your family, because we needed you, rather than steal away with the man you loved."

Callie whirled and confronted her mother. "Are you telling me I made the wrong choice?"

Her mother stared back at her soberly. "What do you think?"

"You and Daddy had a good life together. Nolan and I had a wonderful marriage."

"But something was always missing between you and Nolan, wasn't it?"

Callie didn't know how her mother could be so perceptive. Unless she had experienced the same yearning for what had been lost. It hurt to think of her parents' marriage as anything less than perfect, even though she'd known for a long time that things weren't right between them.

"At least Trace came back for you," her mother said.

"He came back because his father had a heart attack and needed him to manage the ranch."

Her mother shook her head. "Trace could have left weeks ago. Why do you think he's still here, Callie?"

"How should I know?"

"What if you had a second chance? Would you make the same choice?" her mother asked.

"Are you telling me you don't need me anymore? Are you telling me you can manage Three Oaks without me, if I were to leave?"

"I don't know," her mother said. "We'd certainly struggle without you. We might even lose Three Oaks. But things have changed. The ranch doesn't mean as much to me as it did to your father."

"I can't believe you're saying these things! Three Oaks has been paid for with the blood and bone of Creeds for generations. We'd be losing a piece of ourselves if we gave it up!"

"Then I guess you have your answer," her mother said. "You would still make the sacrifice."

Callie frowned. "There's no sacrifice to be made. Trace doesn't love me anymore."

"Do you love him?" her mother asked.

Callie avoided the question. "What difference does it make how I feel?"

"What about Eli?" her mother asked. "Are you going to tell Trace he has a son."

"I can't. He might try to get custody of Eli, if he knew the truth."

"That's too bad," her mother said. "A boy needs his father."

"Eli had a father!" Callie snapped. "His father died."

"Trace and Eli are the same blood and bone. If you love Trace, you'd be a fool to give him up again. Talk to him. Maybe you two can work things out."

"You're being ridiculous, Mom. I can't go back."

"No, but you can move forward."

Callie stared at her mother, her heart pounding, her hands knotted. "I need to go check on Sam," she said abruptly.

Callie pulled open the door and headed down the hall toward the elevator.

She was having trouble digesting everything her mother had said. How could she even talk about moving forward, when the cost of doing so might be the loss of Three Oaks? It was frightening to think her mother didn't feel as strongly about keeping the ranch as Callie did. What if her mother sold Three Oaks to Blackjack? She wouldn't dare! Not after the fight her father had waged against his mortal enemy. Callie would never allow that to happen. Three Oaks belonged to the Creeds. She would never give it up.

She checked with the reception desk on the main floor to find out which room was Sam's, then headed toward the elevator.

"Visiting hours—"

That was all Callie heard before the elevator doors closed behind her. She had to stop herself from running down the fourth floor hall, and she anxiously shoved open the door to Sam's room, wishing she could talk to her brother about the things her mother had said. But the days when she and Sam had been confidantes were long past.

Her brother was hooked up to a monitor that beeped slowly and steadily. Callie had never heard a more beautiful sound. She crossed to the bed and looked down at Sam. His eyes were closed, his lashes dark against his pale cheeks. She hadn't been there a full minute before the door opened and a doctor came in. He didn't seem at all surprised to find her there, and she realized the nurse downstairs must have paged him.

"I'm Callie Creed Monroe. How is my brother?"

"He had a narrow escape," the doctor said. "If you hadn't found him when you did, he wouldn't have made it."

Callie swallowed hard. She grabbed the bedrail to steady herself.

"Are you all right?" the doctor asked.

"I'm fine. How soon before Sam can come home?"

"I'd like to do a few tests to see what shape his liver and kidneys are in."

"Is there something wrong with them?"

Rather than answer, the doctor asked, "How much alcohol would you say your brother consumes in a twenty-four-hour period?"

Callie hesitated, then realized this was a time when honesty was required. "I'm not really sure. He used to have a couple of shots in the evening, but lately . . . it's been a great deal more."

"He has to stop drinking, or he's going to kill himself."

Callie eyed the doctor bleakly.

"Have you thought about AA?"

"I don't think Sam would go," Callie said.

"Have you talked to him about it?"

Callie was ashamed to admit that she hadn't confronted Sam about his drinking in a long time. She used to complain when he didn't get the bills paid on time, but it had been easier to take the burden on herself than to keep after him to do it. She had been too consumed by everything else that had to be done to worry about Sam's drinking problem.

She looked at her brother and saw a man she didn't know. His cheeks were sunken, and there were bags of dissipation under his eyes. His hair badly needed a cut, and he hadn't shaved for days. Callie felt helpless to help him, too overwhelmed by all the other responsibilities in her life to add one more. She felt the knot of despair growing in her throat. Sam's face began to blur from the tears welling in her eyes.

"I'll speak to him when he wakes up," she told the doctor. "Is it all right if I sit with him for a while?"

"Sure. I'll tell the nurse I said it was okay."

Callie stood beside Sam's bed after the doctor had left, staring at her brother. She took a deep breath and let it out. She could handle this. She could handle anything. She always had. She wasn't going to fall apart now.

She brushed the brown curls from Sam's brow. "But you're going to have to do your part, Sam," she whispered, as she bent and pressed a kiss to his brow.

"How is he?"

Callie turned to find Trace in the doorway. "The doctor says he's going to make it."

"Good. Are you ready to go?"

"I think I should go home to Three Oaks," she said.

He didn't argue, simply walked over, scooped her up in his arms, and headed for the open doorway. "You'll thank me for this later," he said.

Callie was too tired to struggle. Besides, she needed peace and quiet to think about everything her mother had told her. To consider what to do about Sam. To consider how to save Three Oaks from the wiley Blackthornes.

"How are the kids?" she asked, surprising herself with a yawn.

"Hannah and I made blueberry pancakes for supper—with only fifteen servings of PAM."

Callie smiled. "Good for you. Did Luke get home? Did he give you any trouble?"

"He was upset, but he got over it," Trace reassured her. "We were both glad when Rosalita showed up. We were about to flip a coin to see who washed the dishes."

Callie laughed, something she hadn't thought she'd be able to do after everything that had happened. "Oh, Trace. You're good for me."

She bit her lip on the admission and eyed him askance. His face was shadowed with the beard he hadn't had time to shave—because he'd been taking care of her family. She reached up and brushed her hand across the rough bristles.

He leaned away from her and said, "Don't."

She laid her head against his shoulder and pressed a hand against his heart. She thought she could almost feel it beating. She closed her eyes and gave a sigh. "I'm so tired."

She heard the automatic doors swish open, and then felt the cool night air on her face. She felt Trace shifting her as he opened the car door and then the soft leather under her thighs as he set her down. She half-opened her eyes and smiled. She was sitting in the oversize Buick 88 convertible. "I like your wheels."

"Thanks."

She tried to keep her eyes open, so she could see where Trace was taking her, but they drifted closed as soon as the car got on the highway. "How far?" she murmured.

"Twenty minutes," he said.

"I might have to take a nap."

"You can use me for a pillow if you like."

"All right," she said, sliding down and laying her head on his thigh. She grasped his leg up high to have something to keep her steady and felt his thigh muscles tense.

Once again, he admonished her, "Don't."

"I thought you wanted to have your wicked way with me," she said.

"I do. But I'd like you to be wide awake and willing."

"I'm awake," she mumbled.

He snorted. "When we get there, would you rather have a shower or a bath?"

"A bubble bath would be lovely." She sighed. "I don't suppose you keep bath bubbles at a hunting cabin."

"I might be able to scrounge some up."

"Mmmm. I hope so."

The next thing Callie knew, Trace was shaking her shoulder.

"Wake up. We're here."

She dragged herself upright, stretching and yawning. There were lights on inside the cabin. Although, she doubted anyone but the Blackthornes would call the two-story wood house a cabin. It looked more like an antebellum mansion, complete with pillars holding up a second-story porch. The house was surrounded by trees and bushes that encroached on the narrow path that led to the front door.

She followed Trace to the front door, which was odd in itself, because the front door in Texas was reserved for funerals and strangers. "How long has this 'cabin' been here?" she asked.

"A hundred years or so."

"How come I've never seen it or heard about it?"

"Nobody's used it since the fifties."

She lifted a brow. "Eisenhower slept here?"

Trace smiled. "Yep. Teddy Roosevelt, too."

Callie laughed. "Can I sleep in his bed?"

"The furniture's all covered, except for the little bit I've been using. I had the plumbing and electricity fixed. Otherwise, it's pretty rustic."

"I thought you were staying at your parents' house."

"I was until Dad got out of the hospital. Once he came home, I moved in here."

That way, he could come and go without his every move being monitored by his father, Callie realized.

"I still have supper with my parents," he said. "When my schedule allows it."

Callie stepped into an enormous Victorian parlor and could only imagine what the room contained, based on the outlines of the sheets that covered the furniture. Trace had uncovered a wing chair covered in maroon brocade, which was angled toward the immense fieldstone fireplace. An enormous buffalo head was mounted above it. "Nice," she said with a cheeky grin.

"My decorator thanks you," he quipped back. "The bathroom's this way."

Callie made a sound in her throat. "I just realized I don't have anything clean with me to put on."

"Eli helped Rosalita pick out some things for you to wear. I'll bring them in once you're settled in the tub."

"It seems you've thought of everything."

"I have my own reasons for wanting you rested, Callie," he reminded her.

Callie wished he hadn't spoken. It had been nice pretending that Trace was being so considerate because he cared for her. "I haven't forgotten anything," she said.

They had arrived at the bathroom, and she turned to face him. "I can take it from here."

"All right. I'll go get your bag."

Callie stared at the old-fashioned, claw-footed tub. She would much rather have lain down in it and gone to sleep than fill it with water. But her back and shoulders ached with tension, and she knew a hot bath would help her to relax. She turned on the water, and the ancient pipes groaned like an old lady getting up out of her rocker.

She adjusted the water temperature and stripped off her clothes, leaving them in a heap on the floor next to her boots. She looked through the medicine cabinet for something to make bubbles, but found only shampoo and cream rinse—which she took out and set on the floor beside the tub—Trace's razor and shaving cream, toothpaste, aspirin, and a pine-scented aftershave. No bubble bath.

She didn't wait for the tub to fill, just stepped in and sat down. Then she realized she didn't have soap or a washcloth. She stood up just as Trace walked back into the room. She grappled for a shower curtain to cover herself, but there wasn't one.

"I've seen you naked before, Callie."

But at the time, she hadn't borne two children. Callie laid one hand across her belly, where she knew two silver stretch marks remained, and the other across her breasts, which weren't nearly as perky now as they'd been eleven years ago.

"Sit down, Callie. I've brought your bubbles."

Callie couldn't move. She was caught by the lambent look in Trace's eyes. He reached toward her tentatively, as though to touch her. "Don't," she said.

He withdrew his hand and poured a powdered substance into the tub, which quickly filled the room with the pungent scent of apples and the tub with foaming bubbles. She sank into the water. "Oh. That's my favorite. How did you know?"

"I asked Eli."

"And he knew?" she asked, looking up at Trace.

"No. He thought you liked the lavender. Hannah told me to take the apple."

"That's her favorite, too," Callie said with a smile. She realized she was no longer self-conscious about her nudity. But she wasn't precisely relaxed, either. "I usually don't do this with an audience," she said, as she lifted a handful of bubbles to cover her nipples, which had peaked beneath Trace's steady gaze.

"Go ahead and wet your hair," he said.

"What?"

He bent over and picked up the shampoo. "Wet your hair, and I'll wash it for you."

Callie slid down in the tub until her hair was in the water, grateful for the blanket of bubbles that hid her from Trace's penetrating gaze. When she came up, the water sluiced off all the bubbles, and her slick, wet body was exposed to Trace's gaze. The avid look in his eyes made her blood sing.

She turned her back to him and said, "Shampoo away."

He dribbled cold shampoo onto her scalp, but his hands quickly warmed it. She leaned her head back as his strong, callused hands massaged her scalp.

"That feels wonderful," she said with a groan of pleasure.

"Lean forward." He angled her head forward as his fingers worked out the tension in her neck and shoulders. His tender ministrations soothed the ache inside her. She shivered as his touch slowed. She was being seduced, but she didn't care. She wanted him. She felt the need rise inside her to be touched in all the places he hadn't yet touched.

"You can stop that in about fifty years," she murmured.

"Rinse," he said abruptly.

Her eyes flickered open, and she turned to look at him over her shoulder. "Rinse?"

His blue eyes were heavy-lidded, his lips rigid and full. She recognized the signs of arousal.

"Rinse your hair," he said in a husky voice. "Then I can wash the rest of you."

Callie gulped and looked at the soap and washcloth that lay on the toilet seat. "Where did those come from?"

"There's a basket of soaps and towels at the other end of the tub."

"Oh," she said.

"Rinse," he ordered.

Callie slid into the lukewarm water and rinsed her hair.

And remembered the deal she had made with Trace. Sex for money. Trace didn't really want her. Well, he did. But only for one purpose, and it had nothing to do with love.

She rose out of the water, hair slicked back, arms crossed over her breasts, and announced, "I can wash myself."

"I don't doubt it," he said. "But I want to do it."

"Give me one good reason why I should let you."

"Because I never got to do it eleven years ago."

Callie understood his regret because she felt it so keenly herself. "All right," she said at last. "Go ahead."

He wet the cloth in the tub, then soaped it. He stared at her for so long, Callie finally asked, "What's the problem?"

He grinned and admitted, "I can't decide where to start."

She laughed and raised her arms. "I usually start under here."

He chuckled and swiped at her underarms with the soapy rag. It didn't take him long to get to her breasts. They must have been just filthy, Callie thought, because it took him forever to wipe them clean. Her breath was coming in shallow pants by the time he worked his way down her ribs to her belly.

He hesitated, and she felt a soapy fingertip trace its way across her flesh.

"Those are stretch marks," she said, her hands tightly gripping the edges of the tub to keep from shoving his hand away. "I got them when I was pregnant with Eli."

"I figured that," he said quietly. He looked into her

eyes. "I wish . . ." His bare hand slid beneath the water to cover her womb. "I wish my child had been growing here."

Callie shoved his hand away and scrambled to her feet, nearly falling as she slipped on the slick tub. "Don't you have a damned towel around here?" she asked, as she looked around for something to cover her nakedness.

Calmly, he stood and retrieved a towel from a shelf behind her. He opened it up and held it for her, forcing her to step out of the tub and into his arms. He wrapped her tightly in the towel, then lifted her in his arms and carried her down the hall.

"Where are you taking me?" she demanded.

"To bed."

She began to struggle. "Put me down. I'm not going to sleep with you, Trace. I'll find some other way to pay my father's estate taxes. I don't want to do this. We can't recapture the past. It's useless to try. I—"

He leaned over and pulled down the coverlet on a standard-size sleigh bed, then dropped her on the sheets and snatched away the towel. She scrambled under the covers and pulled them up to her neck. "Where are my clothes?"

"You don't need any." Snaps popped as he pulled his Western shirt open from breastbone to navel and dragged it out of his jeans. He yanked off his boots, then unbuckled his belt, unzipped his jeans and stripped them off, along with his briefs, and joined her in bed.

"I won't be able to sleep with you in this bed," Callie complained. "It's too small. There's no room for both of us."

"There's plenty of room in the middle," he said, as his

hand curved around her waist. He dragged her back against him, spooning her hips into his. She could feel the heat of him down the length of her back, and the undeniable proof of his arousal against her thigh. She struggled against his hold, but without success.

"Go to sleep, Callie. I'm not going to touch you."

"You're touching me everywhere!"

"I'm not going to make love to you," he corrected.

"What is it you want from me?" Callie said. "I have to tell you the suspense is killing me."

"I want you to close your eyes and go to sleep."

"That's all?"

"For now."

A breath shuddered out of her, and she relaxed her body against him. *For now.* That meant there would be other demands later. If she was smart, she'd get some sleep, so she'd have the energy to argue her way out of trouble when the time came.

His skin felt warm, and the masculine hairs on his arms and legs made her tingle where they brushed against her. He laid his bristly cheek against her shoulder, then caressed it with his lips.

She stiffened. "You said—"

"It's only a kiss, Callie. Go to sleep."

Callie closed her eyes. When she opened them again, it was morning. And Trace still held her in his arms.

She looked out the bedroom window at the pastel sky and realized it was not quite dawn, the time she normally woke up. But she still felt tired. Apparently one night of sleep didn't make up for weeks of nights when she'd lain awake and worried. Callie was glad she didn't have to get out of bed to do the myriad tasks that were her responsibility at Three Oaks.

She carefully rolled over so she was facing Trace, who was still asleep. Or maybe not, she realized, when a callused hand began snaking its way up her leg.

"What are you doing?" she whispered.

"Making up for lost time," he replied.

A moment later, she was flat on her back, and Trace was on top of her. His knee came up to force her legs apart, so his aroused body fit hot and hard in the cradle of her thighs.

"Oh," she said.

"Oh, indeed," he said with a smile.

She reached up to caress the dark stubble on his cheek. This time he didn't stop her. He leaned his cheek against her hand, rubbing himself against her like a sleek cat.

She ran her hand down his throat and over his shoulder, threaded her fingers through the hair on his chest, brushed the crest of his nipple, then traced each rib. Her hand followed the curve and play of muscle and bone all the way down his flank and then around to his buttocks. "I love to touch you," she said.

"I love the way you touch," he replied as his mouth closed over a budding nipple.

Callie's body arched, and she moaned with pleasure. She tugged on his hair, forcing his head up, leaning down greedily to find his mouth.

They were both ravenous. They had spent too many years without each other, and their previous encounter had only whetted their appetites. There was no need for foreplay. No desire to prolong the merging of their two bodies. Trace slid his hands beneath her and joined them with a single thrust.

They made love in a frenzy of demanding touches, love bites, and violent kisses, until Callie's body ached with need.

"Come with me, Callie," Trace said in a ragged voice. "Don't turn away from me now."

Callie didn't want to feel so much, didn't want their coupling to fill the empty spaces inside her soul.

But it did.

She tried to convince herself that it was only sex, that she was giving Trace no more than he had bought and paid for. But the ache inside her was more than the need for physical satiation. And what he gave to her was more than physical pleasure.

Afterward, she lay enfolded in Trace's arms, their bodies spooned together once again.

"I have to pick up some clean clothes at my parents' house this morning," Trace said. "Will you come with me?"

"Do you think that's a good idea?"

"I want to spend time with you, but I've got a lot of work to do today. Anything that keeps us together is a good idea."

Callie felt a small burst of pleasure inside and squelched it. They hadn't been making love; they'd been having sex. "I want to check on Hannah."

"No problem."

With any luck, she could convince Trace to drop her off at Three Oaks. She'd taken a night off to rest. And she'd given him what he'd paid for. Now she had to get back to work.

"I'll be glad to come with you," she said, as she ran a finger down his breastbone. "But I think we'd better get dressed now."

Trace captured her mouth in a lingering kiss. "I have no problem with letting you get dressed . . . later."

Chapter 13

CALLIE REALIZED SHE WAS ACTUALLY NERVOUS at the prospect of entering the legendary, thirty-thousand-square-foot ranch house at Bitter Creek that was better known as the Castle.

She'd seen photographs of the house in *Texas Monthly*, when they'd done a feature on famous Southwest Texas ranches. The chandeliers had been made by Tiffany in the late nineteenth century, and the furniture was Chippendale and Hepplewhite. The engraved silver had come from the first Blackthorne's English estate, and several portraits of Blackthorne ancestors had been done by famous artists, although she couldn't remember which ancestors or which artists.

As Trace drove under the crescent of black wrought iron that spelled out BITTER CREEK CATTLE COMPANY, she asked, "Is there any chance we're going to run into your father?"

"You can count on it."

Callie made a face. "How about your sister?"

"Summer doesn't spend much time in the house. She's usually out riding."

"What about your brother Owen?"

"He visits on occasion. I haven't seen him since your father's funeral. I think your sister gave him an earful, and he's out hunting down your stolen horses."

Callie looked at Trace in surprise. "Owen didn't hold out much chance to me that we'd recover them."

"I doubt you will. But my brother seems determined to try."

Callie tried not to let herself hope. Hope could turn into disappointment too easily, and she couldn't stand any more disappointment.

The road turned from dirt to asphalt about a mile from the ranch house. Trace drove past the magnolias lining the circular drive in front of the house and kept going until he reached the back door, where he parked the convertible in one of several paved spaces.

Callie hung back, but Trace waited at the kitchen door for her. "Welcome to the Castle," he said as she took a step inside.

"It's certainly as big as a castle," Callie said in an awed voice.

Trace grinned. "When I was younger, I kept asking why there were no turrets and what they did with the moat."

Callie gawked at the kitchen, which was nearly half the size of the ground floor at Three Oaks. The fourteen-foot ceiling was trimmed in elaborate crown molding, and an antique paddle fan in the center slowly moved the air-conditioned air. She saw two modern ovens and a commercial-size refrigerator-freezer and realized they were probably needed for all the entertaining the Blackthornes did.

"Come on in, Callie," Trace said. "It's just a house."

"A castle," she corrected.

Trace waited until she took another step inside before he pulled the kitchen door closed behind her.

Callie felt trapped. She was well and truly in enemy territory.

Before she could panic and run, an elderly Mexican woman wearing an apron turned from the sink and smiled at her. "Señor Trace," she said. "Welcome home. Who have you brought to meet Maria?"

"This is Callie Monroe," Trace said.

"*Buenos días*, Señora Monroe," the old woman said. "Can I offer you something to eat? A cup of coffee perhaps?"

Callie thought of the coffee Trace had made for them at dawn. The cinnamon toast they had fed each other in bed. The cinnamon sugar that had ended up on the sheets when they abandoned the toast, finding the taste of each other much more satisfying.

She shot a quick glance at Trace, deduced from the gleam of laughter in his eyes that he was remembering the same thing, and blushed.

"We've had our coffee, Maria," he said. "Thanks anyway." He walked to the portal that led to the rest of the house and held out his hand to Callie. "Ready to beard the lion?"

Callie crossed to Trace, looked down at his outstretched palm, and laid her hand in his.

He met her gaze and smiled.

Callie clasped his hand more tightly. She was giving Trace a chance to take care of her. It was the first step down a treacherous, slippery slope. Maybe, if she was careful, she wouldn't get hurt.

The house was eerily quiet. She followed Trace up the carpeted wooden staircase to the second floor, noting the family portraits along the wall, which had been featured in the *Texas Monthly* article. "Which one of these dashing gentlemen is the original Blackthorne?" she asked.

Trace pointed to a painting of a handsome man standing beside a chair made of horns and cowhide in which a beautiful woman was seated. "The first Blackthorne and his wife, Creighton Creed."

Callie stared at the portrait of the two attractive people. "So that's them. I was hoping this would be one of the paintings featured in the *Texas Monthly* article, but it wasn't. I've never seen a portrait of my great-great—however many greats—grandmother. Everything was lost when the first Three Oaks burned down."

"They made a handsome couple. It's too bad her son Jake was so opposed to the marriage," Trace said. "Otherwise, the Blackthornes and Creeds might not still be feuding today."

"From the stories I've heard, Jake was convinced that Blackthorne forced his mother into the marriage so he could get possession of her land."

"She wasn't coerced," Trace said. "She was in love with him."

"How do you know?"

"I've read her diary. You can borrow it, if you like."

"Oh, that would be wonderful!" Callie smiled ruefully. "I'll let you know when I have some spare time to read."

Which reminded them both that she wasn't likely to have the time to catch up on family history anytime soon.

As Trace headed down the hall, Callie followed closely behind him, unwilling to get stranded in the great house.

"Feel free to take a look around while I pack a few things," Trace said as he stepped into a bedroom and began rummaging through a chest of drawers.

"That's all right. There's plenty to look at right here." Even from the doorway, Callie could see that Trace's room was filled with magnificent antiques. The bed had an eight-foot-tall carved headboard. A dry sink with a flowered pitcher and bowl sat along one wall, and an enormous mirrored clothes press was angled in the corner.

"Your room is . . . exquisite." It was the wrong adjective to describe a man's bedroom, but she couldn't think of another word that fit. There wasn't a single framed photograph, nothing left hanging over a chair or dropped willy-nilly on the floor. Not a pen or pencil or box of Kleenex could she see. Not a piece of Trace Blackthorne, the man, was in evidence. It could have been a room in a museum.

Callie shivered. Trace's bedroom felt cold, despite the sunlight streaming in through the window. Perhaps it was simply that she wasn't used to the air conditioning.

She thought back to Trace's room at the cabin, where she'd spent the night, and realized it had all the warmth and charm that this room lacked. It was smaller, for a start. She'd noticed a bridle he'd brought home for repair on the chest of drawers, and a pair of spurs on the windowsill. He'd left a shirt draped over a ladder-back chair, and his pocket knife and wallet and change had been strewn on the bedside table.

No wonder he hadn't wanted to stay in his parents' home.

Trace finished stuffing a canvas bag with perfectly pressed and folded clothes—it seemed even his T-shirts had been ironed—and zipped it closed. "Maria takes care of my laundry," he explained. "I can't convince her she doesn't need to put it away in the drawers."

But it was obvious to Callie that the woman couldn't very well leave it sitting on the bed. Not in this room.

"I need to speak with my mother," Trace said as he crossed past her and headed down the hall. "Her studio is in the other wing."

Callie followed him, curious to see whether Eve Blackthorne could possibly keep her artist's studio as neat as the rest of the house.

"She probably won't answer the door," Trace said, "but I usually knock anyway." There was no answer to Trace's knock, and he slowly, silently eased the door open.

Callie was assaulted by the strong odors of oil paint and turpentine. His mother's studio was filled with sunlight, which seemed to be magnified by the bare windows and white walls. But where the rest of the house shouted order and conformity, here everything was chaos.

Callie heaved an inward sigh of relief. It was obvious somebody used this space. It looked lived in. Debris littered the shelves and counters that lined the edges of the room. Tubes of paint lay uncapped, and dabs of paint splattered the wooden floor. Callie speculated that the rest of the house must be kept like a showplace for the benefit of all their famous guests.

She watched as Trace screwed the lid on an open can of

turpentine, which explained the strong smell of it in the room. Paint rags lay in piles, and canvases were stacked on the floor, with their faces to the wall.

Mrs. Blackthorne stood before a large canvas set on an easel, a paint-daubed palette perched on the crook of her arm, a paintbrush clenched between her teeth, her eyes narrowed as she perused her work.

"Mother," Trace said.

Callie was a little disconcerted when Trace's mother ignored him and remained focused on the painting. Callie crossed with Trace to stand beside Mrs. Blackthorne and suddenly realized that she recognized the scene.

"It's the Rafter S auction!" Callie exclaimed.

Trace put a finger to his lips.

Mrs. Blackthorne didn't react to the sound of Callie's voice, merely continued studying her work.

Callie stared at the painting, impressed by the effort it must have taken to re-create the red-and-white-checked tablecloths in the food tent, delighted by the perfect lazy clouds in the stunning blue sky, fascinated by the magnificent stallion rearing in the foreground, a number 2 painted on his flank.

The stallion struggled in vain to be free of his handler, every muscle flexed against the taut rope that held him captive. The whites of the animal's eyes, the bared teeth, the striking hooves, all revealed his fury and frustration.

He seemed so alive! Callie could almost feel the animal's pain and fear . . . and rage.

Indistinct—incomplete—figures were seated in the stands along the side of the ring and stood beside the corral. Callie wondered who Mrs. Blackthorne would paint there and whether the people would have the same precision of form—and depth of emotion—that Callie had found in the stallion.

Trace actually had to tap his mother on the shoulder to get her attention. When she turned, her eyes looked dazed for a moment before they focused on him.

She grabbed the brush from between her teeth and said, "Trace! What are you doing here?"

"I wanted to let you know I won't be able to stand in for you at the Cancer Society luncheon in Fort Worth next Saturday. There's a quarter horse auction I have to attend the same day in San Antonio."

Eve Blackthorne frowned, then said, "All right," and turned back to her painting.

Callie felt Mrs. Blackthorne's dismissal even though the woman hadn't said a word to acknowledge her presence. She tried to imagine how Trace must feel. It was hard to believe this distracted woman was anybody's mother. She certainly hadn't treated Trace with any kindness or consideration or concern. Or even mild interest, for that matter.

"Is this the way she always acts?" Callie whispered.

"It's hard to get her attention when she's working," Trace replied in a low voice. "You get used to it."

But Callie was determined to communicate with the other woman. "Your painting is beautiful," she said.

To her surprise, Eve Blackthorne turned to her and said with an ironic smile, "I wouldn't paint an ugly picture."

"I never meant to suggest—"

"It's not that I think people couldn't appreciate something less than perfection. It's simply that I prefer it myself." She turned away and focused on the painting, her head tilted to one side. "Like this stallion. He wasn't quite perfect. But I've made him perfect."

Callie took a second look and realized that the stallion Mrs. Blackthorne had painted, and the one featured at the Rafter S auction, weren't at all the same animal. She and her father hadn't bid on the number 2 stud because he was too heavy in the chest, which would have made him too slow getting off his front feet. Mrs. Blackthorne had painted a flawlessly proportioned cutting horse.

"Yes," Callie agreed. "He is perfect."

But by then, Eve Blackthorne had already turned back to her work.

Once the studio door was closed behind them, Trace said, "I hope you'll forgive my mother. She isn't rude on purpose. When she's working on a painting she doesn't notice much of anything that goes on around her."

"Her work is truly incredible," Callie conceded. "So . . ." She searched for the right word. "Perfect."

Trace smiled ruefully. "It's sometimes hard even for the critics to find enough superlatives."

"I have to admit I can't wait to see the completed work. How long does it take your mother to finish a painting?"

"That's anybody's guess," Trace said. "Some are done in a matter of weeks. Some take months. Some she never finishes."

"I hope she finishes this one," Callie said.

She could feel Trace's palm against the small of her back, directing her. How many times had he put his hand in that same spot when their bodies were joined to urge her closer? Callie felt the curl of desire in her belly and stepped away from his touch.

She didn't realize where they were going until they crossed the threshold of a room lined with shelves that contained hundreds of leather-bound books, and she saw Blackjack sitting behind an oak desk.

"About time you showed up," Blackjack said. "Handy came to me for instructions this morning when he couldn't find you."

Trace checked his cell phone. "I guess I had my phone turned off. I trust you managed all right without me."

"I told him what needed to be done," his father said. "How are you, Mizz Monroe?"

Callie wasn't prepared for Blackjack's cordial greeting. "Fine," she blurted.

"I hear you and my son are courting," he said, in a voice that suggested their eventual marriage was a foregone conclusion.

Before Callie could make a retort, Trace said, "Dusty and I are meeting this morning to work on the infrastructure for the breeding operation. Do you want to come?"

"Where are you meeting?"

"At Dusty's place. He's moved into one of the manager's houses—the one Harry Pope lived in."

"Why don't you have the meeting here?" Blackjack asked.

"Dusty's already arranged for an architect and a building contractor to meet us at his place."

"What time?"

"Nine sharp," Trace replied.

"Count me in," Blackjack said. He turned back to Callie and asked, "How's your mother?"

Before her mother's confession last night, Callie might have convinced herself that Blackjack was merely being neighborly. Now she knew the truth. "My mother's fine," she said curtly.

"When is she getting out of the hospital?"

"In a couple of days." Callie couldn't keep the antagonism out of her voice. Blackjack was still too handsome, and her mother had obviously never gotten over him.

"I've got to take Callie by Three Oaks," Trace said, apparently aware of her agitation. "Then I'll be back to pick you up."

"No hurry," his father replied, a gleam in his eyes as his gaze shifted from Trace to Callie and back again. "I understand young lovers need their time alone."

Callie felt a flush—of anger, or humiliation, or both—creeping up her throat and fled before Blackjack could see it.

"What an insufferable man," she muttered.

And a powerful enemy.

She felt like circling the wagons, bringing in the children and horses, storing up water, and loading her guns for the fight to come.

"Take me home," she told Trace. "I want to go home."

Trace wished his father to Hades. Couldn't the old man let well enough alone? Callie was walking so fast through the house, she was almost running, and she had a panicked look in her eyes.

"Callie—"

"I want to go home," she repeated, cutting him off.

"No problem," he said. "You can visit Hannah before I drop you off at the cabin."

Her lips pressed flat, and she didn't say another word until they were out of the house. When she started to get in the hunting car he said, "I'm changing vehicles." He gestured to a Chevy pickup parked next to the Buick.

Without a word, she got in and sat facing forward, as though she had a steel rod down her spine. "Take me home," she said.

He didn't argue with her, merely drove her across Blackthorne property to the gate at the boundary of Three Oaks. He stopped and turned to her. "I think we should talk here, where we won't upset Hannah."

"We have nothing to discuss," Callie said. "I'm going home, and I'm staying there. End of discussion."

"You need some rest, Callie."

"I got a full night's rest. And you got what you wanted this morning. Now take me home."

His eyes narrowed. It hadn't been sex for money. That wasn't what he'd wanted from her, and that wasn't what she'd given to him. "If you don't want to stay at the cabin, where I can keep an eye on you, then I guess I'll have to move in with you."

"What are you suggesting?"

He started the truck and bumped his way through the gate. "I thought I made myself pretty clear. I'll be moving in at Three Oaks this evening."

"You've got a lot of nerve, thinking I'd agree to such a thing!"

"I'm not asking you, Callie," he said in a hard voice. "I'm telling you. In case you've forgotten, I've invested a great deal of money in you, and I intend to protect my investment."

She crossed her arms and stuck her nose in the air.

"You're only going to make things a thousand times worse."

"Maybe. Maybe not."

When he stopped at the back door to Three Oaks, she shoved open the door to the pickup and scrambled out. Before she could slam it, he said, "I'll be back at sundown."

"Don't expect to be welcome!"

Trace drove away with a knot in his stomach.

He spent a frustrating morning trying to make headway on the infrastructure for his breeding operation. His father vetoed every plan submitted by the architect. The contractor announced he had to start work in ten days or be forced to take another job. Trace stared down Blackjack, until he finally agreed to one of the plans the architect had submitted for a foaling barn, with certain changes, and the contractor agreed to have it completed by the end of the year. Although the meeting demanded his attention, Callie was never far from his mind.

Trace spent the rest of the day working with Russell Handy, cutting down mesquite trees and then dredging their roots under with a giant disc harrow. Clearing the mesquite was a dusty, dirty, thankless job, but it had to be done. The scratches left by mesquite thorns, and the protection the impenetrable undergrowth gave to flies, made the worm hazard to cattle a dozen times worse in the brush. Once Trace had all the mesquite in this pasture plowed under, he planned to plant Blue Stem grass, which put roots down more than ten feet, choking out the brush.

Trace was grateful for the physical effort the work required, because it distracted him from the confrontation with Callie he knew was coming at sundown. He could conquer the brush with sheer brute strength. It wasn't going to be that simple to deal with Callie.

Trace wasn't sure himself why he was forcing the issue by moving in with her. It was bound to cause problems. But he had never felt with another woman the joy he'd felt waking up with Callie this morning. He didn't want to give that up. And she owed him. She'd stolen something precious when she'd walked away from him eleven years ago. And until the day came when he left Texas for good, he intended to make up for lost time.

"See you tomorrow," Trace said to the *segundo* at the end of the day, as he slid wearily into the cab of his pickup.

"I'll be here," Handy replied, touching the brim of his Stetson in obeisance.

Trace needed a bath. He was covered in dust, which his sweat had turned to mud, and he itched all over. He considered stopping by the Castle before he headed to Three Oaks, but he found himself more anxious to get to Callie than he was uncomfortable.

He regretted that decision when he stepped inside the kitchen at Three Oaks to find Callie nowhere in sight, an argument in progress between Eli and Luke, and no supper cooking. He realized he was not only hot and tired and dirty. He was also hungry.

"What the hell is the problem here?" he demanded.

Luke and Eli stopped yelling at each other and turned on him, like wolf pups facing a menacing mountain lion. It was plain from the look on their faces, that while they weren't happy to see him, they weren't surprised, either.

Callie might not want him here. But she'd expected him to come. She must have decided it was better to tell her family he was welcome, than to fight a war when he arrived.

Luke glared at him and said, "Callie told me to make hamburgers for supper, but Eli forgot to take the hamburger out of the freezer this morning." He held up a fist-size lump wrapped in aluminum foil and said, "How am I supposed to make hamburger patties out of frozen hamburger?"

"Make Sloppy Joe's," Trace said flatly.

"I don't like Sloppy Joe's," Eli whined.

"You made the mistake. You suffer the consequences," Trace decreed. "Get supper started, Luke, before we all starve."

Luke was happy to have the matter decided in his favor, and got down the electric skillet to start browning the hamburger.

Before Eli could stomp off, Trace caught his arm and asked, "Where are Rosalita and your mom and your sister?"

"Rosalita went home. Mom went grocery shopping and took Hannah along."

Trace was frustrated to hear that Callie had sent Rosalita home, but glad for the chance to freshen up before she saw him. He looked worse than a calf with the slobbers. "Which is the best shower?" he asked.

"The only one that works is in Mom's room." Eli suddenly noticed Trace's canvas bag. "What's in there?"

"Everything I need to move in," Trace said matter-of-factly.

"Where are you planning to sleep?" Eli demanded.

He intended to slip into bed with Callie, but he didn't think Eli was ready to hear that. He glanced through the kitchen door into the living room. "I guess I'll bunk down on the sofa. Unless you've got an empty room upstairs?"

"All the bedrooms are taken," Eli said with satisfaction.

"What about your aunt Bay's room. She's away at school, isn't she?"

"You don't wanta sleep in a girl's room," Eli said certainly.

Any bed was preferable to the Victorian sofa in the living room. And he would much rather be on the same floor as Callie than have to maneuver his way up a flight of creaky stairs in the dead of night. "Why don't you show me Bay's room?"

"All right," Eli said. "But you're not gonna like it."

Trace wasn't crazy about the lacy canopy that topped the double bed, or the piles of stuffed animals that adorned the pillows, but he was across the hall from Callie's bedroom. He sent Eli back downstairs to help with supper while he unpacked a change of clothes and a few toiletries from his bag.

He left his boots in Bay's room and walked barefoot across the wooden floor to Callie's bedroom. He left his dirty clothes on the rag rug next to her bed and carried his toiletries into the bathroom. The water in the shower wasn't as hot as he liked it, and there wasn't much water pressure, but he was grateful for even the halfhearted spray as he used a bit of Callie's apple-scented shampoo to wash his hair.

He had just wrapped a too-small towel around his waist, when the bathroom door opened. He expected it to be Callie, but it was Hannah.

"Hi," she said, smiling up at him.

He clutched at the towel. "You should have knocked," he growled, yearning for the hot, pulsing showerhead, much larger towels, and blessed privacy of the bathroom at the cabin. He wondered whether Callie's children walked into her bedroom at all hours without knocking. He'd have to make sure there was a lock on her door before he made any midnight visits.

"Are you mad at me?" Hannah asked.

He saw her chin begin to wobble and felt his resentment melt. "I need to shave," he said. "You can stand on the toilet seat, if you want to watch."

"Okay," Hannah said.

Trace lifted her up, then lathered his face with foamy shaving cream and located his razor. Before he'd taken the first stroke, Eli had crowded into the bathroom and was standing beside him.

"My dad used to shave in the morning."

"I have to do it morning and evening, if I don't want to show up at the supper table with a beard," Trace explained.

"Mom wouldn't care," Eli said, hanging over the sink and staring up at him. "She liked it when Dad rubbed his beard on her face. It made her laugh."

That was a bit of information Trace could have done without. It was painful to think of Callie laughing with Nolan Monroe. Loving Nolan Monroe. He shaved quickly, wanting the job done before Callie herself showed up to see what was keeping him.

"What does that feel like?" Eli asked.

"It's like mowing hay," Trace replied. "One blade lifts the beard up, the next cuts it off."

"But what does it *feel* like?" Eli insisted.

Trace stopped shaving, picked up the can of Gillette shaving cream, and said, "Hold out your hand."

When Eli held out his hand, Trace spritzed a small amount of lather into it. "Spread that on your cheek," he instructed.

Eli edged Trace aside so he could look into the mirror while he was working.

"I want some, too," Hannah said.

"Girls don't shave," Trace said.

"They do, too," Hannah countered. "Mommy shaves her legs and her—"

"All right," Trace said, gripping Hannah's tiny hand to keep it steady while he filled it with shaving cream. He watched as the child studied the coveralls that concealed her legs and the shirt that hid her underarms, before she spread the lather across her cheeks and chin.

When Trace turned back to the mirror, Eli was facing him, waiting expectantly. "Now what?" the boy asked.

Trace glanced once at his own half-shaven face before he handed Eli the razor and instructed, "Stroke gently and steadily downward on your cheeks and upward from your throat."

"I don't have any shaving cream on my throat," Eli pointed out.

"Just work on your face for now," Trace said.

The boy reminded him a little of himself at the same age, eager to begin the rituals of manhood. He noticed the stubborn cowlick on Eli's crown. He'd had one just like it. Nowadays he kept his hair long enough to slick it down.

"What about me?" Hannah asked, patting his arm to get his attention.

Trace tousled her blond curls and said, "Wait your turn, scamp."

He turned back around just as Eli yelped, "Ow!" The boy dropped the razor, which clattered into the sink, and grabbed his face. "I cut myself!"

Seeing the tears of pain welling in the boy's eyes, Trace quickly tore off a sheet of toilet tissue and said, "Second lesson in shaving." He brushed Eli's hand aside, swiped off the rest of the shaving cream until he found the cut, then stuck on a tiny piece of toilet paper.

Eli looked at himself in the mirror. "My dad cut himself sometimes," he said, turning his head back and forth to see the grown-up effect of Trace's bandage.

"What about me?" Hannah said, tugging on the skimpy towel that surrounded Trace's hips.

Trace barely managed to catch it before it fell off. He tucked it back in around his waist and said, "I think maybe you better do a finger shave."

"What's that?" Hannah asked.

Trace copied something he'd seen his father do with his sister. He caught Hannah's chin in his grasp and aimed her face toward him, then used his forefinger like it was a razor, to scrape off the excess shaving cream.

Hannah beamed up at him. "I want to see how I look!"

Trace picked her up and held her so she could see herself in the little bit of mirror that wasn't filled with Eli's face.

Suddenly, he saw Callie's face reflected in the mirror, looking wistful. As their eyes met in the glass, her gaze turned wary.

At that moment, Hannah let out a squeal of delight. "Am I done, Trace?"

"I guess you're done," Trace said.

"But I see you're not quite finished," Callie said, unable to suppress a grin of amusement.

Trace glanced at his half-shaved face in the mirror, then turned and thrust Hannah into Callie's arms. "I've been too busy playing barber."

"Look at me, Mom!" Eli said, turning his cheek so his mother could see his war wound. "I shaved, too!"

"You're growing up too fast, Eli," Callie said as she kissed her son just above the piece of tissue. "Supper is on the table," she announced to her children as she ushered them out of the bathroom.

She turned back to Trace and said, "Thank you for being so patient with Eli and Hannah."

"I told you it would be no problem if I stayed here."

"Oh, it's a problem, all right. But I've learned to handle all kinds of problems over the years. I'll see you downstairs . . ." She eyed his naked knees and winked at him. "As soon as you're decent."

As the excited babble of children's voices faded, Trace turned back to the mirror. The shaving cream had dried on half his face, and his chest bore rivulets of sweat from the steam that hovered in the un-air-conditioned bathroom. As his stomach growled its hunger, his lips curved into a grin.

This is what it would have been like, he thought. *If Callie and I had married.*

The grin faded. These weren't his kids. This wasn't his wife. And the way things were looking, Callie was never going to be free enough from her family obligations to marry him and go back . . . where he'd come from.

Time was running out. Trace couldn't stay here in

Texas forever. He had responsibilities of his own that were being taken care of by someone else. He'd only intended to stay long enough for his father to get back on his feet. Now, before he left, he also had to get the breeding operation set up and make sure his father saw the benefit of keeping it—and employing Dusty, who would also have to be convinced to work for Blackjack—once he was gone.

Trace hadn't counted on the complications Callie was causing in his life. He hadn't counted on wanting her so much. He hadn't counted on needing her at all.

One thing at a time. First he'd get his fill of her body. Then he'd deal with saying good-bye.

Trace picked up his razor and finished his shave.

Chapter 14

 CALLIE LAY IN HER BED LISTENING TO THE house settle, as it did every night as the heat left the earth and it cooled in the moonlight. She had felt Trace's avid gaze on her all through supper, all through the game of Scrabble they'd played at the table afterward, and even while she got Eli and Hannah ready for bed. She knew he'd be coming to her after everyone was asleep. Her body betrayed her by wanting it to happen.

She wished she'd barred the door to Three Oaks against him, as she'd threatened she would. But it was too late for that. Sometime over the past few days, he'd breached the emotional walls she'd put up to keep him out. From now on, she'd be fighting for her life.

While she'd tucked Hannah in, Trace had stood in the doorway, his arms crossed over his chest, watching. She hadn't expected Hannah to want a good night kiss from him. Or for Trace to press his lips to her daughter's forehead with such gracious ease.

She'd seen Eli's agitation, when her son thought he'd be subjected to the same sort of "mush" in front of Trace. She'd been surprised by Trace's understanding, by the way he bent to remove the cherished piece of toilet paper from the wound on Eli's baby-smooth cheek and said, "That'll be healed by the time you need to shave again."

Eli had carefully brushed his fingertips across the spot, then sat up a little straighter, pulled his knees up a little higher beneath the paperback in his lap, and said, "I expect so."

She wasn't surprised when Eli pretended to be engrossed in his book to avoid her good night kiss. She smoothed his cowlick and kissed his forehead anyway. She saw how he glanced at Trace in man-to-man commiseration as he ducked away from her caress.

Her children and her brother should be asleep by now. She should go to sleep herself, if she didn't want to be exhausted again tomorrow. Trace was right about one thing. She needed more rest than she was getting.

Callie hadn't heard a sound, but she was suddenly aware that she was no longer alone. The moonlight kept it from being totally dark in the room, but the silver glow didn't extend to the doorway. She heard the door being locked and realized with chagrin that she'd never even considered locking Trace out.

"Trace?"

"Yeah," he answered from the shadows.

She sat upright, pulling her knees to her chest and hugging the covers around her. She barely stopped herself from asking, "What are you doing here?" She knew why he'd come. He'd paid for the privilege.

"I'm tired," she said.

"Good. So am I."

When he passed through the stream of moonlight, she saw he was barefoot and wore a pair of jeans low on his hips. She heard a zipper and then the rustle of denim as he slid them off. He lifted the covers on the other side of the bed and slipped in with her.

Before she could say a word, he turned his back on her and pulled the covers up over his shoulder.

She stared at his back, confused by his unexpected behavior. "Trace?"

"Good night, Callie," he murmured.

"If all you plan to do is sleep, you could have stayed in Bay's room," she said irritably.

He rolled onto his back and laced his hands beneath his head. "I tried to stay away. I know you need to sleep. But I felt like I was going to drown in Beanie Babies in your sister's bed."

Callie smiled at the image he'd conjured. "I thought you would want to . . ."

"I do," Trace said as he turned on his side toward her. "But you're tired, and so am I."

Callie slid back down in bed, keeping the covers pulled up to her neck. She stared at the ceiling, eyes wide open, sleep the farthest thing from her mind. A sardonic smile curved her lips, as she acknowledged that her body had been anticipating Trace's lovemaking, and that what she felt as a result of his restraint was not relief, but sexual frustration.

"I was expecting you to make love to me," she said into the stillness.

Trace lifted his head from the pillow. "I'm trying to be considerate."

Callie blew out a breath of air. "The considerate thing would be to make love to me. Then we could both get some sleep."

"Come here," Trace said gruffly, as he reached across the bed for her.

Callie scooted the short distance between them and found herself body to body with Trace, with only the T-shirt she was wearing to sleep in between them. She pressed her cheek against his throat and inhaled the pine-scented aftershave he wore. She told herself she just needed the warmth and comfort Trace could provide in the cold, lonely night. Soon he'd be gone, and she'd be alone again.

"Love me, Trace," she whispered. "Love me."

She felt his arms tighten around her. "You're exhausted, Callie. You need—"

"I need you inside me," she said, sliding her hand down between his legs.

He groaned as his mouth found hers in the darkness.

There was nothing frantic about this coupling. Trace took his time, his tongue stroking lazily into her mouth, his hands slowly searching out the places where he knew she liked to be touched. Callie felt cherished, relished, valued.

She tried to return the favor, but Trace caught both of her hands in one of his and kept them pinned against the pillow.

"I don't want to be hurried," he said. "I want to take my time."

She was writhing beneath him, begging for release, before he finally began to push himself inside her. Even that he did slowly, inching his way inside until she thought she would die of need. He held her hips in his hands, preventing her from thrusting upward, until he was fully seated within her.

They moved together, in a rhythm as old as time. His groan of satisfaction called forth an answering moan from her throat, and he caught the sound with his mouth.

Afterward, he kept her hugged tightly against him, their bodies heaving air in unison, his cheek brushing against hers. He already had enough of a beard to tickle her, and she gave a breathy laugh.

"What's so funny?" he asked.

"Your beard tickled me."

He stilled for a moment, then tightened his arms around her. "You should have been mine, Callie. You should have—"

"Don't, Trace," she said, cutting him off. "We're together now. Until you've had your fill of me," she finished bitterly.

The silence stretched between them.

"Have you ever wondered what it would have been like if we'd gotten married?" he asked.

"No."

"I have." He rolled over onto his back, but kept her body tucked against his side. "We'd have had at least six kids by now."

"You're ambitious," she said with a chuckle.

"Big families are more fun."

"But more work," Callie said, thinking of all she had to do with only two children.

"There would have been two of us to share the load," he reminded her.

"And of course you're rich, so we wouldn't want for anything."

"I wasn't rich when I left home. But yes, I am now."

"What have you been doing? Where have you been all these years?" Callie asked.

He hesitated, then said, "I've been a cattleman. In Australia."

Callie laughed in disbelief. "I pictured you as a playboy in a casino in Monte Carlo. Or in a steel-and-glass building in Hong Kong manipulating the Asian market. I never figured you would travel around the world and end up working as a cowboy! Why didn't you tell anyone where you were?"

"Owen always knew where I was. I figured he could get in touch with me, if I was needed at home. And he did. I didn't want my father knowing where I was, because I didn't want him pressuring me to come to work for him. So I asked acquaintances who were traveling to send postcards from distant locales."

"You could have told Dusty where you were. He wouldn't have told your father."

"I never told Dusty where I was, because I knew he couldn't keep it from Lou Ann, and once Lou Ann knew, the whole county would, too."

"True," Callie said with a chuckle. "So how did you end up in Australia?"

Trace's fingertips idly followed the shape of her collarbone. "I did my share of playing around the first few years I was gone. Then I went to visit a distant cousin of mine, Alexander Blackthorne, in Queensland. Turned out he owned a cattle station nearly twice the size of Bitter Creek."

Callie tried to imagine a ranch that large. "That would be over two thousand square miles of land!"

"Two thousand three hundred," Trace said.

"How do you keep track of cattle over that much area?"

"I fly a lot," Trace said.

"Cowboys don't earn much," Callie said. "How did you make your fortune?"

"The easy way," Trace said. "I inherited it."

"Are you telling me a distant cousin left you a two-thousand-square-mile ranch?"

"They're called cattle stations in Australia," he said. "Alex got stove up in a riding accident about two months before I showed up. His wife had left him a long time ago—couldn't take the isolation—and his sons had both died. We kind of hit it off—"

"I'll say!" Callie said. "Have you already inherited this monstrosity, or—"

"Alex died eighteen months ago," Trace said. "He got a kidney infection that killed him. I have a good crew of men to keep an eye on things, but I'm anxious to get back home."

Callie stared at Trace, stunned by the pronouncement of some faraway cattle station in Australia, of all places, as *home*. "So you really will be leaving here as soon as your father's back on his feet."

"I don't think I can wait for my dad to fully recover," Trace said. "I don't think he ever will."

"Does he know you've inherited a ranch in Australia?"

"I told him I was working for Alex. I haven't told him I inherited the ranch."

"Why not?"

Trace shrugged. "What purpose would it serve?"

"So how long are you planning to stay in Texas?"

"At least until the Futurity is over in December. After that, I can leave anytime."

"Why would you start a breeding operation if you're going right back to Australia?" Callie asked.

"I've been thinking about breeding horses for cutting in Australia for quite a while," he said. "But I couldn't find the quality of quarter horses I wanted." He shrugged. "I figured I'd build an operation here and ship the best of them home to Australia."

There it was again. Australia described as *home.* "You know your father expects you to stay here and run Bitter Creek."

"He'll have to handle the disappointment," Trace said brusquely.

"If you care so little what he thinks, why did you bother to come back at all?" Callie asked.

He met her gaze in the moonlight. "I came back for you."

Callie felt the hairs stand up on her arms. Her heart began to pound. She tried to back away from Trace, but his arms held her captive. "Let me go, Trace."

"I don't want to let you go, Callie."

She made her body rigid, evidencing her displeasure. "Are you planning to ship me back to Australia, along with your cutting stock?"

She felt his body tense at the jibe. The moment she felt his hold loosening, she sat up and scooted away to the opposite edge of the bed.

As he sat up, his eyes, hot and angry, locked with hers. "There's a lot of room for kids to grow in Australia," he said.

"Texas is plenty big for me. Besides, my family—"

Trace grabbed her arms and shook her. "Forget about your damned family! What about us?"

"Keep your voice down!" she hissed at him. "You'll wake up the whole house." She tore herself free and left the bed.

He cornered her by the chest of drawers, pinning her against the wall with the weight of his body, his palms pressed flat on either side of her head. "When is it our turn, Callie? When do you put us first?"

So many emotions were roiling inside her that Callie wasn't sure which one would bubble up first. She fought back defeat and desperation. Ruthlessly banished desire. Made a brief, losing struggle with reason. And finally gave in to anger.

"You had your chance! You could have stayed around long enough to find out—" She bit her lip. "It's too late for us, Trace."

"The hell it is!"

He grabbed her hips and lifted her enough to thrust himself inside her. To Callie's horror and chagrin, she was wet and ready for him. He grunted with satisfaction, as his eyes met hers.

"You belong to me. You always have."

"You bought and paid for me," she retorted. "I hope you get your money's worth before you leave!"

He shut her mouth with his own and took what he wanted, making her want him in ways she hadn't known she could want. She clutched his shoulders, hanging on for dear life, as he brought them both to climax with a cry that was more pain than joy.

He collapsed against her, his head pressed against her

throat, his breathing labored. "Damn you, Callie. This isn't the way . . . I didn't want . . ."

He released her, and she met his gaze with defiance, clenching her teeth to keep her chin from trembling.

He left her and retrieved his jeans from the floor beside the bed. "Get some sleep," he said. He met her gaze and added grimly, "You're going to need it."

Without another word, he left the room.

Callie had dreaded facing Trace across the breakfast table, but when she came downstairs, Luke announced that Trace had already had his coffee and left the house. "He said he'd be back in time for supper."

"Great," Callie muttered.

She managed to smile her way through their usual morning routine, but once Luke and Eli were out the door and on their way to school, she collapsed at the table, her face in her hands.

"Are you okay, Mommy?" Hannah asked.

Callie forced herself to sit up and smile. "Sure am, sweetheart. Know what we're going to do today?"

"What?" Hannah asked.

"We're going to start training Smart Little Doc and give Sugar Pep a good workout."

Callie had always believed that the best cure for misery was hard work. Luckily, there was always plenty of work to be done around Three Oaks. She planned to start with the job that required the most concentration—training her horse and Trace's for the Futurity.

She started with her own horse because she and Sugar Pep were already a team, and it was a pleasure to work with such a willing partner. Together, they produced something more than the sum of each, but it took trust and faith on the part of both to compete in such an unforgiving sport. One break in concentration by either of them, and the cow would escape and rejoin the herd.

In actual competition, horse and rider entered the arena and slowly approached a herd of between forty to sixty cows. Thirty feet in front of the herd, they would cross a line that set the clock to running. Horse and rider then had two minutes and thirty seconds to cut two cows, or if time allowed, three cows from the herd in sequence.

Driven by instinct, the cow always scrambled to return to the safety of the herd, dodging and weaving to get past anything in its way. Under the rules, Callie was required to slacken the reins, and from then on, it was up to Sugar Pep to keep the cow separated from the herd. Callie could direct her horse to quit a cow only when it was clearly stopped or turned away.

Some horses loved the challenge of the sport and only needed a little instruction. Others had to learn the techniques of stopping and turning and pivoting that were so essential to winning the contest between horse and cow.

Stiff penalties were assessed for losing control of the cow, for always cutting from the edge of the herd—which meant you had to "cut deep" at least once during the time allotted—and for switching cows after you'd committed to a particular one. Scattering the herd and using the reins could also lower your score.

It sounded simple in words. It looked beautiful in execution. But hours and hours of practice went into training a truly great cutting horse.

To Callie's surprise, Sugar Pep seemed reluctant to

come to a complete stop before she turned. Callie finally realized that she was communicating her own agitation and impatience to the horse. She tried relaxing, but the problem persisted. When Sugar Pep finally gave her a good stop, she ended the workout for the day.

"She's looking good."

Callie had been so focused on her horse, she hadn't noticed Trace's arrival. "She's coming along," she said, patting Sugar Pep's neck. Today's problems, Callie conceded, were her own fault.

"I came by to say I'm sorry."

It was a good thing Callie had a good sense of balance, or she might have fallen off her horse in surprise. "A Blackthorne admitting he's wrong? A Blackthorne apologizing?" She knocked her hand against her ear. "I think I must have something wrong with my hearing."

Trace chuckled. "I suppose I deserve that. Will you forgive me?"

Callie resisted making a flippant response. If things had gotten out of control last night, she was at least partly to blame. "Tighten the cinch on Smart Little Doc's saddle for me, would you?"

"You haven't answered my question," he said as he complied with her request.

"All right. You're forgiven. Now, go away. I'm busy."

"One other thing."

"What?" Callie asked, letting him hear the annoyance in her voice.

"I'd like you to ride my horse in the Futurity."

This time Sugar Pep jumped, as Callie's hands reflexively tightened on the reins. The rules allowed her to ride both horses, but Callie wasn't sure she wanted the additional responsibility. "I thought you were going to ride him yourself."

"That would be doing a disservice to the horse," Trace said. "I haven't got nearly the seat you have."

"Get on your horse, and let me see," she said.

Trace met her gaze for a moment, realized she was serious, then stepped into the saddle.

She crossed to the corral gate on horseback, opened it, and held it for Trace to enter the arena. Once he and Smart Little Doc were inside, she kneed her horse through the gate and closed it behind her.

She slid off Sugar Pep, took the couple of steps to the corral and hung her arms over the top rail. "Cut a cow from deep in the herd," she said.

Callie gave him points for walking his horse toward the herd of twenty cows crowded together at the far end of the corral, rather than trotting up and scattering them to the four winds. "Cut out that featherback," Callie ordered, directing him toward a hereford with a white stripe of feathered hair down the center of its back.

She watched as Trace set the horse's nose toward the steer. He ended up cutting three cows, instead of one. Callie watched to see whether he could keep Smart Little Doc focused on the featherback.

In competition, there would be two turn-back riders to make sure the other two steers rejoined the herd with a minimum of interference. Callie smiled when Smart Little Doc crouched nose to nose with the featherback, refusing to let him escape with the other two animals.

She critically eyed Trace's form as Smart Little Doc went to work. All cutters hung on to the saddle horn, but she could see Trace's grip was too stiff, and his heels weren't angled down enough. "Relax," she instructed. "Don't anticipate."

"How the hell—"

"Keep your upper body still."

Cutting was all about stopping and starting. Looking the cow in the eye, Smart Little Doc matched the steer's every move—leaping, sprinting, crouching to keep it cut from the herd. Callie whistled soft and low as she watched the horse work. Smart Little Doc could turn on a biscuit and never break the crust.

Trace, on the other hand, was struggling to keep up with his horse.

"Keep your range of focus wide. Stay centered in the saddle."

As she finished speaking, Smart Little Doc took a sudden sharp turn, and Trace was left sitting in the sand. Callie had to give the horse credit. Smart Little Doc never missed a beat. He stayed right with the cow.

"Grab the reins," Callie said with a laugh. "Before you get trampled."

Trace stood and brushed the sand off his Levi's. "I'm glad you think that was funny."

"You just need a little practice," she said.

"I'd need years of practice to match your ability, and I'll never have your natural talent," he said.

Callie tried not to make too much of the compliment, but his praise made her feel good inside.

Trace crossed to the rail with Smart Little Doc trailing docilely behind him and laid his hands over hers. "I'll give you an extra ten percent of the purse to ride him."

Callie shook her head no.

"What is it you want? Name your price."

Callie didn't hesitate. "Move out, and I'll ride your horse."

Trace stared at her a long moment. "Done. So long as you agree to spend time with me at the cabin."

"How much time?"

"As much as I can get."

"I'm a busy woman."

"I'll take that into consideration," Trace said. "Now that that's settled, I have another job for you."

Callie didn't think the matter was at all settled. But so long as she wasn't committed to anything specific, she intended to spend as little time with Trace as she could manage. "What is it you need me to do?" she asked.

"I wondered if you'd come look at a couple of mares for me. Dusty recommended them, but I'd appreciate having your opinion."

"I have chores to do, Trace."

"I'll send one of the Bitter Creek hands over to help out this afternoon."

"I have to take care of Hannah."

"I've already asked Lou Ann if she'd baby-sit."

Callie pursed her lips. She was certain that if she came up with another excuse, Trace would have arrangements made to get around that, too. "I have to be back before Eli gets home from school," she said at last.

Trace grabbed her hand. "Fine. Let's go."

Callie felt like she was playing hookey from school. She should be working with Smart Little Doc. She should be repairing fence. She should be cleaning house in preparation for her mother's and Sam's return. Instead, she was driving down the road in Trace's extended-cab Silverado with the hip sound of "Garth Brooks as Chris

Gaines" blaring on the radio and the wind blowing through her ponytail.

Callie had known Lou Ann was moving into one of the manager's homes at Bitter Creek, but she was pleasantly surprised by the brick-fronted ranch-style house sitting in the shade of an enormous live oak.

Lou Ann was obviously expecting them and came outside to retrieve Hannah when Trace honked his horn.

"I'll be expecting all of you for supper," she said, once she had Hannah perched on her hip.

"See you then," Trace said as he hit the gas.

Callie turned to Trace and asked, "What was that all about?"

"I promised Dusty and Lou Ann I'd come over for a housewarming party as soon as they got settled. I asked Lou Ann how she felt about having a crowd, and she thought it was a great idea. When I mentioned it to your brother Luke this morning, he said he'd welcome the chance to eat somebody else's cooking. I didn't think you'd mind."

"I see," Callie said, eyeing him askance. Now he was planning her social life. She had to admit it would be pleasant to have a home-cooked meal that wasn't either burned or something she'd cooked herself. "Since you're going to keep me occupied this afternoon, eating at Lou Ann's seems like a good idea. But don't make any more plans without consulting me first, all right?"

"That's fine with me. We'll do our planning together from now on."

"You're moving out, Trace. What planning?"

"Planning time for you to rest. Planning time for us to make love. You know, planning."

Callie laughed. "You're incorrigible."

The afternoon with Trace passed in a glorious blur, and before Callie was ready for the interlude to end, they were back at Three Oaks to pick up Luke and Eli.

"Do you want to change before we head over to Dusty and Lou Ann's?" Trace asked.

Callie looked down at the Western shirt, jeans, and boots that were her constant wardrobe and shook her head. "I don't know what else I'd wear."

"Surely you have a dress in your closet."

"Of course I do."

"Then why don't you wear it for me?"

Callie turned to look sharply at Trace. "This isn't a date."

"Never said it was. But being a housewarming, it is a party. How about it?"

Callie wondered when she had last shaved her legs. And she was certain she didn't own a pair of nylons without a run in them. But she did have a flowered sundress and a pair of sandals. "All right," she said. "Give me fifteen minutes to shower and change."

Callie found that once she was wearing the flowered sundress, her face looked bare without a little makeup, which she judiciously applied. She pinned her hair up, but it felt too formal, so she tied it in a ponytail with a lilac ribbon. She didn't realize how different she looked until she saw the gawking stares of her brother and her son.

"What did you do to yourself?" Luke asked. "You look almost pretty."

Callie laughed. "Thanks. I think."

"You're beautiful, Mom," Eli said loyally.

"Thank you, Eli. You look pretty good yourself."

Eli looked down at his buttoned-up shirt and belted jeans. "Trace said I had to wear something nice, 'cause it's a party."

"I'm looking forward to all that delicious food," Luke said. His Western shirt was also neatly ironed, with the sleeves rolled down and buttoned at his wrists.

Trace had slicked his black hair back with water, and Callie figured he must have shaved, because his face was free of the shadow of beard that he wore almost constantly. He looked breathtakingly handsome. He held out his arm to her and said, "Well, ma'am. Are you ready to go?"

She linked her arm with his, grinned, and said, "You bet."

Callie had forgotten what it was like to socialize with other people, to laugh and tell anecdotes about the children and eat until she was so full she was ready to split. She had forgotten the sound of children shrieking with laughter, and she couldn't remember the last time she'd had to admonish Hannah and Eli to stop running in the house. She'd forgotten what normal life was like.

"We should do this more often," Lou Ann said, as she and Dusty stood at the door, their two daughters clinging to their sides, as they sent Callie on her way.

"We should," Callie agreed, kissing first Lou Ann and then Dusty on the cheek.

Her kids were quiet on the drive home, like balloons from which the air had slowly seeped out. Luke and Eli were belted into the backseat of the cab. Hannah was buckled into the center seat, but she had fallen asleep, and her head lay in Callie's lap.

Trace reached across the seat and took Callie's hand. "How are you feeling?"

Alive. Callie felt her stomach clench and drew her hand free. *And also very guilty.* For having such a wonderful time and never once thinking about everything that needed to be done at Three Oaks.

When she didn't respond, Trace said, "Don't you think it's about time, Callie?"

"Time for what?" she managed to ask.

"For us to be a family," he said quietly.

Callie swallowed past the aching lump in her throat. "What is it you want from me?" she asked in a voice quiet enough not to carry to the backseat.

"A chance," he said. "I want another chance."

Chapter 15

TRACE HAD CAREFULLY CONSIDERED WHEN AND where—and even whether—to tell Callie about the existence of his cattle station in Australia and his plans to return there. He certainly hadn't planned to divulge the truth so soon. But in the sweet afterglow of satiating sex, the revelation had come tumbling out, with the one result he'd most feared.

Callie was committed to remaining in Texas to support her family. As far as she was concerned, there was no such thing as a future for the two of them in Texas, let alone on a continent halfway across the world.

Since Callie's mother and brother Sam had come home from the hospital three weeks ago, Trace hadn't once asked Callie to meet him at the cabin. He saw the confusion in her eyes when he stopped by the house to ask about her progress with Smart Little Doc, but he could handle that better than the loathing that rolled off Sam, or the perceptive awareness in her mother's steady gaze.

Trace had hoped that if he made love to Callie, he could get her out of his system. Or perhaps, if things went well enough between them, they might even get back together. But making love to her had only made him want her more. And even though things had gone well between them, he was ready to concede that the chances were slim to none that they would ever get back together.

Trace knew he ought to cut his losses and get the hell out of Dodge. But he'd come up with a plan that he thought might work to pry Callie loose from Three Oaks.

What if her family no longer needed her help to survive? What if they could manage on their own? Then there would be nothing to stop her from going away with him. Everything depended, of course, on making certain that Callie's mother and oldest brother pulled their weight.

The problem was, he had no idea what skills either of them had, or whether they would be willing to apply them to keep Three Oaks afloat.

He started with Sam, because he found it less daunting to contend with the hatred of the crippled man than with the quiet understanding of Callie's mother. The hospital had dried Sam out before they'd sent him home, and as far as Trace knew, he hadn't had a drink since. But Trace rarely saw him when he visited the rest of the family.

While Callie and the kids were playing Scrabble in the living room one evening, Trace excused himself as though he were going to the bathroom. Instead, he went down the hall and knocked on Sam's first-floor bedroom door. When there was no answer, he let himself in.

"Get out," Sam said without turning around.

Trace was surprised to find Sam sitting in front of a computer. On the screen was what looked like accounting information. "What's that you're working on?" he asked.

"None of your business."

"I think maybe it is," Trace said.

Sam exited the program before turning his wheelchair to face Trace. "What hold do you have over my sister, that she lets you hang around here?"

"I loaned her the money to pay the first installment of your dad's estate taxes."

"Sonofabitch! I knew it was something like that."

"So you see, I do have an interest in keeping Three Oaks up and running. What were you working on?" Trace asked.

Sam perused him through narrowed eyes, then admitted, "I was calculating how much it's going to cost to feed those quarantined cows until we can sell them."

"Did you come up with a figure?" Trace asked.

"Too damn much!" Sam replied. "If I could talk face-to-face with Wally Tippet at the feed store, I might be able to get him to cut us a deal on hay. But I'm not sure when Callie can spare the time to drive me into town."

"Is there some reason why you don't drive yourself?" Trace asked.

Sam pounded his dead right leg with his fist. "That ought to be obvious."

"There are vehicles rigged with hand controls for paraplegics."

"And they're damned expensive," Sam shot back.

"Seems to me it would be an economy to buy a vehicle you can drive, if it meant you wouldn't be hanging around taking up space without earning your keep."

He saw the quick flush stain Sam's cheeks.

"Your brother's the reason I don't earn my keep," Sam said sullenly.

"Nobody forced all that alcohol down your throat.

Nobody's stopping you from shaving yourself or getting a haircut. Nobody's keeping you from carrying your share of the load around here."

"I can't carry a goddamn thing!" Sam said bitterly. "Not with these useless legs."

"Shut up and listen," Trace said. "I just spent the past seven years with a man who couldn't use his legs, and he ran a spread twice the size of Bitter Creek practically by himself. I didn't hear him moaning about his useless legs. He got up every morning and put on his clothes and went to work. Which is what I suggest you do from now on."

Sam stared at him in disbelief. "You can't come in here and start ordering me around."

"I'll have a van waiting outside tomorrow morning, along with someone to give you a driving lesson. You can sit in this room the rest of your life and feel sorry for yourself, or you can go to work. The choice is yours."

Trace turned and walked out, closing the door quietly behind him. A moment later, he heard something crash and splinter against the door. Well, he'd done his best. He'd have to wait until tomorrow to see if it was going to work.

He debated whether to approach Callie's mother now or wait until later. When he saw that Callie had taken the kids upstairs to put them to bed, he decided it would be better to get this all over with at once.

He found Mrs. Creed in the kitchen making an apple pie—from scratch.

"You can buy those in the frozen-food section already prepared and save yourself a lot of time," he pointed out.

She looked up and smiled. "I know. But I find it relaxing to peel apples. Would you like to try it?"

"Sure." Trace took the paring knife she offered and the McIntosh apple she handed him and sat down at the kitchen table.

"I always try to see how much skin I can peel off in one piece," Mrs. Creed said, as she retrieved another paring knife from a kitchen drawer.

Trace concentrated on what he was doing so completely that he was surprised when he looked up—with the entire red peel removed from the apple in one piece— to find Lauren Creed studying him. He smiled sheepishly and set the peel on the table. "I don't know about relaxing, but it was certainly engrossing. It made me forget entirely why I came in here."

"Why did you come in here?" she asked, beginning to peel another apple.

"May I speak frankly, Mrs. Creed?"

"Please call me Ren. And I hope you will."

"I need your help . . . Ren. You must have noticed that Callie and I . . . that I . . ."

"I've noticed," she said with a smile. "Go on."

"I've seen your belt buckle collection framed above the mantel, the ones you got for winning all those national cutting horse competitions, and I wondered why you stopped riding."

"I grew up and got married," she said as she finished peeling one apple and picked up another. "My children had to come first."

He picked up a second apple and went to work. "But your children are all grown up."

"Lately, I've been busy taking care of my grandchildren."

"How would you feel about going back to work with

cutting horses?" he asked as he set down another single piece of peel and retrieved another apple from the bowl on the table.

Callie's mother smiled and began coring and slicing peeled apples. "I think I might enjoy it a great deal."

"You would?" he said, accidentally slicing through the peel, which fell to the table. "That's great!"

"It may not make any difference," she said quietly. "My daughter has a very strong sense of duty."

"I want her to see that you can manage without her," Trace said.

"I'm not sure we can," she replied.

Trace had a queasy feeling in his stomach, like his airplane had just dropped a thousand feet over the Australian desert, and he only had a gallon jug of water with him. "I hope you're wrong," he said.

"For my daughter's sake, I hope so, too. I'd invite you to stay and help me finish up this pie," Mrs. Creed said, "but I suspect my grandchildren are waiting for you to come upstairs and kiss them good night."

"I expect so, ma'am." He'd made it a part of his day to read a story to Hannah at bedtime. He was determined to win Callie's kids over. He'd grown genuinely fond of the little girl, and although Eli remained prickly, he was making headway with the boy.

"Please don't call me ma'am," Callie's mother said with a groan. "It makes me feel my age."

"Sorry about that, Ren." Trace set down the paring knife and pushed his chair back from the table. "I expect you know I plan to take Callie away from here."

"I figured that out."

"You don't mind?"

She met his gaze, and Trace was startled by the piercing look he found in her gray-green eyes, "I want my daughter to be happy, Trace. Can you make her happy?"

"I'll do my best, ma'am. Ren," he corrected himself.

"Then I don't mind at all."

Callie was astonished when Sam arrived at the breakfast table freshly shaven, his long hair neatly combed back into a ponytail, which he'd caught in a rubber band at his nape. "You look . . . wide awake," she said cautiously, as she handed him a cup of hot coffee.

"I'm sober," Sam said when he caught her checking his eyes for redness and his breath for alcohol.

Callie laughed nervously. "You must admit—"

"That's not my normal condition," Sam finished for her as he blew on the coffee and then sipped it. "But it's a new day, Callie. I'm going to start doing my share around here."

"What miracle caused this change?"

"Trace told me about the loan, Callie."

Callie swore under her breath.

Sam glanced up at her, then back at his lifeless legs. "I've already figured out what he must have asked for in return. I just wish I were still man enough to do something about it."

"Oh, Sam," Callie said. "There's so much you don't know. So much I wish I could tell you."

"Are you going to marry him?"

"Of course not!"

"Why not?"

"Well, for one thing, he hasn't asked," Callie said. *At least, not in so many words.*

"Would you marry him if he did ask?"

She laughed nervously. "That's a ridiculous question."

"I didn't think so when I asked it," Sam said. "Why won't you marry him, Callie?"

"How many reasons do you need? You're in a wheelchair, and his brother put you there. His father wants to steal Three Oaks away from us. He's a Blackthorne, and I'm a Creed."

Sam snorted. "If he's good enough to sleep with, seems like he'd be good enough to marry."

"Trace owns a cattle station in Australia, Sam. If I married him, I'd end up living on the other side of the world. Do you really think you and Mom and Luke can manage Three Oaks by yourselves and pay off Dad's estate taxes, too?"

"We could give it a try."

"And if you fail?"

"Then we'd lose the ranch."

"That's not an option I'm willing to consider," Callie said. "Daddy would have wanted us to save Three Oaks, no matter what the cost. I know Mom thinks we're fighting a losing battle. But there must have been lots of times over the past hundred and fifty years when things got tough, and no Creed has ever given up this land. They did what was necessary to persevere. Can we do any less?"

Callie was distracted by a knock on the kitchen door. "I'm not expecting anyone. Are you?"

"Yes," Sam said, taking a big slurp of coffee and setting down his cup.

Callie didn't recognize the pretty young woman at the door.

"I'm here to see Sam Creed," she said.

"That's me," Sam said as he wheeled his chair over to the open door.

"What is this all about?" Callie asked, as Sam maneuvered his way through the kitchen door and onto the back porch.

"I'm about to take a driving lesson," Sam said. "Compliments of your good friend Trace Blackthorne."

Callie stared from the van parked in the morning shadows behind the house, to her brother, to the young woman standing on the back porch. "And you agreed to this?"

"Why wouldn't I agree?" Sam said. "Especially if I'm going to do my part to save Three Oaks from Darth Vadar and the Evil Empire."

"Don't make jokes. This is serious."

"I'm on your side, Callie. Trace said some things last night that started me thinking. I realize now that I should have insisted on getting wheels a lot sooner. I made myself a burden on you and—"

"Oh, Sam, no," Callie cried.

"Stuff it, Callie. The truth is the truth." He turned to the young woman and said, "I'm assuming this vehicle has some mechanism for getting me into the driver's seat, since you don't look big enough to lift me up there."

She smiled back at him and said, "Absolutely."

Sam turned to Callie and said, "I think I can take it from here. You'd better get breakfast on the table before the hungry horde gets downstairs."

Callie closed the door and stared out the kitchen window at Sam, who was deftly maneuvered into the van. She waved goodbye, then crossed to pour herself another cup of coffee. Sam sober. Sam driving. Sam anxious to do his share of the work. It was a great deal to absorb in one morning.

She wasn't given much time to think about it, because a moment later Eli and Hannah came trooping downstairs. Luke wasn't far behind.

"Where's Mom?" Callie asked her brother.

"She's already up and gone."

"Gone? Gone where?" Callie asked.

"Out to the stable," Luke answered.

"What for?"

"I'm hungry, Mommy," Hannah said, tugging on Callie's sleeve.

"In a minute, Hannah. What's Mom doing at the stable?" Callie asked.

"Working with the cutting horses."

Callie gaped. "Mom? Is exercising horses?"

Luke grabbed a slice of cinnamon toast from the plate on the counter and handed it to Hannah. "Yep."

Luke settled Hannah in her chair and said to Eli, "Bring that bowl of scrambled eggs over to the table." He reached around Callie, who was still standing rigid in the middle of the kitchen, for the platter of fried ham.

Callie stared at her helpful brother in disbelief. "What's gotten into everybody?" she wondered aloud.

"Trace said I could start earning the money for a motorcycle by working for him in the afternoon, if I helped you out with Eli and Hannah in the morning."

While Callie was still reeling at Luke's announcement, there was another knock on the door. She beat Luke to the door and opened it to find an elderly Mexican woman standing on the doorstep.

"Buenos días, Señora Monroe. I'm Rosalita's younger sister, Gloriana. Señor Trace asked me to come today and take care of your beautiful daughter."

Callie was too stunned to move. Luke slipped an arm around her waist and drew her back out of the doorway as he ushered Gloriana inside.

Trace was right behind the Mexican woman.

"What's going on?" Callie asked when she saw him. "I don't recognize my family. It seems you've waved a magic wand and turned them all into strangers."

"Why don't we take a walk?" Trace suggested. "We can talk and watch the sunrise."

"The sun's been up for an hour."

"Then we'll look at the clouds. You boys better make a run for the bus," Trace said to Luke and Eli. "Be good and mind Gloriana," he said to Hannah, as he urged Callie out the kitchen door and closed it behind them.

"What's going on?" Callie asked, as Trace led her away from the house.

He turned her to face him and gently kissed her on the mouth. "I wanted you to myself for the day, so I manipulated things a little bit to arrange it."

"A little bit?"

"Well, maybe a lot. Forgive me?"

Callie thought she probably ought to thank him, but she couldn't make herself say the words. She settled for, "I suppose."

"Beautiful clouds this morning," he murmured, as he kissed her eyes closed. "Come on, Callie. Spend the day with me. Just the two of us. It'll be fun."

"What did you have in mind?" she murmured, as he kissed his way down her throat.

"I don't know. What would you like to do?"

"My family needs me here."

"I need you, too, Callie. Will you come and play with me?"

Callie surprised herself. She said yes.

Trace took her to his cabin. He said he wanted to pick up a book to read, if they were going to spend a lazy day sitting under the trees, staring at the clouds going by. But when she followed him into the bedroom, he leaned over to kiss her on the neck, and her hand slid down his hip.

They didn't come up for air till it was dark.

When Callie got home, the house was quiet, and she found her mother sitting in a chair in front of the fireplace knitting.

Callie blushed as she remembered what she and Trace had done in the wing chair in front of his fireplace.

"Did you have a good time?" her mother asked.

"Yes, I did," Callie replied.

"I'm glad you enjoyed yourself," her mother said with a smile. "You look rested."

Callie didn't see how that was possible. She'd been engaged in vigorous exercise all day. "I curled up for a little while and took a nap." That was true. She'd fallen asleep after they'd made love for the second time.

"Come sit by me," her mother said.

Callie dropped to the floor at her mother's knee. The clack of the knitting needles was familiar and reassuring. Her glance slid to the empty chair that had so recently been occupied by her father. The world had turned. Their lives had changed.

"How was your day?" Callie asked her mother.

"I spent most of it on horseback," her mother replied.

"How did it go?"

The clacking stopped. "I'd forgotten how exciting it is to ride a cutting horse," her mother said. "I enjoyed myself immensely, though I expect I'll pay for it tomorrow. I'm not used to spending so much time in the saddle."

"You don't have to do this, Mom."

"But I want to, Callie. I thought I'd forgotten everything I knew. I surprised myself by how much I remember."

"I'm glad," Callie said.

The knitting needles began to clack again. "You should go with him," her mother said.

"I'm afraid you'll sell once I'm gone," Callie admitted, as she stared into the fire.

"I'd never sell unless I had to."

Callie looked up at her mother and said, "I'd never sell at all. I can't leave until I'm sure Three Oaks is safe, Mom."

"Trace won't wait for you forever."

Callie felt an ache in her chest. "I know, Mom. I know."

Callie hadn't planned to have a party to celebrate Eli's eleventh birthday, because she didn't want Trace counting days on the calendar. She felt guilty that she hadn't told him about his son, but she was certain that if Trace knew the truth, he would insist on taking Eli with him to Australia. So she'd intended to observe Eli's birthday without a great deal of fanfare.

But Lou Ann had called to say she wanted to host a birthday party for Eli so Dusty would have a chance to practice with his new prosthetic leg around friends, and went on and on about how self-conscious Dusty felt wearing the artificial limb, until Callie didn't have the heart to refuse.

Eli was delighted at the prospect of all the presents he'd receive, all the games he'd get to play, and all the cake and ice cream he'd get to eat. Callie helped him make a list of the friends he wanted to invite.

"Is Trace coming?" Eli asked when they were done.

"Do you want to invite him?" Callie asked.

Eli doodled on the paper in front of him. "He's kind of bossy."

"I think orders come naturally to the ramrod of a big outfit," she said.

"Trace isn't the boss of us," Eli pointed out.

"True," Callie conceded. "But I think he means well, don't you?"

Eli gave a noncommittal shrug. "I guess."

"You don't have to invite him," Callie said. In fact, that would be the perfect excuse to exclude Trace. *It's Eli's party, and I'm sorry, but you're not invited.*

"It might hurt his feelings if I don't," Eli said, nervously flicking his pencil against the kitchen table.

Callie was surprised. Her belligerent son concerned about someone else's feelings? *About his own father's feelings?* Callie let out a careful breath.

"It's your party, Eli," she said. "What do you say?" Callie wasn't sure what answer she wanted from Eli. Trace would probably be hurt—or at least feel piqued—if Eli excluded him, but it was the safe move.

She was terrified that Trace would suddenly wake up and see all the ways Eli was like him. How Eli shoved the hair off his brow with the same thrust of his hand, or how father and son both rubbed their chins when they were thinking. Or how much Eli's features resembled Trace's. Except for his eyes. *He has your eyes, Callie.*

"Aw. Let him come," Eli said at last. "I guess one more won't hurt."

Callie prayed he was right.

By the time dawn arrived on the surprisingly warm, late October morning of Eli's birthday, Callie was wishing she hadn't given in to Lou Ann's plea. She'd been up all night with a colicky horse, but with the Futurity little more than a month away, she didn't dare neglect her workouts with Sugar Pep and Smart Little Doc.

She tried to keep herself focused on what she was doing, but Smart Little Doc was smart enough to catch her dozing, and took advantage of her inattention to set her down in the sand.

Callie looked up at the horse, who came over to nuzzle her and snort a horse laugh. "Very funny," she said. "I hope you don't plan to do that at the Futurity."

Smart Little Doc flicked his ears forward and back and whickered a reproof.

"All right. It was my fault. I won't let it happen again."

When Callie got back to the house, she discovered her mother had already taken Hannah and left to help Lou Ann decorate for the party. Once she was showered and had put on clean jeans, a white shirt with a string tie, and a leather vest, she knocked on Sam's door.

When he answered, she asked, "Can you give me a ride over to Lou Ann's?"

Sam grinned at her. "You trust my driving?"

"No, but I'm desperate. The truck was acting up this morning."

"I'm ready when you are," Sam said.

Callie was amazed at how adept Sam was at managing the van. "You really are a good driver," she said in amazement.

"Don't act so surprised. I drove plenty before I got hurt."

"I guess you did."

"Did Trace tell you he's having ramps and bathroom rails installed in the foreman's house, so I can live there?" Sam said, as he maneuvered the van into a narrow parking spot behind Dusty and Lou Ann's house.

"No. He didn't say a word about that."

"I hope you don't mind. I know there are still a few of Nolan's things there. I'll be glad to box them up for you."

Callie waited for the tears to come at the mention of Nolan's name. But they didn't. "I'd appreciate that," she said to Sam.

When they arrived, Dusty slid an arm around Callie's waist and dragged her from the van. "You look very pretty today."

"Thank you," she replied. "I see you're walking on two legs—and without crutches."

"All a matter of balance, my dear," he said, escorting her to the house.

And who knew more about balance than a cutter, who had to keep himself centered on a two-thousand-pound whirling, wheeling dynamo? Callie thought.

"I'm proud of you, Dusty," Callie said, leaning over to kiss his cheek. "Lou Ann's told me how hard you've worked to get back on your feet."

"I couldn't have done it without Trace," Dusty admitted. "I owe him a big debt." Dusty grinned. "I can't believe I let Trace talk me into working for Blackjack when he goes back to Australia."

"So he told you about that."

"Finally," Dusty said. "Speaking of which, is there anything you'd like to tell me?"

"Like what?" Callie asked.

"Like whether you're going with him."

"No. I'm not."

"Too bad. Speak of the devil," he said. "There he is."

Callie froze. Trace was sitting at Dusty's picnic table with Eli, their heads bent close together. Callie felt a chill of alarm. What if Eli accidentally said something that revealed the truth? She hurried across the patio, anxious to separate her son and his father.

Eli held up the woven wool horse blanket so Trace could admire the Western pattern.

"Very nice," Trace said. "What else did you get?"

"Pokémon cards and a Star Wars light saber and an R. L. Stine novel—I've already read it, so I'm gonna have to go trade it for another one—and a Monopoly game and lots of other stuff."

"You made out like a bandit," Trace said, smoothing down the boy's cowlick.

Eli grinned up at him. "I sure did." Eli glanced at

Trace and said, "I wish my dad were here. I really miss him."

"Yeah. That's tough," Trace said.

"Every year on my birthday he'd tell me the story of how he drove like a bat out of hell and ran four stoplights to get my mom to the hospital, 'cause I came three whole weeks early.

"I only weighed five pounds and twelve ounces," Eli said. "And look at me now!" He held his arms out like Arnold Schwarzenegger and waited for Trace to feel his muscles.

"Pretty strong, all right," Trace said, dutifully testing each biceps.

Mentally, Trace was doing the math, trying to figure out when Callie should have delivered. If today was October 22, that meant Callie shouldn't have delivered until mid-November. Which meant Callie had conceived on or about . . . Valentine's Day. On Valentine's Day eleven years ago, he and Callie had left the dance at the UT Student Union and driven up into the hill country, where they'd found a spot in the cool grass along the banks of the Colorado and made love the rest of the night.

And created a child together.

Trace stared at the boy with new eyes, noticing the familiar cowlick in his black hair and his sharp nose and Blackthorne chin. Eli was tall, with big hands and big feet, like a puppy that still had growing to do. Like Trace had been at the same age. He was horrified to think Callie had kept such a secret from him.

I have a son. Eli is my son.

He'd missed so much! The pain was searing.

Breathtaking. Why hadn't Callie told him? She had to have known she was pregnant long before he'd gone away.

"Eli! Lou Ann needs you in the kitchen to help her light your birthday candles."

Trace turned at the sound of Callie's voice and stared at her, with all the fury he felt for what she'd done there in his eyes for her to see.

"You want to come help me, Trace?" Eli offered.

"No, son." His throat ached as he said the word for the first time knowing he was addressing his own flesh and blood. "You go on ahead. I need to talk to your mother."

He saw the fear on Callie's face but felt no compassion for her. "I've found out your secret, Callie." He rose slowly and said, "Come with me."

"Trace, I can explain."

"Not now," he said curtly. "Wait till we're alone."

Trace kept his hand at the small of Callie's back, forcing her ahead of him until they reached the shade of a live oak he thought was far enough from the party that he could raise his voice without being heard. Because he felt like howling.

When they stopped, he waited until Callie turned to face him before he spoke. "Is Eli my son?"

"Yes, but—"

"Shut up. I have a few things to say before you start making excuses."

When she stared at the ground, he grabbed her chin and forced her face up until their eyes met. "You'll marry me as soon as I can get a license. Then, my son is going back to Australia with me. You can stay here and take care of your family, or come along for the ride. I don't really give a damn."

He let her go and stepped back, because he had the urge to hit something, and he didn't want it to be her. "How could you, Callie? How could you steal all those years from me?"

"You ran away and never came back! What did you expect me to do? How was I supposed to find you? You never wrote to me. You never called me or contacted me. Nolan offered to legitimize your son. Should I have let Eli be born a bastard?"

"He should have been a Blackthorne! You must have known long before I left Texas that you were carrying my child. You should have told me about him, Callie. You should have given me a chance to be a father to my son."

"If you'd really cared about me you would never have left in the first place!" she accused. "How do you think I felt? Alone and pregnant. And with your child! A Blackthorne child! I couldn't tell anyone the truth."

"Not even me."

"You weren't here!" Callie cried. "And you couldn't have missed me much. I heard about all the women, Trace."

"What women?"

"The women you took up with the minute I was gone."

"I was trying to make you jealous, Callie. I wanted you to care."

"If you wanted to hurt me, you did. More than you know."

"And you've had your revenge," Trace said bitterly.

"For what it's worth, I'm sorry."

He took a menacing step forward. "Sorry? Sorry can't make up for what you took from me."

Callie held her ground. "What is it you want from me? Nothing can change the past."

"I've told you what I want. My son."

"You can't have him."

"He's mine, Callie."

"You're a stranger. He hardly knows you."

"Whose fault is that?" Trace snarled.

"You have no right to him. We were never married "

"We will be."

"You can't force me to marry you."

"Can't I?" He grasped her arms. "Think about it, Callie. All the power of Bitter Creek aimed at the destruction of Three Oaks."

"You'd never sink that low."

"I'd hand my father the sledge hammer."

He saw, from the stricken look on her face, that she believed him. "You owe me, Callie, for all the years I didn't get to spend loving my son."

"I can't give him up to you, Trace. I won't give him up. Not even to save Three Oaks."

At last, something she cared about more than Three Oaks. Not him. His son. He let her go and took a step back. "Then I'll fight you for him in court. And when I get custody—and in this part of Texas, that's a foregone conclusion—you'll never see him again."

He saw the moment she realized she was beaten. Saw the moment when she knew it was useless to fight.

She met his gaze and said, "All right. I'll marry you. But I want something in return."

"How much is it going to cost me to buy my son?" Trace asked icily.

"I want all the inheritance taxes paid on Three Oaks. I want the title free and clear in my mother's name."

"Done," Trace said. "Now get the hell out of my sight."

Chapter 16

Callie rubbed her thumb across her ring finger, where Trace had placed a plain gold band only yesterday. He'd insisted on being married in a church, but he hadn't invited his family to the ceremony, or allowed her to invite hers. He'd told her to dress as though they were going to Bobbie Jo's Café in town, and he'd driven a pickup, since taking any of his father's luxury automobiles would have provoked questions. Then they'd driven south across the border, to a small chapel in Matamoros, Mexico.

Callie didn't know how Trace had arranged to have a Christian minister read their vows in the ancient Spanish mission, but she'd been grateful for the cool shadows created by the thick adobe and relished the rainbow of light through the stained glass windows. They were small comfort during such a dark moment in her life.

As he repeated his vows, Trace had looked at her with wintry blue eyes, as remote from her as though they still lived a continent apart. And yet he had promised to love and honor and cherish her. How had he choked out the words? They had stuck in her throat.

He had wiped her tears away with his callused thumbs before he bent to kiss her. His breath had felt warm against her cold flesh, before his lips touched hers in the barest caress. Then he'd taken a step back, clasped her hand, and led her out into the blazing heat and blinding sunlight.

Thirty miles north of Brownsville, while they were sitting in line for a spot inspection by the Border Patrol, waiting to have the pickup sniffed for drugs by a German shepherd, Trace had announced, "You'll need to take that ring off before we get home. I want this marriage kept secret until my son is ready to hear about it."

"When do you think that will be?" Callie asked, tugging the ring free and setting it in a pocket on the dash between them.

"When he's ready to accept me for who I am," Trace replied. "When I've earned his trust."

Her ring finger was bare now. Callie might almost have imagined the events of the previous day. But the tension radiating from the man standing next to her at the corral was quite real.

"I wish you hadn't given Eli such an expensive gift for his birthday," Callie said, as she watched her son urge the spirited quarter horse gelding from a trot to a lope in the ring. "It's too much."

"Eli doesn't seem to mind."

Callie made a face. "What eleven-year-old boy wouldn't be happy to get not only a brand-new saddle but the registered quarter horse to put it on?"

"My son deserves more than he's had so far."

Callie bristled at the suggestion that Eli had led a life

of deprivation. "*My* son hasn't wanted for anything. He's been loved and cherished his whole life!"

"Not by me!" Trace shot back.

Callie didn't argue. There was nothing she could say. Her chin started to quiver at the mere thought of Trace taking Eli all the way to Australia.

"Give him a little more rein," Trace instructed Eli.

"Can I go in the ring now?" Hannah asked from her perch atop the shiny black pony she'd received at the same time Eli had gotten his quarter horse.

Callie noticed the question was directed at Trace, rather than to her. "Not yet," she answered her daughter.

"Why not?" Hannah demanded, her lips pouting.

"It isn't safe," Trace replied.

Callie noticed Hannah didn't argue with Trace, merely accepted his word as law. But if Hannah had fallen completely under Trace's spell, Callie felt sure the same was true of Trace in regard to Hannah. His gift to Eli was understandable. His generosity to Hannah was not. Hannah was another man's child. Hannah was a reminder that Callie had been married to Nolan Monroe.

But Trace didn't seem to mind when Hannah walked in his shadow, when Hannah demanded to be picked up and hugged and kissed, when Hannah wanted Trace to tuck her in or read her a bedtime story. He had already won Hannah over. It wouldn't be long before he had Eli's trust. And once that happened, he would take her son and leave Texas.

"How am I doing, Trace?" Eli called out.

"You're doing great. Slow him down and cool him off."

"When can I take Hickory for a ride in the pasture?" Eli asked, patting the sorrel's neck.

"How about if we both ride out and take along a picnic?" Trace suggested.

"Can I go, too?" Hannah asked.

"Sure. We'll all go," Trace said with a smile. "I've already asked your grandmother to pack the two of us a lunch. She can always add another couple of sandwiches. It'll be fun."

Callie stared at Trace, annoyed at how quickly he'd arranged her day. "I have work to do."

"Fine. You stay here. I can take care of the kids."

Callie wasn't about to leave Trace alone with Eli. What if he took the boy and disappeared? "I'll rearrange my schedule," she said.

Trace eyed her sideways. "Whatever you say."

Callie fumed inside at how she'd been manipulated. But once they were on the trail, and she saw what a good time her children were having, she admitted it had been too long since they'd done anything like this. She'd been too busy since Nolan's death to take time off with the kids just for fun. Or rather, she hadn't aligned her priorities to put fun at the top of the list, as Trace seemed inclined to do.

"I spy a hawk," Eli said, pointing to the sky.

"I spy a cow," Hannah said pointing into the brush.

"Cows don't count, do they, Trace?" Eli asked.

"I did say be on the lookout for *wild* animals. But that cow looks pretty wild to me," Trace said, winking at Hannah.

Hannah giggled.

Eli rolled his eyes. "Sheesh. Cows."

"Bird!" Hannah exclaimed, as her pony flushed a grouse.

"Hey! That's cheating," Eli complained. "You have to spy 'em before you scare 'em out of hiding. Does that count, Trace?"

" 'Fraid so, Eli."

"Deer!" Eli said, as he surprised a herd of white-tailed deer. He counted aloud as each one bounded over the wire fence. "Wow! Seven! I'm gonna win for sure! What'll I get if I have the most, Trace?"

"My sincere admiration," Trace replied with a grin.

"Awww, shhh—"

"Eli," Callie warned.

"Sheesh," Eli said, changing the expletive in mid-word.

Callie realized where they were going when they were halfway there. It was a pond she'd shown to Trace on the night they'd been searching for her parents. It was the place she'd gone to dream about might-have-beens, while she was waiting for Eli to grow inside her womb.

Cattails lined the far edge of the pond, and a nearby live oak provided shade so thorough that the land beneath it was nearly bare of undergrowth. The surface of the pond was perfectly smooth, except for the ripple caused by two blue-winged teals paddling toward the safety of the concealing cattails.

Callie pulled her horse alongside Trace's and murmured, "This was my special place. Why did you bring us here?"

"Now it's going to be our special place, too," he answered. "Mine and my son's."

Callie turned her face away to hide the stinging tears

309

that threatened and let her horse fall behind the other three riders. Before Trace had learned the truth about Eli, he'd suggested that she go with him to Australia. That offer had apparently been withdrawn. Now his son was going to be all the company he wanted or needed on the journey.

Not that Callie would, or could go with him. Her family still needed her. Even though Trace had signed a prenuptial agreement promising to pay the taxes on Three Oaks when they came due, there was no telling what other disasters might befall them. Without her there to keep the wolf from the door, Blackjack would surely find a way to take what he'd always coveted.

But how could she allow Trace to take Eli away? Her heart would break in two. She was torn between love and duty, and couldn't choose between them. So she simply avoided making any choice at all.

Callie's heart hurt. She put a fist against what was almost a physical pain in her chest, knowing it was despair that caused the ache inside her. Could she have made a different choice eleven years ago? Should she have told Trace right away he was going to be a father? Should she have reached out for love, married the son of her father's nemesis, and hoped for the best where her family was concerned?

Maybe she should have done that. Her sister Bay certainly hadn't flinched at leaving her family behind to pursue her own dreams. Bay had left home and never looked back. Even now, she was at Texas A&M finishing her degree.

But Callie wasn't Bay. She was the eldest. She'd

always put her family's needs first. Even when it had meant sacrificing her own.

It was what her mother had taught her to do. It was what her mother had done herself. Callie had even done her best to be happy with a man she wasn't "in love" with, just as her mother had done. Callie realized she'd made the same choices as her mother. The same mistakes.

You can make a different choice, Callie.

What a tempting thought. How easy it would be to let herself fall in love with Trace all over again. How lovely to think of building a whole new life in an exotic, faraway place. She'd never had the chance to travel. She'd never had the chance to spread her wings and fly. She wanted more children, and she knew Trace did, too. From the way he'd so easily won over her children—Hannah followed him around like a puppy, and Eli seemed to crave his attention and approval—she knew he would make a wonderful father.

Callie couldn't understand the rebellious inclinations that kept surfacing lately. Couldn't understand why a devotion to family that had never seemed onerous suddenly made her feel like a fly struggling in a spider's web, certain that unless she escaped soon, she'd be devoured.

The sound of Trace's voice yanked her from her reverie. "Who wants to swim before lunch?"

"I don't have a swimsuit!" Eli lamented.

Trace grinned. "Ever hear of skinny dipping?"

"No skinny dipping!" Callie announced, as a provocative image of Trace swimming naked flashed through her mind.

Trace shot her a smug grin. "Just kidding. I had your

mother pack swimsuits, too." He threw Eli his swimsuit and said, "You can go behind the tree to change."

Eli was off his horse in an instant and headed for the live oak.

"Loosen the cinch on Hickory's saddle first, son," Trace said, calling Eli back. "And tie the reins up so he doesn't stumble on them while he's grazing."

"Sure, Trace," Eli said, grabbing the reins and tugging the horse along as he headed behind the tree.

"I can't swim," Hannah wailed.

"I'll help you," Trace offered.

"I can help her," Callie said in a cool voice.

"I want Trace to help me," Hannah said. "Will you, Trace?"

"Sure, Hannah. Whatever you want."

"You'll spoil her rotten," Callie said under her breath.

Trace shrugged. "Little girls were made to be spoiled."

"Maybe in the Blackthorne household. At Three Oaks everyone has to pull his own weight."

"Hannah's too young to be pulling any weight at all," Trace snapped back. "And I won't see her put in traces like you were, before she's had a chance to kick up her heels."

Callie found herself staring at Trace's back as he stalked away from her. The metaphor was horrifying when she thought about it. Was that how Trace saw her life? Like she was a plowhorse harnessed with a load too heavy to bear?

Hannah got both legs on one side of the saddle, then grabbed hold of a few strips of leather streaming from a silver concha on the saddle, and let her hands slide down until her feet touched the ground. "Where's my swim-suit?" she asked Trace.

He handed it to her and said, "Your mom can help you get into it."

This time, Callie didn't miss her cue. "Where's my suit?" she asked. "I might as well change at the same time as Hannah."

Trace eyed her over his shoulder, then gestured with his chin. "Check my saddlebags."

"And your suit?" Callie inquired.

He pulled his hand out from behind his back, and she saw a pair of cutoff jeans. "Right here. I'll be with Eli."

Callie had to admit the cool water was refreshing. And Hannah did, finally, take two splashing strokes from Trace's arms to her own. Then she watched as Trace and Eli roughhoused in the water. She tried to remember a time when Nolan had done such a thing. She tried to excuse the fact it had never happened with the thought that Eli had been so young when Nolan got sick.

Eli was eight. He could swim even then. Nolan could have done this anytime.

But he never had. Callie wondered which of the two of them had been remiss. Had Nolan been too busy working to suggest this sort of fun? Or was she the one responsible for putting work first and foremost? *Responsibility before pleasure. Duty before personal happiness.*

There was something wrong with a life that didn't include laughter. Something sorrowful about a life that didn't include fun.

Callie felt Hannah being swept from her arms an in-stant before she felt Eli's palms on her shoulders, forcing her underwater. She barely had time to gasp a breath of air before she was submerged. When she came up, her hair streaming around her face and water dripping off her nose and eyelashes, Eli and Hannah were laughing hysterically.

"We got you, Mom!" Eli said, chortling.

Hannah clapped her hands and parroted, "We got you, Mom!"

Callie joined their laughter, as she shoved her sopping hair out of her face. "I'm hungry. Who else would like to eat?"

She was nearly trampled by Eli's race to the edge of the pond. She followed Trace as he stepped out of the water and set Hannah down on solid ground.

"Change first," Callie shouted at Eli.

"Aw, Mom!" Eli shouted back.

"Change first," Trace agreed.

"Sheesh!" Eli muttered from behind the tree. "Grownups!"

"Sheesh!" Hannah said, hands on her hips as she turned to stare up at them. "Grown-ups!"

Callie and Trace exchanged a look and broke into guffaws of laughter. A moment later, Callie's expression sobered.

This was what had been missing from her life. Laughter. Joy. Delight. She wanted back all those years with Nolan. She wished she'd tried harder to make him happy. To bring him joy. To give her children laughter.

Trace had offered her a glimpse of what she'd lost when she'd turned her back on him. What she saw was so wonderful, it left her aching. And wishing. And even, God help her, hoping. What if Trace could forgive her? What if they could be a family? What if they could live happily ever after?

Trace spread a blanket for them to sit on, while Callie sorted through the picnic fare her mother had packed.

"Hard-boiled eggs, carrot sticks, pickles," she announced as she unpacked each item.

"I want a pickle," Eli said, reaching out a hand.

As Trace handed him a pickle, Hannah said, "I want a pickle, too."

"You don't like pickles," Callie informed her.

"I might," Hannah said, keeping her hand outstretched.

Callie shrugged and said to Trace. "Give it to her."

Hannah took one lick and scrunched up her face. "Ick. Here, Mom," she said, holding it out to Callie. "You eat it."

"No thanks," Callie said quickly. "See if Trace wants it."

"I think we should give it to your mother," Trace said, taking it from Hannah and holding it out to Callie. "As I recall, she likes to suck off all the pickle juice before she eats it."

Callie couldn't look at the pickle. Or at Trace, for that matter.

"Hey, Mom, why's your face so red?" Eli asked.

Callie shot one mortified look at Trace, grabbed the pickle and took a large bite, chewing furiously and nearly choking when she swallowed too fast.

"That's not how I remember you eating a pickle," Trace said in a husky voice.

Callie met his eyes for an instant and saw the passion lurking there, just as it had when she'd teased him by sucking salaciously on a pickle in the college cafeteria a lifetime ago. Unfortunately, he'd had a test right after lunch and couldn't skip class. When they'd finally gotten together in her room, the sex had been frenzied and wild.

"Maybe we should have our sandwiches now," Callie said quickly, dropping the pickle on a paper plate and reaching into the saddlebag that contained the rest of the food.

"This tastes great," Eli said as he wolfed his down.

"Slow down, or you'll get a stomachache," Callie warned.

She should have realized Eli would look to Trace.

"Your mother's right," Trace said. "Chew before you swallow."

Eli made a disgruntled noise through a mouthful of sandwich but waited before taking another bite. Where was the hatred for all things Blackthorne? Callie wondered. The answer was simple: Blotted out by the need for a man's approval . . . and a father's love.

Callie watched the expression in Trace's eyes as he drank in the sight of his son. Wistful. Proud. Sad. Callie wished there were some way to make up for the time with Eli that Trace had lost. But there wasn't. As much as she knew Eli would benefit from having a father's attention and love, she couldn't bear to give up her son. But she was afraid to leave her family prey to the machinations of Jackson Blackthorne.

Callie glanced at Trace and caught him looking back at her, the remnants of desire lingering in his eyes, and felt her body quicken. Maybe she wouldn't be going with Trace. But he was here now and he wanted her. She turned to Eli and said, "After lunch, you and Hannah need to lie down and take a quick nap."

"What are you and Trace going to do?" Eli asked.

Callie couldn't stop the flush that stained her cheeks. "Trace and I have things to . . . discuss." She looked up at Trace, the invitation clear in her eyes.

"Aw, Mom," Eli complained.

"Aw, Mom," Hannah echoed.

She knew Trace understood her intentions perfectly when he said, "Eli, Hannah, your mother's right."

Callie could feel Trace's carnal gaze on her the whole time she told a bedtime story to Hannah to help her fall asleep on the blanket. Despite his protestations that he wasn't sleepy, Eli's eyes closed even before Hannah's. When they were both asleep, Callie lifted her gaze to meet Trace's.

He stood and held out his hand. "Come with me."

Her legs felt like jelly when she stood. She was grateful for Trace's strong, supporting hand. "We can't go far," she said, glancing back at the two sleeping children.

"We won't," he promised.

In fact, he didn't go any farther than the opposite side of the massive live oak, which completely hid them from the children's view. He backed her up against the tree, settling himself in the cradle of her thighs with a satisfied sigh.

"I've missed this," he murmured against her hair.

Callie settled her hands on his hips as she leaned her head back for the kisses he was raining on her throat. "Me, too."

There was no way their lovemaking could be culminated, not with the children sleeping so close. But it was sweet to be held, lovely to be kissed. She hadn't expected Trace to talk. She was stunned by what he said.

"I love you, Callie. I've never stopped loving you. I shouldn't have run away when trouble came. I should have stayed to see things out. I should have been there with you when our son was born."

Callie couldn't breathe. She shoved Trace away and gasped for air, staring at him, wide-eyed with disbelief. She should have felt euphoric. The man she had never stopped loving, had never stopped loving her. What she felt was sick to her stomach. "Oh, Trace."

"I realized when I saw you in the pond, when I saw all of us together in the pond, that I don't want to run away again without trying to make things work between us. I want us to be a family, Callie. I want to make this a real marriage. I want you to come with me to Australia and bring Eli and Hannah. Will you?"

The sob erupted without warning, and Callie let herself be comforted in Trace's strong arms. She muffled the sound against his shoulder, not wanting her children to awaken and find her crying. Callie wasn't certain herself whether she was weeping with joy or in despair. In a fairy tale, Trace's speech would have signaled the beginning of happily ever after. But wonderful as his admission of love was, Callie was too aware of what still stood between them.

The feud. Their families. Her responsibilities.

"Can't you stay here?" she asked at last.

"I have a ranch of my own in Australia, Callie. I'll never have that here at Bitter Creek so long as my father's alive, and God willing, he'll live to a ripe old age. My future is in another place. I want you with me. Come with me," he urged.

"I can't Trace. Don't you see? I can't!"

"I'll be leaving after Christmas," he said. "And I'll be taking Eli with me."

She reached out to grasp his shirt with both hands. "Don't take my son away from me, Trace. Please. I'm begging you."

He freed himself from her grasp and took a step back, as his blue eyes turned to winter frost. "He's my son, too, Callie. The choice is yours."

"I want to be with you, Trace. I do. I . . ." The words *I love you* stuck in her throat. She couldn't tell Trace she loved him. If she truly loved him, wouldn't she sacrifice anything—everything—to be with him? But she wasn't willing to do that yet. She wished she could be with him and help her family too. But until she could figure out how to be in two places at once, that was impossible.

"My family needs me," she said on a whisper of breath. "Don't make me choose between you and them. It's tearing me apart!"

"I'll never understand you Creeds," he said bitterly. "Never."

As Trace wheeled and stalked away, Callie felt a sharp stab of loss. When he was gone, a wave of loneliness overwhelmed her. Callie's knees buckled and she sank to the ground. It hurt to breathe. It hurt to think. It hurt way too much to feel. But feelings bombarded her, nevertheless. Anger. Disappointment. Frustration.

"Hey, Mom, are you sleeping, or what?"

Callie looked up at her son and said, "I was just resting. All that swimming wore me out."

"Trace says it's time to go," Eli said. "We already packed the saddlebags and tightened all the cinches. Come on."

Eli tugged her to her feet, and Callie braced herself to confront Trace again. To her chagrin, he acted as though his confession of love and her inability to make a choice had never happened.

"You ready to go?" he asked.

She nodded. "We might as well get back. I've got—"

"Work to do," he finished for her.

"Well, I do," she muttered, as she mounted her horse.

"Oh, and Callie," he said, when they were separated a little ways from the children on horseback.

"What now?" she retorted.

"I just realized we never had a wedding night. Wouldn't want the wedding annulled for failure to consummate," he said. "Expect me after the children are tucked in."

Chapter 17

TRACE HAD TAKEN A RISK TELLING CALLIE HE loved her. He'd hoped it would make a difference. He should have known better. Callie was still clinging tooth and claw to Three Oaks. He might have considered finding a good manager for his cattle station and staying in Texas until Callie could leave, if she'd said those three words back to him. *I love you.* Was that so hard to say?

He watched Callie from the corner of his eye. She'd been keeping her distance from him since he'd told her he intended to come to her bed. But he wasn't going to give up what little time he had left with her just because she was too stubborn to realize what a mistake she was making. He was going to take what he wanted for the little time he had left in Texas and hope it was enough to fill the empty spaces inside him for a lifetime.

"Hey! What's that Texas Ranger doing here?" Eli called out, as they approached the barn.

Owen was leaning against the shady side of the barn, his hat pulled low. As soon as he saw them, he stood and tipped his hat back, revealing the grim look on his face.

"More bad news," Callie said, shaking her head.

"You don't know that," Trace said.

Callie shot him a look of disgust. "Take a look at his face. I guarantee I'm not going to be glad to hear whatever he has to say."

"Eli, you and Hannah take your horses around to the trough and give them a drink," Trace said. "Not too much, or they'll end up with a bellyache."

"Okay, Trace," Eli said.

"Okay, Trace," Hannah chirped.

Trace saw Hannah mimic the frown Eli aimed at Owen. Owen was Eli's uncle. They should have been good friends. But because Callie had kept his son a secret from him, the boy hated Blackthornes indiscriminately. Trace hoped and prayed the day would come when Eli could accept and trust and cherish his Blackthorne relations.

Before Owen could say a word, Eli came running back around the barn, hell-bent-for-leather. "Mom!" he shouted. "It's Freckles Fancy! She's in the corral. They're all back. All four of them!"

Callie slid off her horse and hurried to meet up with her excited son. "Are you sure?" She turned to look at Owen. "You've recovered my stolen stock?"

"Yes, ma'am," Owen said, touching the brim of his Stetson. "And caught the horse thief who stole them."

Callie laughed. "This is wonderful! Where? How?"

"Fellow was trying to sell them at a small auction house," Owen explained. "One of the buyers had seen my fliers on your missing fillies, thought he recognized Freckles Fancy, and gave me a call."

Trace wondered why Owen's eyes remained so bleak. He'd caught the bad guys and recovered Callie's stolen horses. That should be cause for celebration. Something was obviously amiss. Owen glanced at Eli, then at Trace, then gestured away with his head. Trace figured Owen wanted the boy gone and said, "Eli, did you leave your horse drinking at the trough?"

"Oh, yeah," Eli said sheepishly. "Gotta go, Mom."

Once Eli had disappeared around the side of the barn, Owen said, "There's more."

Callie turned toward Owen, a brilliant smile on her face, obviously expecting more good news. "What?"

"The cowboy who stole your stock was paid to take it."

Trace turned toward Callie in time to see that she wasn't entirely surprised.

"Who paid him?" she asked.

"Russell Handy."

Trace felt his heart sink when he heard the name of his father's *segundo*.

"I knew it!" Callie said. "I knew Blackjack arranged—"

"Handy says Blackjack had nothing to do with it," Owen interrupted.

"Then he's lying," Callie said. "He's your father's *segundo*, his right-hand man. He'd do anything for Blackjack!"

"Nevertheless," Owen said evenly, "Handy claims he acted on his own, without orders from anybody."

"You have to get him to tell the truth," Callie said. "You know your father's guilty. You know he's desperate to own Three Oaks. He must have ordered Handy to have someone steal our stock."

Trace caught another look from his brother that made

his stomach clench. He felt it roll when Owen said, "It gets worse."

Callie stared at Owen, her eyes wary. "I'm listening."

"The horse thief was going down for the third time, so he offered to deal us some information, so long as he got immunity from prosecution. Seems Handy hired him to do more than steal your horses."

Trace saw the blood draining from Callie's face and took a step toward her in case she needed support. He turned to Owen, knowing what he was going to hear, dreading it, but needing to hear it anyway. "What else did he do for Handy?"

Owen met Callie's eyes and said, "Handy hired him to kill your father."

An ululating wail of despair issued from Callie's throat. "Oh, Daddy, nooooo." She jerked free when Trace reached for her, then backed away, staring at him in horror, as though he'd changed into a monster before her eyes. She stared first at Owen, then met Trace's gaze with eyes full of pain. "Your father had mine killed."

"Russell Handy had your father shot," Trace countered.

"He's your father's man. You know Blackjack is guilty. What reason would Russell Handy have to murder my father?"

Trace couldn't think of a single one. He exchanged a questioning look with Owen, but his brother the Texas Ranger looked back at him with stony eyes.

"You see? I'm right," Callie said. She turned to Trace and said, "Oh, God, this is the end of everything. I could never—We can never—How can you ever expect Eli to deal with . . . *this*?"

Callie had refrained from saying *one grandfather having the other killed in cold blood.* But Trace knew what she meant. This was a disaster. The worst possible revelation at the worst possible moment. How could he cling to the hope that Callie would ever let herself love him now? He was the enemy again. And this time it wasn't just one brother crippling another. It was one father having the other killed.

"I've arrested Russell Handy," Owen said.

"Big deal," Callie snarled. "What about Blackjack? When do you arrest him?"

"There's no evidence that Blackjack had anything to do with your father's death."

"To hell with evidence!" Callie shouted. "What about common sense? Common sense will tell you what you need to know. Your father hated mine. He had him killed. End of story."

"That isn't how the law works," Owen said.

"Right," Callie snapped back. "That isn't how the law works in Bitter Creek, Texas, when your father is the murderer, and his son is the law."

Trace waited for some rebuttal from Owen, but Owen remained mute.

"What happens now?" Callie demanded.

"Russell Handy will be prosecuted for murder," Owen said.

"And your father will pay him to hold his tongue."

Again, Owen made no effort to refute Callie's accusation.

"You make me sick," Callie said. "Both of you," she said, including Trace in her furious gaze. "Get off my land. Go! Get!"

She batted her hands at them as though she were swatting mosquitoes into bloody pulps, and both men knew enough about a woman in a rage to get out of her way.

"Can you give me a ride?" Trace asked Owen. "My truck's parked by the kitchen door. I'd rather not cross paths with Callie again before she's had a chance to cool down."

"Sure," Owen replied. "Get in."

Trace stared out the window at the fertile grassland, letting the silence grow between them. As they were nearing the Castle, he asked, "Do you believe Dad is innocent?"

"Did you ever think maybe Jesse Creed wasn't the one who was supposed to get killed?" Owen replied.

"Run that by me again," Trace said, his brow wrinkling in confusion.

"The one thing missing—if Handy really is the culprit—is motive. Why would Russell Handy want Jesse Creed dead?"

"Beats me," Trace said. "But I take it you're going to enlighten me."

Owen glanced at him, then focused his eyes back on the road. "There's only one other person I can think of besides Dad that Russell Handy would sacrifice his own life to protect."

"Don't keep me in suspense," Trace said. "Spit it out."

"Mom."

"Now I'm intrigued," Trace said. "Mom and Russell Handy? I don't think I've ever seen her speak to the man."

"They were lovers."

Trace felt as though someone had grabbed a handful of his gut and twisted. "That's not funny, little brother."

"I caught them together in the barn when I was nine. I heard Mom making strange noises, animal sounds, and I thought maybe she was hurt. So I kept looking till I found her—them—in an empty stall. I'd seen enough mares being covered to know what they were doing. I stood there too long, and Mom saw me."

"Jesus," Trace said.

Owen glanced at Trace, then looked back at the road. "She just smiled at me over Russell Handy's shoulder and kept right on with what she was doing."

Trace felt like he was going to throw up. He opened the window and stuck his nose into the wind. He closed his eyes and took a deep breath to fight his sudden nausea. He swallowed down the bile in his throat, then swallowed again when it wouldn't stay down. "Jesus," he muttered.

"I think she expected me to tell Dad," Owen said. "I think she might even have wanted me to tell him."

"Why didn't you?"

Owen shrugged. "I don't know. I was afraid of what would happen, I guess. I've never told anyone what I saw. Until now."

Trace turned to Owen and said, "I swear to God, if you're making this up—"

"I only told you now because you asked if I thought Dad is guilty. I don't. I think Mom asked Russell Handy to get rid of Mrs. Creed."

"Why would she do that?"

Owen aimed a cynical look at Trace. "Why do you think?"

Because she was jealous. "So you think Mom asked

Handy to have Lauren Creed killed, but the thief was a bad shot and accidentally killed Jesse instead?"

"More likely, Handy couldn't stomach the idea of killing a woman, so he ordered the thief to kill Jesse, figuring that would accomplish the same thing—getting Lauren Creed to leave the neighborhood. That would square with the thief's version of who he was supposed to shoot."

Trace took off his hat and shoved his hand through his hair, then put his hat back on and tugged it low on his forehead. "I can't believe Mom would do something like that."

"Why not?"

"Why do you think? She's my mother, for God's sake!" Their mother was distracted. Disconnected. Even befuddled or bewildered by what was going on around her when she was in the middle of a painting. But he had never, ever seen the kind of jealous rage that would allow him to imagine his mother asking her illicit lover to kill Lauren Creed. "Mom couldn't be that corrupt inside and create such beautiful paintings," he murmured.

"What does one have to do with the other?" Owen asked. "I know a man with hands so talented he can sculpt a marble horse that you'd swear could breathe. He used those same hands to strangle his wife."

"Mom has never even acknowledged Dad's infatuation with Mrs. Creed," Trace insisted.

Owen lifted a brow. "You mean, until she hired Russell Handy to kill the competition."

"If she's that unhappy, why does she stay with Dad?" Trace challenged.

"To punish him."

Trace was taken aback. "Explain that."

"As long as she stays married to Dad, he can't have the woman he really loves."

"Lauren Creed."

Owen nodded. "I figure Dad's loved her all along."

"Then why did he marry Mom?" Trace demanded.

"Why do you suppose?"

"The land," Trace said flatly.

"Yep. Fifty thousand acres of DeWitt grassland."

"Is there any physical evidence against Mom? Anything to tie her to Jesse Creed's death that could be used in court to convict her of murder?"

"Nothing," Owen said. "There's no proof of any kind that she was involved. If Handy refuses to talk, if he's willing to take the blame, there's nothing to tie her to Jesse's murder."

Trace shifted uncomfortably in his seat, still stunned at the enormity of the accusations being made against his mother. "You're guessing. You have no proof."

"Are you willing to take the chance if I'm wrong?" Owen asked, glancing at Trace.

"What did you have in mind?"

"I've called Clay and asked him to come home, so we can have a family meeting and decide what to do. He said he could make it tomorrow night."

"Are you planning to confront Mom?" Trace asked.

"That's the general idea."

"Are you going to invite Summer to be a part of this witch hunt?"

"She's old enough to handle the truth."

"I can't believe we're having this discussion," Trace said. "We don't even know for certain if Mom's responsible!"

"Ever heard of circumstantial evidence? It all points to Mom. Not enough to convict her in court, but enough to prove to me that she's guilty."

"What if you're wrong about Mom?"

Owen turned to him and said, "Then Dad's guilty."

"Shit."

Trace was having a hard time believing either of his parents could have arranged to have someone murdered. But Owen seemed certain one or the other of them had. "I suppose you're going to be the one asking the questions."

"It's what I do," Owen said.

"And you'll be able to tell which one's guilty from their answers?"

Owen nodded.

"Then what?"

"If it's Mom, like I believe it is, we need to lock her away somewhere."

"Lock her away? Where? For how long?" Trace asked.

"We put her somewhere she can get psychiatric help—until she's no longer homicidal," Owen said.

"Who decides that?"

"The doctors at whatever sanitarium we put her in."

"What if she denies being guilty?" Trace asked.

"I'm sure she will," Owen replied.

"Why can't we just hire someone to keep an eye on her?" Trace suggested.

"Mom needs help, Trace. She had a man *killed*. We can't leave her free."

"You really think she'd try again to kill Lauren Creed?"

"Why not? Jesse's death hasn't solved her problem."

Trace rubbed a hand across his forehead. "This is a nightmare."

"I guess after this, you and Callie won't be tying the knot anytime soon," Owen said.

"Callie and I got married yesterday."

Owen hit the brakes, and the Jeep skidded and swerved before he regained control. "Holy shit!" Owen gave a startled laugh, then grinned. "Well, big brother, you can still surprise me."

"Eli is my son."

The grin faded, and Owen stared at him so long Trace finally said, "Keep your eyes on the road."

Owen refocused his gaze on the asphalt road. "I thought the kid looked familiar. I should have figured it out sooner. So what happens now?"

Trace sighed. "You mean, after we have our mother committed for having Callie's father killed? I suppose I'll try to mend fences with my wife. If that's possible."

"And if you can't?"

"I'll head back to Australia . . . and take my son with me."

"Callie Monroe isn't going to stand for that."

"She doesn't have much choice."

"What about the kid? Does he want to go with you?"

Acid churned in Trace's stomach. "I haven't asked him yet."

Owen whistled. "Good luck."

"Thanks. I'm going to need it. What time is this family meeting tomorrow night?" Trace asked.

"I'm arranging for everyone to come to the library at seven."

Trace frowned. "I just had a thought. What if Mom gets a lawyer and fights us?"

"Dad can make sure that doesn't happen."

"What makes you think he'll cooperate?"

Owen's gaze was cynical, his mouth set in a bitter line. "I'm sure Dad will take whatever measures are necessary to protect the woman he loves."

Callie didn't think Trace would dare to show his face at Three Oaks anytime soon, not even to consummate their marriage, as he'd promised he would. When he appeared at the kitchen door at suppertime, acting as though nothing had happened, she couldn't believe her eyes.

"Hey, Trace, you're late," Eli called to him from the supper table. "I made a plate for you and put it in the oven."

Callie had let Eli do it, even though she'd been certain Trace wasn't coming back, because she'd wanted to postpone explaining to her children why Trace Blackthorne had vanished suddenly from their lives. They were too young to hear Owen's news about their grandfather's death until it was absolutely necessary. Thank goodness she hadn't put them through that sort of agony for nothing. Here Trace was, bold as brass.

Fortunately, her mother wasn't at the table. She'd been devastated when Callie related Owen's news and hadn't come out of her room since. Luke had also taken the news badly and roared off in one of the pickups. He would work off his frustration tearing around back roads and giving the differential a workout. It wasn't the safest way of getting rid of anger, but at least it didn't endanger anyone else.

Callie didn't volunteer to put Trace's plate on the table, but he apparently didn't expect her to, since he grabbed a pot holder and retrieved it himself.

"Did you give Hickory a good rubdown after our ride?" Trace asked as he seated himself across from Eli.

"Yessir," Eli said.

Callie stiffened as the words of respect came pouring out of Eli's mouth with all the naturalness they'd had when Nolan was still alive. "Don't talk with your mouth full," she said with asperity.

"It wasn't full," Eli protested.

"It wasn't full," Hannah concurred through a mouthful of food. "I brushed my pony, too," she told Trace.

"Good for you, Hannah," Trace said.

Callie watched the smile split Hannah's face as Trace ruffled her golden curls. If only he wasn't a Blackthorne. If only she wasn't a Creed. If only his father hadn't arranged to murder hers. How could they get past such a calamity? How could she ever leave her mother and Sam alone to deal with a man who was willing to commit murder to get what he wanted?

Callie noticed Trace wasn't any more capable of swallowing food than she was.

"It's getting late," he said, as he shoved his crumbled-up meat loaf around the plate with his fork one last time. "You two kids better get on upstairs and start getting ready for bed."

"Will you tuck me in?" Hannah asked.

"Will you tuck me in?" Eli asked.

Callie gasped. She couldn't help it. What better sign of

Eli's acceptance could Trace have than that simple request? Even she hadn't been allowed to tuck her son into bed since Nolan's death. She saw the stunned pleasure in Trace's eyes, the sudden glisten of tears as he realized the significance of Eli's plea.

"Sure, son," Trace said.

Callie's throat tightened painfully as their eyes met. *Well, you've got what you wanted. Your son trusts you. He respects you. How long do you think that's going to last after you tell him you're taking him away from me and Hannah and everyone else he loves at Three Oaks?*

Hannah tugged on Trace's sleeve and insisted, "Me, too, Trace. Tuck me in, too."

Trace shifted his gaze to the little girl, and said, "You bet, sprite."

Her children shoved themselves away from the table and raced upstairs, now anxious for the bedtime ritual that had been so difficult following Nolan's death.

"They're going to be devastated when you leave," she said past the knot in her throat.

"Then come with me," he said quietly.

Callie didn't bother to answer, simply stood and began clearing the dishes from the table. She felt Trace walk up behind her as she stood at the sink, saw how he'd trapped her when his palms flattened on the counter on either side of her.

"I need you, Callie. There's an empty place inside me that only you can fill."

Callie bit back a moan as he kissed her nape. His words were fresh, cool water to a thirsting soul.

"What's happened between our parents has nothing to

do with you and me," he whispered in her ear. "I told you that eleven years ago, and it's just as true today."

Callie heard the censure in his voice. "So, I made one mistake, I better not make another? Is that what you're saying?" She managed to turn within the frame of his arms, so they were facing one another. "I made the only choice I could, Trace."

"You made the easy choice," he accused.

"You think it was easy leaving you?" she cried. "I nearly died, I—" She cut herself off, stunned at what she'd revealed.

His hands left the counter and circled her waist, as his mouth met hers in the gentlest of touches. "Me, too, Callie," he admitted. "Me, too. I don't want to die again. Come with me. Please."

His mouth devoured hers, ravaged hers, took as though it were the last time they would ever touch or taste or share the wonder of a kiss together. They were so lost in each other that they didn't hear Eli's footsteps. Didn't know he was there until he spoke.

"Sheesh."

They broke apart like teenagers caught necking in church.

"Eli!" Callie exclaimed. "What are you doing sneaking up on us like that?"

"I didn't sneak up." He smirked at Trace. "You guys were too busy to notice me."

It dawned on Callie that Eli didn't seem surprised—or upset—to find them kissing. She knew Eli had never witnessed her and Nolan kissing like that, because she and Nolan had never shared that kind of passion. She couldn't help feeling relieved, but also a little sad. "What do you want?" she asked breathlessly.

Eli rubbed his chin and turned to Trace. "I think maybe I need a shave. What do you think?"

Callie watched as Trace reached out in all seriousness to brush his hand against Eli's baby-smooth jaw, then rubbed his hand along his own cheek, bristling with a day's growth of heavy black stubble.

"I think maybe we could both use one," Trace said, shooting a look at Callie.

"Yeah, Mom," Eli said with a mischievous grin. "Otherwise it's going to tickle when Trace starts up kissing you again."

Callie felt her face turning red. "Shoo! Both of you. I've got dishes to wash."

Trace ushered Eli out the kitchen door, but paused to say, "I'll see you later. In bed." Then he was gone.

Callie put her hands against her rosy cheeks and let out an exasperated sigh. The nerve of him, presuming that she was going to lie in bed and let him make love to her after everything that had happened today.

"I need you, Callie. There's an empty place inside me that only you can fill."

Callie felt her insides draw up tight. He needed her. And God help her, she wanted him. Yes, tonight she'd have him. Because far too soon, he'd be gone forever.

She found Trace waiting for her in her bedroom.

"This night has been a long time in coming," he said. "I want it to be special."

Callie wondered what he had in mind. Trace had long ago taken her virginity, and they'd made love numerous times since he'd returned to Bitter Creek. "What's different about tonight?" she asked.

"It's our first night as man and wife. That means something, Callie. It means we belong to each other before God and the State of Texas. For as long as we both shall live."

Callie managed a tremulous smile. "If you say so."

"That's the way it is."

His touch was certainly different. More possessive. And more reverent.

"You're really and truly mine now, Callie," he said, as his hands caressed her. Cherished her. Honored her. "The children of your body will bear my name, will carry my blood."

"And your eyes and nose and mouth," she teased.

"Your eyes," he countered, as he stared into them.

He joined them swiftly but took his time bringing her to climax, loving her with his hands and mouth. Touching her as though he'd never done it before, as though this were the very first time. She felt his callused hands on her breasts and then his mouth, as he suckled her.

"You're so beautiful, Callie. So lovely."

She let herself be loved. And she gave love in return. Trace was right. Things were different. She was no longer Callie Creed Monroe. Now she was a Blackthorne, too.

Chapter 18

TRACE ARRIVED AT THE LIBRARY DOOR PRE-
cisely at seven o'clock, but the room—which smelled of
hundred-year-old leather-bound books and his father's
expensive Cuban cigars—was empty. He wondered if the
meeting had been moved somewhere else and had turned
back to search the rest of the house, when his father
crossed the threshold.

"Where is everybody?" Blackjack asked.

"I thought maybe the meeting had been moved," Trace
said. "Guess I was just the first one here."

"What's this all about?" Blackjack asked.

Trace frowned. "You mean Owen didn't tell you?"

"He said he had something important to discuss with
the family and that your mother and I needed to be here at
seven o'clock. He said it wasn't something he could talk
about over the phone."

"Where is Mom?" Trace asked.

"She had a meeting of the hospital board at six. She
said she'd be here as soon as she could."

"I don't believe this," Trace muttered.

"Do you know why Owen called this meeting?"

Blackjack asked, as he crossed to his desk and retrieved a cigar from the humidor.

"I do, but I think it might be better if Owen tells you."

"Does it have anything to do with Russell Handy being arrested for the murder of Jesse Creed?" Blackjack asked, as he clipped his cigar. He picked up a lighter Trace knew was a gift from a former Texas governor and lit the Monte Cristo.

"It docs." Trace refused to sit in one of the two chairs in front of the desk. They were purposely lower than the desk, leaving whoever was sitting there feeling smaller and less powerful than the person behind the desk. He crossed instead to the stone fireplace and perched on the arm of a nearby wing chair.

Trace waited for Blackjack to quiz him about what he knew or to profess his innocence. He did neither, simply sat back in the brass-studded swivel chair, put his boot-heels up on the desk, and puffed on his cigar.

Trace stared at the door, wondering where everyone else was, wishing his father would say something, and resisting the urge to ask if he was guilty of having Jesse Creed murdered.

"How are you and Callie Monroe getting along?" his father asked.

Trace debated whether to admit the truth, then decided he had to tell his father about his marriage sooner or later, and this seemed to be the night for confessions. "Callie and I got married in Mexico a couple of days ago."

Blackjack's feet came down and he sat up straight in his chair, his palms flat on the desk. "Why the hell didn't you let me know? This is great news!"

"You're not going to be getting your hands on Three

Oaks through me and Callie, Dad. I signed a prenuptial agreement that prevents me from ever—"

"Without seeing my lawyer?"

"I have my own lawyer," Trace said.

Blackjack snorted in disgust. "You never did learn to go for the jugular. When I married your mother—"

"Don't talk about her. Don't talk about your marriage."

Blackjack raised a brow in surprise. "What's your problem?"

Trace wasn't going to discuss the subject. He was going to let Owen ask the questions. "I'm leaving after Christmas, Dad. I'm going back to Australia."

"To work as a cowboy on some other man's spread?" Blackjack said in disgust. "Don't think I haven't known where you've been these past seven years. I hired someone to track you down. It took him a while to find you, but he did."

Trace flushed. "Why didn't you say something?"

"I figured you'd come home sooner or later."

"I'm leaving after Christmas, Dad. And I'm not coming back."

"You say that now—"

"When he died, Alex Blackthorne left me his cattle station. I don't want Bitter Creek, Dad. It's yours."

His father stared at him in disbelief. "I can't manage this place by myself anymore. My heart—"

"Your heart's just fine. I've done some investigating of my own, Dad. After the bypass surgery you had, your heart's as good as new. It'll stay that way so long as you don't smoke and you eat right and you take it easy on the liquor."

"Hmmph. Doctors don't know everything."

"Summer would love to help you out with the ranch," Trace said.

"I've got a husband picked out for her. She'll be leaving to go live with him."

"Does Summer know about that?"

"He knows about Summer. That's enough for now. I'll tell her when the time is right."

"I'm leaving, Dad," Trace repeated. "Bitter Creek is yours, not mine."

"I'm an old man—"

Trace laughed. "Fifty-four isn't old. Although . . ." Trace hesitated, then decided he might as well get everything out in the open. "You are a grandfather."

"What?"

"Eli Monroe is my son. Your grandson."

His father choked on cigar smoke.

Trace crossed and pounded him on the back. "Are you all right?"

Blackjack straightened and shifted away from Trace. "I think so. This is a surprise. A shock, I should say."

"For me, too," Trace admitted as he crossed back to the fireplace and laid an arm on the mantel.

"You didn't know about the boy, then, when you took off?"

"No, I didn't," Trace said.

"Well, well. This puts a new face on things. Did that prenuptial agreement you signed say anything about whether your son gets a piece of Three Oaks?"

Trace shook his head in disgust at his father's one-track mind. "Eli's going with me to Australia, Dad."

"Callie, too?"

Trace realized he was skating on thin ice. "That hasn't been decided."

"Who hasn't made up their mind? You? Or her?"

"I've asked her to come with me. After what's happened, I don't have a clue what she's going to decide."

"You mean, after Russell Handy admitted that he hired someone to kill Jesse," Blackjack said.

"Yeah." Trace glanced at the door, wishing Owen would arrive, wondering what was keeping him. It was Summer he found standing on the threshold.

"Is this a private party, or can anyone join in?" Summer asked as she crossed and sat in one of the two chairs in front of the desk. Or rather, sat across one of the two chairs. Her booted feet hung over one arm.

"What's up?" she asked Trace.

At that moment, Owen arrived and said, "I just got a call from Clay. He's got a meeting with the governor, and he can't fly down. We'll have to manage without him."

"What is it you wanted to discuss?" Blackjack asked.

"Where's Mom?" Owen said. "I'd rather wait for her."

"She'll be along soon," Blackjack said. "Why don't we get started?"

"All right," Owen said. "I suppose there's some business we can take care of before she arrives."

Trace felt the adrenaline shoot through his veins. It was starting. Soon, he'd know which of his parents was a murderer.

Owen closed the library door, then turned to face Blackjack and asked, "Was Russell Handy acting on your orders when he arranged to have Jesse Creed shot?"

Summer jumped to her feet and put herself nose to

nose with Owen. "How can you accuse Daddy of something like that? You should be ashamed of yourself!"

"Sit down, Summer," Trace said.

"But, Trace—"

"You're here because Owen said you were old enough to handle the truth. Don't prove him wrong."

Summer's eyes were wide and frightened as her gaze shifted from Trace to Owen and back again, before they finally rested on Blackjack.

Blackjack's narrowed gaze remained fixed on Owen. A muscle jerked in his cheek.

"Daddy?" Summer said in a halting voice. "Tell him you had nothing to do with Jesse Creed's death."

"I'm waiting for an answer," Owen said.

"I'd never have ordered someone else to shoot Jesse Creed," Blackjack said angrily. "I'd have reserved that pleasure for myself."

Trace let out the breath he'd been holding. He did it more quietly than Summer, who blew out a puff of air and then plopped back into one of the chairs in front of the desk.

"Well," she said. "Thank goodness that's settled. For a minute there I was a little anxious."

"We're not done yet," Owen said.

"What now?" Summer demanded.

"Now we wait for Mom."

"What does your mother have to do with this?" Blackjack asked.

Trace exchanged a look with Owen. Surely his brother wasn't going to tell Blackjack about their mother's affair with Russell Handy. Not after keeping it a secret all these years.

Before Owen could reply, Trace said, "Were you aware that Mom is jealous of Lauren Creed?"

"That's ridiculous. Your mother has nothing to be jealous of."

Trace barely managed to avoid laughing in his father's face. "Excuse me, Dad, but you've made it pretty plain—to all of us—how you feel about Mrs. Creed."

"What do feelings have to do with anything? I've never been unfaithful to your mother with the woman."

Maybe not physically, Trace thought. But in every other way that counted, his father had betrayed his marriage vows to his mother.

"There's never been a night in thirty-three years that I haven't slept beside your mother," Blackjack said.

Trace was surprised by the admission. He couldn't help wondering whether they still had marital relations. Well, of course they must still have intercourse. As he'd pointed out himself, at fifty-four, his father was still a young and virile man. Especially if his father had been, as he'd said, faithful to his mother.

But what if his father was merely sleeping with his mother? What if that was the extent of what they did together in bed? Maybe his mother blamed the lack of conjugal relations on Lauren Creed, and had finally decided to do something to solve the problem.

His thoughts were cut off as the library door opened, and his mother walked in.

She was dressed in a plum-colored suit from her favorite designer—Trace couldn't remember the name. It was elegant without being ostentatious. She smiled at Trace and Summer—and ignored Owen—as she crossed to stand beside Blackjack, where he sat at the desk, and slid her arm around his shoulder.

"To what do we owe this gathering of our children?" she said.

"It seems Owen had the bright idea that I arranged to have Jesse Creed killed," Blackjack said.

"But, Jackson, of course you didn't do any such thing!" his mother said.

"That's what Daddy told him," Summer confirmed.

"How about you, Mother?" Owen said. "Are you responsible for Jesse Creed's murder?"

Trace was watching his mother, and for the flicker of an eyelash, he thought he saw fury in her eyes. Then she looked into the distance, her eyes almost dreamy, and said, "What an unnatural son you are, Owen, to accuse your mother of such a thing."

"I call them as I see them," Owen said bluntly.

"What possible reason could I have for wanting Jesse Creed dead?" she asked.

"It wasn't Jesse you wanted dead. It was Ren."

Trace saw his father visibly stiffen.

"Explain yourself, boy," Blackjack said to Owen.

Owen's eyes never left their mother as he spoke. "Do you want to tell him about you and Handy? Or do you want me to do it?"

She stared back at Owen as though he weren't there.

"What the hell are you talking about?" Blackjack demanded.

"I'm talking about Mom's love affair with Russell Handy," Owen said.

Summer gasped.

Blackjack rose and started toward Owen. "Why you—"

"Stop right there, Dad," Trace said, stepping in front of his father. "And listen to what Owen has to say."

"I don't believe that bullshit you're spouting for an instant," Blackjack said to Owen.

"Just listen, Dad," Trace said. "Hear him out."

Blackjack took a step back and crossed his arms over his chest. "I'm listening."

"We know Russell Handy hired the man who shot Jesse Creed," Owen began. "Handy works for you, so the logical conclusion would be that you ordered Handy to have Jesse shot."

"But I did no such thing," Blackjack said.

"Right. So if you didn't order Jesse Creed shot, who did?"

"Maybe Handy did it on his own," Summer said.

"For what reason?" Owen challenged. He turned to Blackjack and said, "Do you know of any personal grievance Handy had against Jesse Creed? Any reason he would want Jesse dead?"

"None," Blackjack conceded.

"Then who else could Handy have been working for?" Owen asked.

Trace saw his father was perplexed. He saw the moment his gaze shifted to his mother, then watched it move back to Owen.

"How do you know your mother had an affair with Handy?"

"I saw them together in the barn," Owen said.

Trace watched his father's mouth thin, saw his eyes narrow as he turned back to his wife.

"What do you have to say for yourself, Eve?"

"At least he loves me, Jackson. Which is more than you can say."

Trace watched as his father worked to conceal the shock and humiliation of such an admission. His hands balled into fists, and his jaw was clamped so tight, a muscle jerked in his cheek. Trace waited for him to speak, but his lips thinned, and he remained silent. His tenuous control of the burning rage that lit his eyes was more frightening to behold than an eruption of fury.

Trace and Owen both stepped in front of their mother, fearing that their father might strike her.

"I'm not going to hit her," Blackjack said at last. "She's nothing to me now."

"I was never anything to you," Trace heard his mother say from behind him. "You were always obsessed with that woman. I wish she were dead!"

Blackjack turned on Owen and demanded, "If you believe your mother arranged to have Jesse shot—and that she's a danger to Ren—why haven't you arrested her?"

"So long as Handy doesn't talk, there's no proof she's guilty. But you heard what she just said. She belongs somewhere she can get help, Dad."

Blackjack nodded curtly. His face looked drawn. His eyes were cold and merciless. "I'll make certain Handy doesn't talk," he said at last. "I'd just as soon the world doesn't know your mother is a murderer. As for you . . ." His eyes focused on his wife. "You won't have to worry about competing with Lauren Creed anymore, Eve. I'm divorcing you."

Summer let out a wail.

His mother's face paled. "You'll be sorry if you try."

Blackjack turned to Owen and said, "I'll see a judge in the morning to arrange to have your mother put away where she won't be able to hurt anyone else."

"I've made arrangements for someone to pick Mother up tonight," Owen said. "That is, if you're willing to sign the papers."

"I'll sign them," Blackjack said.

"I'll make you pay if you do this, Jackson," his mother said. "You'll pay more than you can bear."

"I've heard enough," Trace said, his stomach churning. "Owen, call your people and get them in here. Summer, go cry in your room."

Summer hurried from the room, sobbing.

"Dad, sign the commitment papers and leave. Owen and I will take care of Mom."

Two burly men appeared at the library door. Trace thought they looked like wrestlers from the WWF. One had a shaved head and a Van Dyck beard. The other had tiny eyes and a bulbous nose. They were wearing clean white uniforms, with white web belts and white nurses' shoes.

"Mom, I'll come and visit you," Trace said, as they led his mother away.

"I'd rather see Clay," she replied. "He's the only one of you I can trust."

His mother walked between the two men to the library door, where she calmly announced to Blackjack, "You'll be hearing from my lawyer."

Trace waited for his father to leave, then closed the door behind him. He sank into one of the chairs in front of the desk. Owen sank into the other.

Trace sighed. "What a mess."

"Mom is guilty, Trace. Don't feel sorry for her."

"I don't. I feel sorry for the rest of us." He forked his fingers through his hair in agitation. "I have no idea how I'm going to explain this to Callie. It was bad enough when she thought Dad was guilty. How can I tell her about Mom? Especially when there's been no justice for her father's murder."

"You're wrong about that," Owen said.

"Oh, really?"

"You can tell Callie that Mom has suffered the perfect punishment for her crime."

"What punishment?" Trace asked.

"She lost Dad."

Chapter 19

Callie stared at Eve Blackthorne's painting with something akin to awe. It stood on an easel in the elegant ballroom of the Worthington Hotel in downtown Fort Worth being ogled by an upscale Western crowd that had just paid $250 a plate for a lukewarm steak dinner at the Charles Goodnight Gala.

The ceremonies were over, and Blackjack had been a humble and gracious recipient of the Charles Goodnight Award. Callie had been surprised at the pride she'd seen glowing on the faces of all his children—all except Clay, who'd pleaded a last-minute emergency and hadn't shown up.

Unfortunately, Eve Blackthorne had suffered a mental breakdown—Callie wondered if it was related to the accusations relating to her father's murder that had been made against Blackjack—and was recuperating in a sanitarium.

It had been hard to sit at the same table with the Blackthornes, knowing that their father was alive and celebrating life, and that he was the reason that hers was not. Callie finally understood what her father had felt whenever he met Blackjack. Finally understood what it meant to hate someone so much that the mere sight of him tied your gut in knots and made bile rise in your throat.

But Trace had insisted she attend the gala. "You're my wife," he'd said. "You're family, and you belong there."

Impossible to think of herself as one of them—a detestable Blackthorne—but heaven help her, she was.

Callie was occasionally jostled by the crowd of attendees who ambled the borders of the ballroom, signing up to buy items in the silent auction being held to benefit the Charles Goodnight Scholarship Fund. In a few moments, the live portion of the auction was scheduled to begin.

The "live" part didn't merely refer to the fact an auctioneer would be singing his patter. Among the items up for bid was a "live" fifteen-hundred-pound Longhorn steer with a majestic eight-foot span of horns. It had been brought up in the freight elevator and, Callie noted with amusement, had allowed itself to be led around the carpeted ballroom on a halter.

And then there was Eve Blackthorne's painting, which she had titled "Supernatural Love." Callie hadn't been able to take her eyes off of it. The featureless bodies she'd seen in the stands at the Rafter S when she'd previously studied the painting had become recognizable people. Herself. Trace. Blackjack. Her father. But, oddly, not her mother.

Where her mother had stood between the two fighting men, another figure had been substituted. Eve Blackthorne had painted herself into the picture, gazing up at Blackjack with a look of adoration. Callie wondered why Mrs. Blackthorne had made the change, until she remembered something the woman had said in her studio. "*I like to make things perfect, the way God intended them to be.*"

So she'd painted out the woman who was the source of conflict between the two men and painted herself in. Husband and wife adoring one another. The way things should be. The poor woman seemed to be as much Blackjack's victim as everyone else who came into his realm.

Callie flinched when she felt Trace's arm slide around her waist.

"Where did you go?" Trace said. "I missed you."

"I've been studying your mother's painting."

"It should earn a lot of money for the scholarship fund," Trace said.

"Have you taken a good look at it?" Callie asked.

Trace looked at the painting. "What is it I'm supposed to see?"

"The woman standing between Blackjack and my father that day was my mother, not yours."

Trace stared at his knotted fist. "Yeah? So what?"

"She painted herself in, because she should have been the one singled out for attention by your father, not my mother. I can't help feeling sorry for her."

"Don't," Trace said. "She doesn't deserve your pity."

"I don't know why not. She—"

"She's the one who had your father shot."

Callie's eyes went wide with shock. "What?" she gasped.

"I've been meaning to tell you. I just . . . didn't know how. This is not the time or the place to discuss this."

"You can't say something like that and not explain."

"We've both got horses competing in the semifinal

round of the Open Futurity tomorrow," he said, taking her hand and heading for the escalator. "You need your rest."

"I'll rest after you explain."

"I'll explain in the room," Trace said.

Callie bit her tongue on the escalator going back down to the main floor. She remained silent as they got on the elevator to go up to their room in the hotel. She was having too much trouble absorbing Trace's revelation.

Eve Blackthorne had arranged to have her father killed. Was that why she'd had a nervous breakdown? Why hadn't someone—Owen, in particular—said something before now, if Eve Blackthorne was the culprit? But then, the Blackthornes took care of their own. Maybe they were concealing whatever evidence existed against Mrs. Blackthorne, so she wouldn't have to go to jail.

Callie intended to find out the truth.

The luxuriousness of the Worthington, with its fresh floral arrangements and lush carpets, reminded her that she was living in a different world now that she was one of *them*. This was a far cry from the Holiday Inn down the street from the Will Rogers Center, with its rubber-backed curtains and rattling windows overlooking the train tracks, where she had stayed in the past.

The instant the hotel room door closed behind them, she turned on Trace and demanded, "Why did she do it?"

"She was jealous of your mother."

Callie frowned in confusion. "So she had my father killed? That makes no sense."

"Think about it. If your father was dead, you'd very likely lose Three Oaks and your mother would leave the neighborhood," Trace explained.

"But we're not going to lose Three Oaks," Callie said.

"No. Handy was mistaken about that."

"Did your mother have a mental breakdown? Is she in a sanitarium?"

"No and yes. We put Mom where she could get some help and won't be able to hurt anyone else."

"Why isn't she in jail?" Callie asked in a cold voice.

Trace sighed. "Because there isn't any evidence against her that would hold up in court."

"And I'm supposed to be satisfied with that excuse? Your mother should be punished."

"Ahhh," Trace said.

"What is it you're not telling me?"

"My mother is being punished. Perfectly punished."

"How?"

"My father's divorcing her."

"I see," Callie said, frowning. "She wanted Blackjack all to herself. Instead, she's lost him entirely."

"Right."

"I hope she suffers as much as we have at our loss," Callie said bitterly. "Oh, my God," She moaned. "I just realized something."

"What's that?"

"Once your father's free, he'll go after my mother."

Trace set his black felt Stetson on a shelf in the closet and forked his fingers agitatedly through his hair. "I don't think you have to worry too much about my father marrying your mother."

"Why not?" Callie demanded.

"Because my mother will never give him a divorce."

"She won't have any choice," Callie argued.

Trace snorted. "She can make the price too high. She

can drag things out in court until they're all too old and gray to care."

Callie dropped into a nearby wing chair like a puppet with its strings cut. "How awful. . . ." She looked up and met his eyes. "For us."

"What happens between them has nothing to do with us," Trace said. "We have to live our own lives."

"What if my mother married your father? What would happen to Three Oaks then? Blackjack would get it after all!"

"You're thinking too far into the future imagining something that may never happen. You've got a big day tomorrow. You'd better get some sleep."

Callie was too agitated to sleep. She was spoiling for the fight Trace had just denied her. "I won't let it happen, Trace. I'll stop it somehow. Even if I am one of the goddamned Blackthornes now!"

"That's enough," Trace said.

For a moment, she thought he was going to reach for her, but his hands curled into fists, and he headed for the bedroom.

"I don't think things are going to work out between us, Trace, with all that our families have done to one another."

That stopped him. When he turned, she saw his body was coiled for action, like a rattlesnake ready to strike. "The hell they're not!"

She didn't move fast enough to escape. He yanked her out of the chair by her arms and pulled her up on her toes, so his hot breath fanned against her cheeks when he spoke.

"You better think long and hard before you throw me

out of your life again. Because this time, I'll be the one who ends up with our child. You can come with me and be my wife and Eli's mother. There's not a damn thing stopping you."

"You know there is!" she cried.

"What's stopping you, other than the fact you're stuck in a rut and too damned scared to climb out?"

Callie felt herself flushing with anger. "Someone has to protect my family from yours!"

"Your family can manage on their own. I need you, Callie. *I need you.*"

Callie's heart hurt at the agony in his heartfelt plea.

"I can't go with you, Trace," she said at last. "I can't."

Sugar Pep had let a cow escape back to the herd in the semifinal round and didn't make the cut. But Smart Little Doc had stayed on the bubble, and when the scores were finally posted, Trace's horse had made it into the final round of twenty-two competitors in the Open competition. Callie had drawn number eighteen for Smart Little Doc, and the finalists had been divided into two groups of eleven, with the cattle to be changed between groups.

The arena was filled to capacity, and Trace sat next to Callie in the row of seats directly above the thirty-nine Hereford cattle—3.5 for each of the eleven finalists in the second round of the evening—that had just been herded into the arena at the Will Rogers Memorial Complex. Trace's nose had long since adjusted to the acrid, ammonia smell that rose from the dirt in the arena.

Two hazers were riding through the herd, allowing

Trace and Callie to evaluate how the cattle responded to a horse and rider.

Choosing which cow to cut was always a risky business, but it could mean the difference between winning and losing. No system was foolproof, but Trace pointed out which cows eyeballed a horse before moving calmly away from it, as opposed to those that squirted through the herd in a panic.

"That cow with the white spot on his tail is a runner. Stay away from him," Trace warned.

Callie nodded without speaking.

He gestured with his chin. "That bald-faced, ring-eyed cow looks like a good bet, and you might try that motley cow with the red eyebrow."

"Hmm," Callie replied, as she focused on the cow with the multicolored face.

Trace marveled at how calm she seemed. He could feel the electricity in the arena. Normally, competing later was an advantage, since the judges tended to be conservative on their scores for the first cutters. But tonight they'd witnessed something extraordinary. The number eleven cutter had just received the highest score ever given in the Open Futurity.

Each contestant started with 70 points, and the five judges gave scores ranging between 60 and 80, deducting or adding points depending on the quality of the ride. The highest and lowest scores were thrown out, and the sum of the other three provided the rider's score. It was rare to earn more than 220 points. The eleventh rider had gotten 233.

The cutter had known it was a great ride, and he hadn't even waited for the judges to post their scores before he'd let out a yell and thrown his hat high into the air in jubilation.

"You don't have to win the competition to get the money I promised," Trace reminded Callie. "You just have to be in the top ten."

"I know," she snapped back.

It was almost a relief to see a sign of nerves from her. "How are you doing?" he asked quietly.

She managed something between a grimace and a smile and said, "Fine." Her gaze returned almost immediately to the arena, where the hazers continued riding slowly through the cattle, sending them in whirling eddies, like currents moving around a stone in a stream.

Trace felt a hand on his shoulder and turned to find his sister squatting in the aisle behind them.

"Just wanted to wish you both luck," Summer said.

"Thanks, Summer," Trace replied for both of them.

"Some pretty good riding in the first half of the finals," Summer said, pointing out the obvious.

Trace glanced at Callie, but she seemed oblivious to his sister's presence. "Yeah."

"Still think Callie can make it into the top ten?" Summer asked.

Trace turned to look at his sister and realized she was nervous. "Would it be such a huge disaster if you had to go back to school?" he teased.

She said a word he knew nice girls shouldn't use.

"Callie's good, Summer. She's got Smart Little Doc in great shape to compete. My advice is, keep your fingers crossed."

"I will. Good luck, Callie," she said, patting Callie on the shoulder.

Callie made a sound in her throat, but never took her eyes off the cattle in the arena.

When Summer was gone, Trace focused his gaze on Callie. "It wouldn't have hurt you to acknowledge her."

"I'm busy. Why should she care, anyway, whether I win or lose?"

"If you're not in the top ten, she has to go back to college and graduate."

Callie smiled and shook her head. "For her sake, I wish I didn't need to win. College is important."

"Does it bother you not to have a degree?" Trace asked.

Callie hesitated, then said, "It wasn't missing out on the degree, so much as the loss of choices. One day I could have been anything, done anything. The next . . ." She shrugged.

Trace stared at her, wondering what she might have done with her life, if he hadn't left her behind, alone and pregnant. Then he remembered that her brother had been paralyzed at the same time. Her choices might very well have ended even without the pregnancy.

The competition had begun again, with the first cutter riding his horse ever so slowly into the herd. Trace glanced at the five judges sitting in the raised booths, decorated with Christmas poinsettias, that split the arena in half. The back half of the arena was used as a warm-up area, and the next rider was already loping his horse there.

Trace watched with Callie as the competing horse lost a step on the cow. "That'll cost him," Trace murmured.

But it was the only mistake in a nearly flawless performance. The score was high. Callie was going to need a good ride to make the top ten.

"Ready to go?" Trace asked.

Callie stood. "Yeah. Might as well get Smart Little Doc warmed up."

Trace was going to act as a hazer for Callie, keeping the cattle bunched while she was working, and he stepped out with her and headed downstairs to the stalls where they'd left their mounts.

Trace felt jittery and realized he wasn't sure how things were going to turn out. Callie was good, but the quality of the horses in the competition was phenomenal. If Callie lost, and his father refused to continue supporting the breeding operation, he could always invite Dusty Simpson to come work for him in Australia. But Dusty and Lou Ann had strong family ties in Texas, and he hoped that wouldn't be necessary.

Trace was also aware of how much it would mean to Callie—and to him—if she had the extra $100,000 he'd promised her if she made it into the top ten. Maybe if the Creeds had a little financial cushion, Callie would find the courage to leave Three Oaks and come with him.

He and Callie rode together to the warm-up pen just as the number sixteen rider completed his cut. They watched together as the number seventeen rider chose the bald-faced, ring-eyed cow and then cut the motley-faced cow. His score was as high as any rider who'd preceded him.

Trace said, "Guess you'll have to go with that black-tailed cow and the red-faced cow with the white ear."

Callie nodded without speaking.

When her number was announced, Trace met her eyes and smiled. "You can do it." He left her behind as he rode into the arena to replace one of the hazers.

He watched from the arena as she performed her personal competitive ritual—tugging her hat down and patting Smart Little Doc's neck—before she nudged her horse into the arena.

Trace kept one eye on the cattle bunched at the end of the arena and the other focused on Callie. She went deep first to cut the black-tailed cow.

It was as though there were strings attached between Smart Little Doc and the black-tailed cow. Whenever the cow turned, Smart Little Doc turned. He sat down on his haunches and stalked the cow like a cat stalking a mouse.

The crowd went wild. Trace's stomach did a few leaps and turns of its own.

When the black-tailed cow paused and stared in consternation, Callie turned away and went looking for the second animal she was required to cut. The cow with one white ear was too deep for her to get to, and Trace wondered what other animal she would choose. He watched as she found another motley-faced cow and separated it from the herd.

Trace couldn't breathe. He couldn't remember whether the mot was a runner. He didn't remember noticing the cow at all when they were doing their survey. He took his eyes off Callie for a second to turn his horse into the herd and keep it compacted.

And heard the crowd roar.

Nose to nose. Shoulder to shoulder. Eye to eye. Smart Little Doc's tail whipped out behind him as he whirled and turned. Dirt flew as he lunged to stay with the calf. Above it all, Callie sat deep in the saddle, gripping the horn, the reins hanging loose in her hands.

When the buzzer sounded to indicate her time was up,

Callie didn't do anything so exuberant as throw her hat. She patted Smart Little Doc—and smiled at Trace.

Trace's heart leapt to his throat and stuck there.

He heard the crowd roaring again and turned to look at the scoreboard. 234. He looked for his father in the stands. When he found him, he touched the brim of his hat and grinned. He saw Summer put her fingers to her lips and whistle shrilly, before she grinned and waved at him.

He caught up to Callie in the area beyond the warm-up ring. She was already off Smart Little Doc and had her face pressed against the horse's mane, her arms around his neck.

Trace touched her shoulder, and she turned and threw herself into his arms. He lifted her high into the air and grinned up at her smiling, tear-streaked face. "You did it, Callie. You did it!"

"I did, didn't I," she said, her grin stretching from ear to ear. "Although Smart Little Doc deserves a bit of the credit."

"You're both immortal," he said. "That's a score that isn't going to be bested for a long, long time."

"I bet somebody said the same thing to the number eleven cutter," Callie said with a laugh.

Trace set her down and hugged her tightly against him. "Yeah. But you know I'm right. There couldn't be a more perfect ride. Or a more perfect rider."

Callie didn't say anything, simply smiled up at him through her tears. He leaned down to kiss her, and their lips clung. Trace held Callie close to his heart, knowing that with the end of the competition, their time together was growing short. He wished he knew the words that would entice her to come with him.

"I love you," he whispered in her ear.

He waited for her to say the words back to him. Before she could, they were surrounded by Summer and Owen and Blackjack, and Callie stepped out of his embrace.

"Thank you, thank you, thank you," Summer said excitedly as she gave Callie a hug. "You saved my life!"

"I didn't realize—"

In her excitement, Summer cut Callie off. "Now I can stay at Bitter Creek." She shot a triumphant look at Blackjack. "Where I belong."

"That was quite a ride, young lady," Blackjack said, tipping his hat to Callie.

"Thank you," Callie said, her body visibly stiffening as Blackjack put a hand on her shoulder.

"Congratulations, Callie," Owen said, stepping between the two of them and offering Callie his hand.

Callie took it reluctantly and let it go as soon as she could.

Trace could tell Callie was losing her composure under such an onslaught of Blackthornes, but he wasn't going anywhere until he heard the words of concession, the admission by his father that he'd lost their bet.

"Well, son," Blackjack said, tipping his hat up with a forefinger. "Guess you won this one."

"Of course he did," Summer said with a grin. "I told you he would."

"Although I can't say I'm sorry," Blackjack continued, ignoring Summer's interruption. "That friend of yours, that Dusty, is a man who knows his horses."

"I'm glad to hear it, Dad."

"Well, little lady, I guess the two of you will be leaving soon for Australia."

"What Trace does is up to him," Callie replied stiffly. "I'll be staying at Three Oaks."

Trace felt his heart sink. Well, he had his answer. She didn't love him. Not enough. "I guess it'll just be me and Eli leaving after the holidays," Trace said quietly.

Callie leapt into the saddle and spurred Smart Little Doc back toward the arena. Trace reached out to stop her, but she reined the horse out of his reach. He realized she was responding, in part, to the announcement on the PA system.

Smart Little Doc had won the Open division of the World Championship Futurity.

Chapter 20

"WHY CAN'T I TELL MY FAMILY WE'RE MAR-
ried? You've told yours," Callie argued. "It can't remain
a secret much longer. Christmas is next week. Eli isn't
going to like you any more next week than he does now,
unless you're planning to bribe him with more expensive
gifts."

Callie saw Trace flinch and knew she'd hit below the
belt. She didn't care if she was fighting dirty. This was a
battle she needed to win. "Don't take Eli away from me,
Trace."

She watched as he lifted his hat to thrust a hand agitatedly through his hair, then resettled the Stetson low on his
forehead. There wasn't much light in the barn, just what
little made it through the seams of ancient wood and the
open door at the other end of the barn. Dust motes drifted
aimlessly in the narrow streams of sunlight.

"Eli is my son, too, Callie. It's not as though he won't
have a good life in Australia. I'm sorry if it means taking
him away from you and Hannah, but—"

"What's he talking about, Mom?"

Callie gasped as Eli stepped out from the shadows of a

shoulder-high stack of baled hay. His face was ashen, his eyes wide with shock. She felt her gut wrench, the way it did when Eli came to her with a skinned knee or a scraped elbow. Only this wound was much, much worse.

She reached out to him, but he took a quick step back. "I'm so sorry you had to find out this way, Eli."

Her son turned to stare at Trace. "Then it's true? You're my father?"

Trace nodded.

"Is that other part true, too?" Eli demanded. "That part about taking me to Australia with you and leaving Mom and Hannah behind?"

"I'd like to explain about that," Trace said.

"Then it's true?" Eli said in a panicked voice.

"Yes, but—"

"You're not my father!" Eli shouted at Trace. "My dad is dead. And I'm not going anywhere with you!"

Eli whirled and ran.

Callie saw the stricken look on Trace's face, but had no time for sympathy. Her son needed her. "We shouldn't have been keeping secrets from him," she said as she brushed past Trace.

He caught her arm. "Where are you going?"

"To find my son and try to explain this mess to him."

"I'm coming, too."

Callie shot Trace a look that said she would rather go alone, but he didn't back down. "All right. Come on."

Callie headed for the house, expecting Eli to have locked himself in his room. When she opened the kitchen door, she found her mother deep in conversation with her brother Sam. Sam had gotten drunk one night last week and had conceded he couldn't stay sober on his own. He'd agreed to go to AA and Callie wanted to believe it would help.

She checked him for signs of drunkenness and was glad to see he was clear-eyed. His newly cut hair was combed back from his forehead and his face was clean-shaven. "Have you seen Eli?" she asked.

Callie's mother pointed toward the kitchen window and said, "I saw him on horseback a few moments ago, headed toward the middle pasture. Hannah was right be-hind him."

Callie's heart skipped a beat. "The *middle* pasture?"

"What's wrong?" Trace asked.

"I'm having some work done in the middle pasture." The north and south pastures couldn't be cleared until the hunting season ended in mid-January, but Callie had seen no reason not to get rid of the mesquite in the middle pasture. "I've got a controlled burn scheduled there soon."

"Today?" Trace asked.

"I don't know. Might be. Maybe. I told the men I hired to go ahead and do the burn as soon as they finished clearing. It could be today or tomorrow or a week from now."

The mesquite was being cleared with a tractor the size of a prehistoric beast, with a bar across the front to push the mesquite trees over and funnel them underneath the tractor, where their taproots could be cut with a root plow, slowing down regrowth.

Once the mesquite had been cut up by the tractor, fires would be set in the four corners of the pasture and tended as they burned toward the center, leaving the pasture ready for planting grass. Anyone riding into the pasture might be caught unawares and trapped by the advancing flames.

All eyes were directed toward the window that gave them a view of the middle pasture. In the far distance, Callie saw what looked like low white clouds in the blue sky. Or was it wisps of smoke?

"Wouldn't they call before they fired the pasture?" Sam asked. "Give some kind of warning?"

Callie's cell phone rang, and she answered it. "Is it too late to stop it? I've got kids in there, that's why!"

She met Trace's eyes and said, "That was the foreman, calling to let me know they've started the burn, and that we should stay clear of the middle pasture until it's done."

"We'd better go find those kids," Trace said as he headed for the door.

Callie ran after him. "At least one of us needs to be on horseback," she said.

"You take the pickup and try to head them off," Trace said. "I'll follow on horseback."

"Eli won't want to come with you," Callie said. "I should be the one to go in on horseback."

Trace met her gaze and said, "He'll come with me."

"Give me one reason why—"

"I won't give him a choice."

Callie stopped beside the pickup, which had the keys in the ignition, and glanced toward the middle pasture. She saw what was unmistakably smoke. "Hurry, Trace!"

"Don't worry about me," he shouted as he headed for the barn to saddle himself a horse. "I'll be right behind you."

Callie gunned the engine, and the back end of the

pickup fishtailed as she headed onto the dirt road that led to the middle pasture. The bump gate was located near the center of the pasture, but there were no cowboys there to monitor the burn. Callie realized they must be stationed at the four corners of the pasture, watching for flare-ups along the fenceline.

She hit the bump gate going too fast and pressed her foot on the accelerator to get through before the gate could demolish the side of her truck. She hadn't gone more than a quarter mile down the road, when she spied someone on horseback. She honked the horn repeatedly and was rewarded when the figure on horseback waved back.

It was Eli.

Callie shoved open the door and clambered down. "Where's Hannah?" she called to Eli, as he slid off his horse.

"She was bugging me, so I told her to get lost." Eli turned to look over his shoulder at the growing cloud of smoke. "But I didn't know about the fire then, Mom. I swear I didn't!"

"I believe you," Callie said, taking her son into her arms. "Did Hannah turn back? Do you think she went home?"

"I don't know. What if she's in there? She'll get burned up!"

Callie could feel Eli trembling in her arms but wasn't sure whether it was fright over Hannah's predicament or his own. "Trace is hunting for her," she said reassuringly. "He'll find her if she's in there."

Callie called Trace's number on her cell phone, but got

no answer. He either didn't have his cell phone with him, or for some reason couldn't answer.

"You wouldn't really have let Trace take me away, would you, Mom?"

"Trace is your father, Eli."

"So what?" Eli retorted, tearing himself from her embrace. "That's his problem, not mine."

"I wish I could make this easier for you, but nothing can change the facts."

"Did Dad know? I mean, that I wasn't . . . You know . . . his own kid."

"He knew," Callie said. "He loved you anyway, Eli, like you were his own flesh and blood."

"But I wasn't."

"No. You weren't."

"You should have told me. How come you never told me?" he asked in an agonized voice.

I never thought you'd find out, Callie thought. "I made a mistake, Eli. I hope you can forgive me."

"What if I don't want to go with Trace. He can't make me go, can he?"

Callie didn't know what to say. "We can work all that out later. Right now I need to call your grandmother and let her know you're all right."

Callie made the call, realizing that the fire was moving closer. Smoke drifted over them, and she realized she had to do something, that she couldn't just sit here and wait. "I'm sending Eli home," she told her mother. "I'm going to go looking for Hannah and Trace, in case . . ." Callie couldn't put her worst fear into words. *In case I need to get Hannah to the hospital.*

"I need you to go straight home, Eli. Will you do that for me?"

"You could marry him," Eli said as he mounted his horse.

"What?"

He looked down at her from his perch on Hickory. "Trace. You could marry him. Then he'd stay here with us, and I wouldn't have to go away with him."

Callie was flustered. "I don't have time to discuss this now, Eli."

"I know you like him a lot," Eli said.

"Trace and I are already married, Eli," she said, her agitation making her more brusque than she'd intended. "We got married in a private ceremony a couple of weeks ago, after Trace found out you were his son."

"You mean, he didn't even know until a couple of weeks ago? I mean, about me being his kid?"

Callie shook her head.

Eli frowned. "So he might have wanted me to be his kid a long time ago, but you didn't tell him?"

Callie swallowed over the painful knot in her throat. "I thought . . . I did what I thought was best."

Callie watched the expressions flit across Eli's face. "I don't understand. If you're married to Trace, why isn't he taking you and Hannah with him to Australia?"

Callie hesitated, then replied, "He asked us to come. I told him I had to stay here."

"Why?"

"Because this is our home."

Eli snorted. "We can have a home in Australia. I wouldn't mind seeing some kangaroos. Tell him you'll go with him, Mom. That'll make everything okay."

"It isn't that simple, Eli."

"Why not?"

"Because it's not! Now I have to go."

Eli shook his head and muttered, "Sheesh."

"Go back to the house, Eli We'll talk more about this once I'm sure Hannah is safe."

"All right, Mom," Eli said, kicking his horse into a trot. "But I don't see why you'd want to stay here in Texas, when all of us can go to Australia with Trace and see kangaroos and platypuses and crocodiles and neat stuff like that."

Callie stared after her son. He made the choice sound so simple. She couldn't believe he felt so few ties to Three Oaks. But he hadn't had a lifetime to learn to love it as she had. He hadn't grown up, like she had, with a father who'd insisted Three Oaks must be preserved for the Creeds, no matter what the cost.

Callie mulled her son's words. *We can have a home in Australia.* Could choosing Trace over Three Oaks really be as simple as that?

Callie called her foreman again and asked whether he'd seen anything—anyone—as they'd followed the fire in from the fence line. "Nothing," Callie repeated. "I understand."

Where was Trace? And where was Hannah? What was happening to them?

Callie called home again. "Mom? Have you heard any word from Trace? Has Hannah shown up?"

Callie felt her stomach turn over at the fear she heard in her mother's voice. "I'm scared, too, Mom. I don't know what to do. I—"

Callie heard hoofbeats and said, "Wait a minute, Mom.

I hear someone coming. It might be—Oh, no. Oh dear God. No."

Callie stared at the riderless horse that came flying past her. It was Hannah's pony.

"Blackie just came racing past me, Mom," she gasped into the phone. "The saddle was empty! My baby is on foot somewhere in that burning pasture. I have to go, Mom. I have to find her!"

Callie felt frantic. She couldn't lose her daughter like this. Not when she was about to lose her son. God couldn't be that cruel.

She got in the pickup and took off straight across the fields, doing her best to avoid the skeletons of mesquite that threatened to tear out the truck's undercarriage. She kept a sharp eye out for a second riderless horse. Had Trace found Hannah? Was he keeping her safe? But where could they possibly be safe in this burning inferno?

Callie slowed as the thick smoke made it difficult to see where she was going. She had the air conditioning off and the vent closed, but even so, smoke was seeping into the cab of the pickup. "Where are you, Trace?" she muttered. "Where are you?"

And then she knew. *The pond.*

Callie headed in the direction of the pond where they'd had their picnic. It was the one place Hannah and Trace might be safe from the fire. Only, Hannah couldn't swim. What if she'd gone there alone and gotten into the water . . .

Callie suddenly found herself facing a wall of fire, with no way to get past it or around it. She looked in the rearview mirror and realized the only safe route was back the way she'd come. She considered trying to drive through the fire but realized that would be foolhardy. If the fire didn't kill her, the thick smoke would.

She hit the steering wheel, swearing loudly and profanely as she put the truck in reverse and gunned the engine. She coughed and realized the cab was nearly full of choking smoke. She was having trouble breathing, and as soon as she saw clear sky, she opened a window and gasped a lungful of air. She stared at the crackling fire, which raged across the pasture, leaving nothing behind but embers and ashes.

"Noooo," she moaned. "Oh, please, no."

There was nothing she could do but wait. It wouldn't take long for the fire to burn its way past the pond. She could only hope that Trace had thought of the water, as she had, and that Hannah had managed to find her way there.

It was way too much to hope for. Callie braced her arms across the steering wheel, laid her head on her arms, and said a silent prayer.

She was startled when someone pounded on the fender of the truck. She sat up abruptly, a smile already on her face, expecting to see a soot-faced Trace holding her daughter. But it was her brother Luke. Her smile faded.

"What are you doing here?" she asked.

"Sam and I came to help."

Callie looked beyond Luke and saw Sam waving at her from the van. "I'm glad you're here," she admitted. She was afraid to go looking on her own. Afraid of what she'd find.

"What are you waiting for?" Luke asked.

"I'm waiting for the fire to get past the pond."

"Oh. Yeah. Good idea. That's where I'd go, too," Luke

said. "Looks like it's pretty much done burning. Wanta give it a try?"

Callie started up the engine. "Let's go," she said.

She drove fast, not sure how hot the ground still was and a little worried about whether a piece of burning wood kicked up by her tires could start a fire in her gas tank. The cattails stood tall against the charred landscape. The total lack of vegetation growing in the shade of the live oak had saved the tree from burning.

"The tree," Callie said to herself. "I'll bet they climbed up in that damned wonderful live oak tree!" She was almost laughing with relief. Until she saw the lump near the edge of the pond and recognized the charred remains of one of her striped saddle blankets draped over it. The flesh prickled on her arms, and her heart started to pound.

She hit the brakes, shoved open the door, and went running. As Callie got closer, she could see Trace was actually lying half in and half out of the water. He had the blanket draped over the upper half of his body. Where was Hannah? She didn't see Hannah!

She went down on her knees beside the scorched blanket and slowly pulled it away. Trace lay facedown, his eyes closed, his eyebrows singed, his face blackened with soot. She couldn't tell if he was alive, and she was afraid to find out. There was no sign of Hannah.

"How is he?" Luke asked.

Callie looked up at Luke through eyes blurred by tears, but she couldn't speak.

I love him. I need him. How will I live without him?

Too late. She'd realized the depth of her feelings for

Trace far too late. She should have told him how she felt long ago. Eleven years ago.

Luke reached for Trace's shoulder and pulled him onto his back—revealing Hannah beneath him.

"Hannah!" Callie cried.

Her daughter's eyes flickered open. "Mommy," Hannah wailed. "Mommy!"

Callie pulled her daughter into her arms and clutched her tight, smoothing her tangled, singed curls away from her soot-covered face, reassuring herself that she wasn't dreaming.

"Trace doesn't look too good," Luke said. "We better get him to a hospital."

"I'll take Hannah to Sam and be right back to help you," Callie said, struggling to her feet with her daughter in her arms.

"Is Trace gonna be all right?" Hannah asked as Callie jogged toward the van.

Callie forced words past the lump in her throat. "I'm sure he'll be fine, sweetheart." She resisted the urge to ask what had happened. She didn't want Hannah to have to relive what must have been a terrifying experience.

"Trace saved me from the fire," Hannah blurted. "Blackie threw me off and ran away and I was scared and then Trace came and found me but the fire was all around me."

Callie shuddered. That explained her daughter's singed hair and Trace's singed eyebrows. "You're safe now, baby. That's all that matters."

Hannah put her hand on Callie's cheek and said, "Trace said he loves me and he loves Eli and he loves you.

He promised he'll be my daddy and love me forever and ever."

"Oh, sweetheart." Callie crushed her daughter against her, hiding her face against Hannah's neck so her daughter wouldn't see the tears spurting from her eyes. What if there was no forever?

She yanked open the passenger door to the van and buckled Hannah into the seat next to Sam. "Will you take her to the hospital and make sure they check her out? We'll be right behind you with Trace."

"I'll meet you at the hospital," Sam said, as Callie shut the door.

"Thank you, Sam," Callie said through the open window. A look of understanding passed between them. Her brother was no longer a burden but another member of the family willing to carry his share of the load.

By the time Callie got back to the pond, Luke had already lifted Trace upright. He still showed no signs of regaining consciousness.

"I'll take his shoulders. You take his feet," Callie said.

"He probably just breathed too much smoke," Luke said. "They can probably give him some oxygen or something at the hospital and he'll probably be fine."

Callie didn't contradict Luke. "Probably," she agreed, using the adjective he favored. She hoped he was right. But the icy shiver that ran up her spine confirmed her fear that he was wrong.

"Do you mind driving?" she asked her brother as they loaded Trace into the bed of her pickup. "I want to stay in back with Trace."

"No problem," Luke said.

As Callie held Trace's head tenderly in her arms, she

wondered if she ought to be doing some kind of mouth-to-mouth resuscitation. But when she bent her head down, she could feel his faint breath on her cheek. Maybe Luke was right. Maybe all he needed was a little oxygen at the hospital and he'd be fine.

She touched his singed eyebrows, shivering when she thought of the risk he'd taken to save her daughter, knowing how close he must have been to the fire. She marveled that he'd managed to find Hannah, and that he'd figured out a way to keep her daughter safe from the suffocating smoke.

"I love you, Trace," she murmured in his ear.

He didn't seem to hear her. His eyes remained closed, his breathing faint and shallow.

"Please, Trace. Live."

Trace disappeared into the emergency room as soon as they got to the hospital. There was no question of filling out insurance forms for Trace Blackthorne, no question of deposits to ensure payment of his bill when he checked out.

"Has Mr. Blackthorne been notified that his son was injured?" the nurse asked Callie.

"Uh. No," she replied.

"I'll take care of that," the nurse promised.

Callie wanted to ask the woman not to call Blackjack, but she wasn't sure how serious Trace's injuries were. What if he was dying? Trace would want his family with him. Even if they were Blackthornes.

Hannah had already been examined before they arrived and deemed not to be any the worse for wear—except for a few singed hairs. Sam and Luke had taken her home, while Callie waited at the hospital for news of Trace.

"Mrs. Blackthorne?"

Callie didn't realize at first who the doctor was addressing. Then she remembered she'd told the hospital she was Trace's wife to ensure she'd be kept informed of his condition. "Yes," she said, rising from her chair. "What is it, doctor? Is Trace all right?"

"The few burns he has are superficial, but he seems to have breathed a great deal of smoke," the doctor said.

Callie waited for an explanation. The doctor cleared his throat and continued.

"We're not sure yet of the extent of the damage to your husband's lungs. There's some upper airway edema, but I don't see the need yet to intubate him. We'll know more over the next twenty-four hours. He regained consciousness—"

"He's awake?" Callie interrupted, unable to contain her excitement.

"He was awake, but we've sedated him and moved him to a private room where he can be watched for signs of difficulty breathing."

"I want to stay with him," Callie said.

"He won't know you're there," the doctor said in a gentle voice.

"I want to stay with him," she repeated.

"Very well. The nurse can tell you which room he's in."

Callie followed the nurse to Trace's room and sank into the chair beside his bed. It was soothing to hear the rhythmic beep of the heart monitor. Trace was alive. He'd regained consciousness, if only briefly. Callie knew he'd get well. Nothing could go wrong now. It just couldn't.

Because if he survived—and if he still wanted her—she had made up her mind to go with him to Australia.

"How is he?"

Callie was startled by the sound of Blackjack's voice, when she hadn't heard the door opening or closing. "He's been sedated," she replied. "They don't know yet how bad the damage is to his lungs."

Blackjack exhaled as he sank back against the closed door.

Callie noticed the deep lines in his forehead, the creases on either side of his mouth, the gray pallor of his skin. "Are you all right?"

He patted a hand against his heart. "I just got a little scare when the call came. That's all." He straightened and crossed to Trace's bedside. He put a hand out to touch his son's cheek.

Callie found it difficult to watch the tender gesture. It made Blackjack seem human, when he'd been the bogeyman all her life.

"Are you going to stay here when he leaves for Australia?" Blackjack asked.

Callie was surprised by the question. Confused about what to say. "I don't think that's any of your business."

He lifted his brow. "We're talking about my son. That makes it my business. And, of course, I'm always interested in anything that might hurt Three Oaks."

Callie felt her blood chill. "Why are you saying something you know will make me want to stay here? Don't you want your son to be happy?"

"I don't want my son to go at all," Blackjack replied. "You're wrong if you think he'll stay here in Texas on my account," Callie said. "Trace has already made it clear he's going back home to Australia."

She'd used the word *home* on purpose, to hurt Blackjack, but a flicker of annoyance was the only response she got.

"I think you underestimate your hold on my son," Blackjack said. "If you stick to your guns, he'll come around."

"I'll bear that in mind," Callie said. "I think you ought to know that even if I decide to go with him, you won't have an easy time getting your hands on Three Oaks."

"It was clever of you to get Trace to pay the inheritance taxes," Blackjack conceded. "And it was a good move to get him to split the winnings from the Futurity. But that barely gets Three Oaks out of the red."

Callie smiled. "But we are, in fact, out of the red. And now that my brother Sam is back in the saddle, so to speak, things will run more smoothly and efficiently."

"If you say so."

"And my mother—"

"Yes. About your mother."

Callie's chin came up. "What about her?"

"I heard a rumor she's gone back to training cutting horses."

"She has," Callie confirmed. "What about it?"

"It seems providential, since I now have a breeding operation, to have a trainer in such close proximity."

Callie stared at Blackjack, her eyes going wide as understanding dawned. "Are you suggesting that you might hire my mother to train your cutting horses?"

"Why not?" Blackjack said. "I imagine Three Oaks can use the money."

And he would have an excuse to see her mother. Callie felt sick. "You have to stay away from her," she whispered.

Blackjack met Callie's gaze and said, "I can't."

"If you love my mother so damned much, why didn't you marry her the first time you had the chance?" Callie blurted. The instant the words were out of her mouth, she wished them back. But it was too late for that.

"I made a mistake," Blackjack admitted. "A tragic mistake. I didn't realize what was really important until it was too late. I've regretted it ever since." He looked Callie straight in the eye and said, "For my son's sake, I hope you don't make the same mistake."

Callie turned away from Blackjack's intense gaze to stare at Trace. The chance for a lifetime together with the one person he loved above all others had come and gone for Blackjack. But it wasn't too late for her and Trace. There was still a chance they could have a wonderful life together. If she would just reach out and grab for it.

Chapter 21

CALLIE KEPT VIGIL AT TRACE'S BEDSIDE THE rest of the day, doing her best to cope with the visits from his family. His brother Owen couldn't stay long, but his sister came and spent most of the afternoon keeping Callie company.

"I have to go," Summer said at last. "There's ranch business that needs attention. Dad doesn't think he depends on me," she said with a wink. "But he does. Good luck, Callie. Tell Trace to bring all of you with him for Christmas dinner."

Callie couldn't imagine such a thing, Christmas dinner at the Castle, but rather than argue, she merely said, "I'll be sure to mention it to him."

She had spent several hours sitting alone at Trace's bedside, with nothing to do but think, when the doctor finally arrived. He did a quick examination and announced that the edema in Trace's lungs was no worse, so he was taking him off the sedative. "He should wake up soon. You can expect his voice to be a little hoarse, but otherwise, he should make a speedy recovery."

Callie was glad Trace's family had come and gone and

that she would be alone with him when he woke up. She had something very important to say to him.

"Callie." Trace sounded like he had laryngitis, his voice cracked and husky.

Callie stood and reached out to grasp his hand. "How are you feeling?"

"Chest hurts," he said, as he forced himself into a sitting position in bed.

"Next time, try not to breathe so much smoke," Callie teased gently, as she rearranged the pillows behind him.

"Hannah?"

Callie squeezed his hand reassuringly and said, "She's fine. She's at home. Thank you, Trace."

"Couldn't let anything . . . happen to one of my girls," he rasped, as he smiled at her.

It sounded like it hurt for him to talk. "You rest, and let me do the talking."

Callie took a fortifying breath and said, "I love you, Trace." It was amazingly easy. She couldn't imagine why she hadn't said it before.

"I love you," she repeated. "With my whole heart and soul. I want to share my life with you. I want us to make a new home together, wherever it may be."

He closed his eyes and made a gurgling sound in his throat. She watched tears seep out from beneath his closed lids and leaned over to kiss them away.

"I want to come with you to Australia . . . if you'll still have me."

He opened his eyes, and she felt her heart leap at his look of unfettered joy.

"I love you, Callie," he said in a gravelly voice. "I'll take you any way I can get you."

She laughed as he reached out to pull her into his embrace. She held on tight, realizing how close she had come to losing him.

"I want to give you a kiss worthy of the moment," Trace said. "But I don't think I can hold my breath that long."

Callie laughed. "Don't worry. I won't ever forget this moment," she said. "Even without the kiss."

Trace laughed with her, then stopped when he ran out of air. When he coughed, it sounded like his insides were coming out.

"Trace? Are you all right?"

He put a hand to his chest. "I'll be fine," he said. "Nothing can keep me down now. I—" He stopped himself in mid-sentence and looked at her. "What about Eli? What does he have to say about all this?"

"He's the one who suggested we ought to make a new home in Australia. He's anxious to see a kangaroo."

"I think I can manage that," Trace said with a wry smile. He paused and said, "What about Three Oaks, Callie?"

"Three Oaks will survive without me." It had taken her a long time to come to terms with that fact. "Mom and Sam and Luke can handle things now. Especially since your father plans to hire my mother to train his cutting horses."

Trace lifted a singed eyebrow in astonishment. "He does?"

Callie nodded. "I think he wants to help her, if he can."

"And you don't have a problem with that?"

"Not anymore," Callie said.

"I can hardly believe you're finally mine," Trace said.

"All yours," Callie confirmed. "Completely and totally, now and forever, yours."

"Hey, Trace!" Eli shouted as he came charging through the door.

"Hey, Trace!" Hannah echoed.

The two children galloped the short distance from the door to the bed. Eli settled himself beside Trace on the bed, and Hannah climbed into his lap.

"Are you okay?" Eli asked.

"Are you okay?" Hannah parroted.

"I'm fine," Trace said, gathering the children into his widespread arms. "How about the two of you?"

"We're fine," Eli said. "Hannah's got some singed hair."

Hannah reached up to touch a wiry curl. "From the fire," she informed him.

Callie watched as Trace leaned down to kiss Hannah's blond curls. "They'll grow back in no time," he said.

"Are we going to Australia?" Eli asked.

"Are we going to see kangaroos?" Hannah asked.

"Yes and yes," Trace answered.

"Wow!" Eli exclaimed. "This is gonna be neat. Wait till I tell all my friends." He slid off the bed and headed for the door.

"I gotta tell Grandma," Hannah said, sliding off the bed after him.

Eli stopped at the door and said, "It's all right, Trace. Mom told me."

"Told you what?" Trace asked.

"How you didn't know I was your kid. So I'm not mad

at you anymore for leaving me. I think it's kind of neat that you're my dad, if you want to know the truth. Dad."

"I see," Trace said.

Callie saw the tears brimming in Trace's eyes and reached out to grasp his hand. He clutched her hand tightly in return, though his gaze remained riveted on Eli.

"I'm not mad at you, either, Dad," Hannah said.

Trace smiled. "Thank you, Hannah."

They were out the door a moment later.

"I guess that settles that," Callie said. "We're going to Australia."

"We've got a lot of lost time to make up for," Trace said as he gazed after the two children.

"We'll manage somehow," Callie replied. "Your sister invited all of us to the Castle for Christmas dinner."

Trace raised a brow. "How do you feel about that?"

"I think it's going to give your father another heart attack to have two active children racing around the house."

"You're forgetting my parents raised four children of their own."

"I guess so," Callie replied. It was hard to imagine Trace's mother and father as parents. She'd thought of them for so long as "the enemy." Now they were her children's grandparents. "None of this is going to be easy," Callie murmured.

"I never promised it would be," Trace said. "But we can do it together, Callie. It'll be easier with time."

"And distance," Callie pointed out. "Don't forget the distance."

"We'll come back to Texas for visits," he said. "And

there's no reason why your family can't come to visit us in Australia."

Except, Callie knew, there was always more work to do at Three Oaks than there were people to do it. She couldn't imagine her mother or sister or brothers finding the time to get away for a trip halfway around the world.

It was finally dawning on Callie just what she was giving up for a life with Trace. Not just the home she loved, but the close ties with her family.

Trace seemed to be reading her thoughts, because he said, "You can call them on the phone, Callie. You can e-mail them or write letters. There will be visits. But no, it won't be the same. We'll be a long way from civilization. Do you still want to come? Have you changed your mind?"

Callie felt the tension in his hand where he gripped hers. She knew what he was asking. It would be harder on everybody if she said yes now and changed her mind later. It would be better, if she had reservations, to let him leave without her.

"I won't take Eli if you decide not to come," he said quietly. "I'll leave him here with you. So you don't have to come, Callie. Not unless you want to."

"What?" Callie was confused by Trace's abrupt turn-around.

"You heard me," he said, his voice even rougher with the edge of tension in it. "I won't take him away from you. Eli can stay in Texas with you, if you don't want to come with me."

He was giving her the freedom to choose, without the threat of losing her son if she didn't choose him. Callie pulled herself free of Trace's hand. "You mean, I can stay here, and you won't take Eli away from me?" she repeated.

Trace nodded soberly.

"Oh, Trace." Callie didn't have to think twice. The answer filled her heart and mind and soul. "I'm coming. We're all coming. The whole family's coming, me and Eli and Hannah!"

"I love you, Callie."

"And I love you."

His lips sought hers, and they came together, two ragged halves of one perfect whole.

AUTHOR'S NOTE

*Those of you who have read my Captive Hearts series set in Regency England are no doubt wondering how Blackthorne became the last name of my Texas family, when Wharton is the family name of the Dukes of Blackthorne. I've mentioned in *The Cowboy* that the first Blackthorne in America was called simply "Blackthorne," which would have been a common way of referring to the duke in England. I've taken the creative license of having Blackthorne become his surname in the American West, where no one asked about a stranger's past or whether he had any other name beyond the one he gave them.

*I've made up my own names for the cutting horses in *The Cowboy*, using as my guide the names of horses that are presently among the winners in cutting horse circles. However, the horses in my story are entirely fictitious.

Letter to Readers

Dear Readers,

I hope you enjoyed reading about Trace and Callie as much as I enjoyed writing about them! *The Cowboy* is the first in a trilogy of novels about the Blackthorne and Creed families set in Bitter Creek, Texas. In the second book of the trilogy, Texas Ranger Owen Blackthorne matches wits—and trades kisses—with Bayleigh Creed.

If you'd like to read more about the Blackthorne family, look for my Captive Hearts series set in Regency England, which includes *Captive*, *After the Kiss*, *The Bodyguard*, and *The Bridegroom*. For those of you intrigued by the creeds and Coburns, you'll find their history chronicled in my Sisters of the Lone Star trilogy, *Frontier Woman*, *Comanche Woman*, and *Texas Woman*.

I very much appreciate hearing your comments and suggestions. You can contact me through my website at www.joanjohnston.com, or find me on Facebook at www.facebook.com/joanjohnstonauthor. I look forward to hearing from you!

Happy trails,
Joan Johnston